Club Cognac

Jeff Hawksworth

Club Cognac

Jeff Hawksworth

Paperback Edition First Published in Great Britain
in 2018 by aSys Publishing

eBook Edition First Published in Great Britain
in 2018 by aSys Publishing

Disclaimer

This is a work of fiction. Names, characters, businesses, places, events and incidents are either the products of the author's imagination or used in a fictitious manner. Any resemblance to actual persons, living or dead, or actual events is purely coincidental.

ISBN: 978-1-910757-92-5

aSys Publishing 2018

Acknowledgements

Paradoxically, whilst I prefer to be alone and isolated when writing, there are times when I need companions too.

The support and encouragement I have received from family and friends have been vital and I thank them all, unequivocally.

The lead position in that regard belongs to Pam, my wife for her unfailing support and honesty, when critiques were called for.

Proof reading can be a tiresome affair but the Lockwoods, Emma Wilson and Linda Skingsley stepped up to the plate once again, after which, Nicola Makin of aSys Publishing turned a manuscript into a book. Not forgetting Teresa O'Neill who produced a wonderful cover.

But above all and as always, I owe my most special thanks to you, because you're reading this.

Characters

Club Cognac members

Annie Stockley – Retired business woman.

Sue Bennett – Annie's sister.

Adam Harding – Retired detective sergeant.

Bob Lucas – Retired council housing officer.

Carol Lucas – Bob's spouse.

Tom Ecclestone – Megan Spencer's father. Corner shop owner.

Barry Parsley – Retired accountant.

George Dyson – Wine snob and expert.

Amy Dyson – George's spouse.

Alan Maitlin – Retired Prudential manager.

Jayne Maitlin – Alan's spouse. Hairdresser and property owner.

Barbara Thatcham – Artist.

Other characters

In the UK

Kendall Spencer – Relief bar manager.

Megan Spencer – Kendall's spouse.

Simon Sheldon – Megan's lover.

Penny and Tom Challis – Gite owners in Aurigny les Bois.

Gail and Les Anderson – Vendors of property purchased by Annie and Sue.

Anton Michaud – cognac distiller.

Henri – Anton's employee.

Albert Pichon – Anton's neighbour.

Maurice Pichon – Albert's father.

Phillipe Rambert – Anton's banker.

Margot Rambert – Phillipe's spouse.

Father Fabian Bissonnette – Priest and friend of Phillipe's.

Jean Claude and Marie Anne Durand – Annie's and Sue's neighbours.

SS Obersturmführer Ernst Meyer – Gestapo AKA Arnold Myers.

Challans – Archivist.

Mathieu Laroche – Head archivist.

Paul Gagnon – Lawyer used by Club Cognac.

CHAPTER 1

October 1952

It was two hours before the wreckage was discovered and it took the men and women from three neighbouring farms nine more to retrieve the body. In spite of the shallow depth of water and gentle, riffling flow, there was no question of survival. But as time passed, their cautious respect for the remains was replaced by brutal desperation.

They had tried other machinery for the recovery, but the ground was too soft for the wheels to gain traction and the bank of the stream had begun to collapse under their weight.

Eventually, as the daylight began to fade, two teams of horses finally rolled the tractor on to its side, though it still trapped half of the youth's body; burying it deeper into the stream bed with the rolling movement. Had machinery been used, all those present would have been spared from hearing the femur snap beneath the edge of the mudguard. Unseen and unheard, another, unknown edge of the machine further crushed one side of the chest and almost severed a limp grey arm from the shoulder.

The men holding the halters began to scream at their charges, prompting the one final effort needed to raise the machine enough for the men in the stream to haul the body free. They were all cold, wet and exhausted, but as soon as the youth's body was free it was handled with a gentler care, as they transferred it to the outstretched arms of the women waiting on the bank.

There were wounds all over the body, all bleached by an indifferent yet cleansing flow of the stream, though some thought the imagery was all the more obscene because of it, turning what was left into nothing more than a butcher's carcase. A few noticed the grazed face and damaged ear, but those injuries were just two of so many and never mentioned.

Silence fell on the scene and those close to the body stepped back, save for one, who fell to his knees and gathered his dead son's head to his chest. A loud wailing or a scream would have been less affecting than the soft sobs that came forth, as the old man began to rock to and fro, as if he was helping his child to fall asleep.

CHAPTER 2

In spite of the rather grand name, Waltham Parva is a very small village in a lost corner of Leicestershire. As recently as the nineteen eighties, it had a garage and general store cum Post Office, but a hundred years earlier, it also boasted a handful of weavers, leatherworkers, farm workers, two blacksmiths, a doctor, castrator, wheelwright, miller/baker, cobbler, thatcher, a village school and three ale houses. Pretty well everyone worked in or around the village and most lived in tiny rented cottages, apart from the vicar who lived in a rather grand Georgian vicarage and the schoolteacher who occupied the schoolhouse.

The name 'Parva' is the Latin term for 'little' and used when there is a larger settlement of the same name nearby; in this case, Waltham Magna. Ironically, thanks to recent development, the scale had reversed quite dramatically but neither would have countenanced a transfer of suffix, though Waltham Magna would have willingly transferred the two large pig farms that continued to deter developers.

Nowadays, no-one worked in the village; save for three remaining farmers who had been compelled by the costs of mechanisation and economies of scale to become heads of corporations, with huge acreages to match.

The village had also surrendered to the modern day demands of the upwardly mobile by becoming a dormitory community, in which rows of tiny worker's cottages were morphed into five bed roomed residences. Others were demolished and the building line was stepped back from the lane in order to add privacy to the long wish lists of new buyers. Eventually, they ran out of cottages and further demand gradually pushed the curtilage of the village out into the green belt, as planning specialists exploited any opportunity they could.

These new homeowners arrived in the eighties, along with two cars and teenage children, who soon added more vehicles to the parking problem, though they went on to graduate from college and make their own way in life; out of the village for the most part, since the demographics were now dictated by a shortage of starter homes, leaving an ageing population to wait until it was time to 'move down' into something more manageable, in one of the neighbouring communities. One that included a general store and a large doctor's surgery.

Of course, they were the 'baby boomers', born after the second World War, between nineteen forty six and sixty four. Most agreed that it was the 'golden' generation, with lots of disposable income, fully funded pension schemes and longevity. *La Dolce Vita*!

Moreover, many of them were either retired or close to retirement age. A significant number had finished work in their mid fifties, thanks to generous redundancy packages, inheritances, medical necessity, or in one case, a lottery win, though that wasn't to say they always had lots in common. Some were self-made, some professionals, some hard grafters and one was just plain lucky.

So whilst they could be a fairly disparate group at times, they did have some fundamental things in common. They were too healthy, intelligent and demanding to surrender themselves to pensionable dotage. Even victims of mild heart attacks or type 2 diabetes bounced back by treating the threats as wake-up calls; a nudge to get on with life rather than sit and stare at the approaching headlights of mortality.

Bucket lists were always a popular topic at the Friday coffee mornings; always interesting and inspirational, though sometimes bordering on the daft. On a few occasions there was an accord, which resulted in a few joining together for an adventure, like the whale watching trip to the Baja Peninsula, in Mexico, the previous year.

At the daft extremity lay Steve Ellis's project; prompted by the misdiagnosis of lung cancer, which proved to be lesions caused by fumes he'd inhaled at the foundry he managed. The doctor's confusion was matched only by Steve's delight, when they began to disappear by their own accord. By way of reaction and thanks to a generous early retirement package, he purchased three acres of woodland, a chain saw, trailer and hydraulic log splitter. Oh, and a log burner. He'd survived three seasons, but each episode left him buggered; in desperate need of hot baths, toddies and back massages from his long-suffering wife Mary. Nevertheless, he argued that the enveloping warmth given out by the log burner each winter made it worthwhile.

Mary differed. In spite of his recovery, the prognosis had been uncertain enough to ensure that a substantial compensation sum accompanied his early retirement plan and she argued that they could easily afford to buy the logs in, but Steve would have none of it. Neither really understood that he needed to keep pushing the envelope, to keep the demons that remained at bay.

Adam Harding was perhaps the one who fell furthest from their norm, if there could be such a state and privately, the group spoke of him as an outsider. Clearly though, he had the means to purchase a cottage in the village, albeit the smallest one; a survivor from the old days, with two up and two down. Nevertheless, it fetched more than a three-bed semi would have done, in Hinckley, a medium-sized town, fifteen miles away. The source of his wealth was a closely guarded secret, but the group did note that he was divorced, overweight, clean but slightly shabby and clad in clothes that were creased in all the wrong places. His easy going manner was acknowledged, but it fell a long way short of gregarious and could sometimes err toward the belligerent if confronted with an idiot, or fuelled by too much whisky. In essence, he had an air of independence that intrigued some and it could be accompanied by a wry, understated sense of humour, which appealed to others. That said, the few who had invited him in for drinks soon resolved to hide the single malt in future and have him consume biblical volumes of cheaper brands. In fairness, he didn't just drink other people's whisky; the consumption often continued at home and accompanied him down memory lane, sometimes to things he would prefer to forget. Not all the memories were bad though. In fact some were fine enough to bring tears that would not come when he was sober.

Those good ones were always welcome and more often than not involved his adventures with Graham Parsons; a good friend who had experienced an out-of-body experience when holding a child at the point of death. He then suffered dreadful head injuries at the hands of the child's attacker and in the months that followed, discovered that he'd been given a remarkable clairvoyance that enabled him and a small group of supporters to save so many kids who needed help. That association lasted for little more than three years, until Graham died. The small 'gang' who had gathered around him still mourned the loss, though they did keep in touch with each other. Adam still maintained contact with some of the kids they'd saved. Most notably Jimmy, who became Graham's adopted son, and Chrissy, the American.

But Graham's death was a watershed in Adam's career as a detective. For those three years he'd experienced so many triumphs, putting a stop to crimes of abuse that might have otherwise gone on unchecked had it not been for Graham. Afterwards, he couldn't return to the traditional policing methods, knowing how many kids there would be out there, helpless and unidentified.

Not that he was a softie. He just had a keen sense of right from wrong, where shoplifting was a one on the scale of things and child abuse was ten. As a colleague, most found him wanting. He could be intolerant, taciturn, and sometimes abusive to criminals and colleagues alike, though any offence was often tempered by a quiet, measured delivery. Rookies soon learned that he had absolutely no tolerance for fools and little time for his seniors for that matter. In short, he was a loner. Only one officer had managed to break through that barrier, into something which approximated friendship. Her name was Pat Geary, a child protection officer and fellow member of Graham's gang.

When serving, he earned the nickname 'Breadbin' because of his diet and weight, but soon after his arrival in the village, Kendall Spencer called him Sir Rhosis.

Adam retired from the Police force at the age of fifty six, with the rank of detective sergeant and the barely concealed relief, glee even, of his superiors, some of which had been involved in the international incident he'd brought about four years earlier, involving Chrissy.

He would have still been in a one bed roomed flat in Leicester had it not been for the one million dollar settlement that came out of that affair and an unexpected legacy from Graham. There had never been many real friends in his personal life; unsurprisingly, given his occupation and disinclination to spend leisure time with his peers, but there were a few and almost all were members or beneficiaries of 'Graham's Gang'.

His new home was pleasant and in lovely surroundings, with open countryside on all sides, but he missed the buzz of the city and in some ways, life in an urban flat was more private than in the village.

Chrissy Haddon was now almost seventeen years old, with a mature grace and character that amazed those who met her. Adam had witnessed this strength four years earlier, when she sought help from the gang, in a bid to escape the abuses meted out by her father, Senator Haddon; the same man who arranged for drugs to be planted in Graham's luggage and his subsequent imprisonment. There followed a transatlantic odyssey that had resulted in the Senator's own and rightful incarceration.

Now, Chrissy was free and extremely independent, thanks to the multi-million dollar settlement arising from her parent's divorce. That was an arrangement her mother had made. As a 'dry' alcoholic she resolved to secure her daughter's security in case she fell off the wagon in the future.

Chrissy was set to graduate at senior school, before going to university, with a longer term plan to study law at Yale. She still exchanged correspondence with Adam, who sat at his kitchen table, on the 12th of December two thousand and ten, to compose a reply to her latest letter;

Dear Chrissy,

Many thanks for your last letter. It was good to hear your news and in particular, that your mum is still well and happy. Good to hear that you two spend so much time together.

I certainly hope this letter finds you in brighter surroundings than here. I know I'm being very British in writing about the weather, but with due cause. It's shitty. Dull grey clouds overhead and drizzling rain, which means that I have to have the lights on all day.

Still, I shouldn't grumble. Instead, I should do something about it I suppose and book a sunshine holiday, where I might find a gorgeous, wealthy widow.

Hold that thought for a moment! I'm still as chunky as ever and my dress code hasn't improved, so perhaps I ought to add myopia to her attributes.

Life in Waltham Parva is still very quiet. Last week, some idiot suggested I get a dog! As you know, the only dogs I love are in America and come in buns.

That said and this bears repeating – I would love to show you and your mum, (or is it mom), some of England if you could manage a visit. Have to be in a hotel mind – too many would need to sleep on the floor in my cottage.

Terrible business about the earthquake and tsunami in Sumatra. The whole planet seems to be in turmoil, not that we notice much in sleepy Leicestershire. Maybe I'll stop moaning about being bored and appreciate what we have.

I've just realised that once you graduate from college and I have no doubt that you will; the next step will be law school. After that, a wonderful position with a private practice will be offered and that would have put you on the opposite side of the table, if I was still a copper. Of course, you could stay on the side of the righteous and join the DA's office I suppose, but the pay isn't as good. Same applies over here too.

Once again, this serves to prove that I'm not a great letter writer, but please don't stop sending yours. They mean a great deal. I'm off to the Friday morning coffee club at the local pub now. The coffee is like the stuff they serve in your diners, weak but the refills are free.

Take care,

Adam.

PS The gang send their love.

He sealed and addressed the envelope before placing it on the telephone table beside the front door; he'd post it next time there was a need to visit the local post office in Coalville. A glance at the clock was enough for him to realise he'd be one of the last to arrive, as usual. By then they would have clustered into groups and he could join the one of choice, which would entail the forcible insertion of a chair and much shuffling to accommodate it.

He struggled into his jacket and removed a black woolly hat from a pocket before venturing out into the rain. He glanced at the letter and said aloud, as he'd become wont to do lately, "Why do my letters read more like bloody crime reports?" With a sigh, he stepped outside, opting to do without a brolly; a decision he would regret three hours later when the drizzle had developed into a downpour. By then though, three pints of *Pedigree* and a hot pie would serve to dull any discomfort.

***

Thanks to a tenacious landlord, the village still had one pub, fittingly named The Rose and Crown, given that in fourteen eighty five, just a few miles away, the Battle of Bosworth marked the end of the War of the Roses and the beginning of the Tudor dynasty.

He didn't make much out of the coffee morning group, not least because of the free refill rule, but a few stayed on for a pie and a pint.

Each cluster had its own topic of conversation, which resulted in an overall decibel level that required everyone to shout, which was why Annie's call to order took so long to sink in.

Before rapping the table with her house keys she had carried out a head count. Thirteen present; a full complement, give or take. She thought it was a propitious omen. Contrary to popular views thirteen had always been a lucky number for her.

Annie's interruption was met by a variety of expressions, reflecting different perspectives. Curiosity, askance, indulgence, polite indifference, and mild irritation at having their own conversation, or worse, storytelling interrupted. But they were all startled when she bent down and extracted a bottle of Cognac from the carrier bag at her feet. They might have expected holiday snaps but not BYOB in their local, particularly by Annie. None could have known that the young barman had been bought off with a tenner. He would have thought twice before taking Annie on anyway and at that moment, was advancing with a tray of clean cognac glasses.

To begin with, there was a rapt silence as they watched her uncork the bottle and pour measures out, but when the drinks were passed down the table Barry Parsley, AKA Parsleymonious when out of ear shot, called out, "Are we paying for this?"

Annie had lifted her glass and was gazing through the dark amber fluid, "Perhaps, sort of, but in the meantime, just tell me what you think of it."

All sniffed and swirled the contents of their glass before taking a sip, except Harding, who knocked his back in one; it was after all, only a small measure. The rest of the group held it in their mouths for a few moments, allowing their taste buds the opportunity of employment and for the most part, they relished the experience. One of the group said that since it was December, a mince pie would have been nice but most simply sought another sample.

Annie waited until the chatter settled back before complying, though before addressing the first proffered glass she realised that the most important view had yet to be heard. She looked halfway along the left hand side of the group to George Dyson; their in-house wine snob and expert. Everyone had expected him to lead with a critique, but instead he remained silent, until finally, she was forced to ask, "Well George?"

He was still staring at his glass, but the look of rapture and reverence of his tone when he did speak was eloquent enough, "This is bloody good. Where did you get it?"

The expert's endorsement prompted further murmurs of appreciation and a few thanked Annie but eventually, Barry Parsley asked the question, "Well Annie, where *did* this come from?"

She beamed, "France of course. I've just been there, with my sister."

George needed to know more, "Yes, but exactly where in France? Here, give me the bottle."

She favoured him with an enigmatic smile and held the bottle to her chest, even though he had no hope of reaching it anyway, "Well, after three days in La Rochelle, we spent the rest of the time in a *gite* near Saintes. Well, actually, it was close to Cognac, too."

He waved his hand impatiently, "No,no, you know what I meant. Where did you find this stuff?"

Annie feigned surprise, "Oh, the Cognac. Well it comes from a small distillery in a village called Aurigny-les-Bois. It's rather nice isn't it?"

Someone else attempted to speak but George held up a hand to silence them. He chuckled, "You're playing with me Annie Stockley. *Nice* is an understatement and you know it. This is stuff for the gods and I've a pretty good idea of how much it would have cost." He raised his glass, "So I'm very grateful to you."

Barry Parsley asked, "Any chance of letting us in on that secret?"

She smiled, "First, let's find out what everybody thinks."

Fortified by the liquor and George's endorsement, they all called out tributes of their own, though Adam limited his response to a polite appreciation. He knew that most regarded him as something of a blunt instrument when it came down to spirits. Then, George silenced them by raising his glass and gazing at the amber residue. He closed his eyes and placed the glass to his nose before addressing Annie, "This is a thirty or forty year old Cognac which probably cost you on the heavy side of a hundred and forty Euros."

Someone murmured, "Bloody hell!"

Alan Maitlin, one of the newer members called out, "How many bottles have you got Annie?"

"Just this one," she replied before adding, after casting a glance towards her sister, "Though I think Sue has a few."

Things were going to plan nicely. Annie began to recharge the glasses and addressed the group as a whole, "George is absolutely correct on one count, it is a forty year old Cognac, but he was adrift on the price. I paid sixty Euros."

George called out, "I'd want a dozen bottles at that price!" He leapt from his chair and moved to her side, reaching for the bottle, "Please, let me see that!"

She held it away from him once more, "Wait, let me serve the others first!"

Chastened, slightly, he looked on as she refilled the line of glasses that had appeared before her. Once satisfied that everyone save George had been served, she poured a measure into his glass and passed him the bottle. His retreat resembled a small predator's snatch and grab from a lion's kill. To his credit, he studied the bottle closely without succumbing to the temptation of adding to Annie's measure. During that time some chatter broke out, but it was intermittent and less voluble than usual. They were all waiting on George, who was savouring his sample and reading the information on the back of the bottle again. Eventually, he looked at Annie and spoke quietly, "Please Annie, I need the exact address and then I shall go."

She raised her hand to attract everyone's attention, "I was going to suggest that we all go."

There was an immediate call of support from most of them,

one of whom called out, "A short break you mean, to visit the distillery?"

"No. I mean to invest in the distillery."

Bob Lucas, a long time member of the group chuckled, "Well, that does sound like an adventure; I'd have to think about that one!"

His wife, Carol, stared at the table, rather than bothering to look his way, "Yes, we will, won't we." The inflection on the 'we' was too slight for the others to notice, but Bob retreated into silence, in the knowledge of a storm ahead.

CHAPTER 3

Annie Stockley was fifty four years old and still, a strikingly beautiful woman; of average height, with what most men would call a sexually mature figure and a round, evenly featured face that was framed by a shock of auburn hair. Any hint of greying had been dealt with by the same expert who gave her such a professional bob cut. But her key features were those dark brown eyes that signalled intelligence, empathy and humour for the most part, though they could cut like lasers when a confrontation was called for.

She'd been a widow for six years; long enough to get on with life, but the loss was recent enough for memories to cause pain. They had owned three sports shops, in Leicester, Coventry and Nuneaton; all managed with a perfect blend of skills. With none of the natural sort to take care of, they had become her surrogate children. Her husband, Donald, was a former mid-league footballer and routinely athletic, but he had little business acumen; a shortfall that was more than made up for by Annie, who was the driving force behind the business. Like so many retail concerns, one of the prerequisites for success lay in the buying, which she excelled at; with enough presence to cow many of the reps who called on her. Better yet, they had been married partners for twenty eight happy years when he went on that last golfing holiday to Florida.

He and three friends went every January, in the quiet trading period just after Christmas, while Annie welcomed the opportunity to clear some of the weak stock out in their January sale and to attend a couple of trade fairs in preparation for the following year.

A clumsy slice put his ball into a lake, albeit at the very edge, in only an inch of water, which is why he decided to play the shot and in watching the ball's flight he failed to see the alligator approach at a rate of knots, bent on illustrating why the lake was 'out of bounds'. The bite of incredible force closed onto his right buttock and thigh and had it not been for a nearby friend, who set about it with a seven iron, the beast would have hauled its prize into the depths of the lake. Not a lot of people know how ghastly the bite of an alligator can be. Notwithstanding the physical impact, from jaws that close with a force of around three thousand pounds per square inch, their mouths are cornucopias of bacteria; nasty ones. In fact, there are so many dangerous microorganisms transferred from a bite that survivors are blasted with broad-spectrum antibiotics as a matter of course, en route to the hospital, let alone when they get there.

Like many before him, Donald survived the physical attack but the infections overwhelmed him in spite of the medication and three days later, he died.

His carefree attitude to life was so at odds with Annie's business-like manner, which gave weight to the notion of opposites attracting, for they loved each other dearly. So much of him remained in the business though and she soon lost heart. Within eighteen months she sold out to a major national retailer. The proceeds of the sale, Donald's life assurance and two significant pension funds ensured financial security, so that in place of work she and her younger sister by four years, Sue Bennett, who was twice divorced, set about seeing something of the World.

Unlike her husband, Annie had rarely taken breaks from the business; never felt the need to, but as the record of adventures grew, she began to realise how much she had missed, particularly when confronted with itineraries that were now too challenging for folk their age.

Nevertheless, their bucket list continued to grow.

The opposites attracting rule seemed to hold good for the

siblings too, for Annie's sister, Sue Bennett, was challengingly different. She was a free spirit yet paradoxically, it would seem, with a highly responsible background as a qualified nursing sister. A career which came to an end after a sleepy porter ran her over with his electric caddy. The compensation and pension package was enough to justify early retirement.

Years earlier, in between marriages, Sue had spent eight years nursing in Sierra Leone, after which she returned to the relative security of the NHS, to recuperate from the traumas she'd witnessed. Ever since then, she would vigorously counter criticisms of our health service; often by describing in graphic detail, the dying struggles of children, who only needed clean water perhaps, or a course of antibiotics. Many dinner parties had succumbed to such monologues, when the appetites of those present for culinary excess fell away in the face of such explicit detail.

In most other ways she was a freethinking, libidinous, libertine. A self- proclaimed man eater, without any ties and that included children, "Thank God" she would say, "The two I married were enough for one lifetime!"

Her shock of once sandy hair was now sprinkled with hints of grey and her green eyes still sparkled, with a, 'take me to bed' warmth. Finally, with a figure that carried enough weight to be voluptuous, the ensemble was complete.

Whilst Kendall Spencer never dared suggest a nick name for Annie, he called Sue 'Rabbit'.

With their new found love of travel came a growing realisation that they would like to spend more time abroad, at a base of their own, particularly in the Charente Maritime region of France, since they both shared a love of the area; a sentiment that was founded upon memories of childhood holidays spent camping on the French Atlantic coast. After some preliminary research on the web they decided that a modest house in that area was feasible, not least of all because it was reachable, either by car or one of the three budget airlines that flew into La Rochelle. Better yet, two offered summertime services out of Birmingham or East Midlands; both of which was less than an hour away from home and offered flights that took a little over an hour to reach La Rochelle. From there they hoped to find somewhere that was no more than an hour's drive away. Travelling there by car would entail an overnight ferry crossing from Portsmouth to St Malo, from where they could be at their destination in less than four hours. It was the route they had chosen for their visit in October.

Since building sand castles or being bowled over by Atlantic rollers held little appeal anymore, they decided to begin their search in La Rochelle where they would do some shopping and decided whether to buy a place in a city or somewhere quieter. The decision was pretty well established before they left England, since a modicum of research suggested that prices in La Rochelle would be too high. Even so, the prospect of a few days there was still appealing.

And they loved every minute of it. The old city, with its great stone towers astride the entrance to the old port, was every bit as charming as they remembered it, from childhood. As adults, they were better able to appreciate the architecture, whilst showing a child-like appreciation of the aquarium, which was unlike any they had been to. One morning, when they were sitting beside the old port, enjoying a coffee in the autumn sunshine, Sue pointed a thumb over her shoulder, towards the archway that led to the Rue du Palais, which connected the port with the Place du Verdun. It was lined with shops on both sides and the sixteenth century covered pedestrian ways were separated from the traffic by stone arches. The enclosures ensured that the paved areas remained cool, even in the hottest days of summer. Sue spoke, "You know, if I saw a troop of Napoléonic soldiers marching down there today, they wouldn't look out of place."

Annie blinked slowly, in a mutual appreciation, "I know, it's lovely isn't it?"

They had been there almost a week; long enough to draw some conclusions. Annie continued, "But would we want to live here, say, for four months a year? I know we could venture out for trips, but how would you feel about coming back here each day?"

They had spent long enough talking to estate agents for Sue to add further to her sister's vein of thought, "It wouldn't be here though, would it Sis'? Our budget will only stretch to somewhere in the suburbs and in an apartment at that. We wouldn't like that would we?"

Annie nodded, "So why don't we move on tomorrow and do some exploring?"

Sue raised her cup in salute, "Sounds like a plan to me!"

Nevertheless, their extended search was postponed the next day, when they drove over the new, huge bridge to the Ile de Ré, an island just off the coast, measuring thirty kilometres by five and packed with beauty spots, restaurants and millionaires. They were in Annie's car which meant that Sue was in place to pay at the toll booth. As they moved off she took another look at the receipt and gasped, "Bloody hell, I wanted to cross it, not buy it!"

Annie chuckled, "Ah, the benefits of driving a right hand drive car. Never mind, enjoy the view and I'll pay for lunch."

They drove up to St-Martin-de-Ré, a port on the eastern side that is still contained within eighteenth century fortifications, with a quaint harbour, surrounded by charming buildings and chic restaurants. There, they sat outside and ordered coffees before striking up a conversation with an English couple, who were seated at the next table. Obviously well heeled too, for they owned a property on the island and spent six months a year there. As is often the case when like-minded souls meet, they were delighted to learn of the sister's plans to do something similar and were soon recommending places to visit, including one of their favourite restaurants, just down the road, at La Flotte. In fact, they were so enthusiastic that Sue promised to try it for lunch that day, an undertaking that caused Annie some concern when they discovered the place had a *Michelin* star. She knew that even lunches in *Michelin* starred restaurants could run to hundreds of Euros and decided that her promise to pay for lunch should carry with it the right of veto.

An hour later, after they had explored the town and with mischievous relish, Sue insisted they go take a look. It proved to be the highlight of the day and something they would talk about in the coming months.

The *L'Ecailler* lay on the northern flank of the harbour at La Flotte and offered a fixed price lunch menu for only thirty eight Euros, which proved to be a mind-broadening experience, worthy of that coveted star. Once again, they were able to sit outside in the sunshine, people-watching, as they savoured every mouthful. The bottle of *Pouilly Fumé* cost more than a lunch, but in the circumstances, seemed worth it, even though Annie, as driver, was limited to only one glass. Sue saw off the other five glasses in fine style.

They spent the next day drifting down the coast towards the Gironde estuary, stopping first at Châtelaillon-Plage, a delightful seaside resort, with properties that were still way beyond their budget; enough for them to realise that *anywhere* on the coast would be too expensive. But the weather was wonderful, so the following day was set aside for a ferry trip to the Ile-d'Aix, a beautiful island with very few cars, gorgeous beaches and lanes that were a delight to cycle on. In fact, it was so quiet it felt time-warped. They hired bicycles, bought filled baguettes and picnicked when they found a cove to themselves.

It might not have been house-hunting, but the experience served to establish that their French house, if they found one, would at worst, be an hour's drive of the coast. Moreover, it had to be this particular coast for in addition to the childhood memories, they had learned that it lay in the lee of two large islands, Ile de Ré and Ile D'Oléron and was therefore protected from the worst of the Atlantic weather. As a result, it enjoyed a micro-climate akin to the south of France.

That night, they stayed in a hotel on the outskirts of Rochefort and after dinner, retired to their room for cognacs while they studied the road atlas. Using a thumb to measure the distances, they decided to focus on an area of countryside bound by Fontenay-le-Comte and Niort in the north and Saintes through to Cognac in the south. The eastern limit would remain within an hour of the coast. Since they were only twenty minutes away from Saintes it was decided to begin there and since stocks were running low, it would be appropriate to visit a distillery in Cognac after that.

They had already discovered that French roads were much better than they used to be, but the drivers on them were unsafe in the half hour running up to noon. Ten minutes later, those roads were almost empty. The French take lunch very seriously, so the two house hunters decided to make an early start and be in Saintes by mid-morning, in time for coffees.

On arrival, the following morning they began by collecting information about the area from the tourist office before touring the estate agents, all of whom had notices in their windows advising that English was spoken. They all wanted to take the women under their wing to visit properties but sadly, prices still seemed high, save for the semi-derelict wrecks which apparently found favour with the English. Not so Annie and Sue, who after a hair-raising two hours in the company of Marc, who sought to demonstrate how close he could get to mach1 in a Citroen C1, decided to look a little further inland. By the end of that day it looked as though their quest might be doomed to failure and their spirits were low, in every sense of the word. At least they would have an opportunity of replenishing one sort the following day, in Cognac.

Their experience with the estate agents in Cognac was little better and few were prepared to give exact locations, rather than escort them in person. During lunch at a delightful bistro on the banks of the Charente, opposite the *Hennessy* distillery they decided to try another approach the next day. The afternoon had been allocated to a tour of the *Rémy Martin* distillery, where they discovered that Annie had been wise to book in advance, since there were no spaces left and quite a number were being turned away.

It began with a short presentation before they were taken on a two hour tour which ended with a tasting of two varieties. The visitor centre was elegant and the fumes, known as the 'angel's share', were enlivening. During the tour they were escorted between row after row of huge honey coloured oak barrels that were most impressive and the whole area was spotlessly clean, but when they reached the buildings that housed the oldest cognacs they questioned the ugly black mould which covered the walls. The guide explained that it was a fungus which thrived on the alcoholic vapours, common to all cognac cellars.

Annie whispered to her sister, "Humph, can you imagine what they'd say back home if my garage walls looked like that?"

Sue leaned back and whispered,"Yes, that you were a piss artist." After a moment, she added, "But a very sophisticated one."

After the tasting came the purchases or rather purchase. As Sue pointed out, the supermarkets were full of cognacs at much lower prices and no doubt quality, but their tastes weren't capable of knowing the difference, at least for those within their price range.

They purchased a bottle of the cheapest there, at thirty three Euros and ogled the *Louis X111* with its price tag of three thousand Euros.

In no time, it seemed, apéritifs were due, along with the lure of another restaurant, though later Sue interrupted the meal with an observation, "I think we've lost the plot 'Sis. Here we are, behaving more like tourists than house-hunters."

Annie sighed, "Yeah, I was thinking the same this afternoon, during the distillery tour, but in fairness, we couldn't afford anything at the places we've been to anyway."

Sue raised her glass, "OK, tomorrow we'll be in the boondocks, so we focus from now on."

Annie raised her glass, "Here's hoping."

So it was that the following morning, they set off with a new strategy. Instead of trolling through the estate agents, they decided to head off into the countryside and look for '*A Vendre*' signs, which translated literally means 'to sell'. If they liked the look of a place they would knock on the door and see if the owner would show them around. At least they would have an opportunity of seeing the surroundings at the same time.

It was a sound plan. There followed a day of exploring the Charente countryside, which they fell head over heels in love with. The rolling countryside contained an amazing mix of woodland, in an autumn suit, pastures populated by creamy coloured *Charolais* cattle along with fields that had been shorn of their harvest and were being prepared for the following year. Whenever they crested a rise they'd be rewarded with staggering views to the west, toward a coastline that remained within an hour's drive. But there could be no doubt about the primary crop. Huge areas were covered in vines, recently stripped of their grapes. They had chosen an exciting time of year to be there, but they wouldn't realise that until the following day.

The lanes became narrower and the villages smaller, to such an extent that they were often 'off piste' so far as their atlas was concerned, but for the first time, they felt as though they were achieving something. Many properties evidenced the pragmatic approach the French have toward maintenance, with scraps of ancient, faded paint clinging to otherwise bare, bleached shutters.

In one village an '*A Vendre*' sign had an arrow which directed them into a tiny courtyard where they discovered that the property was priced at only ninety six thousand Euros, but it had no land and was little more than a 'pied-a-terre'. Further on, in another village, they discovered a modern bungalow priced at one hundred and forty five thousand, but it lacked the charm they were looking for.

That lunchtime they stopped at a tiny bar and enjoyed the finest omelettes either could recall eating, which was in keeping with what looked set to be a perfect day, even though, by mid afternoon, they had failed to find their dream cottage.

It was time to find accommodation though neither could recall the last time they'd seen a hotel. Half an hour later, in the village of Aurigny-le-Bois, they almost missed a small sign beside the entrance to a courtyard that read, *Gites de France.*

Annie was concentrating on driving around a belligerent cat, so it was Sue who called out and moments later they had reversed back to the entrance.

It had obviously been a substantial farmhouse at one time but someone had worked extremely hard in turning the place into what might have been called a grange in England. What was the farmyard now contained a driveway that encircled a grassy area with an authentic, but freshly painted cart standing on it. The house lay on the right hand side of the turning circle and provision for the parking of several cars had been made on the left.

Sue observed, "I know it says '*Gite*', but it looks more like a *Chambre d'Hote* to me."

Annie agreed, "Well, beggars can't be choosers, at least it's a bed for the night and it looks nice enough. Let's take a look."

They parked on the left and were barely out of the car when the front door of the house was thrown open and a great lump of black Labrador bounded out towards them, its tail wind milling like a badly balanced propeller. A woman's voice called after it, "Guinness, behave yourself!"

Annie and Sue stopped in their tracks, uncertain of their immediate prospects but Guinness charged on before clumsily halting in front of Sue, placing a huge paw firmly on one of her feet and pivoting on that axis to lean against her leg, with enough weight to make her stagger. His tail began to form an angel's wing in the gravel as he looked up with a canine grin to complete an eloquent welcome.

By then the lady of the house had appeared at the doorway. She was quite tall and no stick insect, though striking, with long wavy sandy hair that framed a lightly tanned complexion and broad smile. Her spectacles, with bright red frames, reflected the afternoon sun and seemed at odds with the more conventional check shirt and denim jeans. Annie put her age at around thirty eight.

"He's bi-lingual, or at least he ignores me in both languages, but I saw the car plates and opted for English, for your sakes rather than his." She'd been striding towards them as she spoke and held out her hand, "Hello, my name is Penny. Are you here for directions or a bed for the night?" Close up, they noticed a band of freckles across her nose and upper cheeks. Those and the gap between her front teeth gave her a much younger appearance.

Annie shook hands, "Well, we were hoping to find a bed actually. Oh, I'm sorry, my name is Annie and this is my sister Sue."

Sue had been tickling Guinness behind the ears and since he'd become an immovable object she was forced to stretch her arm out from the bent position.

Penny said, "Great, fine. We haven't anyone booked in for tonight, so it could have been either. Anyone without a 'sat nav' can get pretty lost around here."

Sue grinned, "We haven't got one and we haven't known where we were for most of the day."

Penny nodded, and extended an arm towards the gate at the side of the house, "OK, well would you like to take a look at what we have to offer?"

She led the way around to the rear of the house where the former outbuildings had been converted into four *gites* which were screened from the house and formed two opposite sides of an area that was dominated by a swimming pool, contained within a chain link fence. A gate had been installed at one corner and was secured by a number pad. The fourth side of the plot had been left open for the spectacular views to the west. As they walked around the pool Penny explained, "You're welcome to use the pool but it isn't heated and bloody cold at this time of year. The fence had to be put there for regulations I'm afraid. Apparently, a politician lost a couple of grand children in a swimming pool and before we knew it every pool in the country had to be fenced off." By then, they had reached the first *gite* and she showed them in. This time it was Annie's turn to be pushed aside by Guinness, who was intent on escorting the group.

The *gite* they were shown was lovely. There were two bedrooms, a lounge/dining area and a small but well equipped kitchen. The furnishings were simple but mostly new, yet with a rustic theme and whilst it was more expensive than the accommodation thus far in the trip, they accepted it immediately.

Ten minutes after they'd settled in Penny knocked on the door and drew their attention to a flaw in their plans, "I've just thought, have you brought any provisions?"

The sisters looked at each other and shrugged their shoulders. Annie said, "Err, no. We hadn't planned on doing any cooking. Perhaps you could recommend somewhere to eat."

Penny raised her eyebrows and rocked her head, "At this time of year there's nowhere local. The nearest restaurant that's open in the evenings is almost an hour away."

"Bugger" muttered Sue, "We have some bottles of water and a packet of biscuits."

Annie added, "And a bottle of cognac."

Penny nodded, "Thought as much. Well, you'd better eat with us, if you want to that is. I'll figure out a price, but it won't be too much, promise. It won't be anything special either. I have some *Boeuf Bourguignon* in the freezer if that would suit." The invitation was accepted immediately. "Fine, then come up to the house at around six thirty for apéritifs."

When she left, the sisters were lost for words for the moment. Instead, Sue stepped forward and hugged Annie, before putting what they both felt into words, "Blimey Sis', when is this day going to stop getting better?"

There was still enough heat in the sun at six thirty for them to sit outside on the patio for glasses of sparkling *Clairette de Die,* accompanied by delicious canapés. Guinness took it in turns to drop a forepaw onto one of the visitor's feet and gaze meaningfully at the food they were holding. At one point Sue asked about his habit of stamping on people's feet. Penny shrugged, "Don't know, he's always done it, even as a pup. We call it his stamp of approval."

Sue dropped a hand down to tickle him behind the ears, "Then I'm honoured."

Annie wasn't so sure, "Right now, I think it has more to do with the canapés you're eating than a personal appraisal."

Penny introduced her husband, Tom, when he joined them moments later. They learned that he worked for an Anglo-French telecommunications company in Cognac; the reason for their move to France eight years earlier. Like many French office workers, he was dressed casually, in a beige shirt, dark blue chinos and brown, slip-on loafers. Though only in his thirties, his fair hair was thinning on top, but he looked fit and spoke with an easy charm. Annie waved an arm westwards and said how taken they'd been by the area and he clearly welcomed the endorsement, saying that the two hours commuting each day was the price they were prepared to pay for living in such beautiful surroundings. But Annie wondered how Penny felt about such isolation and eventually, emboldened by alcohol and their easy company, she asked, "Do you have stuff to do over here Penny, apart from the *gites* I mean?"

"Do you mean am I bored stiff out here?"

Annie was embarrassed and began to cover her tracks, but Penny held up a hand, "No, it's a good question, particularly since we decided to do without kids, but I was actually the prime mover in choosing this place."

Tom added, "And we've never regretted it. Getting all the conversion work done was a nightmare, but one that we'd been warned about. The rest exceeded our original expectations; still does. Mind, I did a reasonable amount of the work; the non-technical stuff, so I was able to keep the pace up."

His wife chuckled, "Your working practices didn't go down well at times." It was obviously a well used anecdote and she allowed Tom to take it on.

"Well, once, we were laying the concrete floor to the kitchen and by eleven thirty that morning it was clear that if we kept going through lunch we would be finished by around two o'clock. Since it was a Friday I thought it would make for an early start to the weekend for Albert, the chap we'd employed, but the prospect of missing lunch was unthinkable. I thought he was going to cry; couldn't do it to him in the end."

Penny returned to Annie's question, "The *gites* keep me moderately busy in the summer, mostly with British visitors, but we also have seven acres of land, which includes an orchard, two acres of vines, just over two of woodland and a decent sized lake. Adding that to a large garden and recalcitrant dog doesn't leave me with much time. The locals organise lots of things through the year too and they have been wonderful with us. There is still time for traditional values and courtesy over here and that includes the extended family. It is usual to see four or even five generations having a picnic." She went on to describe the land and its demands in more detail but then smiled at Annie, "So that brings me to a question of my own, are you here as tourists or do you have another agenda?"

Annie grimaced, "Well, we started out with one but I'm not sure anymore. We'd hoped to buy a small place over here, but the ones we like are too expensive and the estate agents just want to sell us derelicts."

Penny asked, "When you say small, how small?"

Sue cut in, "As big as we can get for the budget really. We came inland because anything near the coast is prohibitive."

Tom nodded, "So many people have been coming over from England, which hasn't helped, but the market's been buoyant anyway. What is your budget?"

Annie's natural reluctance to discuss money with relative strangers caused her to pause, but Sue was less reticent, "Well, in light of what we've seen, it's been upped to about one thirty thousand Euros, max." She didn't add that her sister could afford much more, but this was a joint venture and sixty five thousand was her absolute limit.

Tom looked at Penny, "What about the Anderson's place?"

She shrugged, "Perhaps, they're desperate enough."

He turned to the sisters, "The Andersons moved out here four or five years ago, when they retired and they spent a bundle on one of those wrecks you talked about; did a decent job of it too, but they haven't settled well. Neither has come even close to mastering the language, which makes living out here in the sticks very difficult and she misses the children and grandchildren terribly. They've had the place on the market for a few months, but it's too rural for the Brits and too expensive for the locals, at least for what it is."

"What is it?" asked Annie.

"A converted barn, with two bedrooms I think. They're asking one sixty, but as I said, they're desperate to get back to England."

Penny interrupted, "The language thing *is* important. Do you two have any French?"

Sue replied, "Yes, we can both get by. It might be a struggle with technical details but we're OK with the day to day stuff, thanks to family holidays, decent language teachers and our love of the country."

Penny showed some relief, "Then if you like, I'll call them and see if you can see the place tomorrow. I'll take you round there."

"Thanks," said Annie, "That would be lovely."

They went indoors for the meal, which began with sweet, fragrant home grown tomatoes, sliced and dressed with a vinaigrette and herbs; simple yet delicious. The *Boeuf Bourguignon* was heavenly, with chunks of beef that dissolved in the mouth like marshmallows. It was accompanied by homemade croquette potatoes, baby carrots and green beans. The red wine was also their own and very pleasant. There followed a small cheeseboard, which included one of the finest *Brie's* the sisters had ever tasted and finally, for desert, they were treated to a *tarte tatin* with crème fraiche.

Throughout, the conversation had been easy and continuous, with each pair sharing more about their lives, families and backgrounds. When Penny announced that it was time for coffee and cognacs, Sue said, "Wait, the least we can do is share *our* cognac with you." With that she dashed off to get the bottle of *Rémy Martin* they had bought in Cognac. It was accepted in good grace, though by then their friendship had become easy enough for him to take the liberty of asking how much they had paid for it. Annie told him and he winced, before suggesting to Penny, "Love, I think a visit to Anton's tomorrow would be in order, don't you?"

Penny took another sip of the spirit before directing her response to the sisters, "He's right. Tomorrow, I'll take you to taste cognacs that'll amaze you, for the quality and price. Anton Michaud, the chap that owns it, is really sweet. Be prepared though, his place will be a bit of an eye opener."

Tom sought to explain, "The French don't have much time for the big names. Hennessy for example, have forty per cent of the global market, but only two per cent of the one in France. Their recent success has been in China, where their sales are huge."

The following day dawned with another cloudless sky, though the glistening dew on the grass was a reminder that summer was coming to an end. The silvered surface was broken by a trail of dark paw prints that led from the house to their door before disappearing into the grounds beyond. Obviously, they had been checked out for a morning fuss and found wanting.

Sue stepped out to take the air and almost fell over a lidded wooden box that had been left on the doorstep; obviously the previous evening, since only dog tracks were evident in the dew. She took it indoors and set it on the table. Inside, she found a complete breakfast. Coffee, milk, croissants so buttery the wrapping had become translucent and a jar of apricot jam, obviously home made. The note that accompanied them bore just two words, *Bon appétit.*

An hour later, Penny knocked on the door before stepping in. Guinness barged past her and chose Sue's foot once again, owned after all, by the master ear tickler. "I've spoken to the Anderson's and they suggested joining them for coffee at around eleven, if that's OK." It was, of course. She added, "That'll take us up to lunchtime so I'll take you to meet Anton at the distillery this afternoon."

That prompted Annie to ask, "Is there anywhere we can buy something for lunch?"

"Sure, there's a *boulangerie* and a *boucherie* in the village. Since there isn't a general store they sell extras too, so you should find all you need. Many folk grow their own vegetables out here so there's not enough call for a vegetable shop. Anything outside of the norm can be bought at the market at Matha, on Tuesdays and Fridays. That's about twenty five minutes from here. Oh, and then there's the bar. It still says Caf*é* Bar outside, from when Claude's wife was alive. It's drinks only now though, served up by himself, dressed in a grubby vest for most of the year. Only the old men go there, to grumble over coffees and cognacs and they all smoke too, in spite of the EU ruling. At least they assemble outside in the summer."

Lunch wasn't the only consideration, since they had both decided to stay on for at least another night and would need to think of things for an evening meal. "Certainly," said Penny when asked, "Stay as long as you like. At this time of year every night is a bonus." She thought for a moment before, "What about the evening meal, you don't want to be stocking up with oils, herbs and stuff for one night do you?"

"What do you suggest?" asked Sue disingenuously.

Penny grinned, "Same time, on the patio."

Annie cut in, "Penny, are you sure? We seem to be taking advantage of you."

"No you're not. I'm charging you, remember?"

It didn't seem appropriate to ask her how much, having enjoyed such wonderful hospitality already, but Penny's broad grin did imply that the meals would continue to be inexpensive.

The sisters strolled into the village and found the *Boulangerie* by following the scent of freshly baked bread. With two baguettes under their arms they moved on to the *Boucherie*, just two doors away, where they bought some equally fragrant ham, *Comte* cheese and lastly, one of their particular favourites; Brittany butter, laced with sea salt crystals.

On their way back to the *gite,* both broke *le quignon,* or crusty end off a baguette, which brought back memories of their family holidays. Annie began, "Do you remember what we used to call the ends."

Sue chuckled, "There were a number of names as I recall. You and I had to go for the bread each morning and Dad used to call the ends 'missings', because they never made it back to the tent. So then, we called them 'mines'. He tried to stop us by saying that the baker always scratches his itchy bottom with the ends."

Annie added a memory of her own, "For a time we would just scrape the crust off with our teeth, leaving a white pointy end. Dad used to call *them* mushrooms."

At ten to eleven they climbed into a battered old Peugeot estate car, with Penny in place as chauffeur. She explained, "This is our builder's truck. You wouldn't believe the stuff we've had in here and it spares Tom's car from abuse." Annie took the front passenger seat and Sue climbed into the back, raising a cloud of cement dust as she settled onto the seat. Their destination was only a quarter of a mile away; easily within walking distance and Annie said so. Penny shook her head, "No way. If Guinness saw us walking out of the drive he'd have howled until the neighbours went round to play with him, or torn the place to shreds; Guinness I mean, not the neighbours. We've tried tying him up outside but you wouldn't believe the damage he can do there and of course, the howling is worse. Yet when we go out in the car he seems to accept being left at home."

The Anderson's place had obviously been a barn, which was stepped back from the farm house but still connected at one corner. The driveway, that passed by the side of the farmhouse had been ceded to the Andersons in the sale and was therefore private.

It was a two-storey place built in light grey stone, with a gable end facing the approach. Half of the ground floor had been left as an open-ended garage, while the other half contained a half-glazed door and small window. As they got out of the car a lady stepped out of the door to welcome them. She was of average height, slim and her short hair was white with hints of blonde. Her open features lit up when she smiled. As they began to shake hands she said, "Hello, nice to meet you. I'm Gail. My husband is out back, stacking wood, but he'll be with us shortly, as soon as he smells the coffee."

They exchanged pleasantries and Penny shared a few snippets of local news, until finally, Gail said, "Well I expect you'd like to have a look around. Please," She extended an arm towards the door and they trooped in.

Annie fell in love with the place the moment she stepped across the threshold, into the lounge/dining area, which was large by cottage standards and though the windows were quite small, the bare stone walls had been sandblasted to near white, giving the room a light airy feel. The open stairs were attached to the lounge wall and looked as though they might have been the originals, leading up to a hayloft. A post and rail banister, in the same light oak as the furnishings had been fitted to it. Around the corner, behind the garage, lay a compact but beautifully fitted kitchen, with a door that led out onto a generous patio, partly covered by a vine-laden loggia.

Upstairs, both bedrooms were large doubles, with windows facing out from the western gable end, with breath-taking views towards the coast. The large bathroom, over the garage had been fitted with an extremely stylish suite which included a double-size shower cubicle, something both sisters commented on. Along the landing, past the airing cupboard, lay a small study with a window that overlooked the drive. Someone brushed against the desk and the *Google* page appeared on the computer screen. Annie suspected that Gail had been on the web when they had arrived, perhaps searching the UK property pages.

They returned to one of the bedrooms and gazed at the view again. The patio led on to a mown grassy area that stretched for fifty metres or so, though on the right, behind the lounge, was a cultivated area with a variety of vegetables and bare areas that had been turned over after harvest. Annie raised a question, "I don't see a fence, where does your garden end?"

Gail explained, "Oh, you can't see the fence through the trees my dear. Most of them are fruit trees by the way; everything from cherries to apricots."

Sue asked, "How much ground do you have then?"

"Oh, just over four acres I think."

They filed downstairs and sat around the table while Gail put the coffee on. Whether by design, or the smell of coffee, Mr Anderson made his entrance, as if on cue, after audibly struggling out of his boots by the back door. He was tall and muscular man for his age, with a full head of curly grey hair and a complexion that mirrored a lifetime of working outdoors. He seemed a little diffident and waited for Gail to make the introductions, "This is Les, my husband."

Penny gave him the usual French greeting of a kiss on both cheeks and he shook hands with the sisters, just as the coffees arrived.

They had already exchanged pleasantries on the tour of the house, during which each spoke of their homes, or former homes, in England. Les and Gail had been tenant farmers, dairy mainly, just south of Ashbourne, in Derbyshire. Their eldest son had taken over the farm and Gail made no secret of how much she missed home and the family, which included three grandchildren. She explained, "They come over here once or twice a year, my daughter-in- law and the kids that is, Gordon can't leave the farm, but it's not like picking them up from school or taking them on outings."

Annie noted that there was no mention of their failure to settle in France, probably for fear of prompting doubts in the would-be buyers. Instead, they talked about the pleasant climate and quiet roads. Eventually though, Gail broached the key subject, "What do you think about the place?"

Annie was way beyond being coy, "I love it! But this is a joint venture and I need to discuss it with Sue"

Gail looked at Sue, who had also fallen in love with the place, but she was concerned about the price, "To be honest, a hundred and sixty thousand is quite a bit more than our budget."

Gail became defensive, "We were told by the agents that the price was reasonable, particularly since it includes most of the contents. We'll only be taking personal stuff back with us."

They hadn't even considered that aspect, but it reinforced Annie's interest and she sought to explain, "I'm sure it's reasonable, please don't think we would try and beat you down for the sake of it, but it really is a question of budget you see."

Les asked, "If we were able to reach an agreement, how long would it take you to complete the purchase?"

It was Sue's turn, though Annie was relieved to hear the positive, "As quickly as the lawyers could manage it. We have the funds available, without the need for a mortgage."

He gave a small nod to Gail, authorising her to make a decision and she dropped her gaze to her hands, which were resting on the table. After a few moments, she reached a decision and looked up, "I think you should go off and talk about things. It's no good talking about price unless you genuinely want to go ahead. If you do decide you want it, come back and we'll try and agree a price."

Annie realised that nothing more would be achieved by staying longer and stood to go, "Thanks for showing us around Gail; we'll get back to you tomorrow, either way."

Gail smiled, "Thank you for that. In which case, come and join us for coffee again; same time as today?"

As Penny kissed them goodbye she warned, "If you lot are talking money I'm staying out of it, so these two will come on their own."

The atmosphere in the car carried enough of a charge to power light bulbs. Penny chose to avoid the subject until later, perhaps over apéritifs. In the meantime, there was a more pressing issue. The sisters were caught unawares when she suddenly swerved into the kerb, opposite the butchers, "We're just in time to catch him; he closes at twelve."

They watched her run across the road, waving at the butcher, who had cleared the chilled counter in the window and was obviously ready to close.

The sudden silence and privacy enabled Sue to look over her shoulder, "What do you think Sis'?"

Annie's eyes were sparkling, "I'm too excited to talk at the moment, let's wait until we get back."

She was right; it wasn't the appropriate time, for Penny reappeared at that moment, with a small parcel, which she dumped onto Sue's lap as she got into the car. It prompted Sue to say, "I am sorry Penny, we're becoming a bit of a burden."

Penny huffed and patted Sue's arm, "Nonsense, we're enjoying your company. Besides, you're paying."

They were back in no time and had barely stepped inside the *gite* when Penny hurried over from the house with a bottle of chilled *Chablis*, "Here, something to have with lunch, you're going to need it."

Annie took the bottle, "Thank you so much, but please let me pay you for this."

Penny was already heading back to the house and waved a hand in the air, "You bring the cognac again, tonight."

They decided to postpone any further discussion until lunch had been set up on the table outside, but as soon as they were seated Annie burst out, "I absolutely love it!"

Sue's enthusiasm was tempered with concern though, "Me too. I think it's everything we were looking for and more, but," she looked as though her bubble had already been burst, "They're not going to come down to one thirty are they?"

"But Sue, we're not going to find another like this, can't we stretch a little more."

"I don't have anything to add Annie. Sixty five thousand is all I can afford."

Annie had the germ of an idea, but that could wait. In the meantime she wanted to share her recollections, "Look, let's not jump the gun. We already know that they're desperate to sell, so you never know. In the meantime, let's just discuss it."

In spite of her misgivings, Sue found herself swept along by her sister's excitement and together, they re-lived the visit, step by step. They also began preparing a list of questions for the next day, when they also planned to walk around the land. By the time Penny turned up to escort them on the distillery visit they were buoyed up by the excitement of it all, - and a bottle of wine.

They turned into a stone arched entrance beside a rather grand but tatty house, that edged the road. Once inside, the building line had been stepped back, forming a corner that required them to turn right before finding the car park fifty meters further on. There were no other cars there and no sign of activity.

A further switch in the building line marked the beginning of the commercial area which changed from an old structure into newer, huge sheds, with roller shutter doors, facing out onto the same open space as the car park. The two areas shared the same concrete surface but were separated by a rusting wire fence. A collection of rusting machinery lay around the edge of the commercial area and might have deemed scrap had they not been fronted by recent tractor tyre marks. In any case, they couldn't recognise any of it, save for a large trailer that was laden with logs. Sue did recognise one thing though, "Hey, Annie, look at the walls!"

Every single one was covered in black fungus. Penny led the way back to the corner facing the main entrance, where they found a timbered frontage set into the recess. It was heavily varnished and glazed from waist height upward. Grubby lace curtains blocked their view of the interior and the small door was locked. Penny pressed the bell button on the wall, but nothing was heard. She explained, "It goes through to the house." They waited for several minutes until Penny sighed, "He must be down in the fermentation room." With that she picked up a wooden baton that had been leant against the wall and rapped on the door, "He won't be long."

He was.

It took three more attacks to the door and ten minutes before they detected movement behind the curtain. He was small, no more than five feet four, with a round face and eyes enlarged by the lens of his spectacles, which were enclosed by perfectly round tortoiseshell frames. His head of short brown hair showed signs of thinning, but the scalp had yet to appear. Annie allowed her gaze to drop, in order to see the check shirt and heavy corduroy trousers held in place with a broad leather belt which shone with a patina that spoke of more than one generation. He wore boots that looked like half-sized wellingtons, which glistened with moisture and accounted for the trail of footprints behind him. All this she observed in the time it took for him and Penny to exchange greetings. The flustered look that greeted them had disappeared as soon as he saw one of his favourite villagers, "Ahh! Madame Challis, Penny, you have come to me at last!" His English was perfect, though accented.

Penny wagged her finger, "But I am still married Anton."

He feigned sadness and regret, "But of course, I forget, please forgive me." He looked at the sisters and then back to her, "But today, you have two beautiful companions with you."

"Who would like to be shown around the distillery and to taste your cognac."

He looked affronted, "But of course." Then he bobbed his head and winked at the new visitors, "Welcome."

They stepped inside and Penny made the introductions. Each handshake was accompanied with, *"Enchanté."* As he closed the door Anton explained, "I am sorry for taking so long, but you have come at a very important time, as you will see."

Penny nodded and smiled. She knew, but wouldn't rain on Anton's parade and they waited in silence as he hurried through the office and into the house to change into a pair of shoes. They had entered a lobby area that was half filled with cases of cognac, stacked to head height. The left hand wall was a semiglazed partition, similar to the frontage, which separated them from the office. It might easily have been a factory foreman's office from the nineteen fifties. One large table took up three quarters of one side and a roll top desk had been positioned in the opposite corner, in front of an elderly captain's chair, clad in tired brown leather. Two filing cabinets lay in another corner and most of the remaining floor space was filled with more boxes. All the wooden furniture was in old oak, with polished patinas on surfaces that had seen contact for many, many years. Two huge trays filled with small glasses sat on the table, next to bottles left there for tastings, but the sister's stared around the place, at what was easily the most significant feature; every wall and ceiling was black, even in the office.

A *Rémy Martin* visitor centre it was not, though they did recognise the heady fumes of the 'angel's share'. They lifted bottles from the boxes while they waited, though the labels meant little to them. Penny continued to hold back, "Don't worry, Anton will explain everything."

He soon re-appeared, wearing a pair of scuffed brown shoes, "Now ladies, I will show you how to make cognac." After a moment he raising a cautionary finger and added, "But not *great* cognac." He sidled towards Sue and winked at her, "Zat is my secret."

They followed him through a dimly lit forest of oak barrels, all stacked on their sides, before turning a corner into a similar avenue, where the barrels were twice as large. They listened politely to his explanation of the 'angel's share', which accounted for three per cent of the volume each year. By then, they reached a large rolling door which he heaved open, enough for them to squeeze through and they stepped into an area filled with machinery, gantries, piping and huge stainless steel tanks. There was a quite different smell too; much fruitier. After closing the door, he showed them where the grapes were brought in and fed into an auger which delivered them to be pulped and stored in huge stainless steel fermentation tanks. "Zis is where the grapes do all the work for us. The skin of the grape is cloudy, which is the yeast. The flesh is the sugar and the skin is the colour, so *voilà*, they make wine by themselves. Sometimes, we have to help, but that is the principle."

He gathered them around one of the tanks and had them place an ear against it, "See, they are working very hard."

To begin with, Annie and Sue couldn't hear anything, but

the silence seemed to grow as they closed their eyes. Soon, they heard a gentle, barely audible roaring. As soon as Anton saw their expressions change he explained, "That is the fermentation, turning fruit into wine. It is near the end. Next week, we will begin to distil it into cognac." He beckoned them, "Follow me."

They negotiated another sliding door and stepped into a smaller space that was dominated by the huge copper still and two other vessels. A semi-derelict wooden cupboard lay in the opposite corner, alongside a small table and two chairs, which had been pushed against the wall. They looked as though they had belonged in a classroom once. An old electric kettle, two mugs and two small, dirty glasses had been left on the table, which Annie imagined were used in long vigils during the distillation period. The two glasses suggested that he'd have the company of a friend for part of the time, presumably for testing the product. A sweeping gaze took in the comical disparity, between the magnificent copper vessels on one side and a shambolic mix of derelict furniture on the other. She 'tuned' back into Anton's presentation, "So we distil the wine not once, but twice, before we have the *eau de vie*, which is clear and seventy per cent alcohol. Then it must live in the barrels for colour."

Sue asked, "May I sit down."

He pointed to one of the small chairs, "But of course, while I explain to you about distillation."

When she pulled the chair away from the wall he cried out, "*Non!* Please, it must be against the wall, or it will fall down!"

From then on his stories of the casks, made from Limousin oak, the ageing and a potted version of the history of cognac was much the same as they had heard on the *Rémy Martin* tour, though they did learn that a cognac bottled after five years in a barrel would remain a five year old, even if it the bottle remained unopened for twenty years. A forty year old will have spent all of that time in a barrel.

Once the tour was over he led them back to the office,

where he poured measures of cognac into three glasses and handed them out, "This is my five year old."

The spirit warmed the palette and their throats, on its way down; similar to the cognac they had already purchased.

He poured measures from another bottle into fresh glasses, "This is my twenty year old." It was darker and much smoother. Annie and Sue said as much and he nodded his agreement and pointed at the first bottle; the five year old, "That is good for cooking perhaps."

He then poured measures from a third bottle and passed them out without comment. This one was much darker and so much smoother, with a wonderfully full flavour; a gentle salve to the palette and throat. Sue held her glass up in a salute to Anton, "That is incredible!"

Anton beamed, "That is my forty year old."

Annie asked for the prices of the twenty and forty year olds. He glanced at a price list that had been taped to the table, "The twenty year old is twenty four Euros and the *Napoléon* is sixty Euros."

They were startled. The *twenty* year old was six Euros less than they had paid for a youngster at the last place. Annie shook her head slightly, "Wow, well I'll have two bottles of the twenty year old please." She looked at Sue, "What about you?"

"Oh I'm having a bottle of the twenty year old and one of the forty year old. One to share with friends and the other I'll keep for *very* good friends."

Anton smiled at her, "Bravo!" Then he pulled three bottles filled with the twenty year old out of a box and an empty bottle from another, before beckoning to Sue with a finger, "Follow me."

He led Sue back through the passages, to a room beyond the still where a barrel had been chocked on its side, in the space within yet another forest of casks. Another barrel lay next to it, but on its end, with the stump of a candle and a few glasses on the top surface. He removed a large bung from the barrel on its side and inserted a thin plastic tube before sucking firmly on the other end. With practiced ease, he bent over and directed the siphoned stream of cognac into the bottle he had placed on the floor. Once it was full, he directed the stream of nutty brown fluid into his mouth and swallowed a significant mouthful before looking up at Sue, "That is my share."

Having blocked the end of the tube with his finger, he looked over his shoulder and chose the nearest glass. After sniffing the interior and inspecting the sides in the light of an overhead bulb, he shrugged and poured a generous measure out before handing it to Sue, "And that is your share."

She was smitten.

And pissed.

They settled up, thanked him profusely and made to leave. The sisters shook hands with him whilst Penny kissed him on both cheeks. Not to be outdone, Sue returned to do the same. Anton beamed and suddenly had a thought, "Ladies, how long are you staying here for?"

Annie said, "I'm not sure."

"Well, you see, if you are still here next week please come back and see my still at work."

Sue turned with exaggerated care and winked at him, "Count on it."

After so many samples and the bottle of wine consumed with lunch, *both* sisters were the worse for wear. Sue crept off to bed for a couple of hours while Annie sat outside, to read a little and doze in the sunshine. It was a timely reminder of what life would be like there. Guinness woke her at one point, by stamping on her foot, but when she ignored him he slithered down to lie there and they both slept.

By six thirty they were both raring to go, though as cognac providers they were confronted with a dilemma. Should they take the twenty year old, or the forty? Penny and Tom had been such wonderful hosts, well beyond what might be expected of anyone charging for catering even, which meant that a the younger cognac seemed to be a cheap shot, though Sue did point out, "It certainly wouldn't have been if we'd bought it at the last place."

It was still pleasant enough to enjoy apéritifs and canapés outside, but only just. There was a distinctly autumnal feel to the air, which Tom assured them was long overdue.

Once they were settled Penny said, "Listen guys, I have to 'fess up to something. When I telephoned the Anderson's this morning, I told them what your budget was. I apologise for not clearing that with you first, but I didn't want to waste anyone's time."

Sue wasn't sure what to think, but Annie was delighted. "That is wonderful news! The fact that they were still prepared to show us around, knowing what our budget was, suggests that they might accept that sum. Thanks for telling us though."

Penny raised her glass, "Well, here's hoping. I still think it would be best if I didn't go with you tomorrow though." Annie nodded her agreement, "Negotiations should be a private matter and besides, the party that concedes the most may not want witnesses."

Tom interrupted, "You mean that a good deal is where one side leaves the table unhappy."

Annie thought for a moment before, "Actually, no. A really good deal is where both walk away smiling."

He grinned and raised his glass, "I'll drink to that."

The meal was another delight, beginning with *bruschetta,* laced with their own tomatoes and garlic, followed by calf's liver in a honey and sherry vinegar sauce, with baby potatoes and green beans. They finished off with a strawberry *granita* topped with crème fraiche.

Over coffees and cognac Tom inspected the cognac in his glass and said, "We're honoured, but there was no need to bring the best stuff you know."

Sue waved a hand in dismissal, "It was the very least we could do, you've been so good to us."

Annie raised her glass, "Here, here. In fact, I've just had an idea. If we could trouble you for herbs, olive oil and the like, I would like to do tomorrow night's meal, if that would be acceptable."

Penny didn't hesitate, "Too right. That would be lovely, thank you."

***

If anything, the Andersons' cottage charmed them more on their second visit. Les Anderson had been a man of few words the day before but he became much more outgoing when he accompanied them on their walk around the land, pointing out the different fruit trees and wildlife; or more often than not signs of wildlife. He explained, "Not much dares to poke its head up in France, for fear of getting it shot off."

Since Annie had already made her mind up, she was keen to get down to business, though not before coffees had been made and everyone was seated around the table. Even so, it was Gail who started and she didn't waste words, "Les and I have been talking about things since we saw you yesterday, to see if there was a way we could come down near enough to your budget."

Annie's pulse quickened, "Penny did tell us that she'd told you what it was."

Gail nodded, "Yes. It's pretty common knowledge that we're desperate to get back as well, but I'm sorry love, it's just too much of a drop. You might well think we should have told you that before showing you around again, but to be honest, we hoped you would want this place enough to increase your budget."

Sue shook her head, "Can't, I'm sorry.

Annie spoke as though she hadn't heard her sister, "How much more?"

Gail looked at her husband and rested her elbows on the table before clasping her hands, "One forty; that would be the absolute minimum we could accept. You see, it's not just a question of how much we need. We didn't stint on anything when we fitted this place out and one forty would still represent a huge loss to us."

Annie spoke firmly, "*If* we found the extra it would be our maximum. No fees, hidden extras or historical gremlins *and* no issues with the building that we should know about."

43

Les spoke, "I can be sure about the building. It's as good as new."

Gail said, "And we haven't got a French granny in the attic either."

Annie thought that was a strange assurance but let it go. Sue remained quiet, so there was little more to add. Annie smiled and stood, "OK, we'll go off and have a word about it. Thanks for showing us around again." They were shown to the front door in silence, but as Annie crossed the doorstep she turned to Gail, "Whatever we decide, I think your place is absolutely lovely."

Gail beamed, "Thank you and I think you would look after it too."

Little was said on the walk back to their *gite*, for it was clear that Annie wanted to go ahead and Sue knew that her sister had the means to do so, but she certainly didn't.

Once inside, Sue went to her bedroom, ostensibly to change, but she was readying herself for what was to come, however difficult it would be for both of them. Ten minutes later Annie called from the kitchen, "Sue, coffees are ready." Which they both knew was Annie-speak for 'right, let's talk turkey'.

Two coffees and a plate of biscuits lay on the table. Annie directed her sister to a chair. Sue sat down, "It's no good Sis', I don't have the money."

Annie put a finger to the side of her nose, "I have a plan, a cunning plan."

Sue rolled her eyes, "Oh God, she's doing a *Baldrick* on me." She waited, but eventually gave in, "Alright, tell me."

Annie was aware of their different circumstances and had given some thought to how she would explain this proposal, without causing offence, "You know that I did OK with selling the business and that money is sitting at home doing damn all in the building societies. We both love that place and I don't think we're going to find another like it. In fact, we'll be comparing it to anything we look at from now on. So, what I'm going to suggest is that I chip in the extra ten thousand and we have an agreement where I get that back if we ever sell the property. No interest, just the ten thou'."

Sue countered, "That will disadvantage you."

Annie shook her head and reached forward to take her sister's hand, "No it won't Sue, not if we get to buy that place." She increased her grip, "Come on Sis' let's do it."

***

After lunch they drove into Matha and found the *Intermarché* supermarket Penny had given directions for. Sue had asked for time to think, without constant lobbying, so Annie bit her tongue and waited anxiously. Once inside the store they had something else to occupy their minds, since neither had suggested a menu, in favour of choosing the best of what was available.

Penny had loaned them a cool box, loaded with frozen ice packs so that getting frozen or chilled stuff home wouldn't be an issue. The fish counter was a gourmet's delight though no more than they expected from a French store. In particular, the *dos de cabillaud* or cod loin looked spectacular and was on special offer, so they chose that for the main course. The rest was easy.

They barely spoke on the way home, to such an extent that it felt as though they'd had an argument, but as they drove up the hill towards the village, Sue cried out, "Oh fuck it, let's call in and tell them we'll buy it."

Annie feigned shock, "Sue, your language gets worse!" They were both grinning though, as were the Andersons, when they heard the news. The sisters were tempted to ask for another tour, but they had a meal to cook. Gail gave them a card from the estate agent and explained that they would need to confirm their decision in writing, on a form provided by the agent. After that, everything would take its course. Annie promised that they would see to it the following morning. In the meantime, they had just two hours to prepare the meal

The Anderson's watched them walk back towards their car from a discreet vantage point and saw the two women hug each other. Gail and Les did the same and as they drew apart she said, "Yes! We've done the right thing."

They began with a raid on Penny's larder and herb garden after establishing, somewhat belatedly, that the Challis's liked fish and chips, but first, they broke the news, so excitedly that Penny ended up in a giggling group hug. There were so many things to ask and not just about house buying because with that came a broadened agenda about the area and community. It was something else to look forward to that evening.

By six thirty it was too cold to sit outside and besides, the sisters had to keep an eye on the cooking, which looked set to take longer than anticipated. Fortuitously as it turned out, for the extended period for apéritifs gave them time for updates and questions.

Tom explained the house buying process, some of which the sisters had already learned from the agents they had met, but they still wanted to hear it all, "Well, it's quite different over here compared to the UK. Now that you've made an offer which has been accepted, even if only verbal, you've entered into a contractual commitment; at least, technically. Tomorrow, their agent will want you to sign an *Offre d'Achat,* which is a formal offer but in due course, the sale and purchased agreement will be drawn up after which you will have a ten day cooling off period, during which you can pull out without penalty. The Anderson's will have had to have a number of reports done on the property but they fall well short of a full building survey, so you may want to have one of those done. Now that termites have been found as far north as Bordeaux I'd check to make sure that the timber has been treated.

The same goes for legal representation. You'll complete the deal in front of a Public Notaire, who will ensure that you're aware of any covenants or restrictions and a bunch of other stuff, but he may not speak English, so you should think about appointing a lawyer, or *Avocat* of your own. You could appoint another notaire instead and at no extra cost, because he'll share with the first notaire, but his brief will be limited whereas you may need much broader help. I'd recommend the one we used actually, not least of all because he speaks excellent English. Listen carefully too. We heard about one couple who purchased a large farmhouse and discovered that the vendor's elderly mother still retained occupancy rights in part of it. She stayed there too! Until she died, at any rate and that was three or four years later."

Sue chipped in, "I can handle bats in the attic, but not grannies."

Tom had yet to finish, "Don't forget the fees. They're a lot higher over here."

Annie cut in, "I raised that issue with the Anderson's and they promised us that the price would include all of them."

Tom's eyebrows headed north, "You're joking!" He shook his head, "Then you've got yourselves a hell of a deal. Some sellers include the agent's fees in the sale price, but not many, because they are so much higher than in the UK; as much as seven per cent plus taxes. The notaire's fees will be the same sort of figure, so they've effectively sold you the place for around a hundred and twenty thousand. I wonder if they realise what they agreed to."

Penny showed her concern, "Hold on a sec'. Does that mean that even if they've made a mistake they're committed to it?"

Tom nodded, "Technically, yes, but don't forget that ten day cooling off period I spoke about."

She looked at the sisters, "What do you think?"

Sue was the first to respond, "I expected the legal fees to be hundreds, not thousands and if we'd had to pay the agent's fees too it would have been *miles* away from my budget."

Annie was concerned too, but for all parties. She asked Penny, "Do *you* think they made a mistake?"

Penny paused, while she measured the effect of her response on her new friend's bubble of joy, but there was no point in lying. Eventually, she nodded sadly, "Yes, I think they have. If they *haven't,* I'm thrilled to bits for you, but having knocked twenty thousand off the asking price, I don't think they'll have anticipated giving that much more away. They're nice people, so I hope I'm wrong."

Privately, Annie agreed. Gail and Les seemed such a lovely, genuine couple, but the revelations did dampen things for a while, until Annie stood and retrieved the second bottle of champagne from the fridge. As the cork took flight, she announced, "Bugger it, whatever happens, we'll deal with it."

Sue, buoyed by two glasses of champagne and the realisation of what Annie was saying, called out, "Rock on Sis', I'm with you." Having already agreed to her sister's supplement of ten thousand, a few more wouldn't matter.

The Challis's were unaware of the hidden agenda, but they welcomed the lightening of the mood, though less time was spent talking about the purchase in favour of a broader range of safer topics.

The starter was a smoked salmon and fresh pineapple salad with a balsamic dressing and the main course was Annie's special take on fish and chips. The deep chunks of cod loin were topped with curried mayonnaise and a mix of breadcrumbs, cheese and fresh parsley, which when roasted, provided a crisp, crumbly topping. The chips were huge chunky affairs, par-boiled enough to give them 'fur coats' when tossed in olive oil and roasted, with a sprinkling of sea salt crystals. All accompanied by green beans and sautéed fennel.

After the cheese, Sue provided a delicious sweet of apricots, baked with muscovado sugar, beneath a layer of brioche that was crispy and brown on the top but still soft beneath, thanks to a liberal application of honey and *Amaretto*.

By the time coffee arrived, they were fuelled once again by alcohol and spirits were high, save for the cognac level. They all expressed sorrow at having to make do with the twenty year old.

***

The evening had turned out to be such a success that the sisters decided to stay up to chat and wash the dishes before they went to bed, but even then, they opted for hot chocolates before retiring. Each sat at the table savouring the sweet fragrance that rose from the mugs, until Sue broached the subject, "Well Sis', what happens now, about the house?"

Annie had been giving the matter just as much thought as Sue and wasn't going to waste her breath with a 'let's wait and see' ploy, "If Tom's right the Anderson's will be in a fix and it'll be a deal breaker." She put her mug down and reached across to take Sue's hand, "Life's too short to play games with something as important as this. If there is a problem I'll cover it, under the same terms."

Sue returned Annie's grip, "I'm not going to decline this one, but hey, we might just be wrong. The Anderson's may have taken the fees into account all along."

Annie shrugged, "Let's see, but it's one o'clock and I'm ready for bed."

As they reached the bedrooms Sue gave her sister a brief hug, "Night, night Sis', I don't deserve you."

Annie smiled and shrugged, "That's true. Sleep tight."

In spite the late night, Annie was up at seven thirty, enjoying a quiet cup of tea when she heard a quiet tapping at the door.

Gail looked as though she had aged ten years. Annie had no doubt that the reddened bags under her eyes were not from sleep and the trembling wasn't caused by the temperature. In fact, Annie saw only a wreck of the strong, warm farmer's wife from the previous day. Gail gazed up at Annie and stammered, "We, we've made a dreadful mistake."

If it had been one of her suppliers in the old days, Annie would have held her ground or told them to take the goods back, but this was different. One on one and each with a moral duty of care when it mattered.

Annie drew Gail into the room by wrapping her arm around the woman's shoulders. She spoke quietly, with a deafeningly effective sincerity, "The biggest mistake you've made is not coming around sooner. By the look of you, I'd say you didn't get much sleep last night."

Gail turned to Annie with an expression of relief and gratitude. She nodded, "Neither of us did."

Annie pulled a chair out from beneath the table and sat Gail down, before, "OK, first things first, tea or coffee." Tea was selected and Annie pulled two mugs out of the cupboard as she called upstairs, "Sue." After putting the kettle on she called again, much louder, "Sue! Get up! We have a visitor." There was the sound of movement and a minute or two later they heard the toilet flush, before Sue struggled downstairs in crumpled jeans and a T shirt that graphically demonstrated the absence of a bra. She was finger combing her hair with one hand and rubbing sleep out of her eyes with the other. Gail stood up and they kissed each other, French style, while Sue explained, "Late night last night. 'Scuse the face, I slept in it."

Gail tried to smile, but didn't comment. She had too many other things on her mind. Annie placed the two mugs in front of them and explained, "Gail needs to talk to us about something." She turned towards Gail with a slight but kindly smile, "Though from what Tom told us last night, I've got a good idea of what it is."

Gail began to tremble again, "We've been so stupid!" We should have known how much the fees and costs were but when we called the agent yesterday he was quite rude. He said that we should have involved him in the negotiations and the fault was completely ours." Her eyes filled as she sighed, "So stupid."

Annie reached across the table and took Gail's hand, "No you're not. We've all been lucky to find each other." She increased her grip, "Now, what will it take to make you feel better?"

***

They drove into Matha that morning, but not before they had called on Penny to tell her the news. Annie explained, "Gail and Les are covering the agent's fees and we're sorting the notaire's fees and taxes out."

Penny clapped her hands silently and murmured, "Bravo," before adding, "We were so certain they'd made a mistake, but

I told Tom you would come through. It's going to be a pleasure having you two in the village."

In Matha, Annie treated the agent with appropriate disdain. Not that it mattered, for the form had been pre-prepared and they were back on the street within ten minutes, leaving ample time for a spot of shopping and a coffee.

Penny was cooking the meal that night so they were looking forward to a day of leisure. The excitement of the purchase had mellowed slightly in the face of a ten thousand Euro increase, but they both knew they'd done the right thing and Annie had it covered, easily. She passed off Sue's concern with a shrug and, "Hey, do I leave the money in the building society, or put it into the cottage? No brainer."

Almost every town in France has a large church, a mayor and a square, which accommodates a market for two mornings a week, where the produce is wonderfully fresh and EU rules are ignored. For example, raw meats share the same counter as the cooked and chicken carcases, with head and feet still attached, look as though they might still be warm. Unlike the UK, prices are often higher than in the supermarkets. The French are prepared to pay for quality and flavour.

The sisters already knew that much of the fruit and vegetables appeared when in season rather than a year round supply of adulterated stuff; shipped around the World in gas filled containers. When the sisters stocked up on fruit, they noted that the stall holder picked from the front of his display, discarding anything that was bruised or imperfect. It just felt like another tick on their 'like' list.

They were back at the *gite* by eleven thirty and Annie suggested another coffee, but Sue declined, saying that she was going to walk up to Anton's for another bottle of forty year old. Annie opted for a sit down and read before lunch, but when Sue failed to return by a quarter to one she found herself eating alone, after which she settled back into a chair with the book, which fell away onto her lap when she dozed off.

She was awoken just after three when Sue strode in, with a

bottle of cognac. She made tea for both of them, without asking Annie if she wanted one, though after an hour of 'catching flies', the drink was welcome. They sat outside where the afternoon sunshine still had plenty of heat and the birdsong was a joy, but Annie was intrigued, particularly since her sister didn't seem inclined to explain her extended absence, "So, what happened to you then?"

Sue wriggled slightly, as though she was settling into her chair, "Oh, nothing really, Anton told me a little more about making cognac and since it was close to lunchtime, he opened a bottle of wine and offered me an apéritif. Very nice it was too."

"And?"

Sue sounded defensive, "What do you mean?"

Annie sighed, "Sue, apéritifs don't take three hours!"

Defence turned into remorse, "Sorry Sis' I hadn't meant to abandon you for lunch, but as we were talking he began to put all manner of meats and cheeses onto the table. I finished my glass of wine and was just about to take my leave when he plonked a plate and cutlery on the table in front of me and asked if I'd do him the honour of sharing lunch with him. He really is a charmer you know and I didn't know how to say no. Saying I had to go back to my sister would've sounded a bit lame."

Annie huffed, "You managed to fill three hours with that?"

Sue repeated herself, though with a hint of indignity this time, "What do you mean?" She saw the grin spread across her sister's face and heard the soft throaty giggle, "Oh you bugger! You were just waiting for me to admit to something far more salacious."

Annie continued to giggle, "Come on, I've known you bed a man in minutes. At three hours I reckon you must be losing your touch."

Sue stuck her tongue out, "Sticks and stones." After a moment though, she added, "Still Annie, I would have told you if I'd have even suspected lunch was going to happen. Did you wait long?"

Annie was still smiling, "No, but your dalliance with Monsieur Michaud did make me think about things; stuff we need to agree from the outset." Sue began to speak but Annie held up a hand and continued, "Just because we'll be sharing a house together here doesn't mean that we must share each other's lives. I have no intention of becoming one of an old maid duo and I'm sure you don't."

Sue nodded and said softly, "Thanks Sis', it's good to know, but I still feel the need to tell you that today, lunch was all that happened."

Annie shrugged that one off; then said, "There is a caveat. Whilst you are welcome to have dalliances with whoever you wish, it would be difficult to accept him," she paused before, "Or her, into our house. It's too small for me to share that with."

Sue chuckled, "Quite agree, I'm far too vocal in the sack, always have been and I'll bet you were too. Anyway, same thing applies to you. I hope you find someone."

Whilst shaking her head slightly, Annie said, "We'll see." After a moment she added, "And yes, I was too."

After an extended pause something else crossed Sue's mind, "Oh, it'd be a 'him'. I've never really been attracted to the home side."

They sat in companionable silence then; Annie reading her book and Sue lost in thought, until eventually she said, "Do you realise that we've bought a house in an area we know almost nothing about?"

Annie looked up, "Are you having second thoughts already?"

"Hell's bells no! But I was just wondering. I know we'd planned on going back on Monday, which only leaves us two days to have a look around. Neither of us *has* to be back so soon do we? So how about staying on a while longer and doing some real exploring."

After a thoughtful pause, Annie said, "Let me think about it."

That evening, over dinner they had little to add to the stuff they talked about the previous evening though Tom had written the details of his lawyer down and had telephoned to put him on standby to receive a call from two English ladies.

Sue was still waiting for a response to her suggestion, so was startled when Annie asked Penny, "May we stay on for a while please, perhaps for three or four weeks? Sue pointed out this afternoon that we hardly know this area so the sooner we do the better."

Penny was delighted, "No problem. An extended let at this time of year is a real bonus for us. Mind, you're going to need the heating on so I'll have to take a meter reading and charge you I'm afraid. I haven't done so far but it's getting colder each day now and utilities over here are pretty expensive."

Annie said, "To be honest, we've been having the heating on in the mornings already."

Penny shrugged, "My omission, consider it a freebie, but there is one thing that springs to mind."

Sue chipped in, "Does it have anything to do with cognac?"

A chuckle, "Not directly, but you're close. If you are planning to 'settle in' as it were, I'd suggest having some evenings by yourselves. If we meet like this every night we're likely to get on each other's tits."

Tom moaned, "Penny, please!"

She continued as though he hadn't said anything, "What I mean is, it would be more appropriate to continue as though you were living here already. You can even stock up with the basics and leave them here until you move in."

Annie put both thumbs up, "Couldn't agree more. This is a good time to mention another thing too. Sue and I have talked about it already. You may be sure that we will never be 'cup of sugar' neighbours, knocking on the door every five minutes."

Penny's thumbs appeared too, "We kind of knew that, but what say we eat together twice a week, for this visit; once here and once at yours?"

The sisters nodded together as Annie said, "Brilliant!"

***

The lawyer, Monsieur Gagnon was at his office and taking calls on Saturday, so they were able to make an appointment to see him on Monday morning.

Annie checked the route on Sunday and checked it again, to make sure. In the event, they left ample time for the journey and found a place to park almost immediately, which left them with an hour to lose.

He was an extremely charming forty odd year old, whose lineage must have begun in the *Basque* region, judging from his natural colour and hair. His offices occupied the first floor of an eighteenth century town house in Cognac and he had taken care to furnish the place in keeping with the building. The elegant furniture, high ceilings and windows gave the place a palatial air which the sisters found disconcerting, but they were soon comforted by his easy manner and the coffees brought in by a secretary. They listened politely to his explanation of the processes, after which he took their details and copies of their passports. As they left Annie said, "From now on, we leave everything to him then. We're in his hands."

Sue nudged her, "Humph! I wish."

They spent some of the next three weeks exploring the area, taking in the cities of Saintes, Cognac and Bordeaux as well as the countryside and more commercial attractions such as *Futurescope*. Both were deeply affected by their visit to *Oradour-sur-Glane*, the town wiped out by Waffen SS troops, four days after the D-Day landings and now frozen in time. Rusting cars, pitted buildings, pots, pans and even knitting machines, all left as they were on that terrible day. But they had other things to think about too.

Sue continued to call on Anton and had even negotiated a deal with him in the first week of their extended stay. She explained to Annie, "Superficially, his house is clean, ish, but horribly untidy. He's even adopted a practice of eating out of whatever he cooks in, to save on the cleaning up and he's applied the same approach to everything in the house."

Annie's eyebrows shot up, "So you've been all over the house then?"

Sue held up a hand, "A tour, nothing more, but we've struck a deal. For every morning spent sorting things out I get lunch and a bottle of his forty year old."

Annie was startled, "That's not very much!"

Her sister squidged up her nose, "I know, but he's become a friend."

This time Annie said nothing, but one eyebrow went up, to accompany the knowing look, one that seemed justified when Sue announced that Anton had invited her out to dinner on the Friday night, to mark the eve of the start to that year's distillation.

At the arranged time on Friday, Sue appeared, dressed to kill and as she stepped out of the *gite* Annie called out, *"Bonne chance!"* She received a 'raspberry' in response, as the door closed.

He took her to a restaurant in the centre of Cognac, called *Le Bistro de Hector,* which overlooked the public gardens. The furnishings were simple and the tables crowded together, but the atmosphere was relaxed and the food was breathtaking.

Their friendship had blossomed over the last two weeks, during which they shared many stories and laughs. He taught her much more about cognac and the care of vines, but Sue had always been mindful of the fact that she was on his territory, perhaps because of her own initiative in offering to be a cleaner. Not that he had been any less than the perfect host. In fact, he had been lovely throughout, with an unfailingly impish sense of humour and he'd encouraged her to interact with the British visitors, to such an extent that during the previous day he had left her to escort a group around by herself, though he made sure to be present for the tastings and sales. But there were the other times too. After a telephone call perhaps, or when the post lady stopped by. He would become quiet and reclusive then and she deemed it best to go off and find something to do elsewhere. Just part of being in business she decided, an assessment that seem to be confirmed within the hour, when he returned to his more usual self.

Yet that night, on the drive into Cognac, she saw subtle

differences in his behaviour. He was more gregarious and expansive, as though he had shaken off a leash. The range of topics broadened and during the meal he pressed her for more details of her own background without appearing to be at all fazed by her tales of Sierra Leone. Quite the contrary in fact, for when he saw that she had left half of her *foie gras* he sought and secured permission to swap her plate for his empty one, signalling for her to continue her narrative as he tucked in. They ate slowly and the service was paced to last for hours, but when the deserts arrived his mood changed. Suddenly he grew quieter and more thoughtful. At first she thought he was giving her an opportunity to tell him more about herself, but it was soon evident that he was distracted, to such an extent that finally, she said, "Penny for your thoughts?"

He'd been toying with his desert in silence and looked up, startled, "Pardon?"

She smiled, "You were miles away."

"Oh, I am so sorry."

She interrupted, "Don't be, but share, if you want to."

He shrugged and smiled, "It is nothing." After a moment, he continued, "It is also a long time since I have been away from the vineyard and even longer since I did so with a beautiful woman."

Sue was too long in the tooth to be coy and simply said, "Thank you." After a moment though, she added, "But I don't think your thoughts were just about me."

He put his spoon and fork down before taking a mouthful of wine, then, whilst gazing at the velvet depths of the liquid he explained, "I think it is easier to speak of some things here than when I am at home. My thoughts need many pennies."

Sue remained silent, leaving him time to continue.

He continued to gaze at his wine, "I think I will have to sell the vineyard."

She clapped her hands together, once, "Good for you. Retirement will suit you."

He looked up, alarmed, "No, you misunderstand. I do not

want to sell it, but I think I will be forced to and that will break my heart, I think."

The fun Sue had so often seen in those lovely brown eyes had gone; replaced with a glistening sorrow. She was so startled, "Shit, I mean *merde,* I mean, why? How? Your cognac is so incredible."

He shrugged, "It is complicated, but then it is simple too. My family have always dealt with the same merchant in Bordeaux, here we call them *négociants,* but two years ago they stopped buying from me. They won't give me a reason and the other merchants are already supplied by others, so now they want to pay me less than it costs to produce my cognac. I have managed to sell some, but I do not sell enough to pay my bills and my savings have gone. When bad things happen, I can no longer put them right."

"Such as?"

He turned his mouth down, "Last year a neighbour sprayed weed killer along the edge of his land. It was very windy and the chemical spread onto some of my vines; - almost half a hectare. All his vines were upwind and safe. Monsieur Pichon is not a good man I think. The compensation only paid for the new vines, but they will take years to replace the ones I lost. Then this year, some of his cattle broke through the fence separating our land and damaged over a hundred vines. Thankfully, no more, but he refused to pay me anything because it was my fence.

He is just waiting now, I think. You see, he has always wanted to buy this land and his father before him. He is wealthy enough to do so too, with three hundred hectares compared to my fifty, so now maybe, he will have his *chance.* Anton pronounced the last word in French, which translates to 'luck', but he added with some fervour, "That will never, never be with my blessing. I would rather sell to another for less than he will offer, if I could, or the bank would allow me to."

Sue didn't try to offer suggestions, taking it as read that he'd have looked at all the alternatives. Instead she reached forward and grasped the hand that lay on the table, "Anton, I'm so sorry."

He rolled his hands to clasp hers, but after a few moments he rallied and then smiled, "What is this? What am I doing? I have had a wonderful meal, with a lovely companion. Let us enjoy the moment and not dwell on such other things." He winked, "Tomorrow, you shall light the still. We always toast it with a glass of my finest!"

With his current run of luck, Sue prayed they would make it back without an encounter with a *Gendarme* and his breath-alyser, but by eleven that night, they pulled into the yard, intact and still licensed to drive. Whilst she was certain that his disclosures in the restaurant had been a cathartic experience, there had been evident pain, so she was relieved to see that he was back to his usual self. They sat at the kitchen table and drank small espresso coffees, accompanied by the *de rigueur* cognacs. Both were delicious, but Sue complained, "I've had so much caffeine today I'm going to be too wired for sleep."

Anton disagreed, "*Non, non*, it is a *digestif.* It will help your tummy to digest the rich food."

She grinned, "It was rich too, *and* delicious. Thank you for a lovely evening."

For the want of anything else to say they rose from the table and Anton moved towards her, until they were within arm's reach. He reached forward, took her hand and gently placed a lingering kiss on the back of it, before returning to the upright position and whispering, "Sanc you so much Sue."

At that moment, Sue came to a decision. She smiled and stepped forward into his personal space, one she intended to share that night.

Later, after a clumsy encounter, for which he was embarrassed and apologetic, in spite of Sue's reassurances, she reinforced her bond with him by cuddling up in the dim light of a single bedside lamp; the only one with a bulb in. Neither felt like sleep and later, Sue would conclude that perhaps this latest anxiety helped to bring back the other demons.

Suddenly, he said, "My father always told me and, I think,

my brother, that the old man Pichon was a bad man and we were not to have anything to do with him. He is dead now, of course, but I do not like his son, Albert, very much."

Sue said, "Is he the one with the cattle and weed killer?"

"Yes."

Her head rubbed against his chest as she nodded, "Then I don't like the little bastard either." After a moment, something occurred to her, "Your brother? I thought you said you were the last of the line."

"He died when I was only two years old. I never really knew him. It was a tractor accident. He was twenty years old. There was an eighteen year gap between us."

"Blimey, that must have been a surprise for your parents."

He chuckled slightly, "Yes, they often told me it was."

After a few moments Sue asked, "Did your father tell you why the old man was a bad person?"

She felt him shake his head, "No. Well I don't think so. The only story my mother did tell me was not so serious you see, though it frightened my father at the time. It was during the war. Food was scarce and most of our cognac had been requisitioned by the Germans. They seemed to have first claim on all produce and we were all hungry. Maurice, my brother and his friend took some fruit from the Pichon's orchard and were spotted. Apparently, old man Pichon came over and said that since the Germans had first call on the ripening fruit, he was going to report the theft to them. Apparently, my father pleaded with Pichon and paid him far more than the fruit was worth. Eventually, the threat was withdrawn but my father had been so frightened he gave Maurice a real thrashing."

She allowed a moment, to ensure that he'd finished before, "Hmm, scrumping; not exactly serious crime, but not the stuff of a lifetime feud either."

He murmured drowsily, "No, I think not."

Sensing his descent into sleep she eased up and pecked him on the cheek, "Night, night and sleep on this. You and I have something to look forward to."

He stirred, "What is that."

She had already rolled on to the other side of the bed and was settling into a comfortable position, "Me teaching you all about the female orgasm."

***

Annie had already been up to the *Boulangerie* for a baguette and was dunking chunks of bread into a bowl of hot chocolate when Sue returned. Guinness was in the corner but this time his welcome was no more than a glance and a wag of the tail, after which he returned to his saucer of tea. It only took one, a few days earlier, to establish the routine. Since then he had scratched on the door as soon as he sensed movement inside and was allowed to wander in for his own breakfast.

Annie didn't bother looking up when she asked, "Nice meal?"

Sue had prepared herself for this, "Lovely thanks, Anton can be very entertaining and informative."

"Been learning about Anton's little secrets then? About cognac making that is."

"Yes, he taught me some of the more technical terms in French."

"My, my, the mind boggles."

Sue wasn't one to be discomfited, "Hmm, I think I might have taught him a thing or two, as well."

Unlike her sister, Annie could be embarrassed by matters sexual, but she wasn't about to be cowed into silence either. In fact, stung by her sister's riposte, she said something wholly out of character, "Did he have his own 'KY' jelly then?"

Sue looked back at her, askance, "Of course not, silly." After an extended pause, during which she poured hot chocolate from the pan into a bowl, she added, "We used olive oil."

"Sue! For heaven's sake, that's too much information!"

Sue sat down at the table and reached for the bread, "Sorry, Sis', but you did start it. Now, how much do you want to know?"

Annie wasn't exactly sure how much she ought to know, but eventually, she giggled, "Everything."

At one point, Sue said, "Do you know that he was married once but there were no children, *and* he had one brother who was killed in an accident, which makes him the last of the line. The place has been in the family for over two hundred years and there's no heir."

Annie snickered, "Until last night perhaps."

Sue huffed, "I think not! That *would* be a miracle."

Annie agreed, "And a shock, you old tart."

Sue feigned offence, "Less of the old if you don't mind. Oh, and another thing, I met Anton's employee, Henri, this morning."

Annie looked up, "I didn't know he had one."

"Neither did I. Apparently, he's worked for the family all his life, which by the look of him, has been a very long time. Doesn't say much, but by all accounts he turns up for breakfast each morning to discuss the previous day's work and to receive instructions for the current one. Then he disappears into the fields, which is usually the last anyone sees of him. He even has lunch in the van followed by a nap that has grown longer as time goes on."

Anton had extended his invitation to Annie for the start up of the still, which was set for ten that morning. In the meantime, after clearing up the breakfast dishes, they settled into armchairs to pass an hour; Annie with a crossword and Sue with a John Grisham book.

At some point, Annie looked at her sister and wondered how they could be so alike and yet so different. She had no doubt who had taken the initiative last night, something she wouldn't have ever been able to do, even as a student, yet they had so much in common too. This trip was a case in point.

Eventually, Sue became aware of the scrutiny and startled her sister with a comment that was intuitive enough to suggest that she could mind read, "It's not much fun you know, being on your own. Leastways, I haven't found so, which means that little adventures like last night can be treasures; the occasional arsehole excepted."

Annie put her crossword down, "Is that a warning, because it's a bit late if it is. Remember, I've been on my own for six years now."

Sue dropped her book onto her lap, "Sorry Sis', that was a clumpy of me, but what I meant was, don't be afraid to spread your wings. Find someone you can spend time with."

"Sue, I was married to the same man for twenty six years. The only other love I had was the business and that wasn't the same when Don died. I don't think I'm programmed for another long term relationship."

Her sister held up a hand, "I understand that, I really do, though with my background I'm not sure why I should, but don't worry, I'll never try and match make."

Annie acknowledged the promise with a nod and, "Thank you."

After a lengthy pause Sue added a caveat, "But you ought to try and get laid now and then."

"Enough!"

Sue held up both hands before retreating behind her book. But it wasn't over, because Annie had said something that became the germ of an idea.

Twenty minutes later she had assembled her thoughts, "Annie! I have a red hot date for you." She saw her sister's expression and hurried on, "No, it's not what you think."

Annie simply returned to her crossword, without a word, while Sue stared at her in a silence that became excruciating. Eventually, she dumped the pen and paper onto her lap, "Oh for heaven's sake Sue; spit it out, then I'll say no and bury another silly idea."

"Anton's about to go bankrupt."

"I beg your pardon?"

Sue nodded, "He is, but it just doesn't make sense. His cognac is wonderful and a vineyard doesn't stay in business for over two hundred years unless it's getting something right. It may be that his working practices are a bit out of date, but he's had a run of bad luck lately too. It needs someone from outside to have a look at it and I thought, with your experience...."

Annie interrupted, "Now hold on a minute, I ran a sports goods business. I don't know anything about Cognac."

Sue continued as though she hadn't heard, "With your experience, you might see things he hasn't. I'm not talking about making cognac; he's doing a great job of that already, but once he's barrelled it, it becomes stock, just like football boots or hockey sticks." She went on to relate all that Anton had told her and in spite of huge doubts, Annie became intrigued. She had spent a lifetime observing three mantras and Sue was right, they applied to almost any business. Sound products, marketing and knowing the difference between a profit and a loss were the key ingredients for any business. It was clear from what she'd been told that Anton's enterprise seemed to be missing two of them.

They were late for their visit by then and they left in a hurry, but by the time they reached the distillery she'd been persuaded to have a look, at least.

It took over an hour and several cognacs to fire up the still and ensure that the distillation process was in hand. At one point, while they were waiting for the evaporation to begin, he took a framed picture out of the cupboard and placed it on the concrete platform beside the still with a certain sense of ceremony. It was a picture of an elderly man and a much younger Anton, standing where he was now. Sue moved over and looked closely before asking, "Is that your father?"

He nodded, "Yes, I get this picture out each year. Would you like to know why?" She nodded, so he continued, with the hint of a smile he always wore when being mischievous. He pointed at the image of his father, himself and lastly the still, "Here you have the father, the son and the holy spirit!"

It was after noon and he invited both sisters to join him for lunch. Sue declined on Annie's behalf, saying, "You and I need to have a chat in private."

By four that afternoon Sue had detailed Annie's CV and bullied him into a free assessment and consultation, beginning the following morning. In the meantime, he explained that the first twelve hours of distillation called for close attention, after which the still would only need checking every eight hours or so, leaving plenty of time to answer questions.

And there were lots of them.

Annie accompanied Sue to Anton's the next morning and began by requesting the year end accounts for the previous ten years. In response he clumped upstairs and returned with two large storage boxes, which he dumped onto the kitchen table with, "They are in there, I think." They were far too heavy to be carried back to the *gite* so Annie walked back to collect their car. When she returned, in a somewhat poor humour, Anton was tending the still and Sue made an extremely half-hearted offer to accompany her sister and the boxes back to their place. Thankfully, Annie would have none of it. She called over her shoulder, rather tersely, as she headed to the car, "I'm better left alone with this sort of thing."

The first seven years showed a steady turnover, with the bulk of sales to one merchant house, but that name disappeared in year eight, accounting for a catastrophic drop in sales. She did notice though, that the price paid by the merchant during those seven years remained constant, while the overheads increased, in line with inflation she presumed. Since then there were occasional bulk sales which lacked a pattern and were for much smaller quantities and sometimes, even lower prices.

Unsurprisingly, the stock levels had increased, though the quantity of forty year old was less than she'd anticipated.

She found the exceptional costs of buying new vines and fencing repairs that Sue had told her about, but they only formed part of a general decline. She had no knowledge of the local protocols and markets, but how could a product that was so good be ignored? The accounts were remarkably well ordered and it only took a couple of hours to complete her review. She telephoned the distillery and spoke to Sue, "I've finished looking at the accounts so when will his nibs be available?"

Sue said to hang on while she went to find out and soon

returned with authority to arrange another meeting, for the following morning. Ample time Annie thought, to give some thought to the issues and prepare the bad news.

***

The meeting began well, with Annie saying that she was still amazed by how his wonderful product hadn't found a larger market, but then the questions began, "Your merchant managed to avoid paying you any increases, even over seven years. How could that be?"

Anton explained, "The markets have become very difficult. Cognac, or brandy is produced by so many countries now and most are much cheaper than here. Did you know that South Africa is the World's largest brandy supplier?"

She didn't, but that prompted her next question, "So how come *Hennessy*, *Rémy Martin* and *Martell* survive, with prices that dwarf yours?"

"They are large enough to make their own markets and it is a question of economies of scale. They buy their wines and cognacs in at prices they dictate and then blend them. I am a very small concern and use only my own grapes. There are bad blenders too, who take an old but very bad cognac and turn it into a 'good'...." he signalled the brackets with both forefingers, "Cognac, by adding things; even sugar and caramel."

Annie referred to her notes, "Why are the bulk sales so erratic?"

His mouth turned down, "Most merchants have well established contracts with their suppliers. I did, before they cancelled mine at the review date. So they only come to me when there is a shortfall; a low harvest perhaps."

After making some notes she continued, "Have you tried to find another merchant?"

He bridled at that and said somewhat indignantly, "But of course!"

"And no luck?"

He deemed that one unworthy of an answer and remained

silent. After a few moments, she moved on, "Have you tried to market your cognac independently, perhaps to foreign buyers?"

"But I am doing, with my tours for foreign visitors."

She nodded, "They have been more successful than I realised, but it's still a small market." She'd used Penny's computer to check *Trip Advisor* and the few reviews on there were all complimentary, but not numerous enough to put him in the rankings, "Do you *ask* visitors to mention you on *Trip Advisor*?"

He shrugged his shoulders, signalling that he'd never thought to do so.

She made a quick note, before, "OK, so what about overseas buyers? In the UK, or US perhaps.

His eyebrows shot up, "How? I am just me, I cannot afford a salesman."

"What about an agent?"

He rolled his head from side to side, "How? I am still just me, on my own and too small to export."

Annie shook her head, but smiled too, in an effort to be conciliatory rather than antagonistic, "I don't agree. I reckon you are perfectly placed to find niche markets."

And so it continued, for another hour, by which time Anton was operating on an extremely short fuse. It was a question of Gallic pride really and this woman was doing nothing but dwell on his inadequacies. Annie had recognised the signs, of course, but she'd had enough too. They would leave Anton alone the next day and do some more exploring instead. She promised to return the day after that, with a report and hopefully, a few ideas. By then they both realised that the experience would be challenging.

Sue didn't plan on discussing things in the interim, having often warned that she had the business acumen of a dormouse, though Annie insisted on her attendance at the next meeting, if only to hold his hand.

In the end, Annie chose to close as quickly as possible and leave him to think about things.

The following day was wasted, so far as Sue was concerned.

They drove for hours, stopping for coffee and lunch in two sleepy towns, but any attempt to engage Annie in discussion soon slipped away into monosyllabic exchanges. Annie was wrestling with commercial hurdles, one at a time. Each, it seemed, followed by the water trough of Anton's finer feelings and to some extent, by association, Sue's too.

Finally, the time for jousting arrived. They sat around the kitchen table and she began by talking about stocks, "I noticed that you had some much older stocks, though the age of the oldest didn't mean anything to me until I worked the numbers out and realised the significance of the date; nineteen forty six."

Anton sighed, "Yes, that was the year we started again. My father was alive then, but in many ways he was dead; a beaten man. The Germans took everything. A number of growers, my father included, realised what would happen when your soldiers were at Dunkerque, so they hid their cognac in shallow caves at Mouthiers-sur-Boeme. They were the nearest but still thirty five kilometres away, so it was a very big undertaking. The Germans discovered it, only a month after occupying the region. The officers kept the fine cognac and the soldiers drank anything else they could get their hands on, even the *eau de vie* as it came out of the still.

Only one of the growers from this village refused to hide his stocks and the Germans allowed him to keep them, as a lesson to the rest of us."

Annie spoke softly, "That must have been terrible."

He nodded, "The war cost lives, in more ways than one."

It was time to get down to more contemporary issues. She opened her notes and began, "This is not nearly exhaustive Anton, but here are some preliminaries. First, let me check my understanding of the current operation. It looks as though you produce around two hundred thousand litres of *eau de vie* per year."

Anton nodded.

"And you are considered to be a small producer."

This time he shrugged, "Yes."

The quality, and scale of your operation, along with the fact that you do not blend, should imply a certain exclusivity. In fact, it's the only way to market your cognac, if the merchants won't buy it. Either that or upscale dramatically, perhaps by bringing wine in, but that would require a significant capital injection for equipment and it still wouldn't guarantee you a market. If the merchants won't deal with you now they may not then. I'd love to know why they stopped buying from you when your product is so good." She allowed a moment for him to respond, before continuing, "Advertising, - there isn't any. Networking; - you admitted yesterday that you didn't. So whilst we all agree that the product is wonderful, who knows that? All those things need addressing and soon, in spite of the cost."

Anton asked, "How can I do that, I have no money."

Annie nodded, "That's true, I can't see how you could fund it alone and the bank won't help, not with your current state of affairs, so the only way would be to find someone to share a joint venture with."

He was horrified, "A partner you mean?"

"That would be one choice, but maybe you could find some local growers who are traditionalists and in a similar position to you."

He spoke with certainty, "They would not join up with others."

"Not even by forming a co-operative?"

"*Non!* These people have been independent for decades, maybe even hundreds of years. They would prefer to die in poverty than betray their heritage."

"What about selling a share to a sleeping partner?"

After explaining what a sleeping partner was, she watched Anton pat one hand on the table, "Non! This is the Michaud vineyard. It has been in my family for over two hundred years."

Annie wasn't fazed and she didn't intend to coddle him, "You no longer have a family to leave it to, so it won't be for much longer." His jaw dropped, but she pretended not to notice, "Surely, now is the time to view it as a business rather than a family heirloom."

He seemed lost for words, so she sucker-punched him, "Besides, if you don't do something to improve sales soon the bank are going to take it away from you anyway and sell it for a fraction of its value."

"*Non! Non, non, non.*"

"Then I suggest you just sell the whole thing off as a going concern, provided the bank don't get to it first and anyway, a sale is exactly what will happen when you die. With the stress you're living under, that may be sooner rather than later."

Anton stood, "I have to check the still." Then he moved towards the door but turned, "Thank you for your time Annie, but I do not think you have been much help."

Annie began to collect her notes together, "I'm sorry Anton, but I was asked to provide solutions, not a panacea."

He took a moment to digest that before asking, "What is a panacea?"

Sue cut in, "Aspirin."

He gave them a curt nod, "Then, thank you. *Bonne journée.*" His meaning was clear; don't be here when I get back.

Chastened, they waited until he had gone before showing themselves out. On the way back to the *gite* Annie made one last observation, "Well, I buggered that one up. We've made an enemy before we've even moved in."

Sue couldn't help herself, "I guess we've both screwed up, one way or another."

It was their turn to eat with the Andersons that night, which was a relatively subdued affair that left their hosts perplexed, but the episode with Anton was in confidence and an explanation therefore, impossible. The sisters were back in their *gite* by ten and they went straight to bed, but thirty minutes later Annie heard Sue creep downstairs and out of the door. Perhaps a little coddling *was* called for.

***

Sue returned in time for breakfast again and she provided an update as soon as she sat down; hindered slightly by the mouthful of brioche, "I smoothed his feathers down. In fact, he woke me in the middle of the night and asked me to pass his apologies on to you for his rudeness. I don't think he'd slept at all by then. Truth is, he knows that all you said was correct, but remember you're a woman, an English one at that and he's a Frenchman."

Annie was so relieved, "Thank goodness. So we're friends again?"

"I think so. He was asleep when I left, but it's my morning for cleaning, so I'll know more by lunchtime."

"Do you think he'll want me to give anymore thought to his situation?"

Sue was concentrating on keeping the jam on her brioche as she dunked it in her hot chocolate, "Don't know; can't hurt though."

As soon as they cleared the dishes Annie set off for a walk, leaving Sue to go and earn another bottle of the forty year old, though *sans* lunch it seemed, given the promise to return with an update at lunchtime.

By then, Annie had some news of her own. She poured the wine and directed Sue to her chair. Lunch still sat in the fridge, so the news was pressing.

With her notes already laid out, Annie dove straight in, "Anton needs money, but he also wants to keep control of what he does best, which is making cognac. Soooo, I think I've found a way for that to happen. He can sell an interest to keen, but not gullible, amateurs. I spent some time on Penny's computer this morning and discovered something called a *Confrérie*. There doesn't even need to be an equity stake.

It's where a group of enthusiasts pay an annual fee in exchange for a membership of a sort of affinity group. The vineyard sends them newsletters and they can visit whenever they like. Oh, and all purchases attract a fifteen per cent discount. The fee seems to average about a hundred pounds, so a thousand or so members would help to put Anton back on track. Remember, that's a hundred thousand pounds, every year.

Just imagine how well that would go down at Christmas, as presents for the men who have everything. All it would take would be a couple of ads in *The Sunday Times*. Of course, each member would receive a certificate and perhaps a book on the history of cognac."

Sue said, "So it would be a sort of posh wine club."

"Yeah!"

"OK, so shall I mention it to Anton?"

Annie shook her head, "No, best not to yet. I'll do some more research this afternoon and I think I'll telephone one of the vineyards who have one."

"In that case," said Sue, "I'm starving. Can we eat now?"

Of course, it was too good to be true, though when Sue returned wine was called for again, as the requisite accompaniment to any form of news. As at lunchtime, Annie didn't waste time, "No good Sis', it wouldn't work."

Sue slumped into her chair, "Shit, why not."

Annie had printed some advertisements from the web and had spoken to a vineyard owner in Bergerac, "It is way more complicated than it sounded. Apparently, events have to be organised throughout the year and at harvest time everyone assembles for a whopping great meal and an outing on the following day. Some go to take part in the harvest, but most settle for the social aspect. The members have to pay for the outings, but there's no way Anton could hold that lot together."

Her sister already knew the answer, but asked it anyway, "So what now?"

"Sell; either the whole thing or part of it. Or have it taken away from him."

Sue gave an exaggerated shiver, "Good luck then. He's asked to meet up with you again, tomorrow morning."

The following morning they both approached the vineyard with trepidation. Sue had spent the night at the *gite,* rather than risk facing a confrontation on her own and neither of them slept well, though for completely different reasons. Sue was startled to find that she had real feelings for Anton, beyond the carnal, whilst Annie had woken at three in the morning with the germ of an idea. One that should have remained a dream, but didn't and it wouldn't go away. By five, she was sitting up in bed making notes and doing the maths.

Anton raced to the door when the bell rang and they all exchanged kisses on each cheek, but he hugged Annie too, allowing him the opportunity to whisper, "D*ésolé*," sorry.

Annie smiled and murmured, "*Moi aussi*," me also.

In so doing they had set the tone for all that followed. Sue made the coffees and they gathered around the kitchen table once more. The place was a sparkling testament to Sue's endeavours, evidenced also by a growing stock of forty year old cognac in her bedroom.

Anton and Annie began to speak at the same moment and stopped as quickly, but he held his hand out, palm upward, "Please."

She nodded, "Anton, please forgive me if I was too abrupt in our last meeting, but I've been in business for most of my life, so when I talk about such things I have a different hat on. I only have two hats and now you've seen me with both on."

He nodded thoughtfully, "Perhaps I should have a hat like that. Do you know where I might find one?"

She reached forward and took one of his hands, "You can borrow mine, anytime."

The grins around the table signalled a welcome accord. Sue then came up with an inspired prompt, "OK Anton, you're the chairman of this meeting, so it's over to you." She added weight to that by pinching some paper and a pen off Annie and passing them to him. He noted the date, location and the names of those present, before addressing Annie, "Sue said that you continued to study my problem. Have you any other ideas?"

Annie nodded, "Only a couple I'm afraid and one of those turned out to be a non-starter." She explained about the *Confrérie* concept which he already knew about and agreed with her assessment. He asked, "And your other idea?"

She still wondered whether it was a bizarre one, but she

had to get there by a process of elimination before Anton would see any value in it. "After I realised that the *Confrérie* idea wasn't going to work Sue asked me what was left. I said sell; either all or part of it. To begin with, I wondered whether you could get away with selling some hectares off, but that might exacerbate your problem rather than cure it and yet the question of selling the lot is too painful too. I've come to realise that you see yourself as the custodian of your family's land."

He seemed quite moved by Annie's summary and nodded vigorously, "And besides, the bank would snatch any money I realised in a partial sale away from me, to clear the debts."

Annie finished that line of thought off with, "So that would only buy a little more time, before the inevitable, particularly with a reduced production. In England there is a saying for that process, we say, 'withering on the vine'". She moved on, "Are you afraid that if you sold a shareholding to another grower, it would be the beginning of the end as well?"

His eyebrows shot north, "*Exactement!* I am an artist, not a businessman. Any person who bought a share from me would do so as a businessman, who would probably see it as a step towards taking the whole thing off me."

She smiled sadly, "I understand Anton and I think you may be right. In the meantime, your life would be very unhappy."

He whispered, "Thank you Annie." He'd had time enough to be practical though, "But that only leaves me with a wait, until the bank takes it away from me."

Annie retrieved the notes she had made during the night, "I have had another thought; one I haven't shared with Sue yet.

What if a group of interested individuals provided you with enough money to clear your debts and then some, assuming you still owe around three hundred thousand Euros. With the charge held by the bank disposed of, they would protect their investment by taking a primary charge on the vineyard. In the event of a forced sale or seizure, any creditor would have to get in line, behind them.

This time, his bushy eyebrows knitted together, "As partners do you mean?"

"No, not as such, because partial ownership would mean that they were partly responsible for future liabilities and they wouldn't want to be guarantors for anything either. I don't doubt that they would want to be involved and that wouldn't be a bad thing, because many of them will seek to improve your turnover. They'd probably want the power of veto on a few things, such as further borrowing, but you would retain operational control. More importantly, if things turn the corner, you could always repay them, plus a chunk of profit. Remember, they wouldn't be doing this out of charity."

They sat in silence while he came to grips with the concept. Eventually he asked, "How much exactly, are you suggesting?"

"I don't know yet, but I must warn you that my business hat has just been put on. How much is the vineyard and equipment worth?"

He'd had plenty of time to think about that, "Perhaps two and a quarter million."

That agreed with the research she'd carried out on Penny's computer, "OK, well I can tell you that the investors I'm thinking of wouldn't agree to putting in more than a quarter of the forced sale valuation, which I would guess is around half of the full market valuation. So you would look to raise around three hundred and fifty thousand." She saw his expression and explained, "This is a private business, not a public listed company, where shares can be bought and sold at will. Anyone putting money into this place will have a hard time getting it out, which also gives you the comfort of knowing that they couldn't foreclose on you either. In exchange though, they, as a group, would expect to receive twenty five percent of net profits, if there are any. That may not seem a lot to you at the moment, but I believe, or at least hope, that it will become significant with time. Lastly, there would be no interest to pay on the loans, but they would each expect a one hundred per cent gain on their loan amounts, for every ten years you use the money.

They would have to accept that the return wouldn't materialise, probably, until the vineyard was sold, though you will be able to repay the money at any time, subject to the interest accrued to that date."

He was struggling to write it all down so she said, "Don't worry, I'll write it all out for you, from start to finish."

He put the pen down and shook his head again, "I am not sure."

"I can understand that; you need time to think about it, but remember, this is a high risk investment for them. I promise you one thing though, they will be far must trustworthy than a bank."

He sought a measure of defence with a question, "If it is such a high risk, why would they be interested?"

The reply startled him, "Well, for a start off, I might be one of them and I have an enormous amount of faith in your product."

"Not me?"

She tried to soften her reply with a gentle smile, "As the producer of that fine product, of course, but sorry Anton, I think you are a lovely person and a terrible businessman." After a few moments of silence she said, "I think I've covered everything but take your time to think about it and let me know if you have any questions." A thought occurred to her, "One thing is for certain, you don't have a lot of time. The bank could pull the rug out from underneath you at anytime. It would be a good idea if I had copies of the important pages from your accounts, just in case you decide to go ahead. They will be the first thing investors would want to look at."

He nodded and blew out his cheeks, "Thank you Annie, I will await your written recommendation. In the meantime, Sue, would you be kind enough to make some more coffees and I will fetch the cognac."

***

The sisters returned to a dismally grey UK on the fourteenth of November and by December, they concluded that Anton didn't want to proceed. Secretly, Annie's concern was tinged with relief. Now, they could go and live there without 'baggage'.

Sue had written to him a couple of times but no replies had been received; until the 9th of December that is. As they read it, each could picture him trying to find the right words and checking them in his French/English dictionary.

Dear Annie and dearest Sue,

I hope you are well. I am too.

I have been thinking about you ideas for a long time now and I am very pleased to say that I think they are good ones, especially now that the bank has told me to halve my debt with them, or else!

Please see if you can persuade your friends to embark on this adventure.

Cordialement,

Anton

Before I forgot, the bank has given me until the end of January.

Sue was delighted. Annie was aghast. It began as a good idea; an adventure even, but the passage of time had dulled the shine somewhat. Now it was back though and real. Very real.

CHAPTER 4

Annie's proposal at The Rose and Crown that Friday morning stunned everyone into silence, until Barry Parsley said, "I trust we'll be given a bit more information before you need a decision Annie."

Kendall Spencer piped up with a barbed quip, just as Annie had expected, "'Course not you fool, that would spoil the fun wouldn't it. If we're going to chuck money away, best not know how far the drop is."

Annie ignored that one and addressed Barry's question, "Absolutely."

She and Sue spoke for over half an hour, describing Anton Michaud, his house and outbuildings and the fifty hectares of vines which produced six hundred thousand litres of wine each year, prior to distillation. Sue spoke of the inheritance issues, or rather lack of them and his cash shortage, while being so asset rich, "You see, France is full of small producers who are less able to deal with the modern markets, which makes them vulnerable and the banks nervous."

Kendall asked, "So shouldn't we be?"

She rocked her head to one side, "Perhaps, but I don't think so. The demand for fine wine and cognac isn't going to go away and land is land; they won't be making any more of it. So the way I see it is provided we ensure that the investment is well covered, a drop in values shouldn't hurt us."

She then described the structure of her proposal, "This is not a short term investment. Theoretically, you could get out, but only if the remaining members funded it, or agreed to include the outsider you were selling to. However, the potential for capital growth is substantial. The owner is fifty eight years old and has no next of kin, so at some point the place will be sold, either through retirement or death. In exchange for an equity backed loan of three hundred and fifty thousand Euros, the investors will then receive their capital back plus a return of one hundred per cent for every ten years the money is left there. Incidentally, that loan amount equates to one eighth of the present day value of two and a quarter million, so there is ample protection.

In the meantime, if we can help to market his cognac profitably and that is something I'll come to in a moment, the group will receive twenty five per cent of the net profit, to be shared equally. Oh, that reminds me, the investment amount is the same for everyone, so it will be a case of dividing three hundred and fifty by the number of investors." She glanced at her notes, "So for example, if eight people decided to join they would stump up forty three thousand, seven hundred and fifty Euros, which at today's exchange rate translates to thirty three thousand, six hundred and fifty pounds."

Sue passed out some sheets of paper, "Here are some website addresses for you to check the values of similar concerns that are currently on the market, but that is theoretical, because Anton desperately wants to keep his land. All he wants to do is to resolve his liquidity problems and keep his land out of the clutches of a predatory neighbour, who he hates. Beyond that, there are no other concerns, given that there are no heirs."

Kendall Spencer's next comment did merit an answer, "So what happens if he gets run over."

Annie nodded, "We'd have title to twice our loan amounts anyway, for any sort of disposal."

Barry Parsley called out, "What about due diligence?"

The perfect question she thought, "Good question Barry. Naturally, we'll have it all assessed by a professional in that field, but I wondered if you could see to the financials, being our own expert."

Barry sat up a little straighter, to better appreciate having his ego massaged, "Well, yes, of course, I'd be delighted." He was a certified accountant, though he'd spent most of his working life as the finance director of a small engineering company in Coventry, right through to bankruptcy, three years earlier. Annie smiled and nodded, with the comfort of knowing they had the first fish nibbling at the bait.

"Oh, and there is another thing. You can either be arm's length investors or you can get down there and muck in. Anton said you would be very welcome, since there is always work to be done. It really is a quiet and beautiful area."

Eventually, with all the immediate questions answered, Annie suggested a more formal meeting the following week, over coffees rather than cognac, though she or Sue would be happy to answer questions in the meantime.

George interrupted, "You said you were going to mention marketing."

Annie struck her forehead with the palm of her hand, "Duh. Sorry George. I'd have kicked myself for forgetting that." She looked around then, "We all know that George knows his stuff when it comes to wine and cognac. I'm sure we've all agonised over what to buy when he's been invited to dinner." There were murmurs of agreement around the tables. "So when he says something is good, I believe it. That said, this stuff is *so* good even I realised it. The reason Anton is in trouble is that like so many of his peers, he's reliant on the big boys to buy his stuff in bulk, for blending. In those circumstances, if the merchant dumps you, too bad. Most sit there and wait for the bailiffs. One of the reasons Anton has managed to struggle on is that he offers tours to passing tourists, many of whom are British. There aren't enough entries on *Trip Advisor*, yet; that is something we can encourage, but several moan about being unable to buy any in the UK. We need to remedy that by finding a couple of agents."

George agreed, "I know a few in fact and I reckon they would leap at this. There is another thing to sort out too. That price; retailing that forty year old at sixty Euros is an absolute joke. Even direct from the vineyard it should be twenty five per cent higher."

Annie smiled, "Thanks George." Fish number two.

As the group began to rise she dropped another bombshell, "Oops, nearly forgot, Sue and I have bought a cottage in the same village." It prompted another round of questions, which she fielded for the moment, promising them more information at the next coffee morning.

The proposal had startled everyone, including me Annie thought, when she cast back to the glimmer of an idea that had woken her in the middle of a night. Now, as she and Sue trudged back to her house in the pouring rain, she could barely believe that the thing had progressed this far. Sue suddenly nudged her, "You done good Sis'"

Annie shuddered, "God, I hope I haven't done something stupid. If this fails I may as well move away."

Sue stayed upbeat, "Well you've sorted that one out already."

***

Carol Lucas was unusually quiet on their way home from the pub; in fact, she didn't say a word. Bob tried to keep up for the first hundred yards until finally, he muttered, "Fuck it" and slowed to a more comfortable pace. After all, there was no hurry to get home and face more music. His raincoat kept his body dry, but his salt and pepper hair darkened in the rain, though it was still thick enough to keep his scalp covered as it matted down. They both walked often and ate wisely enough to keep in trim and Carol always bought the highest factor sun cream she could, to protect the freckles that covered his face and body. Even his light brown eyes were distinctly freckled. Neither of them was particularly shy and would voice an opinion if called upon to do so, but they avoided such things as cocktail parties and the banality of small talk.

It began before he'd taken his coat off.

He knew, of course, that Carol was so anti-French she

wouldn't even buy their *Golden Delicious* apples at the super-market. She'd never been to France and didn't intend to. "What happened to the 'we' Bob? Was it because you knew what I'd say?"

His shoulders drooped, "No love. I wasn't thinking. It was just something to say."

"Well, now you know what to say next time. 'No, thank you'. There is no way we are going to put money into a dodgy French vineyard. They don't like us and as far as I'm concerned, the feeling's mutual. And take that coat off before you ruin the floor."

He glanced down and saw the circle of drips that were pooling around his feet and did as he was told, before following her into the kitchen for lunch. She was already bent over, reaching for the butter and cold meats in the fridge when he asked, "Don't you think we could discuss it, at least?"

She didn't bother to look at him as she transferred the food to the counter, "Why, there's nothing to talk about?"

"But you're the one who said 'we' when I was silly enough to say 'I'. That would imply a joint decision, surely?"

This time she did turn to face him, "No, it doesn't. It means that you paid no heed to my values. We are *both* entitled to an opinion and you already knew what mine would be, or you should have."

He backed down, for the time being, but it wasn't over yet. The proposal had intrigued him and unlike his wife, the thought of spending a little time in France appealed to him. It wasn't as if they couldn't afford it either. After buying the two kids a house and creating a trust fund for the grand kid's education, they still had three million left over from the lottery win. A few in the village knew about it, but no-one knew how much it had been. Meanwhile, they continued to live in the same house and drive medium-sized cars. Carol was nothing if not conservative.

***

At fifty two, Kendall Spencer was the youngest member of the coffee morning group and the only one still at work, as a relief manager for *Drummer Breweries*; a role that required him to be all things to all men, until their back was turned that is. He knew when to be a Leicester City fan, a cricket follower or a formula one fan even though he had little taste for any sport, save the horses and part-time barmaids. Both liaisons had proven expensive, but the losses at the bookmakers had been camouflaged by the erratic nature of his income and whatever he could fiddle through the tills.

He never thought of his actions, either commercial or extra-marital as betrayals, in that they were never excessive or discovered, though an encounter with gonorrhoea six months earlier had given him a fright. If sex at home had been a regular feature he'd have had some explaining to do, but after their daughter had been born he thought Megan had let herself go, by putting two stones on her waistline and three cup sizes into her bras. As a result, their sex life had dwindled to such an extent that the enforced abstinence during treatment went by without comment. Even that experience failed to encourage safe sex; he hated condoms and decided to remedy the matter, for a time, by pursuing married females only. Discretion was assured as well as genital wellbeing, he reasoned, since they had as much to lose from discovery as he did.

He and Megan rented a cottage in the village, not much larger than the original design, though it did have a bathroom and toilet tacked on to the rear of the kitchen. Conversely, the garden was enormous with a jungle of coarse grass and weeds

They had been married for fifteen years. Megan was ten years younger and after repeated attempts to start a family they had given up trying and contraception was deemed unnecessary, so both were startled when Sophie came along.

For her part, Megan knew everything. She had a daughter, who she worshipped, a battle with weight, that she was losing and a cheating husband. Her long brown hair hadn't seen more than trims for years, at the cheapest hairdressers and many of her clothes had been found in charity shops. She'd spent most of the coffee morning trying to control their wayward three year old, so it was left to Kendall to fill in the gaps, over lunch. By the time he'd finished she knew the answer to her question, but asked anyway, "What do you think?"

He was so excited, "It's a winner Meg' an absolute winner. Not for a capital return certainly, or at least not a quick one, but that Annie has nous. If she thinks it will produce an income, I believe her." He didn't add that the bottles of cognac he would exchange with the ones behind the bars would guarantee a supplement to their income too and there were others who would be up for a regular supply.

"But we haven't got that sort of money. Most of the savings we do have belong to Sophie, from her christening."

"Don't forget love, we paid for that christening."

"But Kendall, there's less than two thousand there. Where do you propose to get the other thirty odd thousand from?"

"Your father."

"No."

He was startled by the sharpness of her response, but not put off. This was too good to miss and nothing was insurmountable, even Megan. The thought triggered unwelcome images of actually mounting Megan, but 'hey' he reasoned; whatever it takes.

It took three days to persuade her to at least talk to the old man. The idea would be to have him speak with Annie, on a one to one basis. Wisely, Kendall would stay away from the meeting, though he hoped that Megan would be allowed to attend, for reporting purposes.

Her father, Tom Eccleston, had run a corner shop for forty years, latterly in the face of competition from supermarkets who were now open on Sundays. As a result, he and his wife were suffering a miserable decline of income, where odd percentage points of profit were all they were working for. But they didn't owe a penny and had saved in better times. They had also paid for a small bungalow to retire into, so the sale of the shop and outbuildings would be a bonus, no matter how small.

Megan was his only child and he would have laid down his life for her, anytime. In fact, his protection was broader than she could have suspected, in that he knew about her husband's weaknesses and hated him for them, though he would never divulge the details to his daughter. And now there was little Sophie, who played his heart strings like a concert harpist. It was a weakness that was about to be exploited.

Megan arranged to take Sophie to her grandparents for lunch on the Tuesday, when she spent the afternoon relating Annie's story. Tom knew what was coming within minutes, but he still asked pertinent questions until finally, he said, "I'm sorry, but no," as expected.

Then, as instructed, Megan said, "It isn't so much for us Dad, as for Sophie and any other kids we have. It's a long term investment and whilst we may have a bit of income from it, the real money will be made when the place is sold. Wouldn't that be a wonderful start for the grandchildren? It will probably buy a house for them, outright."

Tom winced, he'd given them a wedding present of five thousand pounds, for a deposit on a house, but nothing came of it. They were still tenants and would no doubt remain so, until he and his wife were dead and Megan inherited the bungalow. They'd left it to her alone, though he knew that divorce courts didn't recognise such arrangements, but at least she would know what it was to own a home, for a while.

In the meantime, this venture seemed to mean a lot to Megan. He could at least go to the meeting with this 'Annie' and then say no again, as gently as he could.

The meeting was arranged for the following morning, on his way back from the wholesalers. At the appointed time he called to collect Megan and was startled to find her husband at home too. Kendal's phoney welcome was transparent enough to non-plus *Uriah Heap* but his father-in-law let it pass by, consoled by the knowledge of what he intended to say after the meeting. At least the treacherous little shit stayed at home and looked after Sophie.

He was in for a surprise though.

From the outset, he was charmed and impressed by Annie. Moreover, the investment had more merit than he'd expected. The returns *were* long term, but they were significant and well protected. He'd even been given a sample of the cognac to try while Annie spoke of her plans to find markets for it in the UK, which sounded credible.

That night he sat down with his wife and together, they formulated a plan.

The following morning he contacted their solicitor who confirmed that the plan was feasible and accepted instructions to get on with the paperwork. He then telephoned his daughter to arrange a meeting at her house that afternoon; the time of day he was most certain to find Kendall there too and that was vital. The terms were simple enough, but Tom was determined to make sure that his son-in-law understood them and knew that any breaches would not be tolerated.

Predictably, though privately, Kendall was enraged and outmanoeuvred. Tom saw this and was delighted, though he did a better job of hiding his feelings, behind a business-like approach, "Here's the deal." He had looked at Megan, "Your mum and I have talked this through and we're both in agreement. Speaking of which there will be an agreement between all of us; a written agreement. We *are* going to let you have the money." He saw the tension leave Kendall's body and heard him mumble some sort of thanks, "But, the investment will be placed in trust, for the sole benefit of Sophie and that includes any income that comes back. You, Megan, will be the trustee until her eighteenth birthday, but don't worry; the trust wording will be very specific; there won't be any financial decisions to make. The capital element will be invested in the vineyard, naturally, but any income received must be invested in the *National Savings,* in Sophie's name."

Megan was delighted, "Oh Dad, thank you so much! That's wonderful."

Kendall's gratitude was a tad less effusive and he was left

wondering how much more stock he would need to filch out of the place to make up for the lost income.

***

Adam Harding ambled home after his Friday lunch. Always the same; three pints of *Pedigree* and a large steak and onion pie; sized thus because the landlord couldn't stand the smell of chips and therefore omitted them from the menu. Not that it mattered much, for most of his regulars were more concerned about their arteries. Harding, of course, was the exception.

He and George Dyson were the only two members of the coffee club morning who had stayed on for lunch that day, by the end of which they'd made their minds up. The first thing he did, after dumping his sodden coat and hat on the boiler, was tear open the letter he'd written to Chrissy Haddon, to add a post script. He had to share the news with someone.

P.S. Chrissy, I have some startling news. Annie Stockley, a member of our Friday morning coffee group, has just been to France and bought a house there. She also discovered an ailing distillery that makes incredible cognac – I've never tasted the like.

It's a small operation in need of financial help. At the moment the owner is being dumped on by his bank. Also, I've been convinced that with them out of the way his produce could be marketed very successfully, with our help. At least Annie thinks so and I trust her judgement; she's been in business for most of her working life.

Besides which, it will give me something to do. I haven't enjoyed retirement that much, to be honest and the size of the investment is comfortable enough for me, or in other words, I could afford to lose it without too many tears. In the meantime, I'll look forward to spending some time in France. Only been there once and that was to Paris, when I was married.

If it goes ahead I'll send you a bottle of the forty year old. It's good!
With that, I'll sign off, again.
Adam

After addressing a fresh envelope he headed for the stairs, saying aloud, "Right m'lad, time for a nap."

***

The Maitlin's minds were made up immediately. They loved the idea.

Weighing in at eighteen stones, Alan was spectacularly unfit. His six foot two frame carried the excess weight quite well for the most part, but his trouser belts sagged beneath a belly that refused to respond quickly enough to diets. A horseshoe pelmet of white hair enclosed a shiny pate and seemed to corral a group of light brown moles, which had been tested and declared to be non malignant. Brown eyes, and a deep resonant voice that was easy on the ear gave him an air of sincerity that had been used to great effect in a career of selling life assurance and investments. He'd been an active and successful investor himself, for most of his working life with the *Prudential*, who allowed him to retire from his post as regional manager at the age of fifty, with one of the largest pensions in the village which was likely to remain so, for it was index-linked.

By contrast, Jayne was only five feet two tall, with the figure of a fit thirty year old. Streaks of grey would normally have been evident, but the treatment received from her favoured hairdresser was superb, leaving her with a head of velvety brown hair, which framed a face that had been blessed with a bone structure that pared ten years from her looks.

Jayne still owned and ran a hairdressing salon fifteen miles away, in Nuneaton, though she left most of the day to day affairs for her manager to deal with. The property was hers and thanks to Alan's guidance, she had an impressive investment portfolio of her own. They had maintained separate bank and savings accounts throughout their married life and during the week that followed the meeting they had tried to use that status quo to justify two individual punts at the vineyard, but to no avail. Annie argued that whilst they may have separate finances they were still partners and could skew future decision making.

As Francophiles, they couldn't wait to check the new venture out with a visit. In the meantime, after the meeting at the pub, they had hurried home to check the location on their French atlas. After that, they retreated to their laptops and *googled* the afternoon away. Jayne even located Anton's place on *Google Earth* and printed the image out before pinning it to the notice board in the kitchen.

It was a grand project!

***

By the following Friday Bob Lucas had made up his mind. He had an hour to confront Carol and get it over with, before they left for the pub. Carol was in the kitchen, washing the breakfast dishes when he ambushed her. Prevarication wasn't an option, it would be treated as weakness, "I'm going ahead with Annie's investment."

She still had an elegant figure, but with a slight gauntness of age. Now her blond hair was grey and the lines on her face sometimes reminded them both of ageing, but her features were still striking as they appeared in silhouette when she slowly turned. Finally, she faced him, "I beg your pardon?"

"You heard me love. I'm going to use thirty five thousand of the money we have lying doing nothing in the building societies." He hurried on before she could interrupt, "I've thought about it a lot and I decided that if I take that much out of our savings, you should be able to as well. Put it into a separate account, in your name alone and do whatever you like with it. Blow it all on clothes if you like. We'll hardly notice the loss from the loads we have."

She hadn't given Annie's idea anymore thought. So far as she was concerned, the matter was closed. Now, shock was soon replaced by anger, "You're not serious."

He nodded and spoke with an assurance he'd been practicing for two days, "I certainly am"

"I don't believe it."

"You must, dear."

"No! No, no ,no! Why on earth would we want to put money into a failing vineyard, and a French one at that?"

"Why not?"

"I've just mentioned two reasons, but give me time and I'll give you loads more. For a start, you know absolutely nothing about making cognac."

"Well think of it as *my* folly, not yours."

"Oh, of course, it's *your* money now too. Up until now, it's always been *our* money and I don't see any reason to change."

"I've just given you one."

"No you haven't, at least not a valid one. All you've suggested is that we should change everything for this stupid jaunt. One I will never agree to."

"It isn't stupid."

"Isn't it? Well tell me then, just what do you hope to achieve; live for another thirty years in the hope that you might see some of it back?"

"Sooner or later, it doesn't matter."

She began to shout, "It bloody well does matter! We both agreed to safeguard that money. No Stock market investments or funny bonds. Compared to this, they're gilt-edged."

"It's not so much about the money."

"Well do tell; what is it about?"

"I just wanted to break out; broaden our horizon a bit."

"See, there you go with 'our' again."

"Sorry, I meant 'mine' but I'd love it if you were involved too."

"Fat chance!" She took a breath and lowered her voice, "So tell me, if this is to be a new horizon, what do you plan on doing on it? Go over there to pick grapes maybe, or tramp around London trying to sell the sodding stuff to merchants?"

He shrugged, "Whatever, I'm sure they could find something for me to do."

She closed her eyes and placed a wet hand on her forehead, "This is getting worse. You were a housing officer for the council for Christ's sake. A glorified clerk! How the hell do you think that qualifies you for this?"

"Thirty five thousand would be a good start."

"You're beginning to sound pathetic, do you realise that."

His own wife had just called him a glorified clerk and

pathetic. She'd gone too far. He shouted, "I'm tired of this village, the area, gardening, gossip, muddy walks, crime, crowds and long grey filthy winters." He'd slowed for the list to come to mind, but his pace returned, "In fact, I'm tired of my whole fucking life at the moment. Now I would love to have you share this with me, but please, if you have any respect for my wishes, don't try and stop me; I won't let you."

She was stunned, "So what are you going to do?"

"I'm going up to the pub and putting my name down, with or without you."

She turned back to the sink, "So be it. If you feel that strongly about it, go on your own."

He turned and left the room. There was nothing else to say.

Moments later, when the front door was closed, she sank down at the kitchen table and stared at the wall without focus. The room was silent, save for a steady drip from one of the taps which hit the water below with a measured splash that seemed to mirror her own slowing pulse. The hollowness in the pit of her stomach grew until finally, she covered her face with both hands and wept.

CHAPTER 5

Annie was anxious, on two counts. The theoretical had now become a reality, with all the complexities of handling large sums and drafting the legal documents. She knew that would be left to her, but what if too few wanted to go ahead with it? The thought of breaking that news to Anton made her shudder.

She and Sue sat in the same place and counted heads, just as they had the week before. Thirteen; the same number, but this time Carol Lucas was absent and Amy Dyson had accompanied George. She wondered whether those differences signalled one partner for and, one against.

There was the usual chatter but unlike the previous week, they were silenced by the first tap on her glass.

Kendall called out, "No free samples this week Annie?"

Annie had her business hat on, "No, from now on you have to pay. It's make your mind up time. First though, any questions?"

George's question sounded as promising as she'd hoped, "When do you want the money by?"

"Preferably by the end of this month, but certainly no later than the middle of January. The bank intend to pull the plug on Anton at the end of January, so any later would make things much more complicated and expensive."

Harding asked, "When can we go over and have a look at this place. I think I'd need to see it before helping to save it. At the moment we only have your description."

She gave him a wry grin, "Which is not something to be taken as read then?"

He wasn't fazed, "Nope. Put it down to my background. Trust no-one and suspect everyone until proven otherwise."

Annie addressed all of them, "Does anyone else want to have a look first?" A forest of hands went up. "Fair enough, when?" The consensus was that with Christmas only eight days away, it would have to wait until the first week in the New Year. It was certainly convenient for the sisters, since their house purchase would be ready for completion by then.

A date was set, plus or minus two days, to enable Sue to find a fit with *Ryanair's* schedules between Stansted and La Rochelle. A stay of three or four days was deemed sufficient and a sheet of paper was passed around for email addresses, so that the information might be shared easily.

Annie suddenly realised that she couldn't wait that long for the money any more. She called them to order again, "For this thing to happen I need firm commitments from you by the end of next week and I now need the money in a holding account before we leave for France.

Barry Parsley mumbled, "It was the middle of January a moment ago,"

She nodded, "But this trip means that we're going to lose the first week of January. During that time, the lawyers can be sorting the paperwork out and be ready to act the week after we get back. Thankfully, there's no conveyancing of title to be done, which would have taken longer, but we must still make sure that the legals are done properly." She took a breath, "That said, I realise that the visit will be a good thing and I'm certain you'll all be impressed, but I may as well add now, that if anyone is unsure or worried about the basics, it would be better to not get involved. We can draft something that would enable anyone to back out after the visit, but for the sakes of the others, it would need to be a valid reason, in which case, in all probability, we'll all be backing out anyway."

George held up his hand, "What about accommodation?

Do we sort our own out or do you have something in mind?"

"Perhaps, but I need to make a call. I'll get back to you."

There were more questions, though most were already answered in the written briefing she'd already given them, which they had yet to read.

Eventually, it was time to ask if any had made their minds up already and wanted to put their names down. Hands shot up immediately. George Dyson, Adam Harding, Alan Maitlin, and Kendall Spencer confirmed their interest and waited for yet another sheet of paper to make its rounds. When it reached Bob Lucas, Annie was startled to see him write his name down. He'd been quieter than usual though and the look on his face when the list reached him was difficult to read, but there was no hesitation in adding his name to the list. Carol's absence could be significant, but that was a question best left for another time.

Barry Parsley was the last to seek inclusion, but with a caveat, "I would like to have a look at the financials before I finally commit, if that would be OK?"

Annie added his name to the list and said, "Of course Barry, I have copies of the last ten years accounts at home. Call in this afternoon and I'll go through them with you."

Steve Ellis put his hand up, before, "Sorry Annie, we're going to sit this one out, but may we come and visit?"

George called out, "Too right you can. I'll always find somewhere to bed you down, have no fear. It was an offer which served to announce that he and Amy had already decided to look at houses over there.

Finally, Annie added her own name to the list and counted. There were seven, one less than she had calculated for. A gremlin, she thought, the first in what would probably be a long list, but it needed addressing, "OK, so that makes seven. There's still time to find more, but if we don't, the amounts will change." She quickly scribbled out the revised calculation and announced, "If it stays at seven, the revised investment amount will be thirty eight thousand, four hundred and fifty, give or take change. That's an increase of almost five thousand. Is everyone happy with that?"

Everyone except Kendall confirmed that it would be. He glanced at Megan before saying, "Almost certainly, yes, but we'll just need to check something out."

That single note of caution made Annie think. She looked at the list and shook her head, it wasn't enough. "Hold on guys, I think it would be better if you all emailed me confirmation of your interest then while you're at it, I would ask you to acknowledge the details." She counted them on her raised fingers, "The amount involved and deadline; the 'back out' option, but with good reason *and,* that whatever the outcome, you will bear your share of the legal costs. The reason for that is by teatime today I will have given instructions to our French solicitor, if you have no objection that is. He's acting for us in the house purchase because he speaks perfect English and came highly recommended."

There were no objections. In fact, with the exception of Kendall, every investor asked for a sheet of paper and together, they formulated a document that would be common to all and in line with Annie's requirements. Bob Lucas knew that he would send his commitment to Annie, but he would do so with misgivings. It was the most exciting thing he'd ever done, but at what cost to his relationship with Carol?

Annie telephoned Monsieur Gagnon in Cognac, at three that afternoon and explained everything. He was very charming and agreed to act, though he asked for a written brief, which she promised to email before Monday.

Sue asked if *she* could call Anton, who was as delighted to hear from her as he was to learn the news she had for him. The call went on for far too long and Annie was on the verge of signalling so, by drawing an extended finger across her throat, when it finally came to an end. Amongst the other things, which Sue chose not to share, he also promised to let them have his lawyer's details and to clean up his place before her visit."

The last call of the day was to Penny Challis. After the preliminaries Annie explained, "Something else cropped up when we were with you. I can't tell you much at the moment but hopefully, I'll be able to when I see you, which will be during the first week in January. Thing is though, we'll have eleven or twelve people with us. Can you accommodate that many?"

Penny sounded distraught, "Oh bugger, I'm so sorry Annie, but Tom's moved all the furniture into one *gite*, while he decorates the others. There's no chance of us having them ready for then."

Annie asked, "Any suggestions?"

"At that time of year? Phew, it'll have to be a hotel in Saintes or Cognac."

Another gremlin, "OK, I'll get on to the net. We'll still be able to meet up won't we?"

Penny chuckled, "Of course!" After a moment she added a caution, "But we won't be able to feed that many."

Annie reassured her, "No chance of that happening. It'll be just me and Sue; if I can drag her away from Anton."

Penny laughed out loud, "We know. He's been pining like a lost puppy." After a moment, she added, "He's also told us all about the deal you've put together, which is what I suspect you were going to share with us. He was surprised you'd kept it secret."

Now on her back foot, Annie explained, "It was a matter of discretion. I couldn't tell you about it without Anton's permission."

"Hey, no, I'm not criticising you. I'm left thinking I can tell you confidences with safety. Just get your backsides into gear and get over here."

In fact, it was Sue's backside that had been in gear, checking flight schedules and fares. There was a flight out of Stansted to La Rochelle on Tuesday the fourth and one back on Friday the seventh. Once again, because of the time of year, prices were low, at only twenty nine pounds each way. They passed the information on and left it to the individuals to make their own bookings.

***

By close of play on the following Monday, Annie and Sue had found an *Ibis* hotel in Cognac that was delighted to take so many bookings for the quietest time of year; for a modest forty five Euros per room per night. Sue sent the information on and requested a head count, or rather room requirement, promising to make the hotel reservations for them all.

The application forms and mandates had been obtained from the bank and dealt with by a 'pass it on' arrangement, where each investor had to sign the papers before delivering them on to the next name on the list. Each would then have to attend the bank with identification, for money laundering checks.

By Christmas Eve the full investment from four of the investors, Annie included, had been deposited with the bank and both French lawyers had agreed to a meeting on Thursday the sixth of January, by when they would have everything prepared for signing, thanks largely to Annie's brief being so complete *and* in accord with Anton's expectations.

Ironically, in spite of bringing together such large number of people, Annie and Sue found themselves alone on Christmas day, without even an invitation to share sherry and mince pies. They both lay in, before exchanging presents of no particular note. All were practical, pleasantly scented or warm. Instead of turkey they opted for pheasant, dressed with a creamy apple and Armagnac sauce, accompanied with braised celery and broccoli mousses. After the cheeseboard they could only give the Christmas pudding a glancing blow, but it would do for the next couple of days. They did however, have space for espresso coffees and some of Anton's forty year old, pulled from Sue's excessive stocks.

On Boxing Day they received a telephone call from 'Barmy Barbie', another barbed nickname dreamt up by Kendall Spencer.

Barbara Thatcham was of landed stock; still with a family seat in Bedfordshire. At least that is what her birth and christening certificates indicated. Little else about her existence thus far, sixty four years on, supported that claim.

She had always been a wayward child; enough to drive her

father to distraction. He often claimed that if she'd been a boy, attending public school, the floggings would have taken her to within an inch of her life. Instead, after being dismissed from three elite girl's schools; one of them *Roedean*, her parents gave up and employed tutors at the stately home. It would have been nice to report that her different take on life tugged at a string in one of her parent's hearts, but neither of them showed her any affection and for the most part, carried on as though she wasn't there.

Barbara treated her tutors in the same way. Only the art tutor found favour with her. In fact, they got along splendidly. By the time she was eighteen, even the family recognised her artistic talent and after graduating at a nearby college they were all startled when she gained admission to the Royal Academy of Arts, in London, where she studied for a further three years, at which point she was honoured to have two of her pictures included in the summer exhibition. With two older brothers and an academic sister, Barbara was never going to be a significant player in the family affairs, even if she'd been 'normal', but at least she looked set to become a noted artist.

She would have been too, if she'd sold any of the work and there was a lot of it, but she steadfastly refused to do so. Instead, friends would be sent home with one, in much the same way as a grandma might send visitors home with a jar of home-made jam.

Worse, her behaviour had not improved. Her father often spoke of sending her off somewhere, a long way off, to paint lost tribes or something and privately, after one very ugly episode, involving cannabis and a couple of local lads, he bemoaned the fact that *Bedlam* could no longer offer them discreet accommodation. Even the countess was shocked by that notion and made him promise never to mention the name again.

So when Barbara announced that she would like to settle in a cottage she had found in a place called Waltham Parva, seventy blessed miles away, her father leapt at the chance and his cheque book.

Now, thirty years on, she was still a free spirit, but her shaking hands had finished her as an artist. The studio that had been built onto the side of the lounge was now used to house her chickens. They all had names, peculiar diets and even stranger treatments. Annie had called in one day to find Barbara massaging *Friar's Balsam* into a poor bird's breast. She explained that it had sounded a little wheezy that morning and probably needed its tubes cleaning.

The house was at best chaotic; at worst, a midden, but somehow, an offer to help and sort things out seemed inappropriate. It would have been so *not* Barbara.

In spite of the mess, Annie had a real fondness for the old girl and called in as often as she could. The British have always loved their eccentrics and Barbara was right up there, near the top of the list. There was a family of badgers living at the bottom of her garden, which she fed, regularly, with better food than she could afford to buy for herself. A couple of sparrows would hop into her kitchen each day, demanding food and her four bird boxes were occupied every year. She used to boast that she was on first name terms with most of the local wildlife and Annie believed her. They shared an interest in wildlife and Annie had taken to supplying some of the feeds. She felt wonderfully rewarded on the day Barbara had asked for help finding a blanket in the loft. It had been floored and there was a light, but the space was as chaotic as the rest of the house. Besides boxes and bags, there were canvasses strewn all over the place, some finished and others not so. Annie almost trod on one scrap of paper that was little more than the corner torn off a larger sheet, but she picked it to discover an exquisite water colour of a dog rose branch and bloom with an attendant bumble bee. The detail was incredible and Annie said so.

Barbara dismissed the praise with a wave of her hand, "Oh tish, you can have that if you like."

Annie certainly did like, and soon had it framed and hung on her dining room wall.

Barbara's father had provided her with a modest income,

which he'd increased occasionally, until his death in nineteen eighty five. Since then, the family had ignored her pleas for more, until a few years ago, when her older brother sought to put an end to her begging by sending their accountant along, with just one remit. He was to produce a report which showed that she had ample to live on. Her brother also told the accountant to take a colleague with him. "Why?" asked the fellow, "To provide a second opinion?"

"No," came the reply, "To act as chaperone."

The two professionals were about to embark on an adventure they would never forget.

By the time they had struggled through the weeds to the back door, the dew had soaked their trousers. Barbara threw the door open, "Hello my dears, how nice of you to come and see me."

She led them along a very narrow 'S' shaped trail in the kitchen, through piles of cans that were stacked to waist height. There were all sorts, from cat food to garden peas but instead of offering an explanation she said, "I've spent all week tidying up in honour of your visit." They followed her into the lounge and gazed at the chaos. Every horizontal surface was covered in books and magazines which had failed to find space on the bookshelves that covered one wall. Even the grand piano seemed to sag beneath the weight of them, though a little of the surface was in view, where they noted the sweeps made by a duster; dark shiny paths framed by collars of dust. Only one easy chair had been cleared, so they remained standing while she went off to make tea. Both were startled when she returned with a tray laden with a beautiful silver service and box of *Mr Kipling's* cherry bakewells. They would learn, in due course, that the piano and tea service were from the ancestral home and the cherry bakewells were from the *Co-op*.

After pouring their teas out, she turned to them, "Now, tell me again, what are your names?" Their response called for an immediate correction, "Oh dear me no; I meant your Christian names."

"My name is Nicholas," said the elder of the two, "And this is Jeremy."

She then asked, "Who's in charge?" When Nicholas confirmed that he was she directed him to the easy chair and said, "Then I daresay you have lots of questions." As he sat down, he couldn't fail to notice the cat hairs that migrated onto his dark blue suit, in a static exchange.

"Now, Jeremy." She picked up a lettuce that had lain nearby and pushed it into his hands before directing him to the dining chair that had been left next to the studio door, "You can feed the girls while Nicholas and I have a chat." Nonplussed, the younger man moved to the chair, which was when he saw the chickens, who had in turn, seen the lettuce.

Barbara pulled the stool from beneath the piano and positioned it a few feet from Nicholas's knees before settling herself down.

Meanwhile, Nicholas watched his colleague tear a leaf from the lettuce and gingerly open the studio door. Clearly, it was a delicacy, which was snatched out of his hand immediately, causing him to snatch his hand back and slam the door. He looked visibly shaken. Barbara glanced at him and clapped her hands, "Excellent, well done you."

It was all about income and expenditure, but Nicholas hadn't bargained on such detail. She read from a list she had prepared, having promised to let him have it when they were finished. He learned how many sheets of toilet paper she used per visit and type of bowel movement; how many days per week she allowed herself meat; how long she made her knickers last, which wasn't as long as her bras, because she refrained from wearing those around the house and how many inches of water she bathed in and at what temperature. She added at that point, "Of course, I'm wearing one today." The list was long and mind boggling. Moreover, he never once gained control of the meeting.

That night, he wrote in his diary;

Occasionally, one has the privilege of meeting someone who has stepped to one side, leaving the rest of the World to continue being 'normal'. Today, I met such a person and am thankful for it.

It was noon by the time they had finished and Barbara said, "Excellent! Then I know the perfect place for lunch." She saw his expression and said, "But they did tell you to take me to lunch, surely?"

Nicholas recovered his wits, "Oh yes, of course." He glanced at Jeremy, who had disposed of the lettuce and sat clasping his hands around his knees.

The conversation over lunch was undemanding, though a little aberrational at times. Once, after a slightly awkward silence, she announced, "I was nineteen when I lost my virginity; to my art tutor. I'd persuaded him to pose in the nude for me but he seemed shy, so I stripped off as well, to put him at his ease. In the end though, I had to do something about that silly erection. I certainly couldn't paint it; Daddy would have had a fit." She thought back to that day for a moment, before adding, "It wasn't very inspiring though, the sex I mean. He had hair trigger issues I'm afraid."

Both accountants reacted in similar yet different ways. Jeremy's jaw dropped open while Nicholas's clamped shut; to suppress a giggle rather than express shock. She then rested a hand on Jeremy's knee, "Anyway, I'm sure that you're a much more accomplished lover, not that I mean to pry. Well actually, that's not true. I *love* to pry. Secrets can be deliciously salacious, can't they?"

The Earl was extremely put out by the report that followed, which concluded that Barbara was desperately in need of more funds. A modest increase was agreed, but with great reluctance.

That was five years ago and even then it would have been regarded as inadequate by most. Thankfully, in the meantime, Annie had arranged for a social worker to call and the benefits Barbara was entitled to dwarfed her brother's niggardly award.

Just eight months ago, the fates finally dealt her a winning hand, or rather The Luton and Dunstable University Hospital did, when they failed to resuscitate an aunt who had bequeathed one hundred and eighty thousand pounds to her favourite niece.

***

Annie tapped on the door and announced herself as she stepped inside and after a cautious passage through tin can alley, she found Barbara in the lounge, watching the fiftieth repeat of *Where Eagles Dare*. They exchanged kisses and hugs before Barbara pointed at a tray laden with a bottle of sherry and two glasses, balanced on one of the smaller piles of magazines that covered the piano, "Would you do the honours please dear. I get it all over the place these days."

Annie reached into her bag and retrieved a half empty bottle of Anton's forty year old, "No need, I've brought you something special to try; a forty year old cognac."

Barbara clapped her hands together, "Oh, how wonderful and how appropriate!"

"Oh and why is that?"

"In a moment dear, let's try it first."

Annie watched as her friend clasped the glass with both hands and took a sip. She closed her eyes and savoured the gentle warmth of the spirit. It had been so long since she'd tasted such a fine cognac and in that moment of cognition, she was transported back to the dinner parties hosted by her father. Those wonderful scents and flavours; miraculously produced from the kitchen and served by liveried footmen. Images sprang to mind, of candlelight and shimmering crystal that cast prismatic beams of light onto a snowy white tablecloth.

She beamed, "It's every bit as good as he promised."

"Who?" asked Annie.

"George, he always pops in at Christmas and brings me a bottle of sherry." She pointed at the tray, "That's it, but he promised to bring me a bottle of this next year."

Annie always delivered a box of chocolates during the week before Christmas and she was comforted to know that someone else did something similar. She put a finger to the side of her nose, "Ahh, I see what you mean about it being appropriate; an advance taster."

Barbara wore a mischievous grin, "Oh no my dear, that isn't what I meant. I would like to be a member of your group, if you'll have me." She saw Annie's puzzled look and explained, "I have the money."

Annie couldn't disguise the doubt in her voice, "Do you?"

"Oh yes. You see, last month, I received a rather large sum by way of an inheritance, but I didn't have any idea of what to do with it, until George told me about your adventure."

Annie's first thought was to suggest spending thirty thousand on the house, to return it to a habitable state, but Barbara seemed to read her thoughts, for she said, "I'm perfectly happy with things as they are here, but now that I no longer paint, life is a little tedious. The prospect of doing something as exciting as this would be simply wonderful. Just imagine, I might even let my stingy brother have a bottle. Please, tell me all about it."

Two hours later, Annie walked back to her house, where Sue was curled up on the sofa, watching television and grazing her way through a box of *Maltesers*. She sat down beside her and took a handful out of the box before saying, "You're not going to believe this, but we have our eighth investor."

***

Bob Lucas was the last to invest, when he delivered the cheque on New Year's Eve. He accepted Annie's offer of a coffee and they sat at the kitchen table exchanging details of pleasant but unremarkable Christmas's, until finally he said, "I think you should know that Carol doesn't approve of this. In fact she's dead against it."

Annie put her mug down, "Sorry to hear that Bob."

He dipped his head into his shoulders, "She'll come to terms with it, eventually, but it was something I really wanted to do."

She cautioned, "But don't let it tear you two apart Bob. This is the sort of thing that would qualify as a reason for opting out."

He shook his head, "No, I knew her views when I signed

up and I'm sticking with it, but when you meet up with Carol would you mind tip-toeing around the subject please."

"No of course not, but remember what I've said."

Now that Barbara's investment had been received, refunds had been made to the early birds, hotel reservations made and all confirmed that flights had been booked. They were set to go. Sue remarked, "I'm amazed it's all come together so well."

Annie looked up and groaned, "I wish you hadn't said that.

The next gremlin appeared three days later, embedded in a telephone call from Monsieur Gagnon. After they'd exchanged *Bonne Années,* he didn't waste time, "Madame Stockley, we have a small problem. The farmer next door, Monsieur Durand still has a right of way across the land you wish to buy and he refuses to relinquish it. It is not a serious matter, of course, but I have to tell you about it."

Annie's heart sank, as she beckoned Sue over, to listen in. She asked the most obvious question, "Why wasn't it picked up when the Anderson's bought the place?"

"I do not know, perhaps they can tell you."

"OK, so where does this right of way lead to."

"Nowhere; he does not own any more land around yours, so the passage cannot go further."

"That is ridiculous!"

"That is correct."

Sue hissed, "He wants a ransom."

Annie asked the lawyer, "Did you hear that?"

He replied, "Yes, but that is not the case. I have already asked him if he would accept a payment for it and he refused."

Sue sounded incredulous, "Sod it."

He said, "*Oui Madame,* It is a surprise."

Annie took control, "Well, the problem will still be there for any buyer, so the Anderson's are going to have to sort it out, I'll get in touch with them." After confirming that everything else was in order he signed off and Annie tried to telephone Gail, many times, but with no luck.

Just after lunch, Gail telephoned them from the farm in

Ashbourne, where they had spent Christmas. Their agent had been in touch with the same news, though he told her that this sort of thing was commonplace in France and shouldn't be regarded as a problem. Annie didn't agree, "Sorry Gail, but for all I know, he could lead a flock of sheep across there and there would be nothing I could do about it."

Gail groaned, "But he said it happened often."

Annie remained resolute, "Neighbours have disagreements quite often and that is when things like this can be used as weapons. I suppose that begs the question, have you had any rows with him?"

"No, none at all; we've always got on well In fact. I'll go round and see him as soon as we get back."

"When will that be?"

Another small groan, "A week on Thursday."

"Well, we'll be in the area tomorrow. How would it be if we called on him, to introduce ourselves and then bring it into the conversation? It's just possible he'll be more concerned about keeping in with us than the people who are leaving anyway."

The relief was evident in Gail's tone, "Oh Annie, would you?"

After taking down the neighbour's details, which included a physical description, Annie signed off with a promise to keep in touch. Annie had half expected Gail to dismiss the problem as irrelevant, just like their agent, but she had failed to take their background into account. All farmers prize their land and resist all attempts to claim usage, save for public rights of way. It was a matter of heritage, for British farmers at any rate.

CHAPTER 6

Some might have thought that Kendall's silent departure from the house had been out of concern for his wife and daughter's slumber, but Megan had known better. She'd been woken by the alarm and had listened to his movements in the kitchen, common to most homes; a running tap; the kettle lid and switch; a mug on the counter and in time the rattle of a spoon, dissolving sugar. She didn't expect a mug of tea, or the sound of him looking in on Sophie before leaving, for he'd shown little *real* affection for them lately. Sometimes, she'd caught the natural scent of other women when he slipped into bed in the small hours, but she had feigned sleep rather than confront him, yet she wondered why he was so unfaithful. Her own scent was as strong and valid as it had been since puberty, yet they rarely made love and when it did happen she was left wanting. She'd wondered whether he resented sharing her with Sophie, who she loved with an intensity that was beyond measure, but surely, wasn't that how a mother should feel?

She heard the front door snick shut and lay on her back, in the quiet darkness, allowing her thoughts to wander. In time, barely conscious of her actions, she raised the hem of her nightdress over her hips and began to caress herself. Gently, almost hesitantly, at first, but with growing intimacy as her senses came alive, until finally, she arched upward and groaned as an orgasm overwhelmed her. At its peak, she called out softly, "Oh Simon, Simon."

***

The party that assembled at the check-in desk at six am that morning numbered eleven, with Sue, Jayne Maitlin and Amy Dyson accompanying their partners, as non investors. They had travelled down in three cars and parked in the long stay car park, or as Adam put it, 'the next bloody county'. Thankfully, at that time of year the queues for security checks were small and they had time to find a restaurant for breakfast and coffees, but the atmosphere seemed subdued. At first, Annie put it down to the hour and the fact that they'd had to set off at four that morning, but the cure-all of sausage and bacon rolls failed to lift their spirits. An observer might have thought they were setting off to attend a funeral.

Only Barbara seemed cheerfully unaware, as she tucked into slices of honey on toast.

Finally, Adam put it into words, "This is bizarre. In the space of two weeks we've put a pot of two hundred and seventy thousand pounds together, on the back of two meetings at the pub. You do still realise Annie, that if we don't like the look of things we will want out." There were one or two murmurs of agreement.

Annie had been just as concerned and was grateful for his comments, "Yes Adam, I do understand that, but it needed saying, thank you."

George's response changed the group sentiment dramatically, "In that case, I'm going to enjoy the jaunt. It's going to be a pleasant break with some fine tasting thrown in. Then, I'm going to come home, delighted. Either with the investment or by having thirty odd thousand back in my pocket; can't lose."

Whilst waiting to step out onto the apron Adam discovered that he was seated next to Barbara, who told him that she had never flown in an aeroplane before. She was fascinated by everything. The huge, cavernous engines and beneath the wings, wheels on great stalks, which he explained, were called the undercarriage. She continued to share her observations, such as the smell of aviation fuel, or the striking blue and yellow livery, and the charming cabin staff who greeted her, warmed themselves by her beaming smile.

Onboard, he swapped his window seat for her centre one and promised to hold her hand if she needed it, though he was relieved to find that the aisle seat next to his had been left unallocated, leaving more room for his chunky mass. Once they were airborne and the view of land was lost in cloud, she leant over and spoke into Adam's ear, "Do you know, that surge, when we began to drive down the runway, felt a little like an orgasm." She carried out a swift mental review and corrected herself, "Or perhaps I should say like a little orgasm."

Adam sat spellbound, but hugely entertained, as she chattered away. It was the verbal equivalent of watching a moth, with glancing and momentary references to wholly unconnected subjects. When they were over Nantes, the cloud cleared and she became enchanted by the view, calling out when she recognised a feature, such as a river or forest, but when they began to descend he had to teach her how to clear her ears. By then they were heading out over the sea and the *Ile de Ré*, before turning back towards land on their final approach to La Rochelle airport.

They assembled at the car hire base within twenty minutes of landing, where three cars were signed for and loaded, before they left for Cognac, less than ninety minutes away. Sue led the way, which entailed an anxious twenty minute dash along the dual carriageway that looped around the northern and eastern flanks of La Rochelle, after which they slipped onto very quiet country roads until reaching the town of Saint-Jean-d'Angéley, where coffee was called for. The crisp wintry sunshine was just warm enough to warrant sitting outside.

***

Phillipe Rambert knew he had postponed making his call for too long, against a fading hope that the problem might come to nothing. His experiences with English investors thus far had been mixed. Many had been naive, driven more often than not

by a vacation gusto that withered away within days of returning to the UK, when they discover a painful ignorance of
French property laws. The penalties they had to pay vendors
for release from the contracts amused him and rewarded many
of his clients.

But the lawyer, Gagnon, had just telephoned him to advise
that a small army of them were arriving that day, intent on
floating Michaud out of his grasp.

Rambert dialled the number with a leaden dread. He recognised the heavy voice immediately, coarsened by heavy
smoking, while his was soft and on this occasion, conciliatory,
"*Bonjour Albert, ça va?*"

The reply was blunt; in colloquial French, "You have bad
news for me."

"Why do you say that?"

Albert Pichon's voice held contempt, "Because if it was
good news you wouldn't be making this call until the end of
the month."

Rambert fell on to the defensive and settled for part truths,
"No, no, not at all my friend. I am merely keeping you up to
date." He knew well, how to use silence as a tool and waited,
until eventually, Pichon growled, "Go on."

"Well, you may recall that two English women have bought
a house in Aurigny and while over here, last month, they became
acquainted with Michaud."

"One of them was screwing him."

Rambert feigned ignorance of that intelligence, "Really? I
did not know that. Perhaps it would have been wise to share
that knowledge with me?"

"Why? How could casual sex with an English whore make
any difference to his financial problem, unless he was paying for
it and that would help rather than hinder things."

Phillipe Rambert was a seasoned banker and recognised an
opening when he saw one, "Well Albert, I have some information I will share with you, though what you have just told
me has given my news a significance I would have recognised

earlier, had I known about it."

The response was predictable, "Stop playing with words and tell me what you called for."

The banker spoke as though everything made sense now, "It appears that those two women have returned today, with a group of friends and enough money to dig Michaud out of his hole."

"You must have known about this before now, you bastard."

As a respected banker, Rambert would have normally put the telephone down at that point, to allow an oafish client time to reconsider the insult and call back to apologise, but this was no ordinary client, "I have been told a little, but they appeared to be lightweights, already spending more on a small house than they can afford. I therefore concluded that they could not possibly afford to invest in the Michaud vineyard?"

Pichon growled, "But now you're telephoning me to say that they can. Is that not so?"

"It is possible, no more than that."

The anger in response hid an underlying anxiety, "Don't piss me about Phillipe. For once in your life tell the truth; all of it, not just half."

Realising that there was no hope of mitigation, Rambert hurried on, "My information is that a group of English are considering the investment; that is all. They have come over to visit the vineyard before making their decision, but I have also been told that they are all retired people, which does not auger well for Michaud's hopes for a sale."

"Why not?"

"Quite apart from the obvious, their inability to carry out physical work; people of that age are disinclined to take risks."

Pichon conceded that point with a grunt, before asking, "Do they know that you plan to foreclose at the end of the month?"

"Apparently, yes."

"But they are still here. That does not agree with your assessment."

Privately, the banker agreed but he sought shelter behind

another lie, "It is too early to say, but I suspect that they will back out and hurry home like so many English do."

Pichon would have none of it, "In that case, why are you telephoning me?"

"Merely to share information, something we should both do."

The coarse growl lent weight to the threat, "We share many things Rambert, you would do well to remember that." After a moment, he instructed, "Bring the deadline forward, to the end of this week."

"I cannot do that."

Pichon sighed, loudly, as though he was having to deal with a recalcitrant child, "And why not?"

Rambert began to feel angry but only managed to sound petulant, "Because there are now two lawyers involved, who have all the information and more importantly, the correspondence I have sent to Michaud. The writs would come back at me like tennis balls."

The reply was unequivocal, "You know what is at stake. By now you should have taken steps to counter the threat. This is making me very angry."

"Please, Albert, be patient. This English thing will come to nothing, I'm certain and in the meantime I will continue to keep you advised."

The telephone receiver at the other end was thrust back into its cradle, with a crash.

***

Annie's original plan had been to drive straight to the hotel in Cognac, where they would have lunch before moving on to Aurigny-les-Bois, but Anton had insisted on them having lunch at his place. They arrived just after noon and spent only a short time with the introductions before he ushered them into the dining room, where he and a neighbour's wife had laid out a remarkable spread of cold meats, pates and cheeses; complimented by dishes of olives, pickles and less recognisable accompaniments. To one side lay a small mountain of baguettes. In all, they filled the room with wonderful fragrances. Annie had never been beyond the kitchen before, so like her companions, she was impressed by the scale of the room and its furnishings. The dark oak table and chairs could have seated fifteen or more, easily. Sue whispered to her sister, "I'm pleased to see it's as clean as I left it." Anton appeared then, took her arm and led her to the seat next to his. Understandably she thought, when confronted with so many strangers.

Good food and wine serve to make most travellers feel at ease and soon, the room filled with babbling voices. Occasionally, Anton would answer a question, but for most of the time he chatted with Sue. The time to share his knowledge would come after lunch, when he would lead them on a tour of his distillery. With that in mind, he had deliberately omitted cognac from the lunchtime fare.

Jayne Maitlin sat between Bob Lucas and Kendall, leaving her husband in the company of Adam and Barbara. Bob was pleasant enough though a little dull at times, particularly when he lamented Carol's absence. Clearly, he missed her but then conversation with Kendall gave way to a tiresome litany of risqué jokes and innuendos which left her in no doubt that given the chance he would like to bed her. They were finally stopped when she insisted on him sharing them with Alan, who was seated opposite. They were not things to share with a lady's husband. In time, subjects of a more general appeal came up and spread to include everyone at the table.

True to French form, lunch continued until two thirty, when the lady from next door appeared and began to clear away the dishes. Anton introduced her to the group and acknowledged her assistance in preparing lunch, which called for a round of gentle applause, but her total lack of English limited any further communication to nods and smiles.

Anton wasted no more time in rounding them up for the tour. Annie and Sue tagged along at the back, eager to measure the reactions of the others and relieved to see that Anton was in fine form. It was clear from the outset, that he and George

Dyson had found an accord that extended beyond the usual, to such an extent that after the tour was over and the tastings in hand, Anton invited George to join him in an inner sanctum that even the sisters were unaware of. After leaving the others with a bottle of forty year old, they slipped away without being noticed and headed off through the forests of barrels to the furthermost end of his buildings. Sue went with them, leaving Annie to deal with questions and there were plenty. Bob Lucas, Kendall Spencer and Adam Harding formed into a cluster as did the women, Amy Dyson, Barbara Thatcham and Jayne Maitlin. Barry Parsley announced to anyone who would listen, that he couldn't wait to interview Anton about the financials, while Annie floated from one to another as questions were raised. In general though, she was pleased with the response so far.

As they entered the small area, separated from the rest of the building by an old oak door, Anton said to George, "This, my friend, is where I keep my best *'Hors d'Age'*. Sue had no idea what that was and said so, but George was beside himself. He explained, "It's the title only given to high quality cognac that is beyond the official age scale." Anton nodded his agreement and smiled.

The lighting was barely adequate to move around safely, but Anton approached a small table and lit a fat candle that was secured by its own cold mass of formerly melted wax. Half a dozen glasses reflected the wavering light that lent the place a theatrical atmosphere.

Anton explained, "Sadly, the oldest I have is only sixty five years. The Germans you know, but I think you will find it acceptable." The understatement was deliberate, of course and with some ceremony, he eased the bung from the barrel that rested beside the table and siphoned some off into a small decanter. George watched in awe as the dark amber fluid was transferred to three glasses and handed out with a reverence that belonged beside an altar.

Sue was stunned by the gentle splendour of it, but that was nothing compared to George's reaction. She felt certain that he was affected by the atmosphere and surroundings, as well as the nectar on offer, but she was still startled when he wept.

Anton looked on with delight, until his new English friend set his glass down on the table, stepped forward and hugged him.

George stepped back then, fearful of having overreacted, until he saw Anton's face too. With that, he turned to Sue and shook his head, "I shall remember this moment for as long as I live."

Anton gestured towards George's glass with a needless and therefore unspoken question.

On their way back to the others, Anton broke away to check the distillation. Alone, with George, Sue agreed, "That was rather special, wasn't it?"

He couldn't believe his ears, "That, my girl is the understatement of the century. Not only have you tasted one of the finest cognacs imaginable, but we've just swallowed about eighty pounds worth to boot."

She gasped, "You're joking!"

He shrugged, "*Google* it."

***

It was all over by five that afternoon, in every sense, save perhaps for Barry Parsley, who had his own agenda. Everyone else had seen and heard enough to make their minds up, though none had acknowledged that, yet. Adam was the first to do so.

They all thanked Anton with genuine though slightly excessive enthusiasm of the semi-drunk. He told them to call in anytime with any questions and Adam whispered in Annie's ear, "I have one." She looked at him and he continued, "Where do I sign?" He was rewarded with a grin of gratitude.

That night, over a light meal, they all expressed delight at the visit. Decisions had yet to be called for, but George made his position clear, "I'm good for twice my amount if anyone wants to pull out." There were no takers.

It was Barbara though, who expanded their horizons,

when she asked Annie, "Do you think we might be able to rent somewhere, large enough for us to share?"

They were all startled at first, but the notion gradually took form and became a subject of excited discussion.

Annie said, "Well, tomorrow, Sue and I have something to attend to, so I was going to suggest dropping us off in the village before treating yourselves to a tour of the area. If you could collect us at teatime we can discuss everything over tomorrow night's meal and call for decisions. Don't forget, we have a provisional appointment with the lawyers the next morning, to sign up, hopefully." There were nods of agreement all round except for Barry, who said, "Actually, I've arranged with Anton to meet up tomorrow morning, for a review of the financials. I have a number of questions."

Kendall leaned over to whisper in Alan Maitlin's ear, "Anton would have to give us the place before old Parsleymonious would think it was decent value."

Annie did a quick mental count before, "That would leave eight doing the tour, so why don't they use two of the cars and that will leave Sue, Barry and me with our own transport.

It was Adam's turn to suggest something, "I fancy having a walk around the land itself; have a look at the vines and so on." Everyone thought it was splendid idea so he added, "In that case, why don't we do the tour, meet up for lunch and go on to the land from there." Earlier, Annie had telephoned Penny who had been delighted to learn they were back and had invited them for lunch. She had accepted the invitation and therefore announced, "Sorry guys, Sue and I won't be clear until two at the earliest but I'd love to join you. I can't believe we haven't done it before. Unfortunately, there's nowhere local for lunch. Try Matha, it's about twenty five minutes away, which should put you back in Aurigny by about two thirty. We could meet up at Anton's."

They were all wilting, so with the logistics agreed everyone retired for the night. It had been a very long and exciting day.

***

The next morning, Sue and Annie left the car and Barry at Anton's, preferring to walk to the house they hoped would soon be theirs. Knowing that it was empty, they settled for another wander around the land, shorn of leafage now, but still beautiful. It served to firm their resolve and they made their way to the farmhouse next door.

A small but well built man, dressed in blue overalls and the ubiquitous dark beret was working on a small tractor in the yard. He stood upright when they approached, but waited for Annie to speak, "Monsieur Durand?"

He had the dark weathered complexion of someone who had worked outdoors all his life, with a grey-flecked walrus moustache and eyes that might have wowed the ladies once but were unreadable at that moment. He nodded, "*Oui!*"

She smiled, and continued to speak in French as she held her hand out, "Bonjour Monsieur, we hope to be your new neighbours."

He'd been wiping his hands with an oily rag but after a quick inspection, they were deemed to be too grubby and he held one up, palm outward and said, in French, "Sorry."

She passed it off with a wave of a hand, "My name is Annie and this is my sister, Sue." He waited for more, so she hurried on, "We would like to discuss something with you, please." She began to think there was something amiss with his thought processes, but eventually, he nodded and said, "Then you had better come inside and meet my wife." They followed him into the kitchen, after he had kicked off his boots at the door and he gestured for them to sit at the table, with, "If you please," before moving to a door in the corner and calling his wife. While they waited, he moved over to the sink and began to wash his hands, leaving Annie to consider the encounter. Thus far, he had only uttered one sentence and a single word. It looked set to be a tough one.

Just then, a small round lady bustled into the room. Her calf length skirt and thick sweater were fairly neutral in colour as well as style and might even have been handmade, but her eyes shone and the smile was genuine when she said, "*Bonjour.*"

Annie and Sue stood and by now, Monsieur Durand had turned from the sink and was drying his hands as he spoke to his wife, "These ladies have bought the house next door." He turned then to the sisters and extended a damp hand, "My name is Durand and this is my wife."

Madame Durand hurried forward and held a hand out. With a meaningful glance at her husband, she said, "My name is Marie Ann. It is a pleasure to meet you." It was clear that she meant it too. Annie noted that she smiled with her eyes as well as her mouth. Marie Ann gestured towards the chairs, "Please, sit. May we offer you a drink; coffee, perhaps?"

Annie smiled back, "Thank you; that would be nice." Monsieur Durand sat down as well, but continued to demonstrate an absence of conversational skills. Thankfully, the hostess and coffees were soon in place, along with a plate of cheese pastries that she urged them to try.

They were stunning. Light, crispy and full of flavour. Marie Ann looked on with a hint of anxiety until both sisters expressed genuine delight. Their hostess beamed and then passed their praise off with an infectious giggle, "It is a recipe my mother gave to me."

Sue said, "But you must also have the gift with your hands for pastry like this. Is it a secret recipe then?"

Again the giggle and a nod, "It is true. We say the same here, but no, I do not keep it to myself. Would you like it?"

"Oh yes please. They are wonderful."

Another appreciative giggle, "I will write it out for when you move in."

Annie spoke gently, "I'm afraid that is the reason for our visit. We may not be able to buy it Marie Ann, because our lawyer has warned us about the right of way you hold on that land. We've come to ask if there is any way we could persuade you to relinquish it."

Durand cut in, though he addressed his wife, "The right has been ours for generations; I see no reason to give it away."

Marie Ann said, "But we no longer own the land on the other side."

His eyebrows went up and he flicked his head over to one side, "A right is a right and this one belongs to us. The other people accepted it so why shouldn't these?"

Annie detested being spoken about in that way, as though they weren't present, but she resisted the challenge of making him speak to her rather than his wife, though she made a point of addressing him directly, "The Andersons were shocked to learn of your right. They hadn't been made aware of it when they bought the barn from you."

His eyebrows headed north again and he held both hands out, palm upward, "*Caveat emptor.*"

Sue missed it because of the French pronunciation and asked, "What is that?"

Annie turned to her sister, "He said *caveat emptor*, it's latin for 'let the buyer beware'."

Sue bridled, "I know that; just didn't get the pronunciation."

This time Annie looked at Marie Ann, "Monsieur Durand said he wouldn't be prepared to give it away, but perhaps we could agree on a price; a realistic one."

The exchanges were bordering on the bizarre, for he then addressed his wife again, "Old family rights are beyond price. They are not things to be bartered like apples and pears."

Annie stared hard at him, "Then I am sorry to hear that Monsieur, we were so looking forward to living here. I will pass your comments on to the Andersons, along with our regrets."

It became too awkward to stay any longer, so the sisters finished their coffee and stood to leave. The Durands stood too and whilst his expression was hidden behind the undergrowth on his upper lip, Marie Ann's was an eloquent mix of sorrow and embarrassment. In spite of everything, Sue pointed at the plate of pastries and said, "May I?" Annie would argue that it was the single most inspired act of the day, for Marie Ann's face lit up, as though she'd been offered an olive branch, "But of course!"

They all shook hands and the sisters set off to Penny's house for lunch. As soon as they were out of earshot, Sue said, "The ignorant old bastard!" There was little to add to that, in the circumstances and since neither wanted to discuss pulling out of the deal, they walked in silence.

As they were passing a five barred bate, a figure clad in a hooded oilskin and wellingtons suddenly appeared from the other side and began climbing over the obstacle. A gust of wind blew the hood back and they saw that it was Marie Ann, flushed and out of breath. She rolled over the top of the gate and dropped down onto to the roadside before saying, "Annie; Sue, I must speak with you. Jean Claude is a traditionalist and a proud man, but he can be very stupid too. All men are, but it would have been improper for me to speak out in our meeting. You understand?"

Annie nodded and smiled, "I think so. Perhaps it would have been better if we'd had men folk to do such things."

Marie Ann clapped her hands, "Exactly! But now, it is for us women to do things properly."

This time, Annie grinned broadly, with amusement and relief. "What do you suggest?"

Another infectious giggle, "First we must make sure that his pride is well fed. That is why I have a plan. He needs to give up that right with honour and I need a new rotovator for my garden." She pulled a magazine cutting out of her pocket and showed them a picture of a bright red machine, produced by a French manufacturer, "That is it. The cost is six hundred and ninety nine Euros, but if that is too much I can assist perhaps, though it would have to be our secret. Then, all will be well, I promise."

Annie was so thrilled she stepped forward and hugged her, "That would be wonderful! We can't thank you enough and it would be our pleasure to pay the full amount."

"Then we have an accord. My husband will agree to lose his right of way, in time for you to buy the house. Leave the payment for the rotovator until you move in, but then I think, it would be better to give him the money rather than me." She finished with another giggle, "Now, I must get to the *boulangerie* before it closes, otherwise I would have no reason for coming out!"

Once they had parted company, Sue said, "You know, I think we're going to get on like a house on fire with her." After a moment, she added, "Not sure about 'whiskers' though."

Annie chuckled, "Great name."

Penny and Guinness were delighted to see them. The sisters learned that Anton had called in one evening and told them everything, including the measure of how much he missed Sue. Over lunch, they told her about their encounter with Monsieur Durand which caused some hilarity. As ever, Guinness shared his affections, or rather paw, between each of them, in the hope of a titbit.

***

Secretly, Barry saw himself as the only member of the group capable of ferreting out unpleasant truths and as a consequence, the one to earn their praise and gratitude for saving them from themselves. They were all so smitten with the cognac it was going to be left to him to observe the rigours of due diligence. There had to be skeletons hidden in there somewhere.

He was wrong.

In the first place, Anton allowed him complete freedom of the files and trading records, which were surprisingly detailed and reconciled exactly with the bank statements. Moreover, whilst the stock takes would prove to be accurate, even he, with such a limited knowledge of vineyards, realised that they had been terribly undervalued. In short, the enterprise was worth a great deal more than had been stated. The same could be said of the plant and machinery, which had been down-written to ridiculous levels. When the time came to physically check the stocks he was surprised to learn that Anton kept cognac in five other rented storerooms around the village. When asked which properties he replied, "Why the black ones of course."

Anton had been attentive throughout and disarmingly candid; so much so that by lunchtime, when they sat down to eat home-made soup, the foundations of a friendship had been laid. Barry described Waltham Parva and his life there, along with details of his career, whilst Anton spoke about the local area, his way of life and the local customs. He even included tips that would gain Barry 'cred' with French waiters; a matter of some importance over there. For example, instead of ordering two coffees with cream, one should simply order two creams, or *deux crèmes*.

When the others arrived, just after lunch, Anton left Barry to carry on alone while he escorted them on a tour of the land. Most of the pruning had been done, but he gave them a demonstration. They were surprised to learn that whilst the harvesting was done by machine, all the pruning was by hand, by just him and one other man; the one who had worked there for most of his life. They had noticed a speckled white old van that looked as though it had been dumped between the vines and when Alan asked where the employee was, Anton waved a hand towards a the brow of a distant rise, where they could just make out the bent figure, "There he is and that is the van I let him use."

George murmured, "A company car no less."

Anton smiled and Sue translated, "It was either that, or take it to the scrap yard. How he has kept it running has been a miracle."

Bob asked, "Why did he park down here and walk all the way up there to work."

"He is a quiet man and prefers his own company. I told him I was bringing you here so he must have decided to keep away. But now, I must continue your lesson!"

He explained how vines were often fifty years old before they were replaced with new stock, that would take two years to produce a reasonable crop. The grapes were of the *'Ugni Blanc'* variety which produced wines that could be fresh and fruity, but did not keep long. As a base for cognac though, they were ideal.

By the end of the tour they had forgotten some of the details, but not Anton's passion. The vineyard was his life; the reason for his existence.

Though they wouldn't know who to thank for it, Sue's previous influence became evident when they returned to the house and were offered tea and cakes; a very un-French thing to do.

Barry was still working and declared that he wouldn't be finished until six, at the earliest, so eventually, two car loads departed for the hotel, leaving Sue and Annie to do the clearing up while Anton answered the list of questions that now lay in wait. Another hour passed by, until finally, Barry bundled his notes together and thanked Anton for his time and patience. Though disinclined to divulge it at that point, he had given the place a clean bill of health and more importantly, he'd dispelled any of the doubts he'd had. There was no way he was going to miss this investment opportunity now.

He was surprised when only Annie got into the car and Sue stood next to Anton, waiting to wave them off. He looked at Annie, "Isn't Sue coming?"

"Ah," she said, "That's something we haven't mentioned. Drive on, I'll explain in a minute."

During the drive back to Cognac, Barry raised the subject again and after a little thought, Annie opted for candour, "Let's just say that Sue's investment in the vineyard is of a non monetary nature."

It should have been her turn for questions about his findings, but Barry refused to answer any, arguing that they should wait to be shared with everyone, though secretly, he relished the anxious anticipation. Piqued slightly, she decided not to tell him anything about the tour with Anton and as a result, the journey was a quiet one.

When they entered the hotel, everyone was waiting in the bar, where it was clear that his verdict was awaited with some concern. Once again, he'd originally imagined addressing them with a cool, unemotional yet professionally factual evaluation. Instead, when the time came to stand before them, he wore a surprisingly silly grin for someone in his position and said, "Thumbs up everyone!"

Everyone was relieved but they wanted to know more. He was delighted to oblige. There followed a remarkably detailed report, which earned a round of applause when he'd finished.

Someone called out, "Where's Sue?"

Barry turned to Annie with a cheeky grin, "Should I add that to my report?"

She waved a hand, "Sure, why not. It shouldn't be a secret."

***

They all gathered in Monsieur Gagnon's office the following morning, when the lawyer presented them with the agreement he and Anton's lawyer had prepared. He insisted on reading it to them in French and then English. A few minor amendments were made after which he summoned a clerk to print out several amended copies. They appeared within minutes and he asked if they would like time to read them alone. Since Annie, George and Sue were the only ones with good enough French to attempt such a thing, the group decided to waive that right.

Barbara was a little intimidated by the formality of the occasion and the quiet, solemnity of the office and furnishings. She turned to Annie and spoke in a whisper that would have woken the dead, "It's such a shame that this place couldn't have been *jollier* somehow. He might just as easily have been reading a will. Some brighter colours on the walls would be an improvement too."

Gagnon overheard her and responded with a half smile and Gallic shrug, "It is true Madam, but perhaps a little more theatre is required before people will pay my exorbitant fees."

She clapped her hands in delight, "Oh my, an honest lawyer. I like you already!"

They took it in turns to sign the document and a colleague witnessed each signature after which Gagnon explained that the agreement would be signed by Anton at his lawyer's office, on the following Monday.

***

Since their flight was at ten the following morning, they chose to spend their last afternoon visiting Saintes, rather than the vineyard again, but Anton had promised to join them at the hotel that evening for a few glasses of champagne, before they all ventured out for a meal at the same restaurant he had taken Sue to.

The old city of Saintes lived up to its reputation. In spite of the persistent drizzle, or perhaps because of it, they all appreciated the light stone used in the buildings, which served to lighten a grey day. They spent a short while looking at Roman ruins, but only from the comfort of their cars, after which they parked and ambled through the old town which was delightful, as were the *galettes* they had for lunch. After an hours' shopping, it was time to get back to the hotel for a nap, before the evening excursion.

Sue and Anton arrived on time and both seemed to be in high spirits. By the end of the evening, everyone else was too, enough for George to announce a toast, "I would like to propose a toast to our maker. Thank you, for giving us taste buds and erogenous zones. I for one wouldn't care to live without them." It seemed natural enough to propose a toast to Anton and Sue then, but Amy sensed what was coming and dragged him back into his seat.

Once again, Sue chose to spend the night with Anton and when the rest of the group waved them off from the hotel car park Barbara commented, "Lucky old Sue," which prompted Alan Maitlin to add, "Lucky old Anton!"

Annie's observation was more practical, "She'd better make it to the airport in time tomorrow morning."

***

Back in Waltham Parva, Megan Spencer was having a great day too. She'd spent much of that morning shopping, with intent.

Months earlier, she read a magazine article that chronicled

a few examples of the many renewed relationships arising from use of the website, *Friends Reunited.* By all accounts, old flames were just waiting in there, for re-ignition. She signed up and claimed, when Kendall asked about it, to be searching for her old school netball pals; a cover story that wouldn't come close to explaining the frisson she'd experienced when she found the love of her life on there. Simon Sheldon.

Star on the sports field, good looking and an incredible kisser. She still regretted not letting him into her panties, but the fear of pregnancy and being called a slapper by her peers overrode the yearning she had felt. After months of laying siege to her hymen, he went off and disposed of another.

Now, here he was, so much older but still good looking. They'd been exchanging messages for months and now the fates were handing her another chance. Not for love though, with so many years in between, they could never hope to re-kindle that early dichotomy of innocence and heat. Besides, they were both established in comfortable lives. He had two children, a wife who worked as a teacher's assistant and a lot less hair while she had Sophie and a significant baby bump.

No, this time, given the opportunity, she would have simply surrendered, in a purely carnal sense. Even the thought of it triggered the deep yearning itch she had known back then but could barely comprehend and one she hadn't enjoyed for a long time.

After the initial message exchange on *Friends Reunited*, they had been using *Skype* instant messaging. They could and sometimes did talk and use the camera, but more often than not, they settled for text messaging, for he contacted her from his office mostly and besides, she didn't want Sophie listening in; even a three year old can let things out.

To begin with, their exchanges had been little more than the polite renewal of a friendship, but they both knew there was more.

There had been a lot of catching up to do, beginning with the day they left school and followed by a broadly chronological detailing of their lives. Once, he skipped over a topic and she admonished him. Since then they had relished the exchange of every detail they could recall. Almost nothing was taboo; health, children, worries, lows and highs. She relished every exchange and every detail, as she sought the intimacy they might otherwise have had. Predictably, though it was never actually acknowledged, their partners were rarely mentioned. It was as though the omission was a tacit acknowledgement of what lay ahead.

Recently, she had begun to wonder what on earth she had seen in Kendall. There had to have been good times, obviously, she just had difficulty in recalling them.

Over several weeks the rite of passage she and Simon entered into became a deliciously subtle play of hints and nuances that moved them to a new level of intimacy. In some ways, more so than when they were young, for now they knew so much more.

Megan finally transported them over that heart-stopping threshold, on one of the days they were messaging about their young love and its intensity. She closed her mind to the consequences and wrote swiftly, in case a fluttering heart and nerves failed her,

It still is, for me.

He replied, *What is?*

There was no going back. She typed, *Intense* and barely breathed as she waited for his reply. After an age of anxiety, she threw everything to the fates, *I wish I'd said yes.* Still more time passed, until finally she read,

Oh God, Megan, I wish you had. I wouldn't have let you down.

She began to write something when another, defining message came through,

I wouldn't have let you go, either.

It marked the beginning of many sexually charged exchanges, filled with secrets, desires and a growing lasciviousness that left her breathless as she wriggled on the kitchen chair, to achieve a delicious discomfort rather than comfort. After so many years the continued absence of an actual physical union had become unbearable.

Until tonight.

Sophie may have sensed the turmoil in her mother and

simply wouldn't go down for the night. The longer it took the more anxious Megan became, but eventually, following a dose of *Calpol,* the child slept.

After a quick shower, Megan began to dress, pausing to check that she'd removed all the labels from the underwear she'd purchased in Leicester earlier that day. After considering the scarlet and black ensembles sold by *Victoria's Secret,* she opted for the white cotton panties, bra and garter belt from *Marks and Spencers* with tan stockings. The stockings and suspenders were overtly sexual, but the simple white accompaniments were like those worn in those innocent days, when she had said no. Tonight, the panties would be his to keep, if he wanted them, both a trophy and gift.

These days though, the panties were five sizes larger and encompassed a belly that hadn't been there then. She fretted for a while, but time was running out. After tearing the labels off them, she slipped each item on without daring to take stock in front of a mirror. All that mattered in that moment was how the ensemble made her feel. Beyond that, she could only hope that he was as readily aroused. There followed a russet coloured skirt and pink woollen jumper before she hurried downstairs to make the telephone call to Simon, who had been waiting in a lay by, three miles away, for almost an hour.

She opened the door as he approached and ushered him inside, where they stood awkwardly for a moment, both unsure of the next step. Finally, he took it and stepped forward into her opening arms for a hug. It was pelting down outside, enough to soak his coat in the short walk from the car. She stepped back, dusting the water droplets from her jumper and said, "Let me take your coat."

After dropping it onto to the newel post at the bottom of the stairs, she made an awkward gesture towards the centre of the room which prompted a further distancing as they moved to the either side of the sofa and then finally, with mutual and unspoken relief, they sat down beside each other. Megan poured two glasses of wine from the bottle she had left on the coffee table beside two bowls of nibbles, but suddenly, the ease they had known in their text and *Skype* exchanges disappeared and they found themselves talking about silly day to day matters, the way mere acquaintances might do at cocktail parties. It was dreadful and not at all how she'd imagined. Suddenly, out of desperation, she leaned in to him; her mouth parted slightly with intent and kissed him. The time for conversation was over, or it would have been if she hadn't dumped half of her wine into his lap. They pulled apart, with her apologising and him providing assurances that it didn't matter.

She watched him grab a napkin from the table and begin mopping up, but she took it and tackled the job herself. While gently dabbing his thigh and without looking up she whispered, "In a minute, I'm going to take you to bed."

He placed a hand on hers and sighed, "Oh Megan, yes please."

Finally and at last, he took the opportunity to put his arm around her shoulders before leaning in and nuzzling her neck, causing an involuntary whimper to rise in her throat as she responded with a roll of the head.

She allowed him to undress her, relishing his delight at the sight of her underwear and gradual exposure of her body. It might have been the realisation that they were *both* older and less perfect than they had been, but instead of apologising, or making some flippant remark when he slipped her bra away and her breasts sagged slightly, she reached forward and drew him to suckle. Her rounded stomach was merely a soft introduction to the waistband of her panties. She dictated the pace, with gasps, hands and swollen lips, until she urged him on top and arched her back to meet him. It was over in moments, though she was excited enough to feel the swelling flare of an approaching orgasm.

He collapsed onto her and groaned, "I'm so sorry. It's been a long time."

With that he made to roll off her but she kept her arms around him, "Shh, stay like that. It doesn't matter, there'll be lots of other times; won't there?"

He raised his head and kissed her gently, "Oh Megan yes, there has to be."

They lay like that for a while until he became too heavy for her and she rolled him over onto his back and cuddled up. After a moment, a thought struck her, "You never mentioned anything about it being a long time in any of our messaging."

He made a sound that lay somewhere between a grunt and chuckle, "After our second was born, Sarah told me that she had no further interest in sex. There hadn't been much of it anyway, but I wasn't expecting a famine. It seems I'd served my purpose in that respect by siring the two children we'd decided on. Since then, my only obligation has been to rear them."

She nuzzled him encouragingly, "So, why *didn't* you mention it before? I might have offered favours much sooner."

He covered his discomfiture by hugging her as he spoke, "It would have sounded like a convenient lie, to justify this."

She nuzzled him again, "No matter, you're here now and I'm so glad."

They lay like that for an hour, until she sensed that he was dozing. She carefully eased away and slipped down beneath the bedclothes, guided now by her own scent. He woke when she took the whole of his soft organ into her mouth and rolled it with her tongue, until very soon, he felt himself begin to harden again. He almost said that he wasn't a 'repeater' which was just as well, because fifteen minutes later they shared an entirely magical, simultaneous orgasm. His was good, but hers was life enhancing. She almost lost consciousness.

***

On Monday the tenth of January, Phillipe Rambert was advised of a significant transfer of funds from England, into Anton Michaud's account. The indebtedness to the bank had been cleared and then some. He asked for a copy of the transfer docket and inspected it closely for errors, however small, but then realised the futility of such an action. The days of an individual being able to refuse transactions for such things were long gone. Nowadays, all such transactions were electronic and the system's acceptance of them was final.

So therefore, he was faced with a *fait accompli*. Little Michaud had outwitted them which left him with the task of making another telephone call. This one though, would be much more difficult and a great deal less pleasant. He decided to postpone it until after lunch, when Pichon's customary bottle of wine may have dulled his wits.

Meanwhile, Anton was seated in his lawyer's office, listening to dire warnings about the hazards of surrendering such control to a bunch of foreigners who knew nothing about making cognac. Eventually, after all the conditions had been considered, he said, "I trust these people, more than I trust my bank, with its treachery. In three weeks from now, they would have stolen my family's vineyard and sold it for peanuts. Given those choices, what would you do?"

The lawyer sighed, "But are you sure that there are no alternatives?"

"Absolutely!"

"Then I am sorry for you Monsieur Michaud. I can only hope that this works out well. *Bonne chance!*"

The 'bunch of foreigners' had persuaded the landlord of the *Rose and Crown* to replicate his Friday morning deal for that Monday, enabling them to gather in one place for the news. They met at the usual hour of eleven, forgetting once again that French time is an hour on and twelve noon was lunchtime, an event, Annie reminded them, of almost biblical importance. Thankfully, Sue and Annie were still having to correct themselves in the opposite direction and had telephoned Monsieur Gagnon before they left the house. He confirmed that the contract was complete and the funds were in place, though he did remonstrate in a mild fashion, "Madame Stockley, you should have transferred the funds to me, not directly into Monsieur Michaud's account. If anything had gone wrong we would have had great difficulty in rescuing the money for you."

Annie knew full well what she had done and why, but she

feigned ignorance, "Oh I am sorry Monsieur Gagnon, we didn't think. Still, we have a saying, 'All's well that ends well'. Oh, and please, call me Annie."

After a small grunt, he sighed, "Very well Annie. As you say, we have been fortunate." He chuckled, "You may tell the lady who likes honest lawyers that I have been unable to charge for making the transfer on your behalf."

It was a fine note to close on.

Once again, Annie waited until everyone had arrived, noting that Bob Lucas was still alone. She rapped a spoon against her cup and the meeting came to order immediately, "OK you lot, I have bad news and good news and I'm going to pass them on in that order." A falling pin would have been deafening. "First, it is now ten past twelve in France and therefore lunchtime."

George groaned, "Oh bugger, why do I keep forgetting that hour?"

There were murmurs of agreement around the table, until Annie held up her hand, "Which is why I telephoned Monsieur Gagnon half an hour ago, when he was able to confirm that everything has been completed satisfactorily."

A cheer rose up and the young barman was rewarded with an order for four bottles of wine instead of a round of free refills. Annie added, "As you know, we decided to shove the money directly into Anton's account in case there was a hiccough with the lawyers, and for that, I received a mild telling off. I told Monsieur Gagnon that you lot made me do it."

***

At two thirty, French time, Rambert made his call. It was answered immediately, "Pichon."

The banker felt that it was necessary to observe the usual courtesies, "Bonjour Albert, OK?"

The response was rude and succinct, "Get on with it."

Rambert took a moment to gather his thoughts and courage, "We have just received a transfer of funds into Michaud's account, which has put him into the black."

The familiar growl, "Do something about it."

In spite of his rising anger, Rambert's reply sounded churlish, "What do you suggest?"

"Don't ask me, you're the expert, or at least you should have been."

"There are some things I have no control over and remember, I had no knowledge of it before last week."

Pichon began to shout, "Don't talk to me about control. That is something you lost when you gave Michaud a whole month to do something!"

Rambert reminded him, "Do not forget, I still have some influence with the merchants. If he can't sell the stuff his new allies will soon run back to England."

"Phah! What value can I put on your assurances?"

"That is unreasonable."

Pichon snarled, "Either sort it out, today, or live to regret it you imbecile." Once again, the receiver at the other end was slammed down.

Rambert replaced his receiver gently into its cradle and said aloud, "Ah, la la, I think that went down rather badly." Nevertheless, he was glad the call was over and done with. He could not, would not attempt any more mischief with Michaud's banking. There were too many involved now and in any event, he could no longer justify taking any action. But what lay ahead and how could he keep that oaf under control?

***

After weeks of living with Annie, Sue had gone back to her flat in Leicester, to check on the place and collect her mail. In her absence, the place was unusually quiet. At seven that evening, after toying with a reheated lasagne that had been left over from the previous night, Annie flicked through the television channels, all the way to the adult section, before giving up. She read for a while, with little enthusiasm, but then remembered to check her emails.

The fourth message was from Penny,

Hi Both,

Trust you are well. Anton has just called in with a bottle of champagne and news that you lot are now fellow vignerons. Congratulations!

We shared the champagne immediately, of course.

Thing is, I was going to email you anyway. You mentioned the possibility of renting a place and I put word out locally. Our local policeman, Hubert, did a better job of it than me. Yesterday, a lady from Aprepont, telephoned me with news of a place her husband inherited from his parents last year. It's been empty for over a year, since his father died, so it's probably very basic and smelling of pee, but there are five bedrooms. She told me that they had sold the land to a neighbouring farmer who had no interest in the property.

Anyway, the upshot is that they're prepared to let it at a modest rent, if the tenants would take care of the place.

Oops, forgot, Aprepont is a village that's about eight kilometres away from here. It has a church and a boulangerie.

If you're interested, I'll pop over and take some photos, then send them to you as an attachment. Let me know.

Penny XX

P.S. Tell everyone they need to start brushing up on their French now.

Once she had sent a reply, Annie telephoned the landlord of the *Rose and Crown* to ask if they might hook into his WIFI on the following Friday, by which time she would be in a position to share Penny's photographic tour of the farmhouse. After then, it would be up to the others to sort themselves out. She and Sue had their own accommodation issues to deal with.

She sat back and stared at the screen. That their friends in Aurigny were celebrating gave her some comfort, but in that moment, the enormity of it came home. She realised that the others would hold her responsible for the whole thing; the idea, plan, group enrolment and completion. She murmured to herself, "What have I done?" She was tired and overwhelmed by it all. What she really needed was Sue's quirky yet down to earth perspective on things. In the meantime, Annie felt herself dwelling on the negatives.

She recalled reading about a study of entrepreneurs, which established that most dreamt of what lay ahead with new enterprises, but those dreams almost always involved successes rather than failures. Why then, was she feeling so anxious and imagining the worst. The experience was so out of character for someone who had spent most of her life running an extremely successful business.

But then she realised where the problem lay. So many of the group lacked a business background; they were quite literally innocents abroad and she was wearing their business hats as well as her own.

There was little else to do but make a hot chocolate and go to bed, for a restless night.

In Aurigny-les-Bois, Anton was afflicted with doubts too, as he wandered through his beloved casks. Eventually, he found himself in the store of his oldest cognacs, where he lit the candle and drew a glass of his finest, before sitting on a stool to contemplate his future. Two more glasses and an hour later he broke the silence, "Well Anton, at least you still have a future." He had never told anyone of his plan, but if the bank had succeeded in dispossessing him, he would have ended things, quietly and alone, in that same spot.

Like Annie, he made his way to bed, where he lay and thought of the comfort Sue would have given him, if she'd been there. He might even have shared that secret with her.

Back in Leicester, Sue was enjoying some of her forty year old while watching another repeat of *The Morecombe and Wise Show;* blissfully unaware of their feelings.

***

Annie's natural confidence had returned to dispel most of her doubts by the next morning, in spite of a lack of sleep. She had mentally tweaked and teased at her concerns until they had been rationalised, solved or placed into some sort of logical order. Above all, the group were all adults and had seen enough of the distillery to make their own minds up. Her responsibilities would only have been significant if they had invested on her word alone, without the benefit of a visit or Barry's audit. Even then, a tiny caveat in the back of her mind knew otherwise. Reason and understanding fled from frightened people with empty bank accounts. One of life's truths came to mind. How it was that people often consoled failures and envied success, until their money was at stake. Nevertheless, their anger would be something she would face, if need be, with a clear conscience. She thought of Monsieur Durand then and nodded a distant salute, *caveat emptor!*

Her rally was helped further by the first message in her email box, from Paul Gagnon,

Chére Annie,

I wrote to Monsieur Durand, as you requested and have just received a response, advising me that he is willing to surrender title to his right of way over your land.

As you suggested, he is doing so without any payment for it, which surprises me. Perhaps he simply wishes to be a good neighbour.

In any event, I shall prepare the paperwork and forward it to him. Once I have it back we can arrange an appointment with the notaire, to complete your purchase. You will need to ensure that the funds are with him in time for that meeting. I will let you have the bank details shortly.

Cordialement,

Paul Gagnon

She tapped the 'forward' button and inserted an address. By then, it had become a matter of course to forward a copy of most things to Penny.

CHAPTER 7

August 1943

Maurice Pichon sat at the kitchen table with his back to the door. It was usually his wife's place, but she and little Albert were upstairs, where they belonged on these occasions.

He heard a car draw up outside and the approaching footsteps, but he wouldn't look up when his visitor strode in without knocking, or show any acknowledgement as the man walked around the table to sit opposite and charge the glass left there, from the bottle of cognac.

Whilst the man's French was academically perfect, it was tainted by the guttural German accent, "Where are they?"

Maurice took a moment to answer, as though the delay bestowed some measure of integrity, but finally, he signalled to his left with a thumb, "At the next farm, Fournier's place."

He looked up as the barbarian threw the cognac back, as though it was a shot of schnapps and stood to leave. Maurice held up a hand and said, "Wait, there is something else." He held out a hand, towards the bottle, "Please, another cognac."

SS Obersturmführer Meyer remained standing for a moment before relenting, with a shrug and returning to his seat. This time he recharged his glass with an unseemly measure.

Pichon waited until his visitor said, "Well?"

The Frenchman's face was lined and weathered from a

lifetime outdoors, but his eyes shone, "The farm; you will confiscate it?"

The German nodded, "Of course."

"Then I would like to buy it, at the right price." In the silence that followed his pulse began to rise in line with the anxiety of knowing he might have gone too far, but eventually Meyer asked, "And how would that benefit me?"

Pichon's tone became conciliatory, "I thought that my assistance, past and future, might merit such a reward and of course, I would hope to show my gratitude to you personally."

Meyer smirked and recharged his glass while he considered the offer, even though he'd half expected it. Nevertheless, it never hurt to make *collaborateurs* sweat a little now and then. Such tactics served to remind them that they were already entrapped by their treachery. Minutes passed by until he nodded, "I will see what I can do." With that he stood and walked towards the door once more.

Emboldened, Pichon said, "I could use the hay."

Meyer chuckled, "Take whatever you can, but not until tomorrow morning."

Twenty minutes later, Pichon heard the rumble of heavy trucks pass along the lane, towards his neighbour's farm. Not long after, he heard a small fusillade of shots and in time, a rapidly growing column of smoke appeared in the distance. He sighed, "So much for the hay."

They didn't even spare the farmer's wife and three children, who stood weeping, on land they no longer owned, before being driven by rifle butts towards the barn. Their kind, loving husband and father had already been forced to accompany the six English airmen into the building and as soon as everyone was together they were summarily executed. The inferno that followed destroyed any evidence of the atrocity and their home.

The airmen had bailed out of their stricken *Lancaster,* which had limped on for another five kilometres before crashing into a wood south of Matha, with the skipper still at the controls, desperately trying to distance the crash site from his men. The bomb load had already been dropped on Bordeaux, so the impact in woodland was relatively muted and there was no fire. With luck, the Germans wouldn't have found the wreckage for a couple of days, by which time the others could have been en route to Spain, God willing.

Pichon went up there the following morning, expecting to find the bodies, which he intended to bury in the woods. Not out of compassion; it was a matter of keeping the episode as secret as possible. If there were no bodies, there would be no accusations. The locals would only know that the Germans had discovered British airmen there and probably deported the farmer and his family. Even the suggestion of survival helped to mitigate local outrage, when barbarity was an established part of daily life.

For Pichon, it had started as a commercial necessity, nothing more. He'd looked on as the fools around him had tried to hide their cognac in the caves at Mouthiers-sur-Boeme. It was a pathetically naive thing to do, for the invaders would inevitably find the hoard and then confiscate it.

But if someone with their wits about them were to tell the Germans where to find it, surely, they could be persuaded to leave his alone.

It worked, but at a terrible price.

He'd travelled all the way to Bordeaux, so as to distance his point of contact with the invaders from the village. The occupying forces had just arrived and chaos reigned. Buildings were being requisitioned and the dispossessed were everywhere. Eventually, he was directed to a temporary HQ, where he met Meyer for the first time

The Germans were delighted with the cognac, of course, though as he suspected, they saw his disclosure as a conveniently easy means of achieving what would have been an inevitable result. They'd have found the stuff eventually.

But a network of informers was far harder to come by. A sliver of information such as that was enough to entrap its bearer. From that moment on he would always have more to lose than his new masters. Thus, Pichon's fate was sealed; his cognac safe, but not his soul.

When the Germans let it be known that Pichon had been allowed to keep his stocks of cognac because he hadn't tried to conceal them, the locals accepted it, albeit with the jealous anger of those who had lost everything through misjudgement. Since then, he had delivered a case of cognac to the local *Wehrmacht* unit every week, for onward transmission to *SS Obersturmführer* Meyer. Any intelligence would be in note form, hidden in the bottom of the case. Much of the information was petty mundane and no-one suspected him of such treachery, but in the years that followed, many saw confiscation of hidden livestock or produce and the execution of several locals who had been guilty of little more than petty mischief. At that time, most misdemeanours were regarded as sabotage and dealt with summarily.

Three months after his neighbour had been shot Pichon sent a message in that week's case of cognac enquiring about the promised sale. He received a terse reply in the mail.

Monsieur Pichon,

We wrote to you last month with an offer to purchase. You did not reply. Be thankful that we did not sell it in the meantime.

A copy of the letter is enclosed.

Respond within fourteen days or we will offer it on the open market.

Meyer

He quickly scanned the accompanying copy, which offered him seventy hectares of land for a fraction of its true worth. It was a fine mix of vines, arable and grazing, which would have attracted buyers from all sides if it had reached the open market.

With a trembling hand, he wrote an acceptance note and hurried down to the *Wehrmacht* unit with an early case of cognac. On the way there, he remembered to curse the postal service and congratulated himself on writing the note of enquiry.

Thanks to his foresight, he now owned more land than any of his neighbours, but it wouldn't stop at that. His sights fell on the land on his other side, owned by the Michaud family.

CHAPTER 8

George tried to be upbeat, "Listen, the French love their brown floor tiles. Anything we'll be looking at is likely to have them."

His wife Amy moaned, "But just look at that kitchen. I've seen better ones on a camp site."

He had no reasonable defence for that. There was a sink unit, minus a door, which might have been removed to accommodate the cutlery drawer which had fallen off one of its runners and sat askew. A dilapidated cooker stood in the adjacent corner, with one of the gas rings secured against use with layers of aluminium tape and an enamel top that was chipped enough to look diseased. A tubular steel framed table with two vinyl covered chairs stood against the opposite wall looking like a sad memorial to the folk who had eaten there for so many years. The circular burn marks in the centre of the *formica* top evidenced an absence, or unemployment of trivets or table mats, but eventually, all eyes were drawn to the storage area.

Two walls had been built out from a main wall to form an alcove which housed shelving for pots, pans and crockery, with a tired red curtain to screen the contents from view. The concrete blocks used for the construction were bare of any decoration, apart from an old calendar which hung from a bent nail.

George made another attempt to reassure Amy, "Sorry love, but that's typical too, particularly in the rural areas."

She huffed, "For a country that loves its food so much, that hardly qualifies as a shrine to fine cuisine."

Annie said, "True, it doesn't look much, but they do eat well, in spite of it."

Jayne Maitlin also had doubts and pointed at the picture of the living room, "That furniture is dire; it's so dark."

George agreed, but remained positive, "That and the floor tiles are giving you a false impression. The photos could never do it justice, particularly at this time of year."

They had gathered around Annie's laptop at the coffee morning and trolled through the thirty odd photographs Penny had sent. It was a very old stone farmhouse, with shutters of grey bare wood flecked with the remnants of paint that had hung on for decades. One shutter had lost a wall hinge, presumably through rust, and hung aslant. When the picture was taken, the remaining shutters were closed, leaving the single exposed window looking like a tooth cavity.

The building was fronted on two sides by outbuildings, with a high wall and gate marking the edge of the road. The yard they contained had been colonised by weeds; no doubt nourished by the mud and manure that would have been there once. Apparently, half the ground floor had been used for agricultural purposes and Sue wondered whether that included wintering livestock in there. She reckoned the warmth they gave off would be welcome, but the smell wouldn't. Small wonder she thought, that Penny hadn't ventured in there.

Inside, beyond the kitchen, lay the large room Jayne had referred to, that must have served as a dining cum sitting area. It was dominated by a large, dark oak table and eight chairs, with backs that reached chest height. An equally outsized *armoire* stood against the far wall and must have been seven feet tall. Three doors fronted a base that reached waist height which had probably been used to store the best crockery and linens. A row of upper cabinets were supported by turned pillars that looked more like billiard table legs, leaving a deep shelf in between.

Simple armchairs with wooden arms and upholstered in red home-made covers had been placed in three of the corners with the fourth left clear for two doorways. Penny had left the one furthest from the corner open, to show the staircase that lay beyond.

She had backtracked then, through the dishevelled kitchen and into a larder which was twice the size. Two feet off the ground, a stone thrawl ran along two sides, while the remaining wall space was taken up with shelves of varying depths, though some, nearest the door had undergone surgery to accommodate a small fridge. A few were still laden with *kilner* jars, filled with dubious looking matter.

Upstairs, the five bedrooms were simply furnished, or at least three of them were. One had to be accessed via another bedroom and that, with another, had been used as storerooms, judging by the boxes and debris still in there. Every room had been wallpapered in the same pattern; small blue flowers on a pale and now badly stained background. In places, the damp had succeeded in separating the paper from the walls but that was a feature they had all expected to see. The three bedrooms furnished for their purpose had a double bed, *sans* mattress; evidence perhaps, of the previous owners incontinence. As if to support that view, the metal springs were remarkably rusty, though the scrolled metal bed ends looked old enough to be of value. Each room had a chest of drawers, with a dark wooden framed swivel mirror placed on top, which reflected in part, the huge wardrobe that stood on the opposite side of the room in incongruous splendour. All three were at least seven feet tall, with a carved arched top and bowed doors that were still beauti-fully enhanced with quartered walnut veneer. The huge drawer that spanned the base had also been veneered, to match per-fectly with the doors above them and the whole structure rested on turned ball feet.

George joked, "You can tell which side they were on in the revolution. Those wardrobes look like booty."

Adam said, "Knocked off from the local chateau you mean, along with the owner's heads."

A grin accompanied the response, "You've got it."

Kendall piped up, "By my reckoning, if we're all there at the same time we'll need seven bedrooms. At the moment there are five and one of those will involve passing through another."

"Oh my," said Barbara, "That will be interesting. I don't wear anything in bed; never have." No-one responded, but there was a silent consensus on the matter; Barbara would not be occupying that room. Adam signalled to Barry, "If you have no objections, I wouldn't mind sharing a room with you. Single beds of course and as Kendall said; it'll only be when we're all there at the same time."

Barry shook his head violently, "Not a hope! Sharing a hotel room with you just once has been hideous. I cannot understand how anyone can snore so loudly without waking themselves up."

Adam agreed, somewhat reluctantly, "You're not the first to mention it. An American called me a bear once."

"That's an extremely fitting title and one I will use."

Jayne Maitlin cut in, "So that leaves us short of one or two bedrooms. It's not ideal, but in the worst case scenario we could get rid of that sideboard in the dining room and buy a good quality bed settee. After all, there won't be many times when we're all there at the same time. I imagine that we'll be able to come and go as we please rather than *en masse.*"

Annie made another observation, "Even if you found an alternative that ticked all the boxes, a place that size, in good order would cost a fortune to rent. Penny tells me that the owners are prepared to let it for peanuts if you tart it up.

Barry countered with, "But what would the tarting-up cost? A hell of a lot by the look of it."

She shrugged, "I have no idea. You'd have to see it first and then make a judgement."

Alan Maitlin voiced a concern that was shared by every male there, "My dodgy prostate means that I'm up two or three times a night, which might not be welcome if I have to scramble through someone else's bedroom to get to the loo." There were murmurs of 'hear, hear' around the table and he added, "By the way, where is the toilet?"

Annie answered, "There are two, surprisingly. One outside

and another upstairs, at the end of the landing, which I'd guess would have been the sixth bedroom at one time." She added, "Penny decided not to include pictures of them."

The discussion continued between the curious, the doubtful and the downright daunted. They viewed the images once more before it was time to leave. At George's suggestion, they agreed to postpone making a decision until the following week, by which time they would probably, at best, settle for an inspection visit and not necessarily by everyone. Some, he hoped, would settle for hearing a report.

As they left, leaving Annie to pack her laptop away, Bob Lucas approached her, "Annie, I wonder, would you be kind enough to forward those pictures on to me please? I'd like Carol to see them."

She had heard rumours of how difficult things had become for him at home and couldn't help but ask, "Would that be wise Bob?"

He grimaced, "You've heard then."

"We live in a village Bob."

"Yeah, I guess, but I still think it's important to keep her up to date. This can't be allowed to be a secret 'other' life."

She patted his arm, "You're such a nice man and Carol knows that."

***

Rambert had found a peace of mind denied to him for months, from when he'd been coerced into the hateful conspiracy to bankrupt Michaud. He had nothing against the man; in fact he quite liked him, but it had come down to a choice between one man's ruin or his own.

How that peasant Pichon discovered enough information for his purposes still troubled Rambert, but after a period of consideration, even that oaf couldn't realistically hold him to blame for a mischievous play of fates that *no-one* could have foreseen. Four days had passed without word from his nemesis, which augured well. Short of outright blackmail, there was little Pichon could do. If he did make matters public Rambert would at least know that the oaf had always intended to make them public, a secret the Rambert family had kept hidden for seventy years.

The Germans knew that movement of money could signal illegal transactions or even acts of subversion. Moreover, only the wealthy had bank accounts, when money and position often secured protection, even under occupation. But the Germans could be a very literal race, particularly when confronted with concrete evidence.

Somehow, they had forced Monsieur Rambert senior into sharing the details of any unusual activity. None of the details were known, even by those closest to him, though some might have suspected some measure of collaboration when people they knew were shot or deported. Eventually, his wife and son found out and they still shared a sense of shame, comforted only by the treachery having remained a secret; a fading one at that. Just one more generation; that's all they needed for it not to matter anymore.

He left the house on Friday morning, looking forward to the twenty minute commute in his beloved Mercedes E350. A gleaming black example of engineering excellence that never failed to delight him.

As he stepped out of the house onto the drive, the sight that lay before him took his breath away. He stood, fixed to the spot in shock until finally, with a groan of despair he staggered around the vehicle, whimpering. Every single panel had been so deeply scoured that the metal itself was damaged; leaving bright scars that would cost thousands to repair. He knew immediately *who* had been responsible, but the savagery of it was shocking and what could have caused such damage?

The answer was simple; the business end of a pair of vine pruning shears.

His wife had been passing a window when she saw his distress though not the cause, but when she joined him they held each other for support. He began to weep then and she stroked his back, 'shushing' gently. Eventually, she asked, "Who could have done this?"

He lied, "I have no idea."

She strengthened her hold, "Well we'll find out and make them pay. I'll go and call the police."

"No!"

She arched her back to look him in the face, "What do you mean, no? We can't just let this happen and let the vermin get away with it."

He had to stop her, once and for all. The first thing the police would look for would be a motive and they would keep digging until they found it, "Listen my dear, please; whoever did this holds a grudge against me. Give me time to make my own enquiries and then, perhaps, we can involve the police. Whoever did this is evil, but it is only a car. If we raise the stakes who knows what might happen. Please, for yours and the children's sakes, let's keep this quiet. It might just be an act of mindless vandalism."

She gave him an incredulous look, "Mindless vandalism? Here, in the middle of nowhere? Whoever did this was targeting you, personally."

"Exactly, me alone. I have no intention of expanding that to include my family. Now please, I beg you, trust my judgement in the matter. Today, I will review all of the 'difficult' accounts we've been dealing with lately. I already have some candidates in mind. Then, we can decide on a course of action. In the meantime, *do not* call the police."

Madame Rambert was an intelligent woman, who knew when her husband was hiding something from her, just as she knew when he was frightened and in that moment, she was too.

He left for work, knowing that he had suffered retribution and worse, he was still entrapped.

***

Dear Chrissy,

Lovely to hear from you, as ever and for once I have some news, so I won't need to moan about the weather this time.

The French caper is now complete and I am a fully fledged investor in a vineyard and cognac distillery. It was on the brink of collapse when Annie, a lady in the village put a rescue package together and asked the coffee morning group if they were interested. Quite a few were, including yours truly.

Anton, the man who owns it seems a nice chap, who is probably sleeping at night now the bank has lost its grip on the place.

How can we hate bankers the way we do yet allow them to prosper so much? I'd bet the banks over there are the same – making billions each year, with the morals of sewer rats.

Eight of our coffee morning group invested and now they're talking about renting an old farmhouse so we can spend some time over there. Sounds like a plan. It's very quiet though and in the middle of nowhere, but the coast is only thirty miles away so perhaps I'll roll my trouser legs up and go for a paddle next time I'm there. Check it out on 'Google Earth'. The village is called Aurigny-les-Bois. I'm not sure where the farmhouse is, but it's decrepit enough to blend perfectly with the countryside so 'Googling' it wouldn't do much good.

As for the group, well, they're a mixed bunch and I'll introduce them to you another time, except for Barbara, who deserves a mention now. She's an artist and fairly dotty, but very entertaining. Her take on things can be quite startling at times but she should liven things up a bit. Everyone else is pretty ordinary – me included. She keeps chickens in the house and hoards mountains of stuff. Only the other day I learned that the badger set at the bottom of her garden is regarded as one of the best examples in Leicestershire. Not surprising really, I've seen the bowls of food she puts out at night. It doesn't stop there. Bread, fat and seed go out for the birds and any chicken carcases she can lay her hands on get thrown out for the local fox. I think you'd like her.

Give my best wishes to your mum and keep up the good work.
Adam

He sat back and looked at the note, judging it to be as pathetic as any he'd written. There was so much more he should have written, but his mind emptied as soon as he held a pen. He'd never been a copper to employ his imagination when writing statements. Just the facts; he didn't need to call anything else to mind. They were all there in his notes. Letter writing was far more challenging.

By contrast, Chrissy's letters were informative, amusing and four times as long. He sometimes wondered why she continued to bother, but then the memories would surface. The beating meted out by her father's heavies; his dash across to America to rescue her and their flight back to the UK, where a hit man very nearly succeeded in getting to the girl. Her father was still in prison and would remain there for another year. Adam hoped that a secondary, more fitting form of justice had taken place while he was there; 'let the punishment fit the crime'.

Another victim sprang to mind. Chrissy's mother April had been driven into alcoholism by the senator but by all accounts, had remained dry for over four years. He wondered what she would make of the French investment, knowing that Chrissy passed his letters on.

Eventually, he folded the letter and placed it in an envelope; unsealed for the time being, in case he thought of anything else to add. It was unlikely.

He was still sure of one thing though; how much he would miss her letters if she stopped writing.

***

Annie had forwarded the photographs to Bob as promised, but Carol refused to view them, just as she'd refused to discuss the vineyard since Bob had returned from France. At least the rowing was over, replaced though with a frigid truce.

Carol realised that the money had gone now, probably for good and there was nothing they could do about it, but the hurt remained. She couldn't reconcile herself to his defiance or the fact that she now faced exclusion from an important part of his life *and* the coffee morning group. There was an underlying concern too. After so many years as soul mates how could he have done something so out of character? Just how well *did* she know him and how much of a stranger had yet to appear?

It was that, which finally compelled her to break the silence with something closer to a civilised conversation. It was Thursday evening, thirteen days since he'd returned from France, since when she had claimed his favourite armchair; beside the fire and in line with the television. There hadn't been a murmur of protest and he now sat in what had been her spot, at the end of the sofa. In truth, he had grown to quite like stretching out on it, which in her darker moments Carol regarded as 'slobbing out', just to make a point.

"What made you do it Bob?"

He was taken aback for a few moments, even though he'd asked himself the same question, several times. He sounded tired, "I don't know love, it's complicated."

"Well humour me, I need to know."

After a long pause he began, "I understand that, I really do. It's not as though I've ever done anything like it before. Perhaps that was part of the reason. I'm still coming to terms with it all, but don't you ever feel that time's running out? As you said, I was just a trumped up clerk and here I am, surrounded by others who did so much more with their lives."

She felt a twinge of guilt, "I didn't mean that. It was said in the heat of the moment."

"Truths often are Carol and that one certainly was."

"I shouldn't have said it and I didn't mean it. You, *we* have brought two wonderful kids up and they're a credit to us."

He took a deep breath, "I know love, but so have others and they still had adventures along the way. I'm not talking about holidays in Spain, or London theatre trips. Look at Annie and her sister; they decided that it would be nice to buy a place in France then went and did it."

A quite separate concern sprang to Carol's mind, "Is that how you see our life?"

They'd avoided eye contact until then, but now he turned to stare at her, "No! Not at all; I'm no different now to what I was before this happened and I don't want to be. It might appear to be out of character, but it's just an isolated adventure, that's all. Just something I really wanted to do. This is my home still; where I live and probably where I'll die." His voice softened, "And where I will always love you."

Quite unexpectedly, she felt tears tracking across her cheeks as a revelation sprang to mind, prompting her to murmur, "I've been frightened."

He patted the seat beside him, "Come here, I need a cuddle."

They sat like that for a long time, still with lots to discuss, but for the moment, a cuddle was enough. An advertisement for stair lifts appeared on the television, which helped to crystallize his thoughts enough to put them into words, "That is the future love. Like it or not, time is racing by. I accept that, but I was troubled by the thought of getting to old age, only to look back on this and thinking, 'I wonder what would have happened if I'd gone ahead with that vineyard deal? Suddenly, the 'what if' question terrified me."

He felt her start, with something that might have been half a chuckle, "Well, sooner or later you'll bloody well know the answer to that question now." In no time, the cuddling called for more and they drifted up to bed.

Bob didn't usually eat breakfast, but when he rose the next morning the table had been set with toast and egg cups. Carol had put the eggs into boiling water as soon as she heard him descending the stairs and when he looked at her quizzicallly, she explained, "You'd better tell me all about it, if I'm going to face that lot up at the pub."

***

They were all delighted to see Carol at The Rose and Crown, but only Kendall was crass enough to comment, though he was studiously ignored and they began to discuss the French farmhouse.

Amy still had doubts, "I wouldn't go near that place without a course of wide spectrum antibiotics; two even." It raised a laugh and a little sympathy.

Alan Maitlin had spent some time studying the pictures and had produced a list of works, copies of which he handed out as he explained, "This isn't exhaustive and it's subjective, which means to say that if these jobs were attended to, *I* would be prepared to move in. Some of you may not agree, but I thought that any more work could be done as we went along." He added a caution though, "The 'guesstimates' I've shown are based on UK prices so we will need to do some research if we go over there and the letter 'P' denotes a need for a professional. " He sat silently then as they scanned the list, which read;

FIT KITCHEN (FLATPACK) INC. FRIDGE & COOKER £3500

STRIP WALLPAPER £GRAFT

PATCH AND PAINT WALLS £500 PLUS GRAFT

PAINTWORK £200 PLUS GRAFT

BEDS & LINEN £4000

WIRING – IF NEEDED (P) £ NO IDEA

PLUMBING – IF NEEDED (P) £NO IDEA

BATHROOM AND TOILETS (PART P) £1800

EXTERIOR PAINTWORK £NOT OUR PROBLEM

CLEANING £400 PLUS GRAFT

TOOLS AND EQUIPMENT £USE OUR OWN

GROUND FLOOR FURNITURE £MAKE DO & MEND

(AT LEAST INITIALLY)

MISC £1000

TOTAL £11,300 GIVE OR TAKE £5000

Amy was sticking to her guns and asked the first question, "If Penny thought the bathroom and toilets were too bad to photograph, they must be pretty dire. Don't you think eighteen hundred is being a tad optimistic? I mean, the tiling could cost that much."

Maitlin explained, "I checked the prices for basic toilet and bathroom suites and worked on the basis that we'd rip the old stuff out, shove the new in and just paint the walls with bathroom emulsion."

Bob was more concerned about the contingency provisions, "I could accept eleven grand; after all, if it was split between eight of us the cost would only amount to fourteen hundred and something each, but the electricity and plumbing are likely to be more than five thousand and that would kill it for me."

George agreed but added, "Of course, we don't know how much of either will be needed, or what sort of a deal the owner is prepared to offer on the rent. He's obviously decided against doing the work himself."

Barbara was in attendance for the first time and had her own special concerns, "What colour do you suggest for the walls?" A ripple of tittering spread through the group, until George sought to save her from embarrassment, "We've a long way to go before making that choice but any early thoughts would be welcome, I'm sure."

Alan flagged at the group with both hands, "That would be up to the group obviously, but I would suggest white, or at the very least a pale colour, to lighten the place up."

They all seemed to agree with that, apart from Barbara, "Oh dear, perhaps I could paint some flowers on the walls; sunflowers perhaps?"

Carol spoke for the first time, "I think that would be a lovely idea." Barbara beamed at her.

It became Adam's turn and he addressed Bob personally, "Sorry mate, I have to question your maths. Granted, there are only eight investors in the vineyard, but this is different. We need to include the spouses. Everybody will be sharing the accommodation equally and should bear their share of the costs."

Bob puffed out his cheeks and exhaled before answering, "I'm not sure I agree with that."

Adam spoke in a reasonable way, "OK, let's imagine that this doesn't get off the ground and we have to find accommodation for each visit. We'll have a hard time trying to find a hotel that will only charge those named on the investment notes."

George joined in, "He's got a point you know."

Alan followed, "Which would make it a little over a grand per head."

While Bob wracked his brains to think of a response he was startled to hear his wife respond, "You're right." She nudged Bob and grinned, "Don't worry, if we only pay for one share you can sleep in the field." There followed a round of applause and a few playful comments, which glanced off without injury, for Bob Lucas was an extremely happy man at that moment.

It was Annie's turn. Until then Annie and Sue had remained silent throughout, given that they had no personal interest in the project, but she needed to correct the maths again, "Sorry Alan, but Sue and I won't be in the frame for this. Remember we have our own place."

He raised a hand, "I stand corrected."

The discussion continued for over an hour, until the lunch-time customers began to drift in and Annie decided it was time to conclude matters with a proposal, "OK, well it seems to me that the only way to get a proper angle on this thing is for some or all of you to go over there again. We received word yesterday that everything is in place to complete our purchase so we've provisionally set a date for the second of February. That's a Wednesday, so we're planning on flying out on Tues-day and back on Friday, like we did last time. Why not come out with us?"

Adam called out, "Sounds good to me. See if we can get the same deal at the hotel."

All except Kendall and Barry thought likewise, but this time George took on the responsibility of booking the hotel. Barry had already committed to a stay with friends in Edin-burgh while Kendall, though he would never admit it, didn't have the money. Each would book their own flights, like last time and Annie agreed to contact Penny, so that a meeting with the farmhouse owner might be arranged for the afternoon of their arrival.

***

Phillipe Rambert was born in nineteen fifty eight, married in nineteen eighty three and divorced three years later by which time he was twenty eight years old. The divorce had been so acrimonious and expensive that he remained single for the next sixteen years. During that time he focused on his career in banking where he rose to the position of bank manager and reconciled himself to bachelorhood, until he met Margot.

She was a member of the head office audit team and on the rebound from a much more recent break up from a violent partner who had resisted her earlier pleas for marriage and more recently, for mercy, when his bi-polar temperament took turns for the worse. Finally, the *Gendarmerie* and a stay in hospital persuaded her to get out of the relationship but by then, her fear of him resulted in a dreadfully unfair settlement. As is so often the case, her keen intelligence and consideration for others left her friends wondering why she had suffered the abuse for so long and ignored their pleas with her to get out of it.

She was of medium height and build with striking features that fell short of beautiful and which included a strong Gallic nose and prominent cheekbones. Some would have described her as *jolie laide*, or unconventionally beautiful but the feature that set her apart was a head of strikingly blond hair, unusual in a region with such strong Basque influences. By contrast with her professional persona, she suffered from a low self esteem in her private life. Ironically, since in her capacity as auditor, many had known cause to fear her ruthless skills in discovering fraud. It was almost a sixth sense that drove her on through the masses of documents she knew held secrets that had been hidden by professionals. Even when colleagues had signed off on an audit she had been known to stay on, with a dogged determination that was sanctioned by seniors who had come to trust her instincts. They were rarely wrong.

Mere suspicion had prompted Phillipe Rambert to call her in and within a week she had uncovered a senior clerk's manipulation of some dormant deposit accounts; long held, but with small balances, left there by elderly clients who no longer held current accounts with the bank, either because of transfer or death. Many of the living would have forgotten about the small residual balances long ago and would therefore never know that the accounts had been closed using forged signatures. The dead were dead, end of; their accounts obviously overlooked by whoever wound up the estate.

Phillipe's obvious integrity and authentic horror at her discoveries impressed her professionally, but she was also taken by his personal warmth and attentiveness. In truth, he was equally smitten and startled by the emotion, after being single for so long. As the audit drew to a close he knew that however ignominious his failure might prove to be, he simply *had* to invite her to dinner.

It was a match so perfect, it must have been ordained and six months later they were married. He was forty four and she was thirty eight. Their two daughters, Adele and Cecile were born, in that order, two and four years later. Now aged nine and seven, they, along with their mother were his reasons for living. He would surrender his life and reputation before seeing any harm come to them.

Which was why he came to be standing in front of a church; chilled and dampened by the light coastal rainfall. He didn't frequent this church, for it was an hour and a half's drive away from the one they did attend in their village. This one was situated on the western edge of Bordeaux, on the road to Lacanau; a relatively new building that replaced one that had been destroyed by allied bombing. It was painted white and void of any decorative stonework, but he knew from a distant visit, that whilst the inside had been treated similarly, huge stained glass windows gave the place a truly spiritual air.

Inside, waiting for him, was the priest, Father Fabian Bissonnette. They were the same age and in spite of differences in location and vocation, they had remained friends from child-hood. Even so, Phillipe reminded himself of just how long it had been since they last met and wondered how welcome this visit would be, given the circumstances, but there was no-one else he could think of turning to.

Fabian was anxious too. Why did his old friend need to meet so urgently and why had he insisted on doing so in the church, when a glass of wine at the house would have been much more convivial? He had waited in one of the front pews, but stood and beckoned as Phillipe entered. After they had embraced he asked, "Are you sure you want to meet in here? My kitchen is much warmer."

The banker shook his head, "Thank you Fabian, but no. I need your guidance, both as a friend and a priest." Whatever was troubling him was reflected in his haggard expression and precluded any attempt at small talk.

The priest gestured towards the nearest pew, "Then please, sit." As they did so he continued, "But I have to ask, why do you feel the need to talk in here?" He didn't need to add 'when you have a priest and church of your own'.

Phillipe sighed, "This is difficult for me. I trust you as a friend completely, but what I have to tell you is so troubling that I need the comfort of doing so under the Seal of the Confessional."

"Then you came as a penitent?"

"In a sense I suppose, but by an act of omission. I have kept a terrible secret from the world, out of self interest. The true penitent should be my father, but of course he is dead now."

Fabian remained silent while his friend gathered his thoughts, but listened intently as the story began to be told, "We don't know how it came about, but we suspect the Germans threatened both him and his family. We have a tiny and very distant Jewish heritage that was thought to be untraceable, but it is possible that they discovered it. He was a good man and a wonderful father for as long as I knew him, though I wasn't born until nineteen fifty eight. He was a bank manager by then, but during the war he was only an assistant manager, with a new wife, four brothers and two parents to consider. Faced with the threat of transportation to one of the camps in Germany for all of them, I'm not sure I'd have done anything differently. No, that isn't correct. In light of what has happened recently, I *know* I wouldn't. At any rate, in time he confessed to my mother that he was collaborating with them, passing information across that would have ended badly for a number of clients, I'm certain. When I was older, she shared the information with me, but that's as far as it went. Nevertheless, all sorts of things can be detected from the movement of money. We still don't know the full details, but there will be records, you may be sure, both at the bank and in the occupation archives.

As you probably know, I am a manager for the same bank, but I dare not show an interest in the wartime records in case anyone else follows my trail. But you see, someone else *does* know about it. How, I don't know, because he has, or had, nothing to do with our bank.

Some eighteen months ago he came to see me at my office. There was no subtlety about his approach, in fact he's a brute of a man, but he knew as much as we did about my father's collaboration and more. There were actual names too, with details of what happened to them. That part may have been fiction, I don't know, but if it isn't, heaven help us. I recall that one couple were summarily shot when it was suspected that they'd passed funds to the resistance. I've never felt so threatened and so powerless.

He told me to continue advancing money to one of his neighbours, a chap named Michaud, until we were in a position to foreclose. At that point, presumably, I'd have been expected to offer him the place at a forced sale liquidation price. In the meantime, I had to use my influence with the merchant who dealt with Michaud, to persuade him to end their relationship. All the other merchants had access to more supplies than they needed, so they would only buy more if it was at less than cost.

I'm ashamed to say that the strategy worked and we had

already served notice of foreclosure. The worst of it is that Michaud is a nice fellow and his vineyard has been in the family for generations.

But then a bunch of English people turned up and invested enough for Michaud to clear his debts. It all happened so quickly; there was nothing I could do, but the man behind me was enraged. I cannot describe the base manner of the telephone call that followed, but in spite of that, I hoped that my nightmare was over.

I was wrong. Two weeks ago my car was vandalised, terribly. Every single panel had been damaged. It was him, of course, but even then I harboured the hope that it was no more than a final act of retribution."

He allowed time for a sigh of resignation before continuing, "Two days ago, our youngest daughter found the body of our cat in the back garden; it had been thrown over the wall. We've managed to convince the children that it had been run over and the driver had disposed of the body in the most convenient way, but I could see that the injuries were caused by something else. Before burying it, I checked the wounds and found lead pellets; she'd been shot."

Fabian cut in, "Didn't you hear a shot?"

"No, at least not a close one, but we live in the countryside; there's always someone out hunting. That said, I don't think the poor creature was killed near us. It hadn't appeared the previous morning, which was unusual and I think that perhaps he captured it and did the deed elsewhere; on his farm probably.

Anyway, it was the last straw. I drove over to his farm, intent on having it out with him, once and for all, but it turned out to be a stupid, naive endeavour, not least of all because he came to the door with a shotgun over his arm; an act so calculated and quite frankly, frightening, that I was lost for words to begin with. He simply said, "What do you want?" I was so flustered that instead of confronting him I found myself merely asking to be left alone. He laughed at me then and said, "Go home Monsieur Banker, I haven't finished with you yet." I ended up pleading but eventually, there was nothing left but to drive away. Since then my days and nights have been lost in the fear of what he might do next.

Yesterday, when I was reviewing the new accounts in our branch, I discovered what it was. He is now one of our clients. Heaven knows what he is planning."

Rambert fell back against the pew, a spent force and embarrassed, "I'm sorry, you've been a patient listener, but there's nothing you can do for me."

Fabian rested a hand on his friend's arm, "I can pray for you. This man is evil and I am so sorry to see you in this state. If we were in the confessional now I would grant you absolution, completely, because this man's blackmail is a far greater sin. But you are not here for that, or pastoral guidance, are you?"

Phillipe raised both hands before letting them fall back onto his knees. He murmured, "I'm not sure, but I had to share it with someone."

He felt the comfort of Fabian's hand on his arm once again and his gentle voice, "I need a little time, to think *and* pray, but not for long. Would you mind leaving me alone for a while, until noon say, when we can share lunch at my house?"

Phillipe returned promptly at noon, though with no appetite and little expectation for anything else, though he had derived some comfort from sharing the burden he'd been carrying for so long.

Fabian ushered him into the kitchen, where in spite of the lacklustre messaging from stomach to brain, his sense of smell responded to the delicious aroma that filled the room. The priest directed him to the table, set for two, with a partly sliced baguette, platter of cheeses, an opened bottle of red wine and a bowl each. Phillipe sat down as Fabian removed a large pan from the stove and placed it on a rush mat in the centre of the table with, "Simple fare my friend, but one we can share while talking."

It was a Provencal vegetable soup, full of colour and the steam that rose when the lid was removed was laden with the aromas of herbs and garlic. The ingredients included haricot beans, leeks, celery, tomatoes, courgettes, onions, carrots and French beans, all cooked to perfection, in that they were still intact, with their individual textures. Even the stock looked homemade. Fabian passed a ladle over to Phillipe and nodded at the soup, "Please forgive the saucepan. I love cooking, but hate washing up."

The banker served himself while the wine was poured and tried a little of the soup. It was delicious and he gave a nod of appreciation with a small smile before taking some bread to expand the experience. They ate in silence for a few minutes, until the comforting effect of the soup had established itself sufficiently to permit conversation. Fabian began, "I have a few observations to make first. Not least of all because we need to put things into perspective. To begin with, any wrongs committed by your father were a long time ago and shared by many others. Most importantly, you are blameless in the matter, or at least you were, until this man persuaded you to commit wrongs of your own. Thankfully, the English investors prevented them from coming to fruition." Phillipe made to speak but Fabian held up a hand and continued, "We live in different times now, when most people take a more pragmatic view of the things that occurred during the occupation. They realise that the next generation cannot be held to account for the sins of their fathers. At worst, there may be some embarrassment, but frankly, few want to be reminded of those times anymore."

Phillipe managed to interrupt, "So you're saying that I overreacted; that I shouldn't have allowed myself to be influenced."

"Frankly, yes; I think it was naive to see the information as a threat."

"But it was my father, who rose to exactly the same position as the one I hold now; in the same bank even."

Fabian had snatched the opportunity to take a large mouthful of soup and chewed on a piece of bread before responding, "As I said, it was a long time ago and not as relevant as you think, but now you *do* have a problem, which is largely of your own making. Forgive me Phillipe, but if we're to get you out of this mess we must face facts. The moment you surrendered to this blackmailers' demands the dynamics of your problem changed. In short, you've replaced your father's sins with your own."

In spite of such bad tidings Phillipe noted his friends' use of the word 'we', which signalled a willingness to share the burden and offer assistance. Instead of arguing the point, he asked, "Then what do you suggest?"

Fabian smiled and raised his spoon, "I have a few ideas, but first, shall we enjoy this before I share them?"

Once the soup had been eaten it became easier to talk while sampling the cheeses. Fabian's first suggestion was the most obvious, yet least likely to find favour, "You should go to the police."

As expected, Phillipe raised his voice, "No! As you've just said, I have committed crimes now. My career, reputation, everything, would be destroyed."

"But if this continues to escalate you may have no alternative. Worse, if you continue to meet his demands who's to say your list of crimes won't grow longer *and* more serious. So far, your actions would be regarded as misdemeanours rather than outright crimes and even then, under duress."

Phillipe had been shaking his head as his friend spoke, "They may be regarded as misdemeanours in a law court but not by our auditors. As I've said, I would be finished."

Fabian pressed further, "I think it is reasonable to presume that this man will continue to pursue you. Why else would he have opened an account with your bank and at your branch, if not to make more demands? At some point, you will be discovered and then the police will come calling without your invitation."

The banker wouldn't be swayed, "Then I must see what he expects of me and make a judgement at the time. Until then, no police."

After drawing a large, audible breath, Fabian said, "I thought as much. You are being very predictable, which is why I have another suggestion."

"What?"

"You must pull the tiger's claws."

"What do you mean?"

Fabian held out both hands, palm upward, "Exactly what I said." He began to count on his fingers, "First, we need to establish exactly how much this man knows. I need you to write down everything he's told you. Second, we need to know where he got his information from and how. It may not have been by legal means or better still, the information may be too vague or inaccurate to be of any use. Some of it may be no more than supposition."

Phillipe interrupted, "Does that matter?"

"Most certainly, if going public with it meant he'd go to jail too and remember, blackmail is a crime in itself." He moved to the next finger, "Third, we need to know much more about this man, even if it means employing a private investigator."

Phillipe cut in again, "I would prefer not to involve anyone else at the moment. Perhaps, in time, but only as a last resort."

Fabian shrugged it off, "Fourth, which will be difficult for you, so regard it as an act of contrition, following your 'confession' in church." He used both forefingers to denote the inverted commas.

"I wouldn't call it a confession; it was a disclosure, to a friend."

"You chose the location, quite deliberately as I recall."

"But you also said that if it were a confession, you'd give me absolution."

Fabian shrugged, "I lied. We priests can do that when a penitent shows an unwillingness to correct his ways. But now we're playing with words instead of working on a plan. You must go and see Monsieur Michaud and offer an explanation, if only in part. It will help to cleanse your conscience if not your soul, but the real reason for doing so is that a frank dialogue may throw up some of the information we need. Victims often know more than we think, though they don't always realise it. In any event, you owe him this much, at least."

Phillipe had been holding a piece of *brie* on the tongue, savouring the creamily runny texture and faint mushroom flavour but the import of that last proposal forced him to swallow, "That is asking a great deal."

"But of course, I understand that, but it is one of the many steps we need to take in order to get you out of this mess. By the way, you haven't told me his name yet."

Phillipe said, "I cannot tell you how much your use of the word 'we' means. The man's name is Albert Pichon by the way. He owns a farm in Aurigny-les-bois which adjoins Michaud's; hence the motive for all this." Suddenly and quite unexpectedly, Phillipe began to weep. Embarrassed, he pulled a handkerchief from a pocket and wiped the tears away, "Please forgive me. This is not out of sorrow, or fear. I have lived alone with those for too long, but now, at last, I have an ally."

Fabian reached forward and took his friend's hand, "And you have, I promise you. Now, we must develop our strategy. For a start, tell me exactly what has happened and how much Pichon has told you."

Phillipe shook his head, "But I've already told you."

His friend explained, "But this time I will take notes and besides, something else may come to mind. It is what the detectives do on television." He regretted his levity immediately, "I'm sorry, this is not a time for jokes."

Phillipe took a moment to marshal his thoughts, before, "He came to see me at the office, months ago and spoke in his usual coarse, aggressive manner and treated me like dirt, so much so that I reached the point of ordering him out, which was when he told me that he knew all about my father's collaboration with the Germans. He added that as a result, he'd been responsible for sending many Jews to the concentration camps. He also implied that my father had provided enough information for the execution of some resistance members. All this I denied, of course, but then he began to give me names and dates. He even gave me the name of the SS officer he liaised with."

Fabian had drawn a pad across from the side of the table and had been scribbling down notes. At that point he asked, "Do you have the names he gave you?"

The banker shook his head, "Only the German officer's. I checked with the wartime records and found him." He withdrew his wallet and extracted a note, "He was SS Obersturmführer Ernst Meyer; based here in fact, in Bordeaux."

"This list he had." He paused before, "Of the victims. Did Pichon have a written list or was he speaking from memory?"

"It was a written one; typed I think." After a moment Phillipe added in a whisper, "There were too many to have remembered."

"So there was more than one sheet." It was more of a deduction than question and Phillipe merely nodded.

"Were they official documents do you know?"

Phillipe tried to recall, "I don't know. How could I?" But then, a spark of recollection, "My God, I think they were, or least the top sheet was! I remember the eagle at the top of the page and the swastika beneath it."

He sat silently then, watching his friend write notes. Eventually, Fabian paused, tapping the pen lightly on the paper and staring ahead without focus, as thoughts sought conclusions. He nodded slowly, "That is helpful. If we assume that Pichon didn't forge the documents with the Nazi coat of arms, then he must have been in possession of the originals, or copies, which means that they've probably been held in an archive. Given the geographical aspect, I think those records are likely to be here, on my doorstep, in the *Archive Départementales.* I will go there early next week."

Phillipe sagged with relief, "Thank you so much my friend."

Fabian passed it off with a shrug, "I am happy to help, but I have one more job for you I'm afraid and this one will be difficult." He allowed a pause before, "You must tell Margot, everything and today."

Phillipe shook his head, "I am determined to protect my family from this. There is nothing to be gained by involving them."

The priest spoke quietly, with an implied empathy, "No doubt your cat was treated as part of the family."

"You cannot be suggesting that they are in danger. Pichon wouldn't dare."

"They are, to some degree and you must realise it. He *may* not injure anyone, but he has already killed your cat and caused thousands of Euros worth of damage. If you are not prepared to involve the police the best protection is for *all* of you to be vigilant and on your guard. Make sure you know where everyone is at all times and what their plans are." He saw the look on Phillipe's face and shook his head, "I cannot believe I'm telling you to do all this instead of *making* you call the police." He held up a hand to stall a response, "People often get hurt, even when the intention is only to cause damage to property. What if he sets fire to your house, not realising that one of the girls is in it?"

That mention of police forced Phillipe into making a concession, "Very well, I will think about discussing the matter with Margot."

The priest would have none of that, "Good! After you have thought about it you must do it, this weekend. I shall telephone her on Monday morning, while you are at work, to see how she is and confirm my support." They stared at each other for a moment, to determine which one's resolve would prevail. Finally, Phillipe nodded, "Very well, I'll tell her tonight."

***

Ten of the coffee morning group assembled in front of the check-in desk at Stansted, a full complement save for Barry and Kendall. Adam continued to grumble about having to park 'in the next county' while Barbara startled Carol with her views on take-offs.

There was still an air of adventure as they settled down to breakfast in the departure lounge, though with a different focus this time. The men discussed DIY projects, past, present and more pressingly, the future, while the women were more concerned about the health risks of living in such bubonic surroundings.

As the aircraft lined up and surged forward, Carol nudged Bob and nodded towards Barbara who was seated by the window on the opposite side of the aisle, with her eyes closed and she was smiling, "Barbara's about to have another orgasm." He looked at her askance and she giggled before providing an explanation. He whispered back, "You try it then. Go on, close your eyes and think of England."

She laughed out loud before whispering, "Wrong figure of speech you idiot!"

Barbara felt altogether differently about the landing, in a twenty five knot wind and lashing rain. She'd chosen Adam to accompany her again and was holding his wrist in an iron grip when she turned from the window and looked at him, aghast, "Why is it wobbling so much?"

Instead of telling her that it was a difficult approach, in dreadful weather, he opted for, "It's not wobbling love. The pilot's just making sure he stays lined up with the runway; bit like riding a bike on a rainy day really."

"Oh," she said doubtfully. Moments later the ground seemed to rush up and the undercarriage took a beating, seconds before the engines began to roar in reverse thrust and the pilot stamped on the brakes, throwing everyone forward. Normal breathing resumed when the throttles were eased back for normal taxiing and a trumpet fanfare was blasted out on the PA system. It was the well known tune entitled 'First Call'; used in horse racing, dog racing, the US military and more recently, *Ryanair;* whenever a flight arrived early or on time. There followed a hunched dash across the tarmac, to a customs and baggage hall that would have fitted into a tennis court. Since their baggage followed the same route, it was soaked by the time they reclaimed it, after which they cleared passport control and scurried across the car park to the car hire *portakabin.* The bags rocked from side to side as they bounced over kerbs and the like, resembling a manic pursuit by penguins.

This time they lunched on the way and assembled in Penny's drive at two o-clock. Guinness shouldered his mistress to one side as she opened the door, but came to a sudden halt, teetering on the edge of the top step, when he saw the numbers involved. He gazed at them and gave a single deep bark, his tail wagging uncertainly, until he recognised Annie. With a great 'huff' he launched himself at her. Had she not bent down to greet him he'd have bowled her over but after an exchange of hugs and licks, things were normalised by his stamp of approval in exchange for tickled ears.

Sue made the introductions, but as soon as they were over Penny said, "OK everyone, back in the cars and save a seat for me. I'll telephone and let them know we're on our way."

Since Annie and Sue had independent agendas during this visit they had a car to themselves, so Penny joined them. The eight others were sharing two cars and followed on in a mini convoy. It was a welcome opportunity for the sisters to catch up with the news. Not a lot had happened, though they learned that the Anderson's had already moved their personal belongings out of the house and were therefore ready to hand the place over. Between giving directions Penny asked, "So when is the *pendaison la crémaillère?*

Sue said, "Pardon?"

As a guest in waiting, Penny explained, "It's a party. Literally translated, it means 'to hang the trammel'. In the middle ages the trammel was the last thing to be fitted in a house. It was an iron hook or a rack of hooks for hanging kettles and cooking pots over the fire, so the new owners would cook a meal to thank whoever had helped with the building of the house."

Annie called over her shoulder, "Sis, put a trammel on the shopping list."

Sue said, "And an open fire; consider it done." She tapped Penny on a shoulder, "In the meantime, how about roasting a bag of chestnuts on top of the log burner?"

The eight kilometres to the farmhouse flew by, though they saw the ubiquitous church tower some minutes before they reached their destination. As they dropped down into a river valley Penny pointed the farmhouse out; situated after the stone bridge and on the rise towards the village centre. A second shutter had broken away from a hinge so that there were now two hanging askew. It was those more than anything else that gave the place a derelict air. Penny explained, "That shutter came adrift when we were opening them all for my photography."

A small white Peugeot was parked in the farmyard, half hidden by the waist high undergrowth, most of which was dead, wintering, grass. The car's passage was marked by a swathe of flattened vegetation which was enough for the visitors to go for the easier option of parking on the roadside. They then gathered into a small crowd before advancing, just as a lady got out of the Peugeot to greet them. She was of medium build, with short dark wavy hair flecked with hints of grey. There was a hardy, well scrubbed look about her that fitted with the calloused hand she used to shake the visitor's.

Penny introduced them all and explained that Madame Nicolas didn't speak English. George made a point of stepping forward and addressing the lady in French, asking how she was and saying how beautiful the countryside was. Clearly, it helped to break the ice so he included Sue and Annie in the conversation. They had thought to put her at ease but there was no such need. Madame Nicolas was perfectly confident and startled Sue by asking, "Ah, so you are Anton's *amoureuse*, perhaps?"

Sue struggled to think of a reply and eventually sought refuge behind a shared femininity, "Men! They are not to be trusted with secrets of the heart."

Madame Nicolas's grin lit up her face, "But of course, that is why they need us, to keep their secrets for them."

Thus, an accord of sorts had been reached before they'd stepped over the threshold.

They were instructed to wait where they were, while she entered the house to switch the electricity on, so they all took a moment to survey the immediate surroundings. The farmhouse was fronted by the farmyard, which in turn was enclosed on two sides by outbuildings, with an archway in the corner where they met, blocked, at least in theory, by a rustic and very derelict looking gate. The wall separating them from the road formed the fourth side of the quadrangle.

Once inside, an observer would have noted a mix of reactions ranging from acknowledgement to concerned consolation, but thanks to Penny's photography there were no real frights.

The interior was as dingy as expected; a view shared by Madame Nicolas who spoke to George and Annie, leaving spaces for translation, "I always hated this furniture. It is too big and too dark. We tried to sell it at a local *vide grenier* but no-one wanted it. If you feel the same way; burn it!"

Bob pointed at the *armoire,* "Well personally, I reckon that could go; we could put four easy chairs in its place, but why don't we try stripping the table and chairs and waxing them?" The murmured responses seemed less than certain so he added, "I'll do it and if you don't like the result we'll go ahead and burn it, but don't forget, we will need a table and chairs and this lot is oak. My way will only cost a few cans of varnish remover." The tone of murmuring became less doubtful.

George advanced to inspect the log burner in the fireplace. It looked quite new, though the glazing was badly blackened. He asked Madam Nicolas, "Is this the only heating?"

She shook her head, "There are electric wall heaters in the bedrooms."

Alan Maitlin asked, "What about the walls?" They all took a moment to regard the textured grey walls, until George said, "White; I'm still with white, once we've skimmed over that awful texturing. The agreement was immediate and unanimous.

The kitchen was the next room to be considered. George took one look and said, "Rip it out and start again." Madame Nicolas asked for a translation which he provided, though quickly adding, "But please Madame, I don't wish to be too critical"

She took his arm conspiratorially, "There is nothing you can say about this place that will offend me and that goes for the previous occupants too. My husband's parents hated me from the start and the feeling was mutual." She added by way of explanation, "I came from Paris."

"Ah," he sighed, "A beautiful city."

She gave his arm an affectionate squeeze before addressing the group, "I will be surprised if you keep any of the furniture and in that case my husband will take anything you throw out to the rubbish tip in his trailer. That includes the beds. They are very loud sometimes and I think, not very safe."

George remained by her side for translation, which he did literally, word for word, so the question of 'loud' beds took a moment to sink in, before they all chuckled.

Madame Nicolas began again, "I have just thought of something, my husband will repair the broken shutters; he has an elevator on his tractor, but sadly, we must leave the rest to you if we are to give you a year's free rent."

There was a stunned silence, broken eventually by Adam who raised both hands, palm outward, "Yep, that would work for me!"

Alan cautioned, "We'd better have a look at the rest of the place first." He withdrew a notebook from a pocket, "I'll make notes as we go along, so if anybody sees anything, shout out."

Bob nudged Carol and whispered, "There's going to be quite a din."

They were all fascinated by the features of such an old French building; so different to anything they had come across in England. To begin with, the external shutters kept out almost all natural light and whilst it was therefore necessary to open them, Penny cautioned against the use of force. Adam murmured to those within earshot, "Go for it. The more that fall off their hinges the merrier. Remember, the farmer is going to fix them."

Windows were left open in an attempt to clear the stale air, in part caused by the carcases of several mice and a pipistrelle bat, though the place seemed less damp than had been expected. Having had an initial gallop around the place they split up into small groups and explored in more detail; an act that promised to take longer than Madam Nicolas had anticipated. She found Penny and gave her the keys, with an explanation, "I must get back. Please lock up when your friends have finished and let me have the keys."

Annie left Sue and Penny with their arms stuffed into their armpits, stamping their feet on the tile floor in a vain attempt at creating heat. Outside, she walked to the archway to untie the piece of orange baler twine that held the gate closed. The whole thing had been constructed with branches of varying diameters and twine had been used to make good joints where the original nails had failed. She pushed it tentatively, expecting some degree of collapse and was startled by the ease with which it opened. On the other side of the archway she could see the two acre parcel of land that had been retained with the house. It formed a triangle, bordered on one side by the road and on another by a stout hedgerow the marked the edge of the neighbour's land. The ground fell away to her left, down to the third boundary; a sweeping curve that marked the course of the stream they had crossed over, on the way in.

To her right, at the rear of the house, Annie recognised a few dead tomato plants; obviously self- setters and the remnants of an herb patch marked where the vegetable garden had been. A few shrubs had become unruly and most of the fruit canes lay on the floor, with plants still attached. She recognised the half-hidden blackcurrant and gooseberry plants, but everything was succumbing to Mother Nature being let off the leash.

The grass was too long and wet for the light shoes she was wearing, so she ambled back towards the archway, where, half-way through, she noticed an extremely old door, set back into the stonework. She poked a finger into the hole where ordinarily a doorknob would have been and felt the metal latch immediately, though it required a deal of effort to lift its weight against the binding effect of rust. After taking a single step inside she waited for her eyes to adjust to the gloom, but eventually she was able to see the single light bulb in the centre of the room, with a pull cord just beside it. Thoughts of sharp tools and lumps of equipment called for a slow shuffle across the earthen floor, particularly when organic matter, dead or alive was added to the mental imagery. As a result, she was both startled and delighted when the light came on, along with another, suspended over a workbench that stood against the opposite wall, beneath a shuttered window. Tools of all shapes and sizes hung from hooks on the walls, some of which she recognised, such as the scythe and pitchfork but all of the blades had rusted and the wooden handles had hosted generations of woodworm.

Larger pieces of obscure machinery lay around which gave her a sense of history as she tried to visualise them in use, a century or more ago. Two large wooden boxes had been left next to a pile of hessian sacks. They were four feet square and as high as her waist, but the wasted tendrils in the bottom of one were all that was left of the potatoes that had been stored in them. The workbench had a large vice fitted to one corner and an impressive range of hand tools had been hung neatly on the adjacent walls. She was tempted to open the window and shutters until the funnel web spider nests came into focus, each with a fearsome-looking resident.

At the opposite end of the bench she found a wooden board, bearing a pile of walnuts, a wooden mallet and a scattering of smashed shells. Whoever had worked in there obviously kept a supply of snacks to hand.

Half of the wall to her right was covered with shelves which stopped short of the corner where two stone steps led to a clumsily bricked-up doorway, put there by the same artisan who had built the alcove in the kitchen by the look of it. Another doorway, into the garden lay next to that, in the adjacent wall and it was while standing in that corner, gauging the size of the room that she recalled one of Penny's early messages which noted that half the ground floor had been used for agricultural purposes. Thankfully, there was no evidence of livestock being kept in there, though she had already seen two mice scurrying from one piece of cover to another.

Sue called out, "We thought you'd got lost!"

Annie hadn't heard her sister and Penny step into the workshop and was startled, but sought to explain with, "Oh, just getting a feel of the history here. I was trying to imagine people out in the fields, working with this stuff." She pointed at the bricked up doorway, "I reckon that is the door next to one for the stairs, but I can't understand why they bricked it up. Surely, locking the door would do just as well."

Penny shrugged, "Maybe he wouldn't wipe his feet."

Annie pointed at the other doorway, "Then they both lost out, because that's the direct way into the garden. They'd both have had a long way to go and pick the beans."

Sue grinned, "Well it would explain one thing; two actually. The brickwork here and in the kitchen may well have been done by the man's wife."

Penny joined in, "In that case she should've stuck to cooking." She pointed down at the floor, "Keeping a dirt floor clean would have been challenging, 'specially when hubby came straight from the cowshed.

Enough had been said on the matter and Annie asked, "How's it going in there?"

Sue answered, "A few raised voices, but nothing hysterical yet." After a moment's thought she added, "Excuse me for a moment I need to tell the others that we've found an extra bedroom or two." She hurried out of the door as Penny said, "Hope one or two of them like sleeping on straw." As she spoke, a mouse ran into the floor space between them, realised its error and hurried back out of sight. She grinned, "Will you tell them or shall I?"

Annie chuckled, "I think they'll find out soon enough. Keep it as a surprise." She shuddered, "But for the moment, how about waiting in the car, with the heating set at tropical."

Penny was already heading for the doorway as she spoke, "Now, THAT'S a plan."

***

That same afternoon, Father Fabian began his own little

odyssey, a day later than promised, but a significant funeral had taken up half of the previous day and he always spent Monday afternoons visiting the members of his flock who were in hospital. Yesterday had been particularly demanding, with a need for sacraments to be shared by both patients and families who were in attendance, combined with calls to provide the last rites to two of his parishioners; one anticipated and another quite unexpected, leaving him quite drained.

He had kept his diary clear for Tuesday afternoon, to allow time for the consideration of his friend's dilemma and to begin the research. He began by telephoning the Town Hall and allowed them to fill fifteen minutes by passing him from one office to another. Finally, he asked to speak to one man in particular, in the finance department. He was unlikely to know the answers, but as one of Fabian's parishioners he might take on the task of finding the person who did.

The poor chap was unused to receiving calls at work from his priest and his greeting was tinged with trepidation. Had something dreadful happened? Sensing this, Fabian didn't waste time, "George I am so sorry to bother you at work but I need to beg a small favour."

The relief was evident, "But of course Father! What can I do?"

The parishioner called back an hour later, "You need to speak with Monsieur Xavier Father. He *used* to hold some of the city's records but most of them have either been destroyed or transferred. You will need to be more specific about which ones you wish to inspect and then he hopes to be of assistance."

Once Monsieur Xavier had listened to Fabian's wish list things took a turn for the better. After declaring that the records in question had not been destroyed Monsieur Xavier *thought* he knew where the records had been transferred to. It would only take a few minutes to be certain.

An hour later, he called Fabian back, "I am so sorry for the delay in calling you back, but, it was lunch you know."

Fabian sensed the shrug of shoulders and said, "But of course!"

"Well, I have good news." A pause before, "I think the records you are seeking have been consigned to the care of the *Archives Départementales*, here in Bordeaux. I spoke with one of the archivists, a Monsieur Challans, who has agreed to speak with you."

Fabian sensed Xavier's hesitancy, "Thank you so much Monsieur, I appreciate your assistance, but I sense there is something else."

After another pause for thought, Xavier conceded, "Actually Father, I think he was a most unhelpful fellow. Whilst he admitted that the records were there, he doubted whether you would be allowed to see them. I protested, of course, but he refused to discuss the matter further, saying that he would listen only to what you would have to say. I am so sorry I couldn't have been more help."

"Not at all, you've been wonderfully helpful. I thank you and shall telephone this man immediately."

He did so and was put through to Monsieur Challans, who had obviously girded his loins in anticipation of the call. His tone was brusque, "*Bonjour* Father, what can I do for you?"

Fabian ignored the tone of voice and spoke pleasantly, "I am sorry to bother you, but I have a need to consult the records you hold for the period of occupation, during the Second World War."

The tone didn't ease, "So the last gentleman said. We do not receive many requests for these records, which is perhaps as well. May I ask, why you need to?"

'That is my business you pompous oaf'. Fabian allowed that thought to go and instead he explained, "I have a friend who was affected during that period but he is an extremely busy man and I have promised to do a little research for him."

"I'm sorry Father; that is out of the question."

It was also out of bounds, so far as basic courtesy was concerned. 'No', without offering a reason was being unnecessarily obtuse. The best response to that was to say nothing. Though less than a minute, the silence that followed seemed an age.

Eventually, the weaker of the two broke, "Hello? Are you there Father."

Fabian kept his tone to reasonable; affable even, "I was waiting for you to tell me why."

"Because access to those records is still restricted of course. Members of the public can't just call in and demand to see them. Well, not without the correct authorisation."

Fabian sighed, "And how would I secure that authorisation?"

"You will have to submit an application to the head archivist, detailing the reasons for your research, with supporting documentation. More often than not, they are from recognised researchers and he can authorise them himself. If not, they are considered by the trustees." After a moment he added, with relish, it seemed, "They meet once a quarter"

Bureaucracy one: Catholic priest nil.

Fabian knew the sort of man he was up against. After all, there were people just like it within the church. Folk who would spend more time and effort avoiding a job than it would take to do it. After ending the call with a forced courtesy, he sat back and considered the problem. He couldn't possibly tell the head archivist the real reasons for his enquiries and in any event, he had no documentation to validate anything. Even if Phillipe told the truth, the archivist would probably respond by telling them to go to the police.

Eventually, he gave up on the idea and drove to the library, where he found a wealth of material about that period, but there was little to do with the local collaboration, beyond the shaving of female fraterniser's heads and prosecutions of key players. Ones like Maurice Papon, who wasn't tried until nineteen ninety eight, when *Le Canard Enchainé* published documents bearing his signature as Secretary General for the Bordeaux police. They showed his responsibility for the deportation of over sixteen hundred Jews. In the interim, Papon had continued to prosper and misbehave. While prefect of the *Constantinois* department during the Algerian war he was known to have tortured prisoners and in nineteen sixty one, as chief of police in Paris, he was responsible for the massacre of between one and three hundred *National Liberation Front* demonstrators.

Yet he became one of De Gaulle's favourites, which included being awarded the *Legion of Honour*. That case struck a chord with Fabian. He remembered the court case, but the fact that the documents had remained hidden for over fifty years bore testament to the archivist's claims of secrecy.

Defeated, He returned to his home and in due course, his study, where access to his last resort awaited; the internet.

The immediacy of information retrieval enabled him to discover a wealth of detail for the period of occupation but nothing he could use as a credible excuse for getting at the archives. There was plenty enough for historians to have used but he didn't feel able to feign interest in militaria, atrocities, troop dispositions and the like, let alone collaboration. For that he would need a much deeper knowledge.

He'd allowed his mind to wander as he scrolled through the pages, until quite suddenly, the perfect motive presented itself. It was so abstract he almost skipped over the page for *The Jewish Telegraphic Agency*, yet it was at such odds with everything else he had seen his finger seemed to click on the mouse of its own accord and curiosity.

Fatigue had also brought on a certain lethargy which left him staring at the screen with indifference, until a copy of the *JTA Daily News Bulletin* appeared. It was dated the 16th November nineteen forty four and included several articles, from post war Palestine to Jewish community elections in Rome. He flicked past those until he reached the fourth page, which carried the article that had caused it to come up on the search. The main headline read,

ONLY 1,200 OF 6,200 JEWS IN BORDEAUX SURVIVED NAZI OCCUPATION; SYNAGOGUES PILLAGED

His eyes were immediately drawn to a sub heading, halfway down the page;

CHIEF RABBI FLED WHEN GESTAPO CAME TO DEPORT HIM

He read;

The Gestapo men told Rabbi Cohen to pack a bag and prepare to accompany them. When he returned to the hallway, where they were waiting for him, they told him to remain there while they rounded up the concierge and his family, but the Rabbi did not wait. Instead, he dropped his bag and fled. He re-enacted the episode for this correspondent with grim intensity in the semi-darkness of the debris-strewn synagogue, from which every single interior fitting had been removed or destroyed by the Nazis, tip-toeing hastily through the small synagogue, fumbling with the locks of doors as he did that December night, when seeking egress. Then, I followed him all around the synagogue, stopping for a moment to show me where he fell over the pulpit steps.

Finally, he found one unlocked door, which led to a small courtyard, from which there was a gate to a back street. He fled that way to the home of a non-Jewish friend who sheltered him and brought him to a safe refuge, in the residence of the Catholic Bishop, where he remained until the city was liberated.

The article went on to detail the systematic looting and destruction of everything the Germans could lay their hands on, but Fabian had seen all he needed to. Whether it was divine guidance or plain providence didn't matter. He had found a reason to request access to the archives.

Within minutes, he had a name and biography, warts and all. His Grace the Archbishop Maurice Feltin had served as Archbishop of Bordeaux from nineteen thirty five to nineteen forty nine, when he became the twenty third Archbishop of Paris. He died in nineteen seventy five.

It was clear that the Archbishop wasn't entirely benevolent, given that he condemned the legend of Santa Claus, claiming that it debased the 'Christian significance of Christmas'. Later, in nineteen sixty three, as Archbishop emeritus of Paris, he denied Edith Piaf a religious funeral due to her 'controversial' life. The Roman Catholic Church did finally grant her a memorial Mass, fifty years after her death, in the St Jean-Baptiste church in Belleville, Paris, the parish in which she had been born. Fabian committed such trivia to memory, ready to share with an archivist the next day.

But more importantly, the man was a Catholic bishop. Why then, shouldn't a priest seek to research the subject?

***

The evening meal at the Hotel in Cognac was a noisy affair and the meeting that followed in the lounge was even livelier.

Since the sister's meeting at the notaire's office was at ten the next morning Sue had joined them, with Anton in tow, albeit for the evening only. He would be sleeping in his own bed that night, alone. As the list of works and schedules became complicated, Sue whispered into his ear, "It's set to be renovation by committee. Now nothing will get done."

Alan was desperately trying to minute everything in his notebook, but it was clear that some were losing the plot, with ideas that might have been valid at home, but not realistic for a seventeenth century stone farmhouse that would be used as a holiday home. Wisely, Sue and Annie kept their council, by way of a whispered accord, "Speak only when you're spoken to".

Bob mentioned the damp, or apparent lack of it, but Alan differed, "Didn't you see the watermarks in the corner of back bedroom wall. It's been getting worse, obviously. The watermarks are like flood markers for ten years or so." He was right, in that the marks grew away from the corner in a rough concentricity that looked like rings on a tree section, but incredibly, they had only been in the one room and Bob said as much, adding, "If that is all there is we should be able to get it fixed for next to nothing. It's probably just a few cracked slates."

The single surprise that delighted them all and ultimately brought about their decision to go ahead was the wiring. Instead of burying it in the walls, the contractor had run the lot through surface mounted white plastic conduit. Whilst not attractive, it did end up at an incongruously new fuse box in the larder.

Someone asked about the water supply and Adam responded

with, "At the very least there'll be a well and that would suit me." Jayne Maitlin gave him a look that indicated otherwise, but by the end of the evening the vote to go ahead was unanimous.

Suddenly, by unspoken agreement, the subject was dropped. It had been worked to death and there were other things to consider, such as the next day. With Annie and Sue off on their own project they decided to do some more exploring on their own. It was too cold for most things but George suggested something that found favour, "I read about a frigate they are building in Rochefort. It's a copy of an eighteenth century ship and open to the public. It's supposed to be pretty impressive, at any rate."

Bob and Alan were delighted but Amy Dyson differed, "That sounds like a very male thing to me George. How close is it to the city?"

He'd done the research, knowing what his wife would say, "My dear, it is next door *and* it's market day tomorrow. Jayne, Carol and Barbara declared their preference for a shopping trip and Jayne went a step further, "What say we buy the makings of a picnic and meet up at lunchtime?"

It was her partner's time to respond. Alan shook his head, "Jeez, you must be joking; a picnic in February?"

"Why not? What's wrong with eating in the cars if the weather's off?"

Alan replied a little testily, "What's wrong with the *menu du jour* in a cafe?"

Carol came to his rescue, "Actually, if it is cold and we've spent the morning going around a market we may need somewhere warm to go."

With the agenda established some went up to their rooms while others clustered together for a nightcap. Carol sat down next to Annie and said quietly, "I can't speak a word of French and I've heard tales of them being rude to people like me. Will anyone speak English do you think?"

Annie could see how anxious she was and quickly sought to reassure her. It didn't start well though, "Some French people are disinclined to speak English, it's true, even when they know a little, but Rochefort is a tourist trap so that shouldn't be so evident. If you start by speaking a few words of French it'll make a huge difference. It shows that you've tried. After that, don't shout. Foreigners who don't speak English are not deaf as well."

Carol groaned, "But I don't know a single word."

Annie said, "Right then, let's make a start by setting you up for the market. Got a pen and paper?" She waited until Carol was ready, "Write this down the way it sounds, phonetically, that way you will know how to pronounce it. Writing can come a lot later." She dictated slowly, "*Je voudrais* then a space, followed by *s'il vous plait.*" She had Carol say it back several times until satisfied that a Frenchman would understand and then explained, "If you smile, that's important, and then after saying the first bit, which means 'I would like', point at what you want and say the second bit, which means 'if you please', you'll be on a winner. One thing's for sure; you'll never have to go hungry."

Carol looked at her notes, "I'm not so sure."

Annie took her hand, "You should be, they were the first French words I used, forty odd years ago."

"What did you buy?"

"A bloody awful pastry. The baker mistook where my finger was pointing, which was actually towards an apricot flan. Funny thing is, it still felt like an achievement. You'll just have to give it a shot."

"But what happens if he asks a question, like thick or thin slice? I'll be lost."

"Not at all; you smile plaintively and shrug your shoulders, then say, 'Pardon Monsieur, I have little French'. Don't forget the forlorn smile, Frenchmen are suckers for it. Given the chance, he'll have you in bed within minutes."

Carol nudged her, "Now you're joking."

Annie shrugged, "OK that may be a bit of a cliché, but it's not miles from the truth."

Carol giggled as a thought struck her, "So I mustn't ask for a piece of his sausage then."

Her mentor thought for a moment before, "Only if I'm there to watch his reaction."

Adam was seated next to Anton, on the other side to Sue and had dropped out of the discussion a number of times, to speak with his new friend. Ever since he had chosen to look around the land with Anton they had enjoyed a growing friendship. Anton's buoyant sense of fun seemed an excellent foil to Adam's slightly taciturn ways. As a result, the others noted that Sue, Anton and Adam were always together at group meetings.

One of the topics they had discussed that evening had been about the distillery and vineyard. Adam had said something about Anton putting his feet up once the distillation was over, in March. The Frenchman was appalled, "*Non*! How could you say that my friend? Tonight I have a holiday, thanks to my neighbour, who is watching over my still, but there is so much cleaning and the vines always need care. There are so many pests and diseases you know."

Adam smiled, "That was exactly what I'd hoped you would say."

***

Annie and Sue met Gail and Les Anderson on the walk from the car park to the notaire's office and they greeted each other as friends, the French way. There was a sparkle to the atmosphere that lasted as far as the waiting room. Monsieur Gagnon was there to meet the sisters and he exchanged a few pleasantries as they introduced him to the Andersons. They hadn't employed a lawyer and so the party was complete, but suddenly quite sombre. The place had been carpeted and furnished in a plush yet conservative manner which helped to create an almost hallowed atmosphere. Even the sister's lawyer spoke in a hushed tone. Precisely at the appointment time a lady showed them into a large, high-ceilinged office that Napoléon might have been satisfied with. The shutters on the sunny side had been left half open, leaving the drapes and bookshelves distanced in the subdued light, but the huge oak desk before them was a magnificent centrepiece which dominated the room. Ironically, the elderly man who stood up to greet them was diminutive. As he stepped around the desk, with a hand outstretched, Annie noted the dark formal suit, shock of white hair and the most charming smile. He was soft spoken too, "Good day and welcome, I hope you are all well."

There were five ornate chairs already in place before the desk and after introductions he directed them all to their seats, with Gagnon in the centre and the buyers and sellers on respective sides.

Annie and Sue later agreed that what followed was a blur. A translation of the more technical terms and questions was provided for both parties by the lawyer as the notaire made his way through a jungle of documents until eventually, they all wrote the required declarations and signed where shown. The notaire handed a cheque over to the Andersons and with a beaming smile, declared the matter to be complete. He stood and shook hands with everyone as they filed past, towards the door.

Gagnon left for his office and the four remaining participants headed for a cafe and celebratory drink. They were making their way along the narrow pavement in pairs when Sue turned to Annie and summed up what they were all thinking, "That, was surreal!"

***

At the same time as the sisters were with the notaire, Father Fabian cast an eye over his notes and mentally declared himself ready to make the call. He rarely used his title to gain favour and more often than not, when he did, it was for someone else, but he needed to impress the telephonist enough to ensure he was put through to the right man, "Good day, my name is Father Fabian and I would like to speak to the head archivist please."

She wasn't sufficiently impressed to respond personally but after a few moments Fabian heard the ring tone sound twice before the receiver was picked up, "Good day, this is Mathieu Laroche."

"Ah, *bonjour Monsieur*, my name is Fabian Bissonnette, my parish is in Salaunes, to the west of the city."

It was evident from his voice that the head archivist was much older than the other archivist and he sounded friendlier too, "I know it well, we have family over there, you may know them." He provided the details and Fabian confirmed that they were actually members of his flock, but with the small talk out of the way it was time to get down to business.

"I am sorry to take up your time Monsieur Laroche, but I am keen to pursue a line of investigation into the period of occupation which is of some personal importance."

Laroche interrupted, "Ahhh, you are the chap who spoke to Challans yesterday, he told me about it. I hope we were of *some* assistance though."

Fabian had prepared for this, "Sadly, no, although in hindsight, I could have been more informative. It all seemed so impossible though."

The archivist chuckled, "Knowing Challans, I can understand how you felt, though I cannot promise any more than he did," Fabian sensed the grin, "But I *will* listen first."

The soft gentleness of the voice was that of a wiser man too and Fabian warmed to him, "Thank you. You see, I've been doing some research into the period of occupation recently. My particular interest is in those occurrences which involved the Catholic Church. One of the most significant involved His Grace Maurice Feltin."

Laroche interrupted, "Yes of course, the bishop who sheltered the Rabbi."

"Exactly, but I have very little in the way of evidence. Most is a matter of lore, passed on from the last generation. What I hoped to do was consult your archives for some sort of documentary proof and then perhaps, a little background information surrounding the event. Of course then, perhaps, there may be references to other activities of our church. After all, such a subversive act implies that there were others, including connections with the resistance perhaps, something the Catholic Church signally failed to record at that time. And then there is the Nazi perspective to it all. Like most historical research I hoped to follow several lines of enquiry, in the hope of making slivers of information become threads that were strong enough to weave into facts."

There was a pause during which Fabian heard a page being turned over, which he took to mean that notes were being made. Eventually, Laroche asked, "And do you intend to publish your work, or make any findings public in some other way?"

The priest startled himself by lying so glibly, "Definitely not, though if the records were ever opened up to the public I would hope to share my research with some of my fellow clergy Perhaps, even, the Vatican as well." He stopped short, fearing that he'd taken a step too far, yet mindful of how public a blackmail case might become.

The chief archivist paused once more, before saying, "You ask a lot Father. There are things in there that people prefer to forget these days."

"The Church is a house of many secrets Monsieur, none more so than in our own confessional." His own looked set to be challenging. The only hope was that his misdemeanours might be deemed to be less sinful if they served to end a greater wrong.

Laroche cleared his throat noisily, before, "Very well Father, I am going to do something entirely out of character. I will allow you view the records, but subject to certain conditions. One, you will only be allowed to view specific files with prior permission. Two, you will not make any of your findings public. Three, I would like to see a full, unedited copy of your findings when you have finished. Please understand Father, I am allowing you to view restricted material."

"Yes, yes of course. I'm so very grateful, thank you."

Laroche thought of something else, "And I would like you to confirm that in writing please."

"But of course, I will bring that in with me, unless you require it in advance."

"No, leave it until you come and when do you think that might be?"

Fabian glanced at his diary, "Would tomorrow morning be too soon?"

"No, that will be fine. I look forward to meeting you, at ten perhaps? In the meantime, I can seek out some of the files. Do you have any names to hand?"

Fabian grabbed his notes and in addition to the Rabbi and Bishop he added the two most important names, adding, "Though I'm sure there will be other connections with the Nazi files too." Moments later, he settled the telephone gently into the cradle and thought about things. He'd gained access to restricted files, but how many untruths had it taken? He couldn't bring himself to call them downright lies. At least he would be the one to write the confidentiality agreement, one which would promise much but might fall short on definitions. An undertaking not to make his findings public was not the same as sharing them with a single individual. He sighed, "Phillipe Rambert, you may well get me unfrocked over this."

Out of professional courtesy, Laroche telephoned his subordinate, "Ah, Challans, I have just had a lengthy conversation with Father Fabian, the priest you spoke to yesterday. He took time to say that he hadn't shared as much information with you as he should have, but in light of that additional detail he's given to me, I have decided to allow him access to the files, though subject to undertakings and supervision."

As expected, Challans sounded piqued, "Very well."

Laroche continued, "In the meantime, we may as well have some of the stuff ready for him. Would you pull the following files out as soon as you can please?"

***

Meanwile, just a hundred and forty kilometres south, in Rochefort, the gang parked their cars near the seventeenth century

'*Corderie Royale*' which still housed machinery for making maritime ropes and hawsers. It was an enormously long, single storey building, constructed with the light stone of the area. Bob declared it to be seventeenth century, as they walked the length of the place, along neatly maintained paths and lawns until they neared the far corner, when *Hermione* hove into view. Still two years shy of the launch date, even the ladies had to agree that she was an impressive sight. Nevertheless, retail therapy beckoned and they split up with an agreement to meet back there at noon before finding somewhere for lunch. Contrary to expectations, it had stopped raining and the clouds were breaking up. The intermittent sunshine was surprisingly warm.

The four women turned away from the dock and crossed the road, towards the town centre. Within a few metres they turned into *Avenue Charles de Gaulle* and could see the market, just a few hundred metres away. Before then though, there were shop windows to gaze at and restaurant menus to consider. Barbara was beside herself and her delight in so many sights and smells became infectious.

By the time they reached the market all four were buoyed by the experience. Even Carol changed her mind and decided she *would* have a go with her five words of French, if an opportunity arose. Discreetly, she removed the mini script from her handbag, to have it to hand.

A French market is always a delight for those who love food, but Carol was astounded. The fish were so fresh and the fishmonger's technique with filleting knives was hugely entertaining. The butchers, delicatessens, fruiterers and bakers presented their stocks so beautifully and so differently to those in the UK. The cuts of meat were trimmed and dressed with great care and she noticed that the fruiterer served from the front of his display rather than out of sight from the rear. More importantly, she watched him inspect each apple as he bagged them and discarded any that were substandard. They were all busy too, with queues at each one.

The choice at the cheese stall was amazing, with waves of

mouth-watering fragrances. A plate of cubed cheese had been placed on the counter for sampling and the others followed Barbara's lead in reaching in for one. It was heaven, so much so that Carol joined the queue, though with enough trepidation to ask them all to stay with her. The wait allowed her time to practice silently.

They watched him serve others, with a banter that some returned while others smiled or chuckled and eventually, he looked at Carol and asked her what she wanted. Guessing it to be that she began, "*Je voudrais,*" then pointed at the samples and continued, "*S'il vous plaît.*"

He asked her how many grammes but it might just have well been in Swahili. She smiled and stuttered, shrugged and stuttered, "I'm sorry I don't know any more French."

He snickered and continued in French, "So is that the best you can do?"

Carol blushed terribly when she heard some of the queue chuckle. Whatever he had said was at her expense and she made to move away.

Barbara blocked her exit and held her arm as she spoke to the man in perfect French, "Yes Monsieur, it *is* the best she can manage. My friend has never been to France before and this was her first attempt to speak French, yet you ridicule her. I've been telling her that French people are courteous and caring. Would you make me a liar?"

A round of applause came from the queue, with a sprinkling of critical comments, but they were unnecessary. He blushed this time, "Forgive me, it is my way. I meant no offence." He looked at Carol and dipped his head, "*Pardon Madame.*"

Barbara continued, in French, "I believe two hundred grammes will be sufficient thank you."

He weighed and wrapped the cheese quickly, and printed a ticket off the weighing scales in order to show Carol the twelve Euros that were due. As she took the change he smiled winningly and said, in accented English, "'Ave a good day."

She smiled back, "Thank you." But then he pointed upward

with one finger, "*Un moment!*" The meaning was clear and she watched as he laid a piece of grease proof paper in the palm of one hand and scraped a portion of runny cheese onto it, from a round that lay on his counter. She thought it looked disgusting yet he handled it reverently. Once carefully wrapped, he handed it to her and smiled once more, "*Pour vous, un cadeau.*"

This time the queue applauded enthusiastically.

As they moved on Carol asked Barbara, "What did he say then?"

Barbara took the new parcel from her and sniffed it appreciatively. "He said, 'for you, a gift.'"

Carol was delighted, "Wasn't that lovely? What was it you said to him, before."

Barbara lied, "We were discussing you actually. He was saying that he appreciated your effort to speak French and what a shame it was that others didn't try. That's why the people in the queue gave you a little applause."

Amy knew otherwise and made a mental note to give the dotty artist a big hug as soon as possible. In the meantime, Carol looked like a poodle with two tails.

Jayne asked, "What cheese did you buy?"

Carol shrugged, "The one we tried."

Amy had made a point of checking, "It was *Brebis*, which is sheep's cheese."

"Oh dear."

"What. It tastes good doesn't it? Why should cows have all the fun?" She nodded to a stall around the corner, "I'll go and buy a baguette then how about finding somewhere for coffee?"

They walked along the *Rue Pierre Loti* and found themselves at the *Hotel de Ville* or council house, which overlooked a large open space called *Place Colbert*. A brasserie lay on the western edge and the morning had become just warm enough to warrant sitting outside.

They all wanted a coffee with cream apart from Jayne who opted for a decaffeinated black coffee.

Carol had been studying the menu and asked, "So do we

ask for *Cafe Crème?*" They grasped her intentions and hurriedly gave her a French lesson. In no time, she was ready to ask for '*trois crèmes et un cafe noir*', though she continued to rehearse it mentally until the waiter arrived. She was delighted to see him nod and jot the order down on his pad. But then he asked whether they wanted small or large, Barbara cut in and said, "*Grande, s'il vous plaît.*"

Jayne asked if the 'noir' could be decaffeinated. His mouth turned down and he shrugged, replying in accented English, "Yes, I think so."

Five minutes later he returned with their drinks and served Jayne's last, with a note of disdain, "'Ere is your coffee, wizout coffee."

The previous occupant of the next table had obviously enjoyed a croissant and jam with his coffee, but before the waiter could return to clear the table Barbara leapt up from her seat and removed the dirty plate and knife. Whilst wiping the knife with a tissue she explained, "I'm sure he doesn't have anything communicable. Now Carol, where's that cheese?"

Amidst fits of adolescent giggling each broke off a piece of baguette and took turns to use the knife. The *Brebis* was smooth and flavoursome, but the runny stuff exceeded all expectations, though it was too strong for Amy's taste, and nose for that matter. Buoyed by success, Carol exclaimed, "That's not just an aroma, it's giving off fumes!"

Jayne spoke with her mouthful, "By God it's good though, what is it?"

Barbara had recognised it by sight as well as smell, "It's *Epoisses*, from the Burgundy region I believe."

Carol was puzzled, "Barbara, you told Bob you hadn't flown before, so how come you can speak French so well and know their cheeses."

The elderly artist grinned cheekily, "Well, I grew very fond of my French tutor, over a number of years." She sighed and looked a little wistful, "But Mummy despatched him before any harm was done."

Jayne sniggered, "Oops."

Barbara inclined her head, "Yes well, I was only fifteen you see. As for the cheese-." She paused as memories flooded back; of the huge Rolls Royce being winched on to the ferry and their chauffeur standing on the dock, beside himself with worry. Once safely on shore he would drive them down to the rented house in Normandy, just west of *Mont St Michel* and to the French way of life, "Daddy used to take us over to France for a month each summer and the rule was, 'when in Rome'. Lunches invariably consisted of bread, cheese and wine."

Jayne helped herself to another piece of cheese as she pronounced, "A banquet."

Amy spoke up, "Speaking of which, we're supposed to be meeting the men for lunch. Shouldn't we leave some space?"

In fact, the men had met up with an English family who recommended a place for lunch, called *Hotel du Port,* where they could find a fixed price four course lunch, with wine, for eleven Euros a head. There was no dissent when they met up an hour later, but by the time they found the place it was almost full. The madam who greeted them was a small, rotund barrel of energy in a shiny scarlet dress and haphazard hair style that might have been a bun at some point. The pearls around her neck had to be fakes, for they were huge, but when she set to work they bounced in and out of her cleavage with a mesmerising action, like a set of snooker balls in an earthquake.

There were enough seats, but they were scattered around the room and she knew that '*Anglais*' preferred to either eat alone or '*en famille*'. She also knew that with enough covers available these '*Anglais*' were not going to be allowed to leave. The other diners must have been regulars, because no-one complained when she attacked the room. Pairs were asked to join the ends of other tables, while singles were slipped into any other spaces. Plates, cutlery, wine glasses and bread followed them with an astonishing efficiency. At one point, other diners were passing the food along and all of it was accepted pragmatically. Finally, she pushed tables into a formation that would allow the gang to eat as two fours. George leaned forward so that they could all hear him murmur, "It was worth coming here just to see that."

Thankfully, each table had a French speaker, because Madam either couldn't or wouldn't speak a word of English. A teenage girl stepped out from the kitchen and laid the tables while the older lady delivered an arm full of meals to one of the other tables. She then returned to the gang and pointed over to a chilled display cabinet on the other side of the room while explaining that the first course was from the buffet. The second was from a choice of four main courses listed on blackboards around the room, from which they would be expected to order when she returned with their wine. The cheese was in the same chilled cabinet as the buffet and the desserts were in the nearby upright chiller. All had chosen red, so a large carafe was soon planted in the centre of each table. The time allowed was just sufficient for them to make a choice.

The Maitlins, Barbara and finally, Carol ordered *Choucroute aux Trois Poissons,* after Barbara had translated for her, "It will be three different sorts of fish on a bed of sauerkraut, with a beautiful butter sauce." Amy chose *Moules Marinières* and chips while Adam, George and Bob ordered entrecôte steaks. When madam had finished noting down the orders she asked how they wanted their steaks cooked, which George translated for the other two. Bob asked for well done and George translated. Very calmly, while still focused on her pad, Madam said, "*Non.*"

George chuckled, "Many French chefs refuse to turn their steaks into shoe leather. It's pink or nothing I'm afraid." When called upon to make his choice Adam just shrugged, "I'll do as I'm told, I suppose." George looked at Madam, "*À point s'il vous plaît.*" *Me*dium if you please. She nodded and directed them to the buffet, though she told them to leave the cheese alone until after the main course and before the dessert.

The buffet was spectacular; all manner of cold meats, seafood and fish, along with coleslaw, potato salad and a variety of sauces. George and Barbara were particularly taken with the langoustines, while Bob and Adam piled excessive amounts of cured ham and salami onto their plates. When they returned to their tables a large basket of bread had been delivered to each.

The whole meal was delicious and noisy. Everyone, it seemed had something they wanted to share from the morning's experience.

Whilst all the men had been impressed by their tour of *Hermione*, Bob's memory of the facts and figures proved the most reliable. To begin with, he explained that the long rope-making building, *La Corderie Royale* was only sixty years old; the original had been demolished by the Nazis.

"Why did they do that?" asked Barbara.

Bob shrugged, "I have no idea. It had no strategic value. Just something else to wipe out I suppose." He brightened as another revelation came to mind, "Did you know that it took eleven months to build the original ship and it'll take fifteen years before this copy is launched."

Adam muttered, "Such is progress."

Bob ignored the interruption and continued to address the ladies, "And this one is going to cost twenty two million Euros."

It was Jayne's turn, "So how much did the original cost?"

"I don't know and I couldn't find anyone who did."

Carol asked, "Was there any particular reason for choosing this ship?"

Bob nodded his head vigorously, "In seventeen eighty she was used to ferry a General Lafayette and his troops over to America, to join the rebels."

That much was understandable, but when Bob began to describe technical detail Carol silenced him with a discreet kick."

It was the ladies turn.

In spite of her misgivings, Carol relished every mouthful of her three fish *choucroute*; it fell beyond anything she'd tasted before. Over coffee she did the maths before asking the question, "That meal cost just over nine pounds each. How come we can't do that in England?"

George added, "What's more, we haven't eaten junk. That was food cooked with love."

Even the pink steaks had gone down exceptionally well.

They all raised their coffee cups as he proposed the toast, "To France, *La belle France.*"

***

"That's a nice touch." The bottle of champagne had been left on the kitchen table and was the first thing Annie noticed as they stepped into their new French home. An envelope containing a 'welcome to your new home' card sat underneath the bottle; signed by Gail and Les. They'd contacted the sisters the day before and arranged to leave the electrics on and food stocks in the fridge and freezer, which included the usual stuff; milk, butter, cheeses, cold meats and a startling quantity of frozen fruit and vegetables. The cupboards held ample stocks of dried and canned foods, along with an impressive range of herbs and spices. It felt like home already and without a word, they hugged each other.

The only thing they lacked was bread and at one-o-clock, there was no hope of buying any for lunch. Sue said, "I wonder," as she pulled her mobile out. In less than two min-utes bread had been organised, though Penny wouldn't stand for one of them to call round for it. Instead, she said she'd be there in a jiff. They didn't resist, since the prospect of offering their friend some hospitality held great appeal.

Guinness charged into the kitchen and bounced around the sisters for long enough to re-establish the relationship, but he was soon distracted by the new sights and smells of a new venue. Penny followed him in and handed over most of a French stick, "I thought you promised not to be 'cup of sugar' neighbours."

Sue flicked a thumb in Annie's direction as she walked towards Penny, "She lied." They gave each other a kiss on each cheek and a hug while she continued, "Welcome to our house. You're the first visitor."

"Second actually." Penny pointed at the dog, which was snuffling loudly as he sought to confirm the location of something beneath the cooker. All attempts to retrieve it, by claw and tongue, had failed thus far.

Annie exchanged greetings before explaining, "The Anderson's told us there was plenty of food in the fridge and I took that to mean bread too; silly of me really."

Penny grinned, "Just kidding. In fact, if I'd known you were going to be here this early you'd have had an invitation to lunch. As it is, I've had mine. A coffee would be nice though, if there's one going."

The choice of food was limited, but it was one of the most comfortable and comforting lunches Annie could remember. Guinness gave up on the scrap of food beneath the cooker and sought the generosity of the two softer options to hand. The measure of attention and more importantly, food he received was proportional to the force and regularity of his stamp of approval, so much so that once Sue called out, "Yow, Guinness, that hurt!"

His technique for such moments was to stare up at the complainant with half-closed eyes, as if mortified by the transgression. Sadly, the cowed expression was at odds with the sweeping of a great tail across the floor and his stupid canine grin.

They were so easy in each other's company and there were few silences, but Penny took advantage of one to say, "We've got something for you as a house warming present, but it's a bit heavy. Why don't you come to dinner tonight and have a look."

Annie was quick to respond, "No Penny, you've fed us so many times we can't do it again, at least for a while."

"Nonsense, we were looking forward to it. Anyway, we want to gauge your reaction to our prezzy. Besides, I'll bet you haven't got a complete meal to hand."

Sue knew she was right, but then an idea came to mind, "Well, I'll accept with thanks, but, on one condition." She looked to Annie, "We're all going home day after tomorrow, so why don't we do a buffet or something and have the gang, Penny and Tom round for a house-warming tomorrow night. Nothing complicated, but with plenty of wine."

Annie raised an eyebrow, "And cognac too?"

Sue dipped her head into her shoulders, "Shit, I was forgetting to include Anton."

Penny decided to join in, "And Guinness."

That night was as enjoyable as ever. Penny had thought to include Anton which made Sue's adjournment to his place a far smoother process. Their house warming present was an old stone watering trough, to stand next to the front door. Both sisters were both delighted and aghast. Annie was the first to speak, "Oh no, this is too generous."

Tom agreed, "Damned right, it took me hours."

Penny explained, "That is *all* it cost, apart from a box of *Radox* for the bath. We found it buried at the end of the field."

***

Challans waited until his wife was upstairs putting their son to bed before announcing that he was going for a walk. It was pouring down, much harder than before and veils of rain moved through the glare of streetlights in response to the gusts of an Atlantic gale. There were so few call boxes these days and by the time he reached the nearest his clothes were sodden. He made the call, which was answered swiftly, "Pichon."

"Ah Monsieur, *ça va*?" Are you OK?

The abrasive voice snarled back, "Get on with it. What the hell are you calling at this time for?"

The caller stuttered, "Something has come up, to do with the German occupation and your name was mentioned."

"Come up? What do you mean come up?"

"A local priest has asked to look at the files."

"He might ask, but they are restricted. Tell him to fuck off!"

"I, I can't, the head archivist has authorised it."

"What other names were there?"

"One was Rambert; I can't remember the names of the others. There were only a few; one was a bishop."

Pichon felt his temper rising, "How long have you known about this?"

"Today, it happened today."

"Has he seen any of the files yet?"

"No, they arranged his visit for tomorrow. I've been told to pull the files before he gets there." Finally, something else came to mind, "Oh yes, he wants to looks at the Nazi files as well, for those connected with collaborators."

Pichon growled once more, "Bring me the files."

"What, all of them?"

"Don't be stupid, you know the ones I mean. Those you've handled before."

"But that is a serious offence; it would mean instant dismissal."

"Listen little minnow, if those files are made public, you will be one of the first to be gutted, I guarantee it." After a pause Pichon added, "Just do it, then bring them here. You'll be paid well, as always."

The walk home felt longer and much, much colder.

***

None of the Club Cognac team could manage more than a snack that evening but they all had something nice to say about lunch. Jayne made another observation, "Do you realise; we didn't mention the house once today."

Alan differed, "Sorry love, the men did."

Amy spoke, "Did I detect a hint of relief there Jayne?"

Jayne wore a rueful grin, "Nah, it might not have been on my bucket list but the men are obviously up for it so I'll run with it." She raised a finger, "But! At the first sign of bubonic plague I'll be out of there."

Amy chuckled, "You'd have to get in the queue."

George grabbed the opportunity that seemed to be presenting itself, "So are we *all* up for it?" In the absence of a conclusive response he tried another tack, "OK, is there anybody who doesn't want to get involved?" After a few moments of silence he sought an unequivocal response, "So, hands up if you think we should tell the lady that we'll take it."

Finally, hands began to appear, until just one remained down. She'd done it deliberately, of course, but eventually Carol leaned in to Bob and whispered, "You bugger!" Then used the same hand to vote and thump Bob en route.

In truth, the whole experience had been an education. The people had been wonderful, the shops, service, courtesy and quality of everything had startled her, but the food had stunned her. On the way back from Rochefort she tried to fathom how she could have been so wrong and eventually she put that question to Bob. He'd thought for a while, before asking, "Do you think it could have been the media? After all, that is all you've had to judge France by, until now."

She realised that he was right, but how wrong her judgement had been and how much she had missed for all those years.

CHAPTER 9

Annie was woken at around eight the following morning by a thump on the door. She struggled out of bed and into her dressing gown before hobbling down the stairs on limbs that had stiffened in the night. The thump occurred again and she was about to call out when she heard the scratching. Mindful of the damage he was causing to the paintwork, she did call down this time, "Guinness! Stop that you brute, that's my door you're wrecking."

His delight at hearing her voice prompted another charge at the door, with a loud thump. He'd come for his cup of tea.

The rest of the gang were breakfasting at the hotel, before setting out for a day in La Rochelle. Annie had telephoned the previous day with an invitation to the house warming party and explained that the day would therefore be spent preparing for it. They would therefore be on their own again.

Annie picked Sue up from Anton's, on the way to Matha, where they planned to shop, not only for the party, but at last, they could stock up on things such as herbs, flour, coffee, tea and all the other basics that could now be left in place. They had set off early, so that the supermarket would have time to prepare the party food and since it was Thursday, the car park was almost empty.

They headed for the delicatessen counter and the brochure for party platters which was on a stand. The choice of themes, treatments and speciality dishes was astonishing and daunting, but within minutes the man from behind the counter stepped out and asked if he could be of assistance. Annie began to detail their plans until his jaw dropped and his head dipped, "But Madam, this is not possible for today. Here, we take orders at least two days in advance and have the food brought in from another place."

Sue's lip curled up on one side, "Uh oh, looks like it's going to be cheese and biscuits."

Annie would have none of that, "Forget it; we're going to do better than that, even if I have to spend this afternoon cooking." She turned back to the *charcutier* and began explore other options, without success. There were no other suppliers in town and their own source was over a hundred kilometres away, notwithstanding the fact that they'd already have a schedule of orders for the day. She explained that they were flying home the next day and had hoped to avoid cooking, at which point they all turned to consider the range of meats and pâtés on his counter, but Annie had hoped to provide a much more sophisticated, *French,* spread.

He added, "I am so sorry Madam, but it is out of season and not even the weekend, so my counter is left wanting."

Since there were no customers at that time, the baker and the butcher had been standing in the space between their own counters, gossiping, until curiosity required them to join in. They ambled over to find out what was going on. The *charcutier* explained what the problem was and all three commiserated, until the baker asked what the occasion was.

Sue answered, "We have just bought a house in Aurigny les Bois, just yesterday in fact and we so wanted to have some friends round this evening, for a party. We call it a house warming."

"Ah yes, the *pendaison la crémaillère.*" She turned to where the voice had come from to find that the fishmonger, or *poissonnier* had joined them. Returning his smile as she recalled that Penny had used the same term, Annie said, "Yes, Monsieur, though we won't have a new trammel I'm afraid."

He chuckled, "I am surprised you know of it."

She smiled, a little sadly, "It looks as though we won't have any food either."

His three colleagues explained the situation but the exchanges were so quick she failed to understand parts, though they kept mentioning Aurigny. Finally, the *charcutier* asked, would either of you know Anton Michaud by any chance?"

Annie replied, "We *both* know him." She rolled her eyes slightly before adding, "But I think it is my sister, Sue, you are referring to." She thought they might have been embarrassed by the implication, but none was evident. Instead, the baker said softly, "Ah lala."

He turned to his colleagues, "Gentleman, we cannot leave these ladies in such need!"

The others agreed and began to make plans, beginning with the baker, "I have some *vol-au-vents* and blinis in the back, and the fruit flans came in this morning. Of course, bread is no problem, but I also have some cheese and lardon baguettes you might enjoy."

The fishmonger said, "I have some beautiful crabs I could dress and some lemon mayonnaise that would go well with it. Then there are the frozen langoustines and how about some shrimps with salmon mousse for the *vol-au-vents*."

Not to be outdone, the *charcutier* said, "Well of course, if I steeped the duck liver pâté with a little *Cointreau* and made a dish of melon cubes with dried ham, would that be acceptable? Then how about if I prepared a plate of meat and savoury pastries with things such as olives and *cornichons.*" He continued with the mental stock take before raising a finger, "Ahh, I also have some very nice *tartes provençales* and some stuffed tomatoes, if you wouldn't mind heating them up."

Annie was grinning by then, "No, of course not."

The fishmonger called out, "In that case, I can make up some *Coquilles Saint-Jaques*!"

The butcher had been waving at the cheese counter man to come over, but then addressed the sisters, "Ladies, my meat is uncooked and therefore of no use to you, but would you allow me the honour of selecting the wines for you please?"

Sue thanked him and provided everyone with the numbers of those attending. The cheese counter man, or *fromagier* arrived in time to be told of the need for a *grand plat à fromage* and with that the sister's house warming party was back on. They arranged to collect the order at four in the afternoon and parted as firm friends.

***

Father Fabian did not enjoy the same degree of success. The *Archives Départementales de la Gironde* are situated on the eastern side of Bordeaux, on the *Cours Balguerie Stuttenberg,* a narrow street enclosed by tall grubby buildings and besieged by masses of two-way traffic, that somehow manages to squeeze past cars parked in allotted bays on both sides.

By contrast, the frontage of the archive building is several times wider than its neighbours and very modern. A third of the ground floor is taken up by a bicycle parking area beside a vehicle access to a courtyard and beyond that, an underground car park, while the first floor is clad with eight huge panes of glass bearing background images of historical text and buildings. A barrier blocked Fabian's attempt to park his car.

Fabian found the place in good time, but parking was impossible. He made five tortuous and widening circuits, with an increasing anxiety as the appointment time loomed nearer, then passed. On his fifth time around he considered an attempt at getting past their barrier, but the prospect of having to reverse back out into the traffic was too daunting. His final circuit extended to the quay, on the *Gironde,* where he finally saw a sign for a car park. With little regard for conflicting tram traffic, he sheered right and tore down a ramp into the underground car park at the *Cité Mondiale,* which proved to be a fifteen minute trek away from his destination.

As a result, he arrived at the *Archives Départementales* at ten thirty and hurriedly gave his name along with the nature of his business to the receptionist, who sat behind a large rosewood counter. She made a call and advised that Monsieur Laroche would be along presently, which gave Fabian time to stand away and take in his surroundings. The place was fittingly quiet, but once again, he was struck by the modernity. Light coffee coloured stone and similarly coloured tiles adorned the walls and floor of the very large lobby, yet the ceiling was relatively low. A wide staircase went up to the first floor, where a sign directed visitors to the reading room. It felt more like the lobby of a modern and expensive boutique hotel.

A few minutes later, a stocky, grey haired man dressed in chinos and a black open-necked shirt appeared from the area behind the stairs and hurried towards Fabian, smiling. Since Fabian was the only person in the lobby, it was obviously Laroche, who recognised a priest when he saw one. They shook hands as the archivist said, "Good day Father, how are you?"

"Very well thank you and I'm extremely grateful to you for seeing me so promptly. I'm so sorry I am late."

The head archivist flapped his arms, "It is not a problem, but I think parking was for you, yes?

Fabian let his shoulders fall and nodded slowly. Laroche smiled, "First, let us adjourn to my office for a coffee. From there I will telephone Challans to find out where the files are. I suspect they'll be waiting for us, in the reading room."

Fabian savoured his coffee while Laroche dialled Challans's number, but there was no answer. He dialled again, in case he'd misdialled and finally, he tried another number in that department, which was answered promptly. He asked to speak with Challans and was told that the young man had gone home half an hour earlier, claiming to have a migraine.

Laroche asked if he'd left any files out for collection, or at least transferred the retrieval request to anyone in the office. The lady he'd been speaking to called out and came back on the line moments later, "I am sorry Monsieur, no one knows anything about it."

This was most embarrassing. The young fool should have at least delegated the job, instead of which, Laroche was confronted with the task of explaining things to this priest. He replaced the telephone receiver and chose not to prevaricate, "I am very sorry Father, but the young man I tasked with the file retrievals has gone home ill and nothing seems to have been done. How much time do you have this morning?"

Fabian brought the image of his diary page to mind, which confirmed that his next appointment wasn't until four that afternoon, with a couple he would be marrying in the near future, "I don't have to leave until three and would be quite prepared to miss lunch, if necessary."

"It won't be." Laroche said with some certainty, "But in the circumstances I will escort you and we will find these files together. He may have left them with the reading room staff, so we shall try there first. If not, we will go into the secure storage. We don't allow many into that area and I think you will find it interesting."

Fabian was delighted, "Thank you. I most certainly shall, and thank you for giving up your time like this."

The archivist threw up his hands, "It is the least I can do. But Monsieur Challans will receive censure when he finally gets over his *headache*."

Fabian sought to lighten the mood, "This is my first visit. It is a lovely building, but smaller than I imagined."

Laroche was startled, "But surely you know that it is huge. In fact, it is the number two archive in France, with seventy two kilometres of shelving."

So was Fabian, "That is an incredible amount of storage."

"But of course! We have records of many things, such as diplomatic, scientific, military, agricultural, artistic, films, genealogy, geology, geographic, the middle ages and before. The list is almost endless; in fact there is almost no limit." He seemed gratified by the look of surprise on his guest's face, but they had work to do, "We must make a start." He rose from his chair and gestured towards the door, "Please, follow me."

They returned to the lobby and climbed the stairs to the reading room, which further startled the priest. Laroche set off to make enquiries at the rosewood desks that lined part of the left hand side of the room, which was far larger than Fabian had expected. The walls were covered in a vellum paper to a height of around two metres, after which the surface was covered in closely laid thin laths of what might have been light oak. The ceiling was a startling white which was broken up along the side by triangular vaults.

But the real surprise was the number of large blue topped desks that were set in rows across the entire central area. Each was equipped with reading lights, power points and computer ports. There were perhaps twenty people sitting at desks, each surrounded by research material and notebooks.

He wandered into a relatively small area, to the right of the entrance and enclosed by tall bookshelves. A small office area had been established at the far end by the installation of a glass wall and the desk within was manned by a lady who was explaining something to a tall thin youth who was seated opposite. The shelves were full of archive catalogues, covering a huge range of subjects, such as Indo China and the First World War, but what was most noticeable was the absence of any reference to the period of German occupation during the Second World War. Specifically, the catalogues on offer to the public were for the period nineteen twenty seven to nineteen forty, the year of the French surrender to the Nazis.

His perusal was interrupted by Laroche, who looked vexed, "It is as I expected, that stupid young man did not do as I asked, nor did he have the presence of mind to pass my request on when he left. It is left to us I'm afraid."

Even the journey into the vaults was a fascinating transit through heavily sealed doors which helped to maintain constant levels of temperature and humidity. Fabian noticed signs everywhere that detailed the protocols to be followed for all sorts of contingencies, besides fire and yet he saw only a handful of people. Between the shooshes of doors and squeak of handles, the silence was almost complete.

Two floors up, they entered a short corridor that ended at a large grey metal door which Laroche unlocked by presenting his identification card to a scanner mounted on the wall and once inside Fabian recognised the format. It was just like the archives he'd seen in films and documentaries, with rows and rows of high banks of shelving; each end bearing reference letters and numbers. Laroche pointed at the visitor's pass around Fabian's neck, "That won't get you in *or* out of here, so don't get lost."

A middle-aged man, who might have been seen anywhere yet not noticed, was seated at a large desk next to the entrance. Even his clothing was neutral enough to remain unnoticed. He smiled warmly and extended a hand when he recognised Laroche, "Ah, Mathieu, hello, how are you? Nobody mentioned you were coming."

"I am well thank you, but this visit has become a surprise to me also. Tell me, did Challans sign anything out yesterday? I asked him to pull some files for me."

The guardian pursed his lips and shook his head, "Not while I've been here, but as you know, I leave at five thirty and there is no-one here at night anymore."

Laroche nodded sympathetically, before turning to the priest, "Cut backs you know, they are still going on all the time." He turned back to his colleague, "Still, I've never known Challans to be early, so I must assume that the task has been left undone." He passed a copy of the list over, "These are the ones I'm going after, so you will know where to find me."

Every single file was missing. The archivist checked, double-checked and even searched the neighbouring rows, in case they'd been put away carelessly, which was just as unthinkable as losing them. They went back to the desk and asked the man to see if the files had been signed out by anyone else, but of course they hadn't. The odds against that happening were extremely long. They returned to the shelving, where Laroche privately chided himself for checking the surfaces for marks left by other visitors. This, he reminded himself, was not a *James Bond* movie! Finally, he had to admit defeat, "I am so sorry Father, but none of those files are where they should be. There will be an explanation, I'm sure, there *has* to be. Files don't just disappear."

Fabian had his own views on the matter, which still seemed too fantastic to be true, but he reminded himself of the reason he was here. Crimes had been committed and the trail had prompted a call for these files. He asked, "So what now Monsieur?"

Laroche was now severely embarrassed, both professionally and personally, "I must initiate a search and once we find them, and we will, I can assure you, there will be an enquiry. This is most troubling."

Fabian sought to ease the man's discomfort. He'd been as helpful as he could, after all. Even so, he lied once more, "Please, Monsieur, I am sure you will find them soon too. Perhaps then, you could telephone me."

The archivist's mind was elsewhere when he said, "Yes, of course." He then thought to ask, "You mentioned a possible need for other files the other day. Do you know of any?"

Fabian checked his notes, "Actually, yes. I would quite like to see if you have a file for SS Obersturmführer Ernst Meyer; based here, in Bordeaux I believe. It would seem that he had dealings with the collaborators."

Laroche nodded, "That would make him Gestapo." He thought for a moment and then beckoned, "Please, follow me."

They walked for some distance until Fabian began to notice swastikas on the ends of index files and storage boxes. All of them were obviously old enough to be the originals. Finally, Laroche stopped and began his search. Having failed to find a specific file for the German he set to work on composite files, with nominal rolls for all manner of units. Knowing that he was an SS officer helped to reduce the scale of things but eventually he was beaten. There was little hope, as he explained, "No luck with this one either I'm afraid, for the moment. I will send someone down to cast a wider net, but the Germans destroyed so many files when they left you see."

Fabian made sure to sound sympathetic, "I understand, but I am also grateful for your time and effort."

At the lobby, Laroche took Fabian's pass and they parted

company with a mix of assurances and thanks. Both men walked away with quite different conclusions though.

****

The platters were astonishing. The specialists had even added the condiments and sauces they deemed appropriate, along with a complete salad. Annie and Sue led the way back to their car, followed by the butcher, baker, *charcutier, fromagier* and fishmonger, laden with platters and boxes, with the whole procession looking like something out of a Disney movie, involving two dowager sisters. These sisters would remain too stunned to fully appreciate the effort and thought that had gone into it all until they got home, though they did kiss each man on both cheeks when they parted.

Earlier that afternoon, just after lunch, Annie had a pressing matter to deal with. They had agreed that just one should call on their neighbour in case she felt outnumbered and handing bribes over called for a little discretion. Thankfully, Jean Claude was outside, chopping kindling, though he did pause to shake hands and bid her good day, after which he pointed towards the house and said, "My wife is in the kitchen."

Annie thanked him and headed that way. The great walrus moustache reminded her of the name Sue had given him. 'Whiskers'; it was so appropriate. She knocked on the door, which soon opened to a much friendlier welcome. Marie Ann kissed her on both cheeks and beckoned, "Welcome! Please, come and have a drink. A bottle of *Pineau* and four glasses had been left out on the side in readiness along with a tin of cheese pastries. Annie dived in while saying, "My sister will be disappointed at missing these."

Marie Anne was delighted, "Then you must take some back for her."

Annie grinned, "Provided I don't eat them all."

The host flapped a hand, "Poof! Then I shall make some especially for her and deliver them in secret."

They toasted each other and included one for new neighbours

generally but as soon they were over Annie pulled an envelope out of her pocket and pushed it across the table. "Forgive the haste; it is in case your husband came in."

Marie Ann looked at the envelope which bore the label, 'Monsieur Rotovator' and contained seven hundred Euros. As soon as the she comprehended its meaning the envelope was swept out of sight and hidden in one of the apron pockets. That was followed by one of Marie Ann's signature and infectious giggles. She raised her glass for another toast, "To all the fresh vegetables we shall share next summer." After a moment, she said, "To begin with, I thought it would be better to give the money to him."

Annie put a hand to her mouth, "Oh dear, I'd forgotten that."

"It is no matter. Now, I think it is better that he understands how we outnumber him."

***

The gang arrived a little earlier than the planned seven that evening and were joined shortly after by Anton, Penny and Tom. They were all impressed by the feast that had been laid out and the aromas emanating from the oven, none more so than their new Francophile, Carol.

Annie and Sue began by giving them a tour of the house, so that they could get down to the more serious matter of opening the wine bottles. Crates had been brought in from the garage to serve as seats for the unlucky, though if anything, they added to the atmosphere.

At one point, towards the end of the evening, mention was made of their flight home the next day and a time was agreed for the rendezvous at La Rochelle airport. Alan called out, "Well Adam seems keen enough to get back. He's already packed and his case is in the car."

Penny looked at Adam, "Don't forget the case, will you."

Adam nodded and then had the good grace to look embarrassed, "I was going to save this as a surprise, but I'm not going back tomorrow."

George's jaw dropped, "What?"

Alan said slowly, "Sneaky beaky!"

"Well, I don't have anything to go back for and Anton's promised to find me lots of jobs to do, so I decided to stay on for a couple weeks."

The room fell silent as the news spread and all eyes were on him. Eventually, he said, "I feel as though I've just farted in a flower shop."

Bob called over, "Can't fault you on that one mate."

Barbara asked, "Which one, the fart or for staying on?"

Alan asked, "Where are you going to stay?"

Penny answered that one, "We've managed to get one of the *gites* ready for him."

Alan said, with feeling, "Lucky sod."

Jayne dug him in the ribs, "There's too much for you to do at home, so don't get any ideas."

Annie stood up and called for attention, "Speaking of ideas, I've had one. I've been trying to think of a name for this group. Let's face it, 'The Waltham Parva Coffee Morning Group' doesn't do it, but last night a possibility did come to mind. Why don't we call ourselves 'Club Cognac'?"

There was no need for a vote; the cheer that went up was unanimous and closely followed by a noisy toast.

***

When he heard the car pull into the yard, Pichon rose from the chair by the fire and sat at the kitchen table, facing the door. There had been something in the young man's tone when he'd telephoned earlier, that might need to be addressed. As he pulled the cuff of his sleeve into place and placed the hand on the table he reasoned, all puppies needed discipline at some point. He knew he was right when Challans walked in without the files.

Pichon gestured to the seat at his side, "Please, come and sit."

The older man's courtesy was unexpected and disarming, for Challan's heart was racing and his mouth had dried in expectation of something much worse. He knew that the absence of files would be obvious, just as he knew that this terrible mess had to end tonight, no matter what the poisoned dwarf said or did.

The tone of Pichon's voice implied a degree of pragmatism, "So, the priest has the files." It wasn't a question.

The young man sat as directed and placed both hands on the table as he launched into the delivery he'd been rehearsing all day, "No, he hasn't and neither will you. I am ashamed of what I've done so far, but you may be sure that..."

Challans heard a howl of pain in the same moment he saw the knife sticking out of his hand, impaling it to the table. The mind-wrenching pain remained constant but the howl morphed into a high pitched keening until the next moment, when dark speckles covered his vision and he realised that the cries were his, just before he fainted.

The knife was still in place and his hand lay in a small pool of blood when he came to a few minutes later. He threw up, across the table and the scream returned when his movement caused the hand to twist on the blade.

Pichon made a sound of disgust but didn't move or speak until Challans reached for the knife with his free hand. The elder placed a single finger on the butt of the knife and said, "If you touch that knife I will assume that you intend to use it on me and I will use another knife to ensure that you don't."

Challans looked at the other man's eyes and saw nothing. There was no anger or emotion and certainly no sympathy. All he saw was a vacant stare that might have accompanied the wringing of a chicken's neck. He whimpered and tears began to flow.

Pichon was gratified by the sight. This little puppy would do as he was told in future.

∗∗∗

At around the same time, Father Fabian was addressing the same issue, in his telephone call to Phillipe Rambert. He detailed his conversations with the archivists and the abortive attempt to see the files.

Rambert was in his study at home but still spoke quietly, in case one of the girls listened in, "So are they carrying out a search?"

"Yes, of course, but it is too much of a coincidence for all of them to have been mislaid."

"Or perhaps it makes a great deal of sense. If they were removed for Pichon to see them, or copied for him, whoever was responsible may have thrown them back into storage in a careless manner. Don't you see, he or she might have deliberately misfiled them."

Fabian had been given longer to consider things and felt certain that the files had been taken, "Phillipe, that tactic would be treated as seriously as stealing the files and would be far riskier. Hiding or misfiling them would be a temporary solution only, whereas taking them would ensure that the contents would never be known. There is one important thing to note though."

"What is that?"

"No file could be found for Pichon."

"That doesn't prove anything. There may not have been a file in the first place."

Fabian took a moment to think around that one before, "Yes, that was stupid of me, I'm sorry."

Phillipe had a question of his own, "Don't they have a system where staff sign these files out and back in?"

"Yes, and I'm sure that the head archivist was troubled by that aspect. In any event, he's promised to keep me up to date."

"So, without a signature they have no way of knowing who the culprit is."

"Sadly, no; for what it's worth, the pompous junior I spoke to in the beginning was off ill that day, with a migraine."

"Aha, so there's our first suspect!"

"I don't believe so, on two counts. Firstly there's no evidence to support that allegation and secondly, if he was the culprit, he wouldn't do something as obvious as having sick leave on that particular day. These files were taken months ago, before Pichon contacted you, I'm certain of it."

Rambert wilted, "So what do we do now?"

"First of all, let's hope they find the files. I'll give the matter some more thought; perhaps the newspaper has record of something, though I doubt it. Jewish transports were kept out of the papers. Have you spoken to Michaud yet?"

"Er, no, not yet; I thought I'd wait to see what you found."

Fabian was suddenly disappointed and concerned, "Have you told Margot yet?"

"Well no, for the same reason."

The response was steely, "You promised to tell Margot last weekend and I take it that you haven't even made an appointment to go and see Michaud yet." Rambert began to say something but was cut short; the priest's anger evident, "This is treachery; not just against me but your family as well. If those files have been stolen and Pichon has been responsible for the things you claim, your family could be in danger. Do they mean so little to you?"

The question was gratuitous, but Rambert was stung by his friend's allegations, "I'm sorry. I have no excuse, I realise that." His voice dropped to a whisper, "Somehow, I know that once I tell Margot, the whole thing will become too real and too dreadful."

Fabian gave no quarter, "Promise me that you will tell Margot, now! Either that, or I walk away from this."

"Very well."

"Now, mark you, not tomorrow or next week."

The reply, "Yes, yes!" was said a little testily but Fabian hadn't finished, "And you're to go and see Michaud before the middle of next week. Somehow, we need to find more information."

For the moment, Rambert was a beaten man. He felt as though he was succumbing to threats from all sides, but those promises were made. There was nothing else to say for the moment and the call was ended. Margot waited until she heard him hang up before gently putting the receiver back into its cradle, in the kitchen. When he walked in, five minutes later he looked ashen and then, askance, at the two glasses of wine on the kitchen counter. Margot stepped forward and wrapped her arms around him. She whispered into his ear, "Come on my dear, it is time to share it." His head fell onto her shoulder and he wept.

Eventually, they returned to his study and sat close enough to hold hands as he told her everything.

When he finished, there were none of the recriminations he'd feared for so long. He should have known better and she told him so, for before motherhood, Margot's life had been spent dealing with crime and confronting threats. Suddenly, he felt able to talk freely about the nightmare and the steps they should take to stay safe. By bedtime he had even agreed to her most fervent demand. From that moment on, she was going to work equally closely with Fabian."

***

In spite of the smell of fresh paint in the *gite* and thanks to a firm mattress, Adam slept better than he'd hoped, which is how he came to be in Anton's kitchen in time for breakfast, or at least Sue's breakfast. The brisk walk had given him an appetite. Anton had been up for a long time but Adam found Sue slumped over a bowl of coffee, contemplating a couple of rounds of dry toast. At her invitation, he helped himself to one of the slices and began to add butter and jam while she made his coffee. She sat down and stared in disbelief as he stuffed his face with a sickly amount of jam. He noticed her look of horror and remarked cheerfully, "I must say, you look dreadful."

She returned her gaze to the mug of coffee and murmured, "Piss off."

Anton came in from the yard, "Bonjour Adam, we have lots to do I'm afraid."

"Don't be, I need the exercise and I have the time. I took so many 'doggy bags *and* bottles' home from the party I won't need to shop for the next few days." Sue recognised Anton's expression and while she provided a translation for 'doggy bag' Adam took the opportunity to snatch the second slice of toast. While ladling jam on to it he added, "Mind you, I have to go to the airport with the ladies first and hire a car."

Anton had considered lending his car to the chubby Englishman, but instinct told him otherwise and besides, if he did it for one he'd have to do it for any of the others who visited alone, "Yes, of course, then call in when you get back and we can discuss plans for tomorrow."

Later that morning, the sisters and Adam set off to meet the other members of Club Cognac at La Rochelle airport. Adam waved them off at the car hire cabin and stayed to organise his own transport, which proved to be a tiny red Citroen C1. He managed to fit behind the wheel, just, though he grumbled to himself, "I must look like '*Postman Pat*' in his van."

Check-in seemed lack lustre and security was enforced at a snail's pace, though no-one seemed to mind. They were still slightly hung over if truth be told.

After buying the coffees from the small snack bar George grumbled to his wife, "Adam scored one over on me there."

Amy looked at him quizzically, "What, are you saying you'd have stayed on too?"

"Bloody right I would have done," he mumbled.

She rolled her eyes, "Let's get you and your liver home."

Two tables away Bob sipped his hot chocolate and carefully set his cup down before daring to ask, "Well love, what do you think."

Carol's expression gave nothing away as she spoke, "I thought you'd never ask." He began to speak but she held up a hand, "If you mean 'what do I think about you setting off on this caper without me', I'd say you were still a shit."

"But you refused to consider it!"

She waved a hand in dismissal, "Whatever, you were a shit. On the other hand, if you're asking what I think about France it would be a different matter." She allowed a short pause before, "I love the place. The people have been lovely, the food and wine is incredible and the country itself is beautiful. I don't know how I could have been so wrong." Her expression hadn't changed; clearly mirroring her concern over such a mistaken set of beliefs.

Bob was secretly delighted but sought some gravity in his response, "You know, you are no different to many others. Perhaps it was our parents and theirs, or more likely it was our history teachers who taught us about the wars we've had with France. It's been a blighted sort of history after all."

She smiled, "Like sticking two fingers up at them at Agincourt?"

He chuckled, "Something of the sort, though when anyone talks to me about that sort of thing I remind them that the French were the last people to successfully invade us. There are differences though. Gallic pride for one thing and then there's the omnipotence of the average waiter. And don't forget the way they accept their President's promiscuity. It's almost as though they expect it of him. In the end, you must learn to love the differences."

She grinned then, "Speaking of which, their cheese is bloody good too." A thought suddenly occurred to her, "Who's sitting next to Barbara?"

"I have no idea, why?"

"Well Adam isn't here this time. If it's a Frenchman I hope he's broad minded!"

Adam's surprise news had unsettled the sisters too. Whilst there had been no mention of it, both were vexed at having to leave their new French home, five minutes after buying it, particularly when there was little to justify a return to the UK. As they flew over the French coast Annie leaned across to Sue, "I'm going to check flights out when we get back, so keep your diary to hand."

Sue gave a thumbs-up sign, "Sounds like a plan."

CHAPTER 10

Earlier, as he drove his hire car out of the airport, Adam was secretly delighted with himself. The prospect of some time alone was as welcome as the thought of some tuition in cognac making. A fifty-fifty mix would suit him down to the ground.

Adam's confidence was shaken twenty minutes after leaving the airport. He'd noticed a *Lidl* store on the way to the airport, just off the ring road, at the *Lagord* exit, which suited him perfectly. Three packs of biscuits, a bottle of wine, a bottle of scotch and a large pizza, along with cheese, crisps, butter and bread completed his 'feel good' requirements. He was a made up man, at least for the next couple of days. Although he'd boasted about the doggy bags, most of the buffet items looked stale, leaving him with just one bottle of filched wine.

He drove out of the car park in high spirits, which disappeared in the moment he saw the car heading straight for him. He couldn't believe his eyes until a brain cell, somewhere up there, responded to the adrenalin and advised him to get on to the right, or perhaps wrong, side of the road. The nose of approaching car dipped and the headlights began flashing as he swerved to the right, leaving just yards to spare. He caught a glimpse of a waving fist as the other car swept by, but by then he was more intent on yelling at himself, "Fuck's sake Harding, you're even in a left hand drive car you muppet!"

Two hours later he was sitting at Anton's kitchen table, discussing a work schedule for the next week, one that would hold surprises for both of them.

At seven that evening Penny called down to the *gite* and asked he was OK for food and stuff. He stepped to one side and gestured towards the table where the remains of a pizza lay, "Voila! La dolce vita, but thanks for asking."

She chuckled, "Multi-lingual no less; inspired by the choice of food no doubt. Still, make sure you look after yourself and if there's anything you need, ask!"

He snapped to attention and clicked his heels together, "Ja wohl."

Her grin confirmed that no offence had been taken at his gratuitous use of another language. Instead she waved it off with, "Now you're just showing off. I'll just go back and brush up on my Serbian for tomorrow night; if you would like to join us for a meal that is."

Guinness shouldered past at that point, causing him to lose balance and spill a small amount of wine. While shuffling a foot over the red spots on the tiled floor he said, "Can't I'm afraid. I called in on Anton earlier and one of my first jobs tomorrow will be shopping for a meal he's cooking for us; perhaps another night?"

Penny growled at the dog, who was sitting beside the table, looking earnestly at the edge of a plate that was still laden with wondrous scents, "Guinness, where are you manners?" She looked at Adam and shrugged, "Sorry about that, you know what they say, 'a dog with an appetite has no conscience'."

Adam laughed out loud at that, "I'm sure I've heard something of the sort."

"OK, so would the next night be any good?"

It was. Meanwhile, Guinness studiously ignored Penny's call for an exit. His tail made great sweeps across the floor when Adam approached the table, but those big brown eyes stared in disbelief as the human pushed the plate out of sight and said something that was recognised as very negative, before pointing at the door. Clearly hurt beyond measure, Guinness finally responded to his mistress's calls and dawdled towards the door.

***

Challans didn't get home until nearly midnight, to find his young wife waiting anxiously. He'd been acting strangely of late and was clearly worried about something, but unwilling to talk about it. That night he'd been particularly nervous and had left the house without a word, until finally, he'd returned, with a bandaged hand.

She ran towards him but he backed away and held out his good hand in defence, "Please, don't come near it!" He nodded towards the injured hand, held up against his chest, defensively, "It's agony."

"What's happened? Where have you been?"

He'd had long enough at the hospital to come up with a story; one that was a blend of truth with fiction, but first, he needed to sit down and administer some self medication, "Please, my love, would you get me a cognac, a large one and then I'll tell you about it."

It didn't take long for the alcohol to take effect, mixed as it was with painkillers. His wife sat beside him on the sofa, trying to offer some comfort by stroking the good arm. Eventually, he began, "A man paid me to get some information out of the archives." He heard her gasp and hurried to reassure, "It wasn't anything to be concerned about; just some wartime material that hasn't been released yet. It was personal to him I think and we needed the money."

That much was true. Their son had been conceived sooner than they had planned and the loss of a wage had been a shock. Cynically, he allowed a few moments for that to register before continuing, "He asked, no *ordered* me to visit him this evening and when I refused, he threatened to report me. What could I do? Without my earnings we'd be on the street."

"So you went to see him."

He nodded, "I was right to be concerned. He wanted more information and this time I refused. He came at me with a knife and I held up my hand in defence. After that it all became a blur. Somehow, I must have pushed him away and got out of the house. Then I drove straight to the hospital."

This was so out of character, unlike anything she would expect of him, "What about the police? Have you reported it to them?"

"No! We *must* keep them out of it."

"But that's ridiculous! The man tried to kill you! Who is he anyway?"

"You don't need to know his name; it's enough to know he's dangerous."

She began to feel angry, "That is *why* I need to know his name. Our son is upstairs and this pig tried to make an orphan of him. What if he comes after us?"

"He won't, I'm sure."

"Well I'm not so sure and I have a right to know." Another thought occurred to her, "The hospital will have reported a knife wound to the police, surely?"

He shook his head, "I told them that I was holding a beef joint while you were boning it and the knife slipped."

She huffed, "And they believed you?"

"No, I don't think so, but they couldn't prove otherwise."

"But why did you say I did it? You could have been using the knife yourself."

The imagery of the attack swept over him as he explained, "The entry was through the back of my hand and out of the palm. I couldn't have done that to myself."

Later, she would realise the measure of his horror, but for the moment she was more concerned about an ongoing threat. They argued for another hour, until finally she stood and turned back towards him with an expression he'd never seen before, "Keep his name secret then, but if he comes near me *or* our son, I'll never want to see you again." With that she went to bed.

He waited for half an hour before following her and they both lay in bed, awake and frightened. She feigned sleep, until he began to weep. It wasn't just the pain. There was much more. Her anger melted away as she sat up and took him in her arms.

In time, he gasped, "I haven't told you everything, I'm so sorry. I've been so stupid."

They stayed there, in each other's arms, as he began his story again, without the fiction.

When it was over, she pulled the files out of his wardrobe and dropped them onto the bed, "These are what he's prepared to knife people for; so do we give them to him or report the matter?"

Moments passed as he considered the options. Finally, he said, slowly, "If I report it, we're finished but if we give those to him, I honestly think it will be over. After what he's done I think he'll realise that it's over. I can't be pushed any further."

She nodded, "Then let's do that."

"When?"

"Now of course."

Their infant son was bundled into his car seat and they set off in the small hours.

Pichon always slept deeply and rose early. People like him were not burdened with a conscience, but he was startled to find a bundle of files on his doorstep, until he reasoned that the puppy would have been too frightened to meet up again so soon. There was an envelope taped to the top file, that contained the message;

This is the end of it. I will have nothing more to do with you.

Pichon screwed the note up and sneered, "You pathetic puppy. I will say when you're finished with."

He glanced through the documents over breakfast and then took a box of matches from the table drawer. Minutes later, in the yard, he set light to one of the pages and murmured; "Now *this* is how to close files." At that moment, as the flames appeared he was chilled by his stupidity; if the files didn't exist there would be nothing to support the hold he had over Rambert. He clutched the files tightly and returned to the house where there were plenty of hiding places. In the meantime, he would wait in the kitchen for the labourers to arrive for work.

He couldn't have known that just four years later, in two

thousand and fifteen, all the files for that period would be released into the public domain and the webs of interconnected documents would still be capable of incriminating him and his father.

Back at their house, on the outskirts of Bordeaux, the Challans's now had their own agenda, born out of a newfound unity. They didn't have any appetite for breakfast, though their son was fractious after such a disturbed night. Eventually, he settled down to eat a fruit compote while his parents drank strong coffee. They both reasoned that Pichon would back off now that he'd received the files and particularly since Challans had shown resistance, even though the encounter had been dreadful. Nevertheless, there was a point where an unwilling accomplice became wilful enough to be a risky one. But the other contingency had to be addressed. If he came after any of them they needed some form of protection, short of involving the authorities.

His wife left the room and returned with a pen and pad, "We must write everything down, from the very beginning."

Challans was horrified, "What, you mean a confession? Because that is what it will amount to."

"If anything happens to you there'll be no need to worry about that." Her eyes filled as the enormity of the thing swept over her, "We will write the whole thing down and leave it with our lawyer. Then, if Pichon harms *any* of us he will have instructions to pass it on to the police."

Challans considered the option for a few minutes before nodding, "Very well, it is the least I can do, having put us in this predicament."

It took an hour to complete the report, after which he telephoned the office to say that he wouldn't be in that day. He didn't offer an explanation, so it was assumed that he still had a migraine. In reality, his hand was aching terribly and he was exhausted. While he went to bed his wife dressed their son and drove into the city to deposit their meagre measure of protection with the lawyer. In truth, she realised, it was more a retaliation than defence.

***

Adam realised that he'd not purchased anything for breakfast and therefore hurried to shower, dress and head for Anton's kitchen once again. Later, he would swear that the bloody hound had been waiting for him to appear. As he entered the courtyard, Guinness wandered out from behind the hire car and cocked his leg beside the rear wheel; staring at Adam for the time it took to empty a full bladder. With that done, he trotted off towards the house.

Adam had stopped and watched in astonishment, but as the dog moved away he called out, "I'll piss in your basket tomorrow night, you vandal!"

He couldn't feel anger though. In fact, on the walk up to Anton's he reasoned that if their roles had been reversed, he'd have wanted to do the same. That animal was beginning to appeal to him.

Truth be told, he was not much of a *people* person. In fact, there were moments, usually accompanied by a bottle, when he acknowledged the painful truth that he'd more in common with villains than he did with the rest of society. That was a generalisation of course, that didn't sit easily with his membership of 'Graham's Gang' but that was hardly a fair example he told himself. Those folk were special friends and would always be so. Beyond them though, he derived a certain comfort from knowing what to expect from villains. The lines in the sand were unequivocal while the traps that lay in wait at cocktail parties and committees were far more treacherous.

In fact, Adam and Anton had that much in common, though Anton's isolation was less welcome and far more difficult to explain.

He had a few friends; close enough to share an evening with, but none that could be regarded as 'best' and his past relationships with women had been enjoyable but short, for the most part, until the disaster of a marriage robbed him of both faith and confidence in that department. He also feared and failed at small talk when forced to attend functions, yet was lucid and interesting when he was on his own property, talking about the things he loved. Until Sue arrived he'd hidden his loneliness behind daily interactions with visitors, who were charmed by his kindly wit.

Adam had expected to meet Henri, the employee, at the breakfast table but Anton reminded him it was Saturday, before adding that there were no days off for owners, or volunteers. After breakfast, Anton gave Adam the shopping list and directions to the preferred store, though there was more. He held up a finger, "But first, I must show you how to look after the still. We have a lot of visitors on Saturdays and while I give them tours, perhaps you will keep an eye on the distillation."

Adam was startled, "that's a lot of responsibility for the new boy isn't it?"

"Noooo, it is simple, you will see. She is very easy to watch. I will tell you what to look for and when to call for me." He was amused by Adam's look of concern, "Come, follow me. This will be your first day as a cognac *distillateur's* apprentice"

The passages between the rows of barrels were cold and the warm ambience of the still room was welcome. The light purring of the gas flames encased in the brick dais, supporting the pot and the fumes it gave off were both soothing. Anton began with, "Now, my friend, you are no longer a tourist. I must be more technical." He pointed at the balloon-shaped pot, "That is an *Alambic Charentais*. It is nearly as old as me."

Within ten minutes, Adam knew all that he needed to. The temperature was shown on a digital display, mounted on the wall beside the pot still, which was connected by pipe work to a large copper condensation tank. At the other end of the apparatus a constant flow of clear liquid was being delivered by a small pipe onto a filter dish that had been set into the opening of an oak barrel that lay on its side. He'd already sampled the stuff, known as l'eau de vie, on an earlier visit and chose not to repeat the experience so early in the day. At around seventy per cent proof it left an enduring burn. His job would entail regular visits to check on the temperature, flow and specific gravity of alcohol and the level in the receiving barrel. The last measure was by means of a piece of timber Anton had left standing in the corner, behind the door. He casually wiped the cobwebs off the lower end before removing the bung from a second hole and sinking it into the barrel.

When Adam asked how the barrel, once full, was moved to the store, Anton explained, "Ah now that is a good question. We have to make sure the bung is tight and then we roll it to the doorway. But we have to stand it up to get it through, into the store. It is very hard and we have to work quickly, because the still, she is still working."

Adam looked apprehensively at the wide barrel and then the narrow doorway, before turning back to Anton who wore an inscrutable half smile. It took just a few moments to realise that he'd fallen for something. He began to speak but Anton interrupted, "Ah, but since it's your first day, why don't we stick a pipe into this barrel and pump the eau de vie into another barrel, which is waiting patiently, in the store."

Adam dropped his gaze and shook his head. He'd fallen for it like a fifteen year old apprentice, "I can think of somewhere else we could stick a pipe."

Anton was obviously enjoying himself, "Perhaps, but first, you must do the shopping. The visitors will be arriving soon! Next week, I will show you how to flush the still out and refill it with wine."

Adam was back by around ten thirty, but there was already a group of seven or eight being shown around. By the time their tour was over another group had assembled beside the office and looked on as samples were poured before purchases were made. There was a holiday atmosphere to the proceedings, in which folk didn't mind waiting and when it was their time, cheerfully bought more cognac than intended. It appeared that many had been before and were introducing others this time.

Anton asked Adam if he would mind joining a couple of the tours, which is how he came to learn that many were English. It was obvious that Anton saw a tour guide in the making, which would have terrified Adam normally, but after a couple of tours he became emboldened by the sampling and charmed by the guests. He kept breaking away to check on the distillation, but by five that day, when Anton broached the subject of acting as a guide, Adam agreed.

"Thank you, that is good. You will take the English and Americans and I will still handle the sales, but it will give me a chance to catch up on the paperwork." With a wink, he added, "That Annie, she is *formidable* you know."

Anton had been quite specific with the shopping list, even to the extent of which chicken quarters to buy, "The back pieces, with legs. That is where the flavour is." That evening his guest looked on from the other side of the kitchen table and behind a wine glass while Anton chatted away, as he threw ingredients into pans in what looked like a casually haphazard manner.

The last group of the day had been French, and none could speak a word of English, so Adam sat in the cosy warmth of the still room and dozed. Now, he asked, "Where were they from?"

Anton waved a hand dismissively, "Ah, they were from the Vendee, *'ventruchou'.*" He grinned, "That is the name we give them. It means cabbage belly." After a moment he continued, "People from here, the *Charentais,* are known as *cagouillard.* It is the old French word for *escargot*, you know, the snail. That is because we are late for everything, in fact very late, so people say we move like the snail."

Adam thought he'd make a note of that and entertain the club members, when the opportunity arose. As if on cue, Anton said, "What is the name of the liquid we have from the first distillation." The blank look on Adam's face was enough. A small notebook and pen appeared, "Here, you must keep notes. It is called *Brouillis*." He waited until the pen was poised before spelling it.

Adam wrote it down carefully, "While you're at it, would you spell the cabbage belly thing and the word for snail please."

"Certainly, but put those at the back of your book. They

have nothing to do with cognac. Speaking of which, what is the name of the *second* distillation."

"Ah, I know that one, it's *l'eau de vie*."

Anton conceded that one, albeit with pursed lips, "That is the product, yes, but after *Brouillis* we call the next distillation *La bonne chauffe*. Go ahead, I will spell it."

After writing it down carefully, Adam asked, "How long does it take to distil all the wine?"

"We must finish on the thirty first of March, whether there is wine left or not; it is the law. Let me explain. The first of April is the cognac's birthday, in all of France. So this year's distillation is year nought and on the first of April next year it will be one years old. From there we have the names; VS stands for 'Very Special', which is after two and a half years in the barrel. VSOP is 'Very Superior Old Pale' after at least four and a half years in the barrel and XO is 'Extra Old' or 'Napoléon'. That is after six and a half years. Finally, there is 'Hors d'*â*ge' which means 'beyond age'. That is very high quality and beyond the official age scale."

Adam asked, "So that would be your forty year old."

Anton held both hands up, "But of course!"

With what appeared to be little effort, Anton produced chicken pieces, with crispy skins, laced with a rich orange and mustard sauce, accompanied by baby potatoes and sautéed fennel. A bottle of dry Muscat was a perfect choice of wine. When the plates were cleared, and a baguette and platter of cheeses were set down Adam sat back in his chair, "Phew, that was incredible, thank you."

Anton shrugged, "It was nothing. Tomorrow perhaps, you can do the meal."

With ill-concealed relief, Adam remembered the prior engagement, "Can't, sorry; Penny and Tom have invited me over for a meal."

"Then you could do it on Monday."

"Ha, in that case it'll be pizza."

"Nonsense, if you love food cooking is easy. What is your favourite dish?"

Adam thought for moment before, "Actually, I'm quite partial to hot dogs; the sort you can find in America."

Anton's jaw dropped and then he grinned; "Now you are having fun with me!" The apprentice's expression told him otherwise, "Oh dear, there is much to do. On Monday, I will buy the ingredients and you can cook dinner."

Adam rose early on Monday, in the knowledge that he still hadn't bought anything for breakfasts and certainty that he would be welcome to share with Anton once more.

When he arrived, his host was seated at the kitchen table with an elderly man who looked up with dark brown eyes and a doleful expression that would have suited a bloodhound. A weathered, lined face, grey, bushy walrus moustache and black beret were so typically French it might have been called a cliché. Anton made the introductions in French, in which Adam only recognised his own name and Henri stood and shook hands, before returning to the conversation they had been having. At the same time, Henri spread jam onto pieces of bread before dunking them into a bowl of fragrant hot chocolate. It looked delicious.

Five minutes later, the old man held up the bowl and drained it noisily, before standing and with a nod to the *Anglais,* made his exit. When Anton asked Adam what he'd like for breakfast he pointed at the empty bowl, "That looked good."

"Ah, the *chocolat chaud* - a good choice." A bowl of hot chocolate, slices of fresh bread and a jar of strawberry jam were accompanied with instructions, "Put the jam on your bread and dip it into you *chocolat,* but without haste. Allow the jam to soften, so that a little stays in the bowl, then when it is nearly empty, the result is very sweet."

In that moment, Adam realised how different the coming week would be from all he'd seen so far. Previous visits had either been out of hours or by special arrangement, whereas now he was discovering a truly authentic experience. He began to explain that to Anton, but was interrupted by the telephone. It was obviously an English caller, making arrangements to visit and Anton closed off with, "Cash is good." As if further confirmation was called for, he rolled r's when adding, "Readies!"

Half an hour later Adam was given a set of overalls before being directed to the area one of the group had called the silo room. One long wall was filled with huge stainless steel fermentation tanks; perhaps fifteen feet tall and three square concrete tanks, which filled the end wall. Each had an oval hatch at knee level and as Anton unclipped one he explained, "The top hatch has been open for a day now, but there will still be carbon dioxide in there, so you must work from out here this morning, then this afternoon you will be able to climb inside and rinse the walls."

Adam cut in, "No I won't." When Anton turned to look at him quizzically Adam placed his hands on his hips, "Look at me! I'd make a better bung for that hole."

Anton stepped back and made a visual assessment before agreeing, "It is true. Too many hot dogs I think. Very well, you do the first bit and I will go inside." With that, he bent and shouldered the cover into the tank then twisted it, so that oval form could be removed. He passed a plastic shovel to Adam before pointing at the dark must inside the tank and a large plastic bin on casters, "Now we must remove the must and put it into the bin, there are others outside. Remove as much as you can, but do not go inside."

Adam said, "So this is rubbish then."

"Oh no, we sell it to be used to make oil, colouring and cosmetics." As he spoke, a lump of the dark mass fell away and landed on the concrete floor with a squelch. They both considered it as Anton continued, "I have to go out for an hour so when you finish this one it is OK to do these along here, but do not touch the three to your left; they are still full." He patted Adam on the shoulder, *"Bonne chance!"*

It took two hours to clear the first tank, a task made more difficult by the cone shape of the base and Adam was exhausted, but with that came a curious exhilaration. Not only was the work light years from anything he'd done before, but he relished being left alone to do it. It felt like an act of faith on Anton's part. While checking the distillation, a glance at the clock reminded him that Anton's hour had become two and there was still no sign of him. Perhaps the epithet *cagouillard* was appropriate. In the meantime, the sweating apprentice was covered in must and smelling like a young wine, so instead of going to the kitchen for a drink he slaked a dreadful thirst from a tap on the outside wall. By the time Anton did return, a third of the second tank had been emptied, though Adam sagged back against the steel while Anton offered praise, along with an invitation to lunch.

***

"I would like to speak to Monsieur Rambert."

The bank clerk noted the absence of 'please' but responded politely, "Do you have an appointment Monsieur?"

"No."

"Then I am afraid it is impossible. I can make an appointment for you."

"Tell him that Monsieur Pichon wishes to have a word with him."

She began to rail against this man's attitude and tone, but on the other hand, he could be a friend of the manager. After an eloquent pause she said, "One moment, I will check."

The man's presence here, in the bank, felt like an assault, but Rambert still recognised a pressing need to cloak the matter in secrecy, "Very well, I will see him in the interview room. Give me five minutes."

It was a pathetic gesture, but he let the oaf wait for fifteen before going downstairs. Pichon was seated in the waiting area, still dressed like a peasant. He stood as Phillipe approached and held out a hand which Phillipe ignored. Instead, he used his ID card to open the door to an interview room and gestured for the man to enter. They sat on opposite sides of the desk and Phillipe placed his pad and pencil down before speaking, "What do you want."

Pichon turned his mouth down and shrugged, "A little civility from my bank manager perhaps?"

Civility was no longer a requirement. Phillipe repeated his question.

The would be nemesis leaned forward and placed his arms on the desk, "That fool Michaud thinks he's solved everything by letting these English interfere, but they will be lightweights. In time and with a few 'incidents', they will run away like scalded cats. In the meantime, you will let me have copies of Michaud's statements and any correspondence your bank has with him."

"You know that I can't do that."

Pichon sneered, "I know that you will!" He lied, "I now have more names, not all of them yet, but enough to make sure that the World will want to learn about your papa's treachery. People here may not care so much about the Jews, but they still mourn those who were in the resistance. Today's adults were the kids your father made into orphans. Think on, you shit. The stench is still carried by the Ramberts and besides, you've already broken enough rules here to have a spell in prison. What would your wife and pretty daughters think of you then?" He stood, "Just do it, then no-one need know."

***

Adam removed the overalls and went home to put his trousers, shirt and underpants into soak, in a vain attempt to remove the stains. A hot shower eased his aching back and then it was time to return, as the *Chef du jour.*

Anton had bought a piece of pork loin which was to be accompanied by an apple and calvados sauce. Baby potatoes and buttered baby carrots would complete the dish. Once again Adam sought to duck the responsibility but was reminded of his position, "You are an apprentice my friend, in all things French I think."

Instructions were given and accepted sullenly, before Anton slipped off to pump out the barrel of l'eau de vie. When he returned, the sliced loin was seared badly and Adam had thrown the flour, butter and calvados directly into the stock. The Frenchman took one look at the lumpy mass and cried out, "No, no, no, you are not mixing cement!" He took a closer look and asked, "Where are the apples?"

Adam looked in too, before, "Shit, I forgot those."

Anton took everything off the heat and hurried to the freezer for a pack of Toulouse sausages, which he began to defrost in the microwave. His apprentice looked on silently as his mentor stared at the revolving plate. How could anyone, he thought, destroy food so readily. Finally though, his horror gave way to comedic disbelief and he began to laugh, "I didn't believe that anyone could be as bad as that."

Adam huffed, "Well now you know."

Anton turned, "OK, so now we will start again and I will stay with you."

"Not a good idea mate. Why don't you do the cooking and I'll do the washing up?"

"No! If a person can eat, they should be able to cook. Trust me, I will show you how. I think you must have spent too much time being a policeman and eating junky food."

"Junk."

"*Pardon?*"

"It's junk, not junky. Junky is what we call...., never mind."

Reluctantly, Adam began to cook again, under close supervision. This time apples and onions were sliced and sautéed in butter, while the sausages were fried in a separate pan then placed in the oven to keep warm. For the first time in his life, he made a roux and successfully thickened the reduced white wine, stock and calvados, into which the other ingredients were placed in a wonderfully fragrant *mélange*. Meanwhile, Anton took pity and cooked the vegetables; though he made sure to include instruction in that too.

Finally, they sat down to a truly memorable meal. Both were delighted and toasted each other generously.

When the time came for coffee and cognac they both become

unusually garrulous, to the extent that Adam's usual caution gave way to the alcohol. He looked down at the cognac glass rather than his new friend as he asked, "Do you want to hear a story. You may not believe it, but trust me, every word is true."

Anton waved a hand, "Please, tell me."

Adam seemed to sober up a little as he took an audible breath, "You see, it all began when I arrested a guy called Graham Parsons, who we thought had abducted a child; turned out that he'd saved the kid's life."

Apart from an occasional need for clarity in the translation, Anton listened to the story for two hours in silent wonder. At the end they had both been sobered. Anton had come to know the chubby ex-detective well enough to believe him while for Adam, it was another catharsis; shared only with people he could trust. Instinctively, he'd always known Anton was such a person. He closed with, "That's not the lot by any means, but I've covered the main ground."

There had been sadness but Anton had laughed out loud at the anecdotal tales of Graham's calamities and he'd taken particular delight at the jailbreak orchestrated by *Hell's Angels*. He said, "That is a very fantastic story." But then saw the expression that appeared on Adam's face and hurried to reassure, "I believe you my friend, because it is too strange to be fiction, but you describe Graham as such an ordinary sort of man, yet his adventures were incredible!"

Adam stared over Anton's shoulder as he allowed his mind's eye to picture the man, "He was more than I can say. His gentle kindness affected everyone around him. Until then, I didn't believe that one man could love another in a non-sexual sense, apart from one's father and siblings, but now I know differently." After a short pause, he shook his head, as if to clear the images and said, "Anyway, it's time I let you get to bed."

"Absolutely, will you be here for breakfast again?"

"If you don't mind?"

"Not at all, in fact that will fit with my plans for you. *Bonne nuit,* until tomorrow."

***

Margot Rambert took one look at her husband's face as he arrived home to know that the girls needed to be sent up to their rooms, to watch television.

When she joined him at the kitchen table and placed a glass of wine within reach she suddenly realised that the man she loved had grown visibly older in the recent months. Worry lines had appeared and a spark had been extinguished; in fact, his whole demeanour had changed.

As she spoke she experienced the white heat of intense hatred, "What has he done?"

"He came to the bank today, without an appointment, and demanded to speak with me. I saw him, of course; I couldn't afford not to."

"What did he want?"

"He still wants to destroy Michaud. This time he's told me to send copies of any correspondence we have with Michaud and the bank statements."

Margot gasped and put a hand to her mouth, as an ex-bank auditor she knew how many laws would be broken by those acts, "My God, surely not."

Phillipe took a great gulp if wine, "He said that he now had names of the resistance members my father caused to be arrested."

She noted the avoidance of the words 'shot' or 'transported' and spared him from any further discussion on that subject. But there were so many questions she needed to ask, not least of all, where the man was getting his information from. She didn't doubt that it was by illegal means. In the meantime, she asked, "Did you agree to do it?"

Phillipe sighed, "He didn't wait for a response; just took it as read that I would."

Every tack her mind took threw up more concerns; amongst them the new people that were involved, "What about the English, if ever they find out there will be hell to pay."

Phillipe answered a little testily, "You don't think I know

that!" His tone softened quickly, "Listen my dear, an international scandal would extend the bank's embarrassment, perhaps, but they can only ruin me once. For the sake of you and the children I've begun to think there is only one way out of this."

She backhanded him across the face, with enough force to knock the glass of wine out of his hand. Neither had ever raised a hand to each other before, but now Margot began to hyperventilate as she spoke, "Never! Never even think like that again. Do that out of either cowardice or misguided love and we will hate you for the rest of our lives!" She stared down at the table while trying to get her breathing under control.

Silently, Phillipe walked over to the cupboard under the sink for a dust pan and brush. Once the glass had been collected, he used a damp cloth to wipe up the wine.

Margot sat in shock. She hated violence of any sort, but she had never known fear and anger like this before either. The silence was broken by the tiniest whimper and she turned to see the man she loved standing at the sink, supporting himself on straightened arms as his shoulders shook. She leapt to her feet, all anger gone as she wrapped her arms around him and gently shushed. He soon stopped weeping and turned to hug his wife. Eventually, she fetched another glass of wine and rubbed his back with her spare hand, "Here, take this into the sitting room and let me think alone. I can do that *and* cook."

He smiled and kissed her, "I love you very much."

Their meal was a quiet affair; even the girls sensed enough to stay quiet and neither parent had much of an appetite, but afterwards, Margot signalled for Phillipe to stay back in the kitchen while the girls watched television in the sitting room.

She made coffees and sat down opposite him, "We need to take action Phillipe. Up until now we have accepted the roles of victims, just like the Jews he claims your father exposed."

He was stung by such a direct reference to his father's acts, but the time for arguing was over, "What do you suggest."

"We need to close the loop, or at least part of it." She noted his puzzled look and continued, "Until now we've been out on a limb. Pichon's made sure of that by threatening you with exposure. In response you've been too afraid to mention it to anyone, apart from me and Fabian, by which time you were in so deep you'd lost the will to swim." She took a deep breath, "To begin with, you must do as Fabian asked and go to see Monsieur Michaud."

"What good will that do, other than act as a salve to my conscience?"

"Don't you see, he is part of this whole thing, whether he realises it or not. For all we know, he may be privy to something we don't know, but what's important for now is that we need allies. You said yourself that Michaud is a nice man. If he's as decent as you say we may have an ally in him."

Phillipe doubted that very much, given the facts, but he also realised that the meeting was inevitable, "Just how much do you suggest we tell him?"

"I don't know until we get there. It will be a judgement call at the time."

"Listen my dear; I dare only tell Michaud some of the truth. Fabian agreed that I should go and see Michaud to apologise and explain that the circumstances were out of my control."

"Be that as it may, if there is any hint of him knowing about the other side of things we *must* develop that. For all we know, Pichon's been just as evil to him."

Phillipe remained sceptical, "I'm not sure. It would require some delicacy." A thought struck him, "Wait a minute, you said 'we'"

She nodded, "That's right, I'm coming with you."

***

Henri stood to shake hands and say *bonjour* before returning to his *de rigueur* bowl of hot chocolate, though he did smile encouragingly on seeing that Adam was going to breakfast in like manner.

They had obviously finished with their day's planning, which had included Adam. Anton explained, "I think that today you should learn a little of what we do on the land. Henri will explain everything and show you what to do."

That, Adam thought, would be a challenge, but he didn't say so.

They found a pair of wellingtons and a heavy jacket that fitted, before he followed them out to Henri's van. It was covered in so many blotches of rust it looked scabrous and both wing mirrors were missing. The door hinges screeched in protest before he clambered into the passenger seat and while Anton gave Henri some further instructions Adam tried to locate his seat belt before discovering that it had been used to secure a plastic drum, filled with fluid, behind his seat. With a mental shrug, he reasoned that they would only be travelling a short distance, at the pace to be expected from an old man.

The old man in question eventually climbed in behind the wheel and they were off! Adam tried to return Anton's wave, but was pinned back into his seat as they shot out of the yard without any regard for passing traffic. The man drove like a lunatic, missing an oncoming oil tanker by millimetres, when neither driver showed any sign of slowing. Nothing was said, for obvious reasons, but Adam sat straight legged for the whole journey, bracing himself for the worst, until finally, they turned off the road into the vines. There, Henri slowed to a snail's pace, out of respect for his charges. Soon after, they stopped and Henri signalled for Adam to get out, while releasing the misused seatbelt.

The rear doors were opened and Henri handed over a large copper tank with leather straps on one side and the word *Meteor* embossed on the other. A handle on one side was obviously intended to be used by the occupant of the straps, to presumably influence what happened with the tube and spray gun that projected from the opposite side. Henri pulled one of two twenty litre water containers to the edge along with the tank that had been behind Adam's seat. Both had taps and with a mix of wholly unintelligible French, eloquent hand signals and a measuring jug, he was shown how to mix the weed killer correctly. That much he learned after Henri had moved to a nearby row of vines and after pointing at the ground, repeated several times, "*Mauvaises herbes.*"

Adam repeated it and nodded; he'd learned the French for weeds. After that, everything made sense. His tutor scored lines in the ground to show the width of the treatment area, which was a little less than a metre and pointed to some distant vines which must have been treated much earlier, for the bands of dying weeds were evident. Henri helped him into the straps that dug into his shoulders, which in turn sagged, as the twenty five or so kilos made their presence known. After a little more guidance Henri was satisfied and he set off on his own schedule.

They met up again half an hour later, when a refill was called for. By then Henri had moved the van across to the other side of the field, which was bordered by a small lane. Instead of helping him get back into the straps Henri beckoned for him to follow and trudged off along the lane. After a few hundred metres he stopped and pointed at a piece of granite that had been set into the verge. It was in the middle of nowhere and obviously a memorial, but someone had trimmed the surrounding grass and kept the polished face clean. The inscription was in French but Adam recognised the letters RAF and used his mobile telephone to take a picture after which Henri nodded, as though to say, 'there you go' and headed back to the field.

At twelve prompt, after a sixth tank of weed killer, Henri approached and signalled for him to stop. They walked back to the van where assistance was needed to remove the tank. Adam's back ached but the narrow shoulder straps had chafed terribly, in spite of the heavy jacket. His shoulders burnt to such an extent that he couldn't face an afternoon of that work. Henri signalled with hand motions that it was time to eat and in response, Adam managed to signal that perhaps he should go back to the house. Henri glanced at the parcel on his seat, containing half a baguette, a measure of garlic sausage and a piece of cheese before nodding emphatically, "*Oui!*"

Since an offer of a lift wasn't made, or for that matter wanted, Adam set off on foot. Twenty minutes later he fell into his chair at the table with a great sigh, "I am fucked."

Anton chuckled, "You mean *Je suis baisée.* We must begin to teach you French also, I think. In the meantime, you had better wash your hands; that weed killer is nasty stuff you know."

Adam remembered the granite memorial and retrieved the picture he'd taken, "Henri showed me this; would you mind translating it for me please?"

Anton took the phone and peered closely at the small image until Adam showed him how to enlarge it. As soon as that was done the Frenchman said, "Ah, Henri takes great pride in that. It reads;

To the glory and memory of the aviators of the RAF, dead for France, pursuing peace and liberty. They were six young men aboard a Lancaster bomber beaten down on the fifteenth of August nineteen forty three."

Adam pictured the nightmare of parachuting out of a crippled plane into occupied territory, until a thought occurred to him, "Seems a strange place for a bomber to crash."

Anton considered that for a few seconds before replying, "Is there ever a sensible place to crash?"

In spite of the nagging discomfort to his back and shoulders, lunch was as lovely as ever, though Adam did wonder how Anton would receive his request for lighter duties. His anxiety was unfounded, since Anton had already decided to give his apprentice the afternoon off, though as things turned out he needn't have worried about his aching back. Fate was about to deliver a host of other things to worry about.

At two o'clock prompt, the telephone rang.

Anton answered in his usual way but it was the pause that followed that alerted Adam, who looked up to see the man stiffen. Eventually, Anton interrupted the pleasantries with, "What is it Monsieur? Is there something wrong?" The conversation that followed was lost to Adam, but his friend's stance and stilted replies interested him.

Anton replaced the receiver and returned to the table, shaking his head, "That is very strange." He jabbed towards the telephone with his thumb, "It was my bank manager. He is coming to visit me, here, which is something he has never done before. I asked him what it was about but he wouldn't tell me; said it was something he had to say in person and *then* he said that his wife would be accompanying him."

In spite of his friend's anxiety, Adam couldn't stop himself from mimicry, in a faux French accent, "Zat is very strange."

Anton didn't seem to notice as he continued, "I asked if I should be worried and he said no, but the matter was important and urgent; which is why they are coming here this afternoon, at three." After a moment's thought, Anton added, "He sounded very tense. Perhaps he is as worried as I should be."

Adam sat up straight, "Then I'll make myself scarce."

"Non! Please, I want you to be here. I will translate so you will feel included, but I would like someone from Club Cognac to be present. It will be, how you say, moral support and I want him to meet one of the people who saved my family's distillery from the bank's clutches."

That was good news, on two counts. Another three hours with that bloody tank on his back was too horrible to contemplate and he was intrigued. A visit from the bank manager was one thing, but not with a hand being held by his wife. Somehow, he didn't think they were calling to sell tickets to the next social, "In that case, I'll nip home and change." He stood and made for the door, "Don't worry, I'll be back in good time." A glance back was enough to see the anxiety on Anton's face as he murmured, "Thank you."

They arrived at three, on the dot. Anton ushered them into the kitchen where Adam stood for the introductions. Like most men, he thought that Madame Rambert was striking rather than beautiful and dressed in a long and expensive overcoat. Her prominent 'Duke of Edinburgh' nose formed part of an equally distinctive bone structure that was extraordinarily stunning. Her brown eyes were both warm and intelligent.

The kitchen was warm enough for her to remove the coat immediately, to reveal a cream silk blouse beneath and dark blue cashmere cardigan, atop a pair of beautifully tailored trousers of the same colour. The figure they hugged was slim enough for the clothes to hang well, yet rounded enough to strike Adam as being entirely desirable.

As Rambert yielded his coat to Anton he said quietly, "Forgive me Monsieur, but this must be a private meeting."

Anton had prepared himself for this, "Monsieur Rambert, this person represents the group who *saved* me from ruin. He is aware of all that happened between us and I would like him to be present. If that is not acceptable this meeting will not be, to me."

After an awkward pause Margot exchanged words with her husband before she addressed Adam, in perfect English, "Very well Monsieur. We have no right to expect this, but may we count on your discretion. This is very difficult for us, but it is time for atonement I think."

Adam couldn't begin to guess at the number of times he'd said the words, which were less than she hoped for, "No deals or promises. Let's hear what you have to say first." He saw the concern on her face and added, "For all I know, you could be here to make more threats and in that case vigorous defence comes before discretion."

She looked down at her hands, which were clasped around her waist and thought for a short while before looking up at her husband, to speak in French, "We have no choice."

Anton made to interpret but she beat him to it, though he nodded vigorously at the authenticity as she spoke, "I said that we have no choice."

Adam sat down, "Then let's get started shall we?"

The two men had agreed in advance that the usual courtesy of offering guests a drink should be ignored; a signal to show that the threats and anxieties hadn't been forgotten, or forgiven.

Rambert sat down and didn't waste time, "Monsieur Michaud, I have wronged you terribly. It was nothing personal, but I ask you to believe me when I tell you that the whole thing has caused me terrible distress. As much, I fear, as it caused you. My wife has come with me to demonstrate how *personal* this apology is though and to explain what happened."

He paused to allow time for Margot to translate, at the end of which Anton nodded once more.

Rambert took a deep breath before continuing, "All that happened, over so many months, was not of my doing. I was acting under instructions, but it is still something I am ashamed of."

After translation Adam asked, "Who instructed you?"

"I am not able to say. Trust me, I would like to tell you, but it is not possible."

"Why not?"

"The man who directed this conspiracy is powerful and possibly dangerous. I do not know what his agenda was, beyond Monsieur Michaud's ruin, but he is ruthless."

Anton interrupted, "So the threat still exists."

Rambert sounded certain, "No, no, your business is now financially sound enough to ensure that my bank has no power over you."

Anton's shoulders sagged with relief, but Adam had more questions, which he directed via Margot while maintaining eye contact with her husband, "So does this person work at the bank?"

Rambert shook his head sadly, "I am sorry, I cannot tell you that, or his name, at least not for the time being."

The gaps during translation gave Adam time to study his man, who jerked his head when asked, "So this man does still pose a threat then."

"No, I am sure it is over."

Adam spoke quietly, "As you said, for the time being."

Rambert appeared to be affronted, "I did not say that."

Detective Adam Harding, (retired), shrugged and thought, 'Yes you did, you lying little toad'. At that point he decided to stop the interrogation. There were so many questions now and he knew there would be more, once he'd had chance to make notes and prepare for their next meeting.

The Ramberts on the other hand, had some questions of their own. Margot was the first, with, "Monsieur Michaud, as my husband said, the bank's involvement is at an end, but this man *was* very determined." She paused, to formulate the question, "It may even be that he contacted you personally even though he was relying on the bank to do his dirty work. Has anyone approached you recently, with any business proposals?"

Anton cast his eyes up and thought for a moment before, "No, I cannot think of anything."

Rambert cut in, "So nobody offered to lend you money or buy anything from you; some of your stock perhaps, or machinery?"

This time Anton took longer to consider the question but eventually he shook his head, "No, why would they? Nobody knew about my financial troubles, apart from the bank."

"But the English group knew. How, I wonder. Could it be that they were being guided by someone."

"That was something quite different and the circumstances were entirely known to me." He had no intention of telling them about his relationship with Sue.

Margot reached across and took his hand, "I'm relieved to hear it, but we are here with a new purpose now, to try and help. I asked Phillipe if I could come with him, to make you realise that this is no longer anything to do with the bank. If you do think of anything or anyone should contact you, please let us know and we'll do everything we can to help."

Adam held his chin in one hand and looked on in admiration. She'd used her husband's first name deliberately, to distance him from any connection with the bank and she did so again, "Phillipe began by saying that what happened wasn't personal. Well I can tell you that it is now, for both of us. If this man should try anything else we would want to stop him."

Rambert thought of something else, "Do you have any enemies Monsieur, or is there anyone who bears a grudge?"

Anton simply shook his head.

But Rambert continued, "Have you sold something to

anyone, or promised to and then backed out? Forgive me; I am simply trying to find a motive."

It was Adam's turn, but this time without eye contact, "Mr Rambert, you appear to be the only person to have had contact with this person and therefore the only one likely to know what the motive was, or is."

Rambert's hands had been locked together on the table and the sudden whitening of knuckles would never have been noticed, unless someone had been watching closely. He cleared his throat before speaking, "I wish that were the case, but in fact, it was one of the reasons we came here today."

Adam shrugged, "Then it remains a mystery."

Margot withdrew a card from her handbag and placed it on the table in front of Anton, "here is our home address and telephone number, if you do think of anything."

The meeting ended more cordially than Rambert could have hoped for; at least the distiller hadn't attacked him. As they drove away he said, "Well, at least I've done as Fabian asked and made my apologies, but Michaud knew nothing that would help us deal with Pichon. Do you think we should have mentioned him by name?"

Margot was horrified, "Good God no! That man is a thug. If you even hinted at his identity we could have brought the whole thing down on our heads. We need information; enough to use against him, but we need to be discreet in the meantime."

As soon as their car was out of sight Adam excused himself, saying that he had to return to the *gite*, to make notes. Anton suggested that he stay and make them in the kitchen; there was plenty of paper, but Adam pleaded the need for silent contemplation, which was the truth.

At times like that Adam locked out external stimuli, until the thoughts that were rattling around his head like a revolving bingo ball basket found order, on paper. He burst into the *gite* and grabbed a packet of biscuits, pen and some paper. They were employed in the same order.

He began with the most tenuous items, in that they couldn't be recalled by using chronology. The list ran thus;

Breathing heavily
Hands over mouth
Head jerks
Hand to throat
Fidgeting
Hands hard on table
Too rigid

None of the signals had been obvious or overt enough to alert the average person but they had all happened at the right times for Adam to know Rambert was lying. When he was a copper he wouldn't have bothered listing them, but whilst he knew that it was like riding a bike, he wanted to guard against the odd wobble or two. He read the list again before adding one more note;

Well rehearsed.

After that, it was a simple case of minuting the encounter and jotting thoughts down. Towards the end Adam felt a sudden weight being applied to one of his feet and looked down on Guinness, who was staring earnestly at the biscuit in Adam's hand. The door couldn't have been shut properly and Guinness would have known that knocking it would have been pointless. Instead he had nuzzled the door ajar and crept in. The dog returned Adam's stare briefly, before refocusing on the biscuit, until Adam dropped it into the dog's jaws, for a perfect catch. He laughed, "Guinness, at least you're honest. You didn't try to pretend that I was more important than the biscuit." They began to share the rest of the packet. At one point, he shared his thoughts with the dog, which seemed to show interest. He finished by handing down another biscuit and saying, "See, elementary my dear Guinness."

The gentle woof that followed resulted in a small spray of crumbs and prompted a caution, "Don't speak with your mouth full."

At the same time as Adam had been making his notes,

the Ramberts arrived at their house and Phillipe telephoned Fabian. He cut to the chase immediately, "I, *we've* been to see Michaud and I feel better for it. You were right my friend, I needed to clear things up with him and to apologise."

The priest was delighted, "That *is* good news. Well done. How did he take it?"

"Better than I could have hoped, I think."

"You don't sound so sure."

"No, he seemed to share my relief, but there was another chap there; one of the *Anglais* group that invested in the place. He seemed a little belligerent and asked most of the questions. I think, perhaps, that he was just making a point, as saviour and self-appointed guardian."

"Did you glean any information?"

"No, he didn't know a thing, or at least couldn't recall anything that could help us. How have you got on?"

Fabian sounded glum, "Nothing yet. I've been in touch with a couple of museums but they have nothing beyond artefacts. The only records they *did* have were sent to the archive centre a long time ago."

Rambert cut in, "Who managed to lose them."

"Temporarily we hope. I telephoned the head archivist yesterday afternoon to see if he'd spoken to the chap who had been instructed to retrieve them, but he's still off work. Apparently, he injured himself with a kitchen knife."

Rambert's spirits began to slide, "It looks pretty hopeless."

"Nonsense! Don't give up hope yet; I certainly haven't"

They spoke for a little longer but there was little either could add and nothing else they wanted to talk about.

Anton appeared to be in good spirits when Adam joined him for the evening meal, even to the extent of proposing a toast, "To the end of unhappy times."

Adam shared the wine but he was French enough by then to avoid sharing bad news over good food. Eventually though, over coffees, he pulled out his notes and burst his friend's bubble with the first sentence, "Rambert was withholding information for some of the time and lying for the rest."

Anton's jaw dropped, but Adam ploughed on, "There was a smidgeon of honesty, I'll grant you, but only enough to act as a salve to his conscience. He used the word conspiracy himself, which was a telling error."

Anton looked puzzled, "But whatever happened, he promised that it was over."

"No, he implied that it was. Anton my friend, when we turned up, a shed load of disasters had happened to you. A long term cognac buyer dropped out for a start off. I don't doubt there were other mishaps which on their own wouldn't have seemed significant, until today, when your bank manager turns up and pleads for forgiveness. He's already admitted that someone else was behind this and I don't believe that person works at the bank. Madame Rambert let that much slip when she said..." He consulted his notes and quoted, "He was relying on the bank to do his dirty work."

Besides, there are too many safeguards and audits for that sort of thing to go unnoticed, while an outsider could stay beneath the radar. Besides, why would they ask if anyone else had contacted you if it wasn't someone outside of their influence?"

"So what are you saying?"

"I'm certain that Monsieur Rambert is either having his pockets lined, heavily, or he's being blackmailed." After a moment Adam delivered the final blow, "Whoever is behind this has frightened the daylights out of him. Consider this, while taking care not to divulge anything that could identify the man he still described him as powerful and ruthless. That was Rambert-speak for bloody dangerous. Oh, and another thing, they weren't asking you questions for your benefit. I can't be absolutely certain, but I think they were fishing for information that could be used against this man."

Anton groaned, "Ah la la, are you sure?"

"Yes."

"Then I think you are speaking as a policeman."

"Absolutely, and if I had him in an interview room I'd crack him within an hour. His wife, I wouldn't be so sure about."

"Why is that? About his wife I mean?"

Adam pursed his lips, "She's the brightest of the pair and even at my age, I think I'd be distracted."

Anton let that one go, in the face of a more pressing question, "What do you suggest?"

The ex-detective smiled, "With your permission, I have work to do."

Shortly after Adam left, Anton poured himself a *Ricard* and sat down in the sudden silence and thought about solitude. He'd never given the matter much thought; there was always so much to do, but this time he was affected as memories bore down on him; of cancelled orders and the willingness of the bank to lend him money, followed by ever-increasing demands and threats. Everything made sense now and a fool of him. With a rising sense of nausea he realised how gullible he'd been, accepting everything at face value.

But he'd been alone and frightened.

He was no longer alone. Any lingering doubts about involving the *Anglais* were finally swept aside. Instead, he was comforted by thoughts of the collective skills they had brought with them; not least of all in the person of Adam Harding, whose perception seemed so clear, certain and above all, correct. He raised his glass and said aloud, "To Club Cognac!"

***

Three days later the club members assembled at the *Rose and Crown* for their Friday morning coffees. It had been a week since they had returned from France; long enough for doubts to set in for some. Understandably perhaps, since so much had happened so quickly. Anxieties were expressed in different ways. Amy Dyson suggested that George's business sense had been swayed by his love of fine liquor and he had to agree, at least in part, while Carol had returned to her original belief, that the whole thing was aberrational. Bob pointed out that they had barely dented the cash held in meaningless deposit accounts and could therefore stand a total loss without undue grief. He also reminded her that she'd become quite the Francophile, known to search the supermarket shelves for French cheeses. Alan had reflected on his career as a financial advisor, advising clients to exercise fiscal prudence, yet he was doing the complete opposite. He chose not to share his concerns with Jayne.

At the other end of the spectrum, Barbara was as cheerfully enthusiastic as ever while Barry had switched from being *devil's advocate* to a Michaud acolyte.

Of course, Annie and Sue had no qualms, for they were committed to a second home there, notwithstanding Sue's personal agenda.

Kendall Spencer had simply sulked. He hadn't managed to get his hands on any free cognac yet and didn't look likely to, now that he'd lost control of the investment. He believed, correctly, that his father-in-law had taken delight in freezing him out, by putting the Club Cognac investment in trust for his granddaughter. Meanwhile, his sexless wife seemed to have a new lease on life. He failed to recognise the true significance of her enrolment at the local slimming club, or the improvements to her personal dress and appearance. Instead, he railed against what he saw as a conspiracy against him, particularly when Megan telephoned Annie and proposed her father as an honorary member of Club Cognac.

Naturally, he continued to dip into the tills and barmaids, as if by right. One night, when feeling particularly piqued, he dumped a pair of bloodstained underpants into the laundry basket instead of throwing them away; half hoping that she would notice them and take heed. The new barmaid had taken to after-hours drinking like a fish to water and what followed was quite simply rape, though he had been startled to discover that she'd been a virgin and he'd been forced to use his own underwear to clean himself up. "No matter" he had told her, his tongue thickened by the liquor, "It has to happen sooner or later."

The following morning he woke at around ten in the morning and lay on his back, as the previous night's dalliance came to mind. Suddenly, he leapt out of bed and ran to the laundry basket. He wasn't concerned about the girl. They had both been drinking and that sort of thing happens to drunks, but putting the blood-stained underpants in with the other dirty clothes had been a stupid act of bravado. The basket was empty. Nausea swept over him as he dragged his dressing gown on, before hurrying downstairs. On entering the kitchen he was greeted by the sound of the washing machine in spin cycle and incredibly, a perfectly relaxed wife. The only conclusion he could come to was that she had grabbed a great handful of clothes and shoved it into the machine without noticing the blood.

Since he had never washed the clothes, Kendall knew nothing about the need to separate coloureds from whites and would therefore never suspect that his wife *had* found them and recognised the significance of those stains. Someone on the television had said that at some point, adultery will always be discovered by the partner and on that basis, she decided to save the pants, to wave in a divorce court should the need arise. They were now sealed in a plastic *Ziplock* bag, in the bottom of her underwear drawer; the one place she knew he'd never venture into.

Meanwhile, Megan now had the relationship she'd always wanted, with the love of her life and Kendall was the only person in the village who didn't know about it.

They were all there that Friday morning, except for Kendall, who felt that his attendance when the father-in-law was there would be a tacit endorsement and that, he would never agree to do. Ironically, Tom Eccleston's attendance with Megan was seen as exactly that, though she made certain that they all knew *why* he was qualified to join the group.

Annie continued to act as unofficial chairperson. Most of the members had telephoned her during the week, so her agenda was set to be appropriate. She rapped her spoon on the table and waited for complete silence before speaking, "I know that some of you have had doubts and that is quite understandable, but for that reason I'd like Barry to begin things. She gave him a nod and he unravelled the notes he'd brought.

They waited in silence until finally he began, "Well, do you want the OK news, the good news, the very good news, or the outstanding news first?"

This, from their doubting Thomas was startling. He waited until the chatter subsided and someone called out, "Let's start with the OK news."

A silly grin had appeared on his face, "OK, well, you were going to get it in that order anyway. I've now had time to view things in more detail, in particular, the ratio of stock to sales, but first, I have discovered that Anton's trading levels are better than we thought, even after losing his main commercial buyer. In the meantime, he seems to have struck a chord with tourists, particularly the British, which means that he is selling at a much higher price than the buyer was paying. The tourists are growing in number too. I reckon by fifty per cent in the last year. The main causes for his loss of profits have been a series of mishaps. The weed killer incident and the straying cattle to name just two and then some machinery was stolen. Without those, he'd have shown modest profits."

He paused, before, "Then there is the good news. It appears and I'm sure this is correct, that the stock of cognac, set against current trading levels, will keep the place going for thirty two years."

George called out, "Bloody hell, so what's the very good news?"

Barry's grin was beginning to ache, "The *very* good news is that my last statement didn't take into account a single fluid ounce of future production, including this year's distillation. The place is quite literally, floating on liquid gold." He was quite pleased with that metaphor and extremely gratified by the applause that followed.

He continued, "Finally, the outstanding news. I calculate that the stock I spoke of amounts to around two hundred thousand litres, with a retail value of not less than four million pounds. I don't know whether you are aware, but the stock was included in our agreement. We were happy with a two and a half million valuation but now that has gone up to six and a half; based on retail value of course, but the stock would still have a wholesale value of over two million." A cheer rose up and he basked in another round of applause.

Tom Eccleston was delighted too and turned to whisper in Megan's ear, "Well love, I think we have a winner. I had my doubts too, but your mum is going to love what I have to tell her now."

George raised his hand before addressing Barry, "I think you'll find that it isn't just tourists. There is a fair number of expats living in that region that must have a grapevine, if you'll pardon the pun. My bet is that a fair number know about Anton and they'll keep coming back, compounding the growth."

Barry nodded enthusiastically, "Point taken."

George had another question, "Why did you use a retail stock valuation? Surely, a distillery should be regarded as a wholesale supplier?"

Barry nodded in agreement. "I know, it is a tricky one, but at the moment, most of his business is as a retailer, yet he is charging wholesale prices."

CHAPTER 11

Adam had never believed in preparing for an interview in too much detail. Because there were so many variables interrogations couldn't be scripted. It was always a question of reacting to what the felon did or said. But he did believe in some strategies. They were the tools he used to weaken or disarm his victims, which was why, in this case, he chose to wait until early Saturday morning before paying the Ramberts an unannounced visit. He guessed that they would both be at home, relaxed and having breakfast.

He was right, of course about them having breakfast, but the Ramberts were far from relaxed. The sat nav had guided him through countless villages along tiny lanes that defied any sense of direction. The locals, farm workers probably, at that time of morning, drove with a total disregard for wing mirrors and blind bends. When they did meet an oncoming car they left the road with a pragmatic disregard for the suspension or Adam's heart rate. He decided that an aerial view of the rural road system probably resembled a plate of spaghetti dropped on the floor. Against all odds, he arrived at Merindol, around twenty five minutes south east of Cognac, at ten past eight. It was a village, but much larger than Aurigny. The church was well maintained and the mayor's office was new and like the church, disproportionately large.

The Rambert house wasn't a chateau, but it was close enough. Built in the local stone and standing in its own, well tended grounds. A large black Mercedes and smaller silver one were parked on the gravel forecourt.

A girl, aged around nine, answered the door. He smiled, "Is your mum or dad in?"

Adelle was doing well in English at school, but like most nine year olds, when confronted by an adult, she was dumbstruck. Instead of answering the question, she called over her shoulder, "Maman!"

Margot was stunned when she saw him but quickly gathered her wits and invited him into the kitchen, which was wonderfully warm and filled with a delicious aroma of coffee. Rambert was equally startled but stood to shake hands. Two sets of plates, laden with half eaten breakfasts were placed on a tray for the two daughters, who were told to go into the living room. The tone of their mother's voice and the haste in which the tray had been prepared left no room for dissent and they left without a word. Adam was then invited to sit in one of the vacant seats and offered coffee.

Finally, Margot sat opposite him and asked, "What can we do for you Monsieur, do you have any news for us?"

Adam smiled, "No, I'm afraid not, but now I've had chance to consider what you told us there are a few details I need to clarify."

They both nodded but said nothing, so he continued, "The other day you began by saying that your attempts to bankrupt Michaud had not been personal and the whole thing had been very upsetting for you."

Margot would continue her role as interpreter throughout. This time the response was, "That is correct, it was so troubling. It is not in my husband's nature to behave that way."

Adam opened his notepad and quoted, "You also said that none of it was your doing, you were acting under instructions."

"That is correct."

"The concentration camp guards said the same thing in nineteen forty five. Do you remember, they all hated their job but were just following orders."

Margot stared at him; trying to decide whether or not they should just throw this man out, but eventually, she translated for Phillipe, who flinched before launching into an angry defense, "You come into my house and accuse me of being a Nazi. How dare you!"

Adam looked at Margot and spoke quietly, "Ask your husband who signed all those letters, threatening to foreclose?" Who would have appointed the team to liquidise Michaud's home and business?"

Rambert didn't fall for that one, "Just what is it you are here to prove Monsieur?"

Adam ignored that, "OK, let's talk about the blackmailer."

Margot interrupted, "We did not say he was a blackmailer."

Adam shrugged, "Whatever. Now, you said he was powerful and dangerous. Tell me please, what makes him powerful? Is it his position, or is he gangster or just a thug?"

Margot translated then said, "My husband said that he is none of those things. But again, just what is it you are here to prove?"

"I don't need to prove anything. You of all people must realise that you've been coerced into doing some really naughty things. You haven't simply broken the bank's rules have you? There are a bunch of laws you've broken too."

Translation was hardly necessary when Rambert stood and pointed to the door, but Adam waited for Margot anyway, "My husband," she paused then included herself, "And I, want you to leave immediately. We visited Monsieur Michaud in the spirit of contrition and you come here now making these accusations. Please go, now."

Adam gathered his notes and stood. Margot did as well, to escort him off the premises, but as they reached the kitchen door he smiled and shook his head, "Don't leave the house please. I'll be back with the *Gendarmerie* before lunch." He pointed at Margot, "When you decided to join your husband and lie to my friend you entered into the conspiracy too. The girls won't thank you."

They had reached the front door before she relented, "Please, what is it you want? Do you want to blackmail us as well?"

He saw a tiny signal in the eyes, as she realised her error. This time Adam looked at her closely, "What I *want* is for you to tell the truth." He began to walk back towards the kitchen and spoke over his shoulder, "And I reckon you've just made a start."

Rambert looked capable of violence when Adam sauntered into view, but Margot placed a hand on his shoulder and began to speak quickly. It was clear they didn't agree and Adam sat quietly while they had an argument, but eventually Margot said something that sounded like a question and he slumped back into his chair, defeated. Margot looked at Adam, "Please Monsieur, what do you intend to do with the truth, if we did tell you?"

"Find this man and stop him."

Margot glanced at her husband as she spoke, "My husband doesn't trust you. I'm not sure whether I do or not."

Adam had his notepad and pen to hand, "So does that mean you're going to tell me everything or do I have to ferret the facts out with questions?"

She waved a hand towards Phillipe, "What do you think?"

They were ready, give or take, but to get the lot would require a little more tweaking of their sensitivities, "At Michaud's place I asked if this man still posed a threat and you said no. Is that still the case?"

Rambert's belligerent answer was smoothed out by Margot, "But of course!"

Adam tutted and shook his head, "See, you're lying to me again."

The reply came back, "I can only say what I believe is true. Things may change, but so far as I'm aware, the threat to Michaud is over, finished."

More tutting, "Now try again, but listen to me, three strikes and *I'm* out; out of that door to the nearest *Gendarmerie*."

The sneer and tone of voice almost did away with the need for translation, which was, "You seem very sure of yourself."

Adam huffed, "I should be, I spent thirty years interrogating criminals and much tougher ones than you I might add."

Margot paled, "So you are a policeman."

"Used to be; I'm retired." He waited while she discussed matters further with her husband, but when she turned to face him he raised a hand and began, with a much softer voice "Margot, I mean you no harm, in fact I may be one of the few people who could help you get out of this mess. I have my own theory so how about I share that with you and let's see how far off I am."

After a pause, she nodded.

"Great, but you'll have to stop me when you need a translation break."

She pointed at his pad, "May I have some paper please and a pen?"

He tore a few sheets off the pad and handed them over as she explained, "I will make notes and translate at the end. It will save you from breaking the line of thought."

Adam was impressed and grateful. He began, "Your husband is being blackmailed by someone outside of the bank, which means that there is something you don't want the world to know about. You also said that he was dangerous, which tells me that he's already threatened you and possibly your children. He might even have committed some act of violence to your property already.

I don't believe much has changed, even though Anton is now solvent. This man still controls you and he hasn't given up, which would explain why you two had questions of your own. It's my guess that you are trying to find enough 'black' on him to frighten him off. It's a plan but you two wouldn't stand a chance. If he felt that threatened he'd come after you personally.

Now, on the subject of motive; there are only two that come to mind. This man might hate Michaud so much he wants to destroy him. I don't believe that for a moment. Anton is so inoffensive and honest I just can't see him doing anything to warrant a vendetta. The second is more obvious. That is a nice vineyard and the cognac he produces is wonderful. There's plenty of it too. So could this man be a neighbour, who wants the place for a song?

Now all that is theory, but here is a fact. Please trust me in this; I know what I'm talking about. This man will never go away. Blackmailers never do. Even if he achieves his aims there will be something else. Your husband is well and truly on the hook and too valuable to be put back. What's more, I'll bet that your husband's been so desperate to keep this secret there's no record of communications. No photocopies or recordings and that means you have no evidence. You two might be jailed but he'll walk away."

He gave her a moment to digest that one before, "Oh, there is one other certainty. You *will* be caught and now that you are both involved think what might happen to your kids."

He closed with the game changer, "I believe I can help you and for the time being at least, keep it under wraps, but you need to tell me everything. It hasn't taken me long to figure things out and I'm no genius. Just think how easy it will be for the police, with warrants and specialists. You two need a friend."

Margot continued to write for some time and then stood, "Excuse me Monsieur, but I would like to speak with my husband in private."

Adam said, "Of course" and began to get up from the table. She held out a hand, "No, please stay here, we will go to our bedroom." As they stood a thought occurred to her, "What is in this for you?"

The answer was simple, "I already have a friend and he needs protecting."

In the living room, two young girls sat in a cowed silence, not even daring to put the television on. They rarely heard their father raise his voice and to hear him shouting at the stranger was extraordinary.

***

Challans had spent the small hours downstairs, alone on the sofa, rocking in pain. There had been some initially, but the doctor had told him that the pain would soon become mere discomfort. He was told to take the pain killers for a few days and the wound would have closed nicely within a week. Instead, crimson tendrils in the flesh flared out from the dressing, towards his elbow. His wife had slept badly for the last week so he chose not to disturb her, but the solitary silence prompted all manner of thoughts and memories. He remembered the original, seemingly innocuous request, with the significant reward, when they were so desperate. But it hadn't stopped there and he soon realised that it wouldn't. He was ensnared. The insidious spiral haunted him that night, as he held his hand up against his chest. Eventually, he relived the knife attack and as he did so, the agony seemed to flare. He looked down at the mess of his hand and wondered what the knife had been used for, before the attack. Whatever it was, he'd been infected with something that defeated the antibiotics he'd been given.

He was vaguely aware of his wife rising to feed and clothe their infant son. Ordinarily, he would have made tea for them both and taken it through, so his failure to respond to her calls triggered unease. She cried out at the sight of the swollen mass, "Why didn't you wake me!" She dumped her son on the sofa and ran to the kitchen for a bowl of hot water and the first aid box. Then, she knelt beside him and gently took his hand. The bandage burst open as the scissors cut through it and Challans groaned with relief, until finally, the wound was exposed. She gagged and he groaned again, at the yellow and black mess. They couldn't see where the pus ended or tissue started, but she was too frightened to go near it. Instead, she helped him dress and get into the car.

Two hours later, he was in theatre.

***

The Ramberts were gone for a long time; enough for Adam to think about his own position. He no longer had a warrant card and in any event, he was on French turf. As a civilian, there would be a danger of guilt by association at best, or worse, as an obstruction of justice. Any right-minded person would force these people into going straight to the police, but they were innocents; he'd seen enough to know that, so they would go down with the ship, even if they managed to ensnare the blackmailer with recordings. Besides, he finally admitted to himself that he'd missed the job and the prospect of working again was too tempting. It would all depend on whether they told him everything.

His first glimpse when they walked back into the room told him they would.

Their red swollen eyes were eloquent enough and as Margot sat down, she asked, "What do you want to know?"

Adam opened his pad and retrieved his pen before addressing them both, "Everything, but let's start with what it is he has on you."

Apart from the odd question asked or answered, Rambert remained silent for the next hour while Margot related their story. As is so often the case, the reason for their entrapment was pathetic, at least from an outsider's perspective, starting with minor favours that would have seemed little more than indiscretions. From that point on though, he was on the hook.

Adam interrupted a few times with questions, but Margot's investigative background ensured that her report was comprehensive. At the end, Adam looked up from his notes and said, "You've been very stupid, but I don't suppose you need me to tell you that."

Margot shook her head slowly, "Fabian said the same thing."

"He's the priest?"

"Yes, but also a lifetime friend of my husband."

"OK, well let's start with him. I'll need you to come with me."

"When?"

Adam's eyebrows headed north, "Now would be good."

She hesitated, "I normally take the girls to riding classes on Saturday morning. They know that something is wrong, but it might be best if we keep things as normal as possible for them."

Adam could see the sense in that, but there was the question of language, "Does Fabian speak English."

She stood, "I'll call him to see if he can see you and I'll ask about his English." She returned minutes later, "He would be delighted to meet you and thinks he has enough English to suffice."

"Hold on." Adam had closed his eyes and rested his forehead on a hand as he spoke. Eventually, he returned from his thoughts, "How long will it take to get there."

"Around one and a half hours."

He was still formulating his plans, "Hmm, a three hour round trip. Do you know if the archive place is open today?"

She shrugged, "I don't know, it is possible."

This time he muttered to himself, "Even if it is, the boss won't be there, I'll be bound." A three hour round trip for a single interview was hardly worth the effort, not when they would be going back to Bordeaux on Monday. He explained and enquired whether Rambert could take Monday off. The signals that followed suggested that he was willing to take a 'sicky'.

Adam was content, "Good, then I suggest we get an early start. I'll get here for eight and we can miss the rush hour but still be there for nine thirty."

Margot looked anxious, "But Monsieur, I have to take the girls to school."

He waved a hand dismissively, "No matter, we'll manage without you, but would you be kind enough to telephone Fabian to see if he would be available please?"

***

They didn't arrive until nearly ten on Monday morning, in spite of a prompt start. In Margot's absence Rambert did demonstrate a smattering of English, which would have served if hand signals could have been incorporated, but that wasn't feasible while driving so conversation became too much of a strain for both of them and silence reigned within a few kilometres. Having left the *gite* at seven, Adam was content to doze in the warm luxury of the Mercedes, but unfortunately, the approach to Bordeaux on the A10 was reduced to a crawl, in which they lost half an hour.

Fabian had been looking out for them and stood at the doorway as they got out of the car. The two friends shook hands and exchanged a few words before Adam was introduced. Fabian's greeting was warm and English better than expected, "Welcome, Phillipe has told me a great deal about you over the weekend and of course, I already knew about Club Cognac."

He was tall for a Frenchman, but with black hair and a complexion that hinted at a Basque heritage, typical for the region. More importantly, there was a natural warmth to the man that had been evident immediately. He showed them into the kitchen and gestured to the table, where a plate of croissants and selection of jams had been set out, "I thought, perhaps, that you may be hungry after such an early start. Please, help yourselves while I make the coffee."

Adam was and did.

Once the coffees were served their host didn't waste time with small talk, "Since we all know the background I suggest you begin with your questions." He translated for Rambert while Adam pulled out his notepad and pen.

The introduction sounded like a classic first line of a police interview, "Thank you for seeing me at such short notice Father." The priest smiled and nodded as Adam continued, "I'm interested in your investigations, in particular, your involvement with the archives." He referred to his notes and read, *The Archives Départmentales de la Gironde,* in excruciating French.

Fabian began by describing his first encounters with the archivists and the subsequent failure to find the files. Much had already been divulged by the Ramberts but Adam noted everything, as though he was hearing it for the first time. At a convenient moment, he took the priest back to his original contact, "You said that the junior archivist was unhelpful. Can you expand on that?"

Fabian cast his mind back, "Well, in truth, I think he was being a typical *bureaucrate*. What is it you call them?"

"Civil servant?"

"*Exactement!* My request to see those files wasn't possible because access was restricted and he told me so, rather bluntly. If I remember correctly, he said something like, "You can't just call in here and demand to see them." Fabian waited for Adam to finish writing before recounting how he'd discovered details of the sanctuary given to Bordeaux's chief Rabbi by the Catholic Bishop and then used the information to evidence serious research and justify authorisation to see the files. That time though, he placed a call to the head archivist, who was much more helpful and terribly embarrassed when every single one of the files was missing."

Adam asked, ""I understand that a junior was asked to retrieve the files in advance of your visit."

"That is correct. Coincidentally, it was the same junior I spoke to originally. I had his name in my notes and I remember the head archivist asking for him by name when he called down to find where the files were."

"And what did the junior say?"

Fabian shrugged, "Nothing, he'd gone home with a migraine."

After a short pause for thought Adam said, "Would you still have the name please?"

"But of course, one moment." The priest left the room, giving Adam an opportunity to wolf down another croissant, laden with apricot jam. He was pushing the last crumbs off his lips and into his mouth with an index finger when Fabian returned, "Here it is, Monsieur Challans."

There was little more to tell. The description of the archives was interesting but not pertinent and the litany of failed attempts to glean information from libraries and museums only served to strike them off Adam's list of possibilities. He returned to the name Challans, "We need to speak with this man. Would you be kind enough to telephone the archive place please and ask to speak to him? If he answers put the telephone down without a word. We'll know all we need to. If he's there, I would like to speak to him today, under the pretence of chasing those files." A thought occurred to him, "Actually, for that to work we would need you with us. Would that be possible?"

Fabian nodded, "*Absolument.*" He went off to make the call and returned ten minutes later, looking less certain, "He is still off work. When they told me that, I asked to speak with the head archivist, who told me that Challans had injured himself with a knife over a week ago. His wife telephoned this morning to say that the wound had become infected and he was in the *Hôpital Saint-André.*"

Adam was pleased with the news, "Excellent! We might have had a hard time persuading him to talk at work and now we don't have to find out where he lives. There's nothing more normal than a priest visiting one of his parishioners in hospital, is there?" Fabian looked less than certain, but Adam sought to reassure him, "Just give me one minute and we'll know whether we've got our man."

"But surely, Pichon is our man."

Adam's gaze became predatory, "I'm looking for the tool, not the machine. I'll bugger that up *with* the tool." He realised who he was speaking to and began "Excuse my Fr..-, bad language."

***

The hospital is in the centre of the city, on the *Rue Jean Burguet*, though it looks more like a Napoléonic government building. It was built in local stone and fronted by a huge colonnaded entrance at the top of wide, presidential-style stone steps. Inside, a series of perhaps twelve rectangular buildings connected with a quadrangle, which surrounded a lawned area with a five metre fountain and bordered by trees and park benches. All this the three discovered in their search for Challans, until a passing nurse directed them to the ward. It was lunchtime when they got there and they were told to go and find one of their own. Visiting was otherwise flexible, so they were also told to return at two.

It was agreed that Rambert should wait outside the room since the patient might feel intimidated at the sight of three of them and Adam wanted to establish a dialogue before doing that.

Challans had a room to himself which Adam thought would be just dandy and what would be more normal than for visitors to close the door for privacy. It was open as they approached and the wintry sunshine that streamed in through the window exaggerated the pale, wan expression. He was dozing, which seemed to Adam the only thing a person could do when lying on his back with one hand encased in a large ball of dressing and the other with an intravenous feed taped into place with feeds from three bags, hung on an adjacent stand. He opened his eyes and looked startled when Fabian coughed politely, but the dog collar and smile were reassuring.

Fabian launched into his script, "Hello young man, how are you?"

Challans replied, "*Ça va, et vous?*" Ok and you?

The priest looked concerned and caring, "Ok, thank you, but I am saddened to see you this way. I am Father Bissonnette. I was speaking to Monsieur Laroche this morning and he told me you were here. Since I was visiting another parishioner who's a patient, I thought I'd call in and say hello." He saw Challans's quizzical look and said, "You probably don't remember, but we spoke a couple of weeks ago, about some research I was carrying out."

Their game was up. Challans's expression changed to one of suspicion, "What do you want?"

Instead of answering the question Fabian pointed to Adam with an anxiety of his own, "I have an English friend with me today, his name is Monsieur Harding."

Adam had been peering at the bags. One was marked *paracétamol* and he guessed that the other two contained saline and an anti-biotic. At the mention of his name he drew up a chair and sat at the bedside. Translation was necessary so he spoke clearly and slowly while locking into an eye contact that Challans couldn't break. His opening line ensured that much, "Hello, I've come to help you." Challans swallowed audibly, but didn't say anything, so Adam continued, "I reckon Pichon must have gutted something, a pig perhaps, before he stuck that knife into your hand." Challans tried to speak then, but Adam held up a hand, "What happened? Did you refuse to hand over the files? You had them, we know that much." He hurried on, as soon as the translation was over, "You are not alone. As soon as you get out of here I'd like you to meet two friends of mine who were facing ruin at the hands of this man too."

This time Challans managed to interrupt, "I have no idea what you're talking about. Now get out of here, I'm calling the nurse."

Adam snatched up the call button, "I'll call her for you, but then you'll leave us no option. When we leave here we'll go straight to the *Gendarmerie*." Most would have missed the fleeting hint of fear in Challans's eyes, but they were being analysed by an expert. More importantly, there was no attempt to snatch the call button or an instruction to use it. Instead the young man rubbed the palm of his bare hand on the bedclothes. Adam nodded at it, "It's hot in here isn't it?" He continued, knowing that he was well ahead on points; the knock out was within reach, "You probably don't know *why* Pichon wanted those files and I suspect you didn't even read them, but we know that he's upped his game, so you and the other two victims will still be at his mercy."

Challans shook his head slightly, but couldn't shake off Adam's stare until, "I don't know anyone called Pichon." His eyes slid to one side as he spoke.

Adam tapped the dressing gently, "Don't be naive. This won't stop and next time it might be your wife." After a moment he asked, "Do you have any children?" Challans didn't respond. It was time for logic and a softer tone, "Listen, with your help we can stop Pichon once for all. At the moment, if we count you, there are three victims, none of whom want to see this made public, which is how you've all been able to be blackmailed. I am, was, an English detective for over thirty years, which is why I can help you, *without* involving the French authorities." After translation he asked, "How many children *do* you have?"

The man bridled, "I didn't tell you I had any."

Adam smiled, "Your eyes did."

Challans turned his head slightly and stared at the ceiling, for long enough to imply that the meeting was over, so Adam stood, "Well, thank you for listening at least. One of the other victims is a friend of mine. He has children; two girls and they had a cat, until Pichon shot it and threw the body into their garden. Two weeks earlier he vandalised my friend's car causing six thousand Euros worth of damage and recently his daughters were mentioned, in a veiled threat. As a parent yourself, you'll understand that my friend would go to jail rather than have anything happen to them, which is why he's authorised me to go to the police from here, if you refused to co-operate.

You see, it all began with you. The information you gave to Pichon was used to blackmail my friend. He's outside in the corridor, if you'd like to meet him." Adam walked towards the door. "Tell you what, let me bring him in, I know he'd like to meet you." He was halfway to the door when Fabian completed the translation; just in time for Challans to call out, "Please, don't."

Adam walked slowly back to the bed but remained standing, "Why? Could it be because the information you smuggled out looks set to ruin the man's life?" He sat down then and leaned forward while speaking softly, "He realises that whatever you did is irrelevant now and that the only way we can beat this brute is by working together."

"I need to think about it."

Adam couldn't allow that to happen, "No you don't. 'No choice' doesn't take any thinking about. I'm not bullying you, but time is of the essence. It's now, or the *Gendarmes*, your choice."

"Please! Give me a few minutes; I need to speak with my wife."

Rambert stood as they left the room and whispered, "How did you get on?"

Adam recognised the question from the tone and didn't wait for the translation. Instead he addressed Fabian, "You go off with Phillipe, find a coffee machine and bring him up to date, but be back here within fifteen minutes. I'm waiting here, just in case fellow m'lad decides to discharge himself."

Fifteen minutes later Challans began to talk, but broke down almost immediately. Fabian pulled a tissue out of a box and passed it to him. Moments later he crouched down to whisper, "Would you like to pray my son?"

The young man shook his head, "For forgiveness perhaps, but I will do that alone." He looked at Adam, who had pad and pen to hand, "What do you want to know?"

Detective Harding, (retired), felt the spike of adrenaline he always knew at this point of an interrogation, but he spoke gently; it was time to encourage, not intimidate, "Just tell us your story, from the beginning."

It was pretty well all that they had known or suspected, save for the details of his entrapment and the transfer of information. They were interrupted once, by a nurse who changed the drip bags, but she sensed the atmosphere and hurried out without checking the patient's temperature, noting that conversation re-commenced as she left the room. At the desk she told a colleague, "I don't know what is happening in there but I was not welcome." She giggled, "Do you think it's an exorcism?" The colleague joined in, "Put *that* on his sheet, I dare you!"

The loss of the files was particularly bad news, but towards the end, when Challans was showing signs of fatigue they learned something of real value. He added it as an aside, "Pichon was in the files too, or it might have been his father. It was in the file for that SS officer. There was some correspondence to do with the sale of some land." Soon after, he finished with a description of the knife attack, "It was so fast and so unexpected, but the worst things were his eyes. There was nothing there, just," he searched for the words, "A cold detachment. My hand was nothing more than a lump of meat."

When Adam thanked him Challans asked, "What will happen now?"

Adam had no intention of sharing that information, but he had to give some sort of assurance, "Well, I still have people to see and things to do, but rest assured, the police won't be involved." The lie rolled off the tongue easily, in the knowledge that if anyone was hurt they would be called in immediately. That thought would come back to haunt him later in the day.

They had exchanged telephone numbers and home addresses already, so Adam promised to keep him informed, via one of the Frenchmen, but he added, "If you think of anything else, or if Pichon contacts you, let Father Bissonnette know immediately. If you ever need protection we'll arrange it." That was an assurance that would require funding, from a bank manager. As they walked towards the door Challans called out, "My wife told me to say thank you."

Fabian asked Adam if he would share the back seat on the drive back; there were things he needed to ask.

Adam did so and as they moved off Fabian asked, "You made it sound as though you knew everything. Poor Challans was startled and so was I."

Adam had intended to sit quietly and relive the interrogation, before thinking about the next steps, but it was always a pleasure to explain how they'd got such a good result, "Well, see, it was a mix of fact and guesswork. You mentioned earlier how it was a coincidence that Challans was the original contact *and* the one ordered to retrieve the files. By the time you got there both he and the files were missing. I don't believe in coincidences.

Then, tellingly, the only files that went missing were the ones you requested. That was seriously stupid. What he should have done is culled the files for anything incriminating then left them in place, which leads me to another piece of guesswork. Pichon is a blunt instrument, unwilling or unable to work that one out for himself. It was he who should have instructed Challans to do that."

Fabian thought for a while before, "You say all this now, after Challans confessed, but you *made* him believe we knew most of it already. How was that?"

Adam grinned, "Guessing, bluffing, fibs and faith. You should know all about that Father."

Fabian grimaced, "I won't be a priest for long if I spend much more time with you." After another pause he asked, "What do you think Pichon has done with the files?"

Adam had been thinking about that too, "He might have destroyed them, but if he did, there would be nothing to back up the 'black' he has on Rambert. There's no way of knowing, but for the time being they're certainly lost to us, unless of course, you'd be prepared to expand your repertoire, to include house-breaking."

Fabian didn't bother to reply, but after a few minutes he asked, "What now?"

Adam stared ahead, "My thoughts exactly. I need a little time to think about things. I can't bulldoze my way into encounters waving a warrant card in the air any more. Whatever we do will be frowned upon if the police find out, but we don't want to do anything they can prosecute us for. They'll see me as a rogue copper and worse, one on their turf."

When they reached Fabian's house he invited them in but rush hour was just starting and Rambert said that they had better set off straight away. Adam thought of something, "There is something you could do."

The priest nodded, "Of course."

"The SS officer, Meyer. Could you carry on digging for some information about him please? He's probably dead now, but there may be family. Who knows, there may be letters or diaries somewhere."

Fabian asked, "What about the German authorities? Won't they have records?"

Adam shook his head, "You'll be wasting your time, without official authority."

The queues and conversation difficulties on the return trip were just as difficult and Adam tried to doze again, but his mind was too active. As investigations went, this one had proved to be very fruitful in a relatively short period, but what now? He would make discreet enquiries of his own, back in Aurigny les Bois. It was a village just like Waltham, where secrets were few, but often the older ones were distorted by time and grievances. Even so, many would enjoy gossiping. It would only be hearsay though, not he reminded himself, that he was preparing a case for the courts. Nevertheless, their best hope at that time lay in tracing SS Obersturmführer Meyer, or his family.

When they reached Rambert's house Adam shook hands and headed for his car; he was tired, hungry and in need of a drink, but Margot had come to the door in time to thwart his escape bid. She would have none of it. A debrief was required from the expert, not her husband, "Please, Monsieur, will you eat with us tonight?"

Adam was startled and unequivocal, "No! Thank you, I would rather get home."

She laid a hand on his arm, "Then an apéritif perhaps?"

At least it was alcohol. They entered the kitchen, where Adelle and Cecille looked as though they were coming to the end of a snack. Margot confirmed as much, "The girls will be leaving shortly, to get on with their homework, so it will be better if we stay in here."

Adam sat next to the elder girl, who he recognised as the one who had answered the door to him on Saturday. He was introduced and they shook hands, but were clearly at a loss. His attempts to communicate with hand signals found little favour either, but by then a bottle of sparkling white wine appeared. He toasted the girls, who raised their glasses of squash in response. It was a start.

Margot tried to forge some sort of exchange between them, without success, but in the ensuing silence Adam leaned slightly in Adele's direction, "I'm sorry I startled you the other day."

The girl thought for a moment before saying, "Yes, you did!"

He smothered an urge to laugh and instead asked, "Was it because I am English, or fat?"

Both girls covered their mouths with hands and snickered. He leaned in again, "If I lost weight, would you marry me?"

Both girls giggled hysterically and continued to do so as Margot ushered them out of the room.

As usual, Margot wasted no time, "Please, Monsieur, what happened?"

***

By the time Adam reached the *gite*, it was too late to cook or go to Anton's. He was too tired anyway. After pouring himself a tumbler of scotch, a stale baguette and three eggs beckoned. A dash of water and thirty seconds in the microwave served to soften the bread sufficiently to house an omelette, doused in tomato ketchup. Not *haute cuisine,* but it would do. After that and a few more scotches it would be time to head north, for a welcome night's slumber.

Two hours later he lay in bed with his eyes closed and mind wide open. Suddenly, the irony and risks became clear. In the first place he was putting himself on the line for strangers. The man he had sought to protect was no more than an innocent victim, who had absolutely nothing to hide. The best thing would have been to involve the police and have done with it. But then he thought about two young girls and the banker's wife; a small infant and an archivist's wife; all innocents who would certainly suffer the shame and impoverishment that would accompany their partner's imprisonment. *Their* crimes would be evident and indefensible, but Pichon's were much worse and well hidden. He would undergo some unpleasant questioning, but Adam knew that as is so often the case, the real criminal would walk away and *that* was the worst of it. Somehow, he had to be stopped, permanently.

And anyway, he hadn't felt this good in a long time. The day had been a result!

***

The following morning Adam walked over to Penny's door. She beamed when she saw him, "Hello stranger, how are you?" She was shoved to one side as Guinness charged through the doorway to carry out a detailed, three hundred and sixty degree olfactory survey.

Adam glanced down to make sure it wasn't a prelude to urination before replying, "Great thanks. Sorry I haven't been in touch, but Anton has been teaching me about fine food *and* how to cook it."

She was impressed, "Phew, bravo. Well come in and have a coffee, I have some mediocre shortbreads somewhere."

Once they were seated with coffees and shortbreads that would have shamed Mary Berry, Penny asked, "So how was Bordeaux?" She saw his expression and explained, "I met Anton in the *boulangerie* yesterday and he told me that you'd gone off for a meeting there." Her eyes sparkled mischievously, "Care to share?"

He didn't see any humour in such an early indiscretion, but it did give him an opening, "just trying to find out a little more about the local goings on, but I'd be grateful if you didn't mention it to anyone else."

"Hmm, I'm intrigued."

He smiled, or tried to, "It would be a little embarrassing for me, though I may be able to tell you more in due course. Having said that, I wonder of you'd mind using the village grapevine to make a few discreet enquiries for me; nothing too obvious, but there's a chap called Pichon."

"Anton's neighbour?"

"Yes. Anton's mentioned a couple of things that suggest he's had a colourful background and I'd like to know more."

She did the maths and came up with four, "Does this have anything to do with your meeting in Bordeaux?"

"No," he lied, "It's just that Anton has said enough to pique my interest."

She turned her mouth down and head to one side, "OK, I'll

be your Watson, but listen Sherlock, you must promise to share if anything salacious comes to light."

He chuckled, "You'll probably be the first to come across it. There is one other favour I need to ask."

"Go ahead."

"Would you mind if I used your computer this afternoon. I need to *google* a few things."

She waved a hand, "Of course, I'm here all day so help yourself."

Anton was seated at the kitchen table waiting for him when he arrived, "Sorry I'm late, I had to pop in and see Penny first."

Anton's anxiety didn't leave space for polite tolerance, "Please Adam, sit down and tell me what happened while I make some coffee."

Adam spent an hour bringing his friend up to date and by then it was time for an apéritif before lunch, but a caution was due, "Anton, we've learned enough to know that Pichon is dangerous. From now on anything I do or say must be kept secret, even from Penny."

Anton thought for a moment before realising why he was being warned, "I did not think it would do any harm to mention your visit to Bordeaux; I didn't tell her anything about your reason for doing so."

Adam acknowledged that with a nod, "Best not to tell anyone anything unless I sanction it."

Anton looked sombre for a short while, until something else came to mind, "Ah, this afternoon, I thought you could help Henri replace some of the support wires."

"Sorry, can't do. I've arranged to carry out some research on Penny's computer." Bless you Penny, he thought, bless you, bless you.

CHAPTER 12

Nightingales had been fine wine merchants since before the Crimean war and still occupied the same premises, just off the Uxbridge Road, in Shepherd's Bush. It was Alan's first visit even though he was a longstanding client. Every available wall space was covered in racks of bottles and the central floor space was filled with upended barrels which obviously served as tasting tables, since each had a stainless steel spittoon fitted into the top. He noted that each one was fitted with a small terminal, the size of an *Ipad*, for recording orders.

A couple were standing around one in the far corner, by the window, chatting to an assistant who was pouring samples of red wine.

The man who greeted him was dressed in a crisp white shirt, old school tie and brown apron, bearing the company's logo. He was surprised to receive a visit from a *Prudential* manager; even more so when the man asked to speak with a buyer. Most of their *Prudential* clients never went there, because they were spread all over the country. It was enough to order from a detailed brochure, or respond to news of a new and remarkable vintage. Orders were then shipped out for delivery the next day.

Nevertheless, a great many managers used them for corporate events or seasonal gifts and collectively, were regarded as one of the merchant's most valuable accounts.

Alan Maitlin was about to make a pitch at reversing the process.

Eventually, and by contrast, a sandy haired man burst into

the showroom, dressed in a creased denim shirt and jeans. He had the sort of open expression that could never be without a smile. He held out a hand, "Hello, I'm James Baxter, one of the buyers here."

Alan was charmed, "How do you do? I do hope this isn't inconvenient, I should have telephoned in advance."

They both knew why he hadn't, but James let it go with, "No problem, what can I do for you?"

Alan reached into his bag and produced a bottle of Anton's forty year old, "I have just acquired an interest in this distillery and one of the reasons for doing so was this. I was advised, by an expert, that it is exceptional, but I would like a second opinion."

James took the bottle and read the label without comment, allowing Alan the chance to continue, "I am about to network with every *Pru* manager in the UK, including the head office, but to meet any interest we need a portal into the country, which is where you would come in." He didn't need to add that if another merchant took it on a valuable account might be at risk. Nevertheless, they were besieged by pitches and very few made the mark. Great tact would be needed.

James smiled, "Then perhaps we had better sample it." His smile slipped a little as he gazed at the swirled liquid in the glass and disappeared altogether when he tasted it. Tact would not be an issue; it was good. No, it was better than good. The nose, colour and mellow warmth were outstanding and he said so, adding, "I don't know what sort of deal you negotiated, but on the face of it, I'd say you've done well."

There followed a lengthy interview, in which Alan was called upon to describe Anton's place and operation, how long it had been owned by the family, whether there were any other UK importers and closer detail of the cognac itself. He went on to describe how Anton used a single variety of grape, from his own vineyard, and therefore there was no blending. It felt like an interrogation, at the end of which he felt gratified in knowing almost all of the answers. The next question was spoken in a hushed voice, presumably because retail customers were present. Alan had been tutored by George for this, though the price had been agreed with Anton, "Seventy five pounds, at the point of despatch. Shipping costs and processing through customs we would leave to you."

James made a snap decision and held up the bottle, "May I borrow this for a moment?"

Alan was heartened, "By all means."

The buyer walked over to the couple by the window. The man recognised him, "Ah, James, good to see you."

They shook hands and James said, "Good morning your Lordship; your Ladyship. We've just discovered this *Napoléon* cognac and I would appreciate your opinion." During the tasting he shared some of the information he'd just gleaned from Alan, who was startled when the Lord said, "Excellent, send me half a dozen cases will you?"

James nodded, "Of course, thank you. It may take a *little* longer than usual; we're in the process of organizing the first shipment. In fact, you will be the first to receive any in the UK." His Lordship was duly impressed. There had been no mention of price, but Alan would later learn that James had simply trebled the supply cost.

Alan couldn't wait to telephone Anton with the news; six cases purchased by a London wine merchant!

James invited him into the rear of the premises, where a maze of corridors led past small offices, each with a single desk and accoutrements. A much larger office held a number of desks, occupied by the administration staff. That much was evident from the box files that filled a bank of shelving. Whenever they passed an office that was occupied, James tapped the door and invited the person to join them, so by the time they reached his office a trail of six people was following them. The tasting that followed was a joy. They were all delighted, particularly when James mentioned the spontaneous order and that was when the senior member of the group instructed James, "OK, go ahead, we'll launch it in the summer issue."

By then the bottle was almost empty and they all left, save

for James who sat at his desk and invited Alan to sit opposite. He'd have needed to anyway, when James announced, "Congratulations Alan, you have a sale. We'll start with just a couple of hundred cases and see how we get on. Oh, I suppose we'd better have a look at the twenty year old as well."

Alan was stunned and barely heard James add a caveat, "As a matter of due diligence I'll have our man in Bordeaux call in and inspect the place, but that should be no more than a formality." The paperwork seemed to take an age but eventually it was complete. James confirmed that he'd be in touch with Anton to arrange a shipping date and promised to visit the place himself as soon as possible.

Distillateur extraordinaire Alan Maitlin left the place in a state of shock. By the time he joined Jayne, who was waiting in a coffee shop, he'd done the maths.

He was still trembling when he sat down at the table, "You're not going to believe this love, but we've just sold ninety thousand pounds worth of Anton's stock."

***

That night, after dinner, Penny sat down at her computer. Adam knew enough to carry out searches on *google*, but he knew nothing about search histories. She scrolled down the list;

Michaud

Pichon

Nazi occupation of the Bordeaux

Collaboration with the Nazis in Charente

War crimes in Bordeaux

War crimes in Aurigny les Bois

Collaboration in Aurigny les Bois

Chief Rabbi hidden from Nazis by Catholic bishop

Typical sentences for blackmail in France

Do private detectives need a licence in France

French equivalent of grievous bodily harm

There were more, but she'd seen enough to murmur, "Good

God almighty, what on earth is he up to and what am I getting mixed up with?" She began to keep notes of her own.

That same night, Club Cognac assembled at the Rose and Crown for an extraordinary general meeting, though any formality fell away in the face of joyous banter and clinking of glasses. Inevitably and in due course a bottle of cognac appeared and the landlord's indignation was eased by a couple of generous measures for him to try. He promptly ordered a case.

Towards the end of the evening George rose unsteadily to his feet and raised his glass, "To our absent member, the jammy sod. I hope Anton is working him hard."

The following morning, in spite of her misgivings, Penny began to ask anyone she met about Pichon and their experiences under occupation. The latter was in response to Adam's search history and she had no idea what she was looking for, beyond satisfying her own curiosity. Few would say much about Pichon, though it was clear that many didn't like him.

But she did learn a great deal about life under the Nazi yoke, even though the people she spoke to were only children at the time. One man, whose family owned a small farm at the time, told her about a network of trails across the countryside, through woods for the most part, that were used to carry produce to the market. Any that tried to use the roads were stopped by German troops who took the lot.

There were anecdotal tales too. On one occasion two German soldiers entered a farmhouse at lunchtime and sat at the table, expecting to be fed. The farmer began to say things that could have had him shot, until he was silenced by his wife, "They have families of their own, just like us." He sat in sullen silence as they ate, after which the soldiers stood and one addressed the woman in perfect French, "Thank you Madame, for your hospitality." With that, he placed a generous number of bank notes on the table and left.

The man at the *Boulangerie* still held a grudge, "Did you know that they charged us four hundred *million* francs a day for the privilege of being occupied." He was also one of the most outspoken when it came to Pichon, "Ha, I spit on that family." She tried to press him for more, but he either didn't know or wouldn't elaborate beyond, "Just things we heard you know."

Anton told her the same tales he'd shared with Sue, but he knew little more about the occupation beyond local lore. In the meantime, he was more concerned about the news from England. Nightingale's man in Bordeaux had already been in touch to arrange a visit on Friday. If all went well, there would be lots to do. New bottles and cartons would have to be ordered, printed and filled in time for the despatch date of April the twenty first.

The following day, over tea and scones Penny shared her findings with Adam. So far, it had been an enjoyable departure from the norms, but she also sought reassurance, "A lot of people don't like Pichon. I reckon he's a nasty piece of work, or could be. If things look set to turn nasty, you will warn us all won't you?"

He honestly didn't believe that Pichon would be stupid enough to threaten any of the villagers and gave the assurance readily. He would have cause to regret not heeding her caution.

Sebastien had been the village postman since he was a youth, and had adopted the practice of delivering the mail from mid-morning onwards, always gauging the load to within minutes of lunchtime. Ordinarily, he used the mailboxes that were fitted on the walls abutting the road, but that morning, the one that followed Adam's reassurances, Penny was outside, pulling weeds from the gravel drive, so he chose to stop for a chat. She was always pleasant and, he thought, rather beautiful, even if he was old enough to be her father. Only just, he reminded himself.

She seemed to be unusually pleased to see him, "My goodness, Sebastien, why didn't I think of you before?" As the village postman he would be a fount of knowledge. They exchanged pleasantries and a little local gossip before he moved on to the recent news of unrest in the Middle East and a civil war in Libya. It was obviously something he felt strongly about, "Those Arab people you know, they are still tribesmen, squabbling all the time."

Finally, she found an opening, "You might be able to help me with a bit of research I'm doing.

He was delighted, "But of course!"

She smiled winningly, "What do you know about Anton's neighbour, Pichon?"

His face clouded over, "Stay away from that man. Please Madame, trust me, he is not a good person. He is his father's son."

"What do you mean by that? Surely you can tell me something."

He looked distressed and uncertain, but eventually he did share something, "Once, when I was very young, his father beat me, severely, because he thought I had mislaid a letter. He frightened me so much I didn't dare report it. The Pichon's have always been that way. That is all I will say." He promptly turned and walked towards the road.

Penny called after him, "Sebastien, please, tell me a bit more than that."

He turned, "Please, trust me."

Later, when she described the exchange to Adam, she said, "You know, looking back, I'd say he was a little scared."

***

Nightingale's due diligence visit went off splendidly. Anton had asked Adam to attend, for moral support, which had been wholly unnecessary. The man was charming and a lover of fine cognac. Moreover, his enthusiasm had been further bolstered by the telephone conversations he'd had with James at head office. From the outset, his meeting with Anton was a shared venture into hallowed territory. They parted the best of friends.

Meanwhile, in England, Club Cognac was getting organised. On the sixth of March, seven were travelling by ferry, in three cars that would be loaded with tools and paint; the latter at a third of French prices. The lack of luggage space meant that the building materials would have to be bought locally. This time, they would be staying for three weeks, with the intention of making at least some of the farmhouse habitable. Barry wouldn't be joining them, having committed to some consultancy work, which he bitterly regretted. By contrast, Megan and her father were hoping to fly out for a couple of days, with Sophie. Kendall was now refusing to have anything to do with the project.

Annie and Sue were going by ferry too, a week later than the main body, with a car load of bits and pieces for their own house and while some help would be given, they had a fairly full agenda of their own. The group had spoken to Penny though, who confirmed their reservations for every available *gite*.

George was given the task of booking the ferry while Alan and Bob bought the paints and repair materials. Barbara had her own agenda, which she refused to share with anyone.

Paradoxically, Kendall wanted to use his sexual infidelities to hurt his wife, while not wanting her to find out. It was in his nature to see her as the transgressor and him the injured party, but now that she and her father had emasculated him his behaviour had become worse. He really didn't care anymore and was even paying for sex now, after a fashion. He'd discovered that one of his regulars was in the escort business and her taste for strong liquor led to an arrangement. He could just about fiddle enough out of the optics to pay her in kind. That still didn't ease the anger that continued to fester. He rarely had a civil word for Megan and no time at all for Sophie, reasoning that if her father was that important, the sooner they left to live with him the better.

Megan was beginning to think so too. He refused to respond when she returned from the Pub with her father and announced that they were going to France for a weekend, so she assumed that money was an issue and tried to reassure him, "It's alright, Dad is paying." She didn't realise it then, but she had just stepped over the line. As soon as Tom had left, the row began; another that the neighbours would share, though they didn't see him step over to the dark side and take her by the throat, slamming her against the wall. It was only Sophie's screams that brought him back from that place, yet he couldn't leave without some form of closure. He hawked and spat in her face before leaving the house to find solace in the arms of his prostitute. Megan began to sob, from deep within, as she wiped the mess off her face, but then Sophie's cries and beseeching arms took precedence. As she picked the hysterical child up and rocked her, Megan knew that the time for her own tears would have to wait.

***

That night a celebration was called for and Anton excelled himself, with breast of duck in a red peppercorn sauce, followed by *Crêpes Suzette* flamed in cognac.

When Adam made his way back to the *gite* he wasn't drunk, just comfortably dulled. The outside light didn't come on when he approached, but there was a full moon and clear sky. Ample enough light to engage the key he'd dug out of a pocket. As he neared the door a figure stepped out from the shadows and held both arms out from the sides of his body, in an unthreatening gesture. He was small, but heavily built, wearing overalls, a beret and a smile. The teeth were evident enough in the moonlight, though the voice was coarse, "*Excusez-moi Monsieur, je suis désolé de vous déranger.*" Excuse me, I am sorry to bother you.

Adam had no idea what had been said, but he saw a hand being extended in friendship. He took it and almost cried out as his hand was subjected to an unearthly grip. Then everything happened in a blur. Another hand gathered the lapels of his coat and snatched him down and forward, into a head butt that smashed his nose. Both hands gripped his jacket and slammed him against the wall before Pichon's face closed with his. Using English he had prepared from a dictionary earlier, the Frenchman snarled, "You are nosy, *Anglais*. You must stop."

Shock and pain began to take hold as Adam shook his head to try and clear his thoughts, but his vision was crazed with black dots and an attempt to fight back was forestalled when Pichon shifted his grip, pinning his victim to the wall with a forearm across the throat. He used the free hand to extract a large wrench from the overall pocket and said, in French, "Now I break a couple of ribs, to make sure you have paid attention." He drew his arm back horizontally, so as to sweep in from the side, when a blur of black flew out of nowhere and attached itself to his arm. Pichon cried out as Guinness's weight and momentum knocked him to the ground, but the dog wasn't finished. Still without a sound, it wrenched its head from side to side, inflicting tears where puncture marks had been a moment before.

Pichon had dropped the wrench as soon as the animal had barrelled into him and his cry of surprise turned into agonised yells, until finally, Guinness decided to back off, by just a few feet, with a stance that evidenced a willingness to get back to it. Pichon scuttled away on his backside for several yards, until he was sure that the dog wasn't following and then he leapt to his feet and ran.

Guinness then padded over to Adam, as though to inspect the damage, but was reassured by a stroke and patting and then content to amble off.

A trail of blood spots marked Adam's passage to the bathroom, where he draped himself over the sink, trying desperately to stop himself from throwing up and worse, from passing out. Time passed, without knowing the measure of it, but finally, he felt able to douse his face in cold water and carefully, very carefully, check to see if his nose was broken. He didn't think so, but two black eyes would be in place by the morning. The bleeding had eased enough for him to contain it with a towel, while he went downstairs to make up an ice pack. The agony of its gentle application soon gave way to relief, aided further by aspirin. Even so, the dull ache wouldn't permit sleep and besides, he had some thinking to do, so he sat in an armchair. No doubt the wrench would still be outside, with Pichon's prints on it, but the police were no fools. They would want to know about the motive and the circumstances leading up to the attack. All that would open up a can of worms for Anton, Rambert, Challans and even Fabian. He sat through the small hours, visualising the most profound means of revenge, but only as a distraction. Nothing had changed. Pichon had to be neutralised in the way they had agreed.

Penny cried out when she saw him. He'd changed out of the bloodstained clothing, but as expected, he now sported two black eyes that were partially closed by swelling. His nose looked like cooked beetroot.

"Oh my God! What's happened?"

Adam sounded as though he had a bad cold, "Pichon 'appened. Ca' I come in?"

She fussed over him, offering dressings, medication and a call to the police, all of which he discouraged. There was only one reason for his visit. Finally, Penny settled for making a coffee, over which he said, "No more questions. Sorry, not feeling up to it yet, but I was wrong an' I don' want you to get 'urt."

She wiped at an escapee tear, "Whatever have you got mixed up in?"

He tried to grin as he spoke, but his eyes almost closed completely, "A bit of bovver."

By lunchtime he was feeling well enough to visit Anton, who was as shocked as Penny had been and almost as emotional. Adam briefed him and elicited a promise to keep everything under wraps, with an assurance that justice would come soon.

Both Penny and Anton had assumed that he would eat with them that evening, but he declined, saying that he wanted a little time to himself. He had purchased steak and eggs from the butcher and begged oven chips from Penny.

That night, with the aroma of chips wafting out of the oven, he went to the door and wasn't at all surprised to find Guinness there. He stepped back and invited his guest in, who sat and watched as the steak and eggs were cooked. When the meal was ready, everything was carefully divided between two plates and one was set down on the floor, "There you go chum, you've earned it."

The only glimmer of good news came from the baker, when Penny called in the following morning. He was very amused,

"Ah, Penny, you were asking about Pichon, yes?" She nodded, uncertain now, where this would take her. He chortled, "Hubert came in this morning and told me that Pichon was savaged by a wild dog, in the woods near his house. The infirmary at Matha stitched him up and there was some talk about testing him for rabies because the injuries were so severe. They have people out looking for it now, but he won't let them on to his land. *I* pity the dog though, heaven only knows what it caught."

Hubert was the local officer of the *Police Municipale*, who by his own admission, had one of the cushiest jobs in France. Something like that would have been a major incident. Penny hurried back and caught Adam as he was leaving for Anton's. He invited her in for coffee while she passed on the news.

At the end of it Adam grimaced, "Ah, I wasn't going to mention that."

She glared at him from beneath her eyebrows, "Give."

"Well, see, after smashing my nose, Pichon was going to set about me with a wrench." He pointed at the chromed tool, propped up by the door, "That one there in fact."

This took things up to another level, along with her temper, "Why the hell didn't you tell me that yesterday?"

"I decided to settle for the visual impact of my conk, believing it would be enough to stop you from asking any more questions. There was no need to worry you any more than that."

She fumed, "For fuck's sake, I had a right to know. Who do you think you are, making judgement calls like that? This has taken common assault up to attempted murder!" She began to stand, "I'm going to call the police, this has to stop."

Adam snapped, "Sit down!"

Her jaw dropped and so did she, back into the chair.

He spoke quietly then, "Oh Penny, you don't know the half of it."

She had regained composure swiftly, "You have ten seconds to correct that, or I'm out of the door and on the 'phone."

He sighed, "OK, I'll tell you everything, but it stays here, for everyone's sake. It all began when Anton was being stuffed by the bank." An hour later he sat back, "So now you know it all. If you go to the police too many others will go down with him."

"What about the others, Club Cognac I mean. Do they know about this?"

"No and they mustn't, for the time being. There isn't a threat to their investment, but it would still cause a panic. As I said, no one else must be told."

She was still trying to make sense out of it all. Suddenly a thought came to mind, "You began by saying that you weren't going to tell me something. It had to do with Pichon's injuries."

"Ah, yes, well the beast that attacked him wasn't a wild dog in the truest sense of the word."

She interrupted, "Don't play games."

He grinned, "It was Guinness. He saved me from being beaten with that wrench."

***

Three days passed without incident, during which time Adam accepted light duties around the place. Henri didn't appear to discuss Adam's appearance with Anton, though there may have been a hint of a smile when they met on Monday. Not that anyone could see much beneath the walrus moustache.

Early on Wednesday morning Anton received a call from Fabian, who wanted to pay a visit. Given the travelling time, Anton immediately invited him for lunch and passed word on to Adam, who said, "Let's hope he has some news for us."

Since it was likely to be a working lunch, Anton laid on soup, a cheeseboard and bowl of fruit; accompanied by a *Merlot*. Fabian arrived at eleven forty five, which allowed time for a *Ricard* and made it easier for him to bring them up to date. The first item on his agenda related to Rambert, "Phillipe telephoned me yesterday in some panic. Pichon had been on the telephone, wanting to know where his copy of Anton's latest bank statement was." He looked at Adam, "I think he is a little intimidated by you, so he asked me to pass the news on with a request for guidance. I had another reason to come here today so I waited until now."

Adam allowed a short pause before, "Let me think for a moment. Carry on, what else brought you here?"

"Well, I have been trying to find out about Pichon's place. How big it is, what it's worth and if he's made any acquisitions, after all, Anton may not be the only target."

That was a good plan and Adam said so. Fabian continued, "There is a land record office we have here, called the *Cadastre.*"

Adam said, "We have something similar, it's called the Land Registry."

"Yes well, their records are very limited. They could show me a plan of the land but there were no details of ownership or the price paid. They told me that I could get that information from the local mayor's office and gave me the form I would require, called the *Demande d'extrait de matrice cadastrale.* That is where I have just been and they have promised to let me have the information within a few days. I think that perhaps it would have taken longer if I had posted it, but you know;" he pointed at his dog collar, "This does have its benefits."

Anton made to get the soup off the stove but Fabian said, "Perhaps we should finish first. I have some news. I have saved it until last." He waited until Anton was seated before continuing, "You asked me to find out about the Gestapo officer. I tried the museums further afield, even as far as La Rochelle, but without luck, but then I contacted the archive department of the newspaper office *Sud Ouest* and the people there were very helpful. In no time, their database came up with Meyer's name." Fabian pulled a piece of paper out of his inside pocket and began to read, "In nineteen fifty one, the Wiesenthal Centre tracked him down in Spain and tried to force the Bordeaux authorities into seeking extradition. They refused. Franco was still in power then and things were difficult. Besides, and this is only conjecture; at that time there were many French people who were being implicated in these actions, who were by then in positions of power. Cases were buried often enough and besides, Meyer was a relatively small fish, when people like Mengele and Eichman were still at large. A reporter did manage to locate Meyer, who refused to give an interview, but when pressed he said that he had no recollection of Jewish transports, or alleged reprisals. That was all they had. It became old news very quickly."

Anton leapt up, "OK, let's eat."

The hot soup silenced them for a while and gave Adam chance to think. In time he addressed Anton, "Would you mind giving Rambert written authority to release copies of your statements to Pichon?"

Anton looked uncertain, "If you think that is advisable."

Adam nodded, "For the time being, I want Pichon to think that he's still in control." He turned to Fabian, "We could do with speaking to Meyer, if he's still alive, but I doubt that the Wiesenthal Centre would give out information to all and sundry. The request would have to come from an official source, such as the police." The germ of an idea came to mind, which he kept to himself.

Later, back at the *gite*, he put a call through to the Leicester constabulary and asked for DC Pat Geary, the child protection officer."

She answered the call crisply, "DC Geary."

He said, "Good afternoon DC Geary, this is DS Harding, retired, are you missing me."

"I haven't thrown anything, recently."

"Now, now, you wouldn't have said that when I was your superior."

"I would have and I did as I recall, oh ex-leader. What do you want?"

"What happened to how are you? Or nice to hear from you?"

"They didn't spring to mind, I'll grant you, but what did was the nagging thought that this is going to cost me."

"Sheesh, you've become very cynical."

She sighed, "With due cause and experience. What do you want?"

He told her.

"Do you realise what you're asking? That would take an official request, which means that I would have some explaining to do if the boss learns about it. The arse kicking I would get doesn't bear thinking about."

"Pat, I need your help, for old time's sake."

"Then address your request to my boss."

"Pat, this is serious. I'm facing a bit of bother, if you could see my smashed nose and black eyes you would realise that."

"So report it, through official channels."

"I'm in France."

She murmured, "Sweet Jesus."

He continued, "Pat, you know I wouldn't be doing this without good reason."

"I can't believe I've continued with this conversation for this long. How about I just say goodbye?"

"How about I take you to lunch when I'm back in the UK and tell you a most interesting story."

"Nope."

"And I'll bring you a bottle of *Napoléon* cognac. Did I tell you I have an interest in a French distillery?"

"Sweet Jesus, a wolf in the sheep pen."

Her levity signalled a weakening, "Pat, trust me, please. You doing this will help to put down a blackmailer and a vicious thug to boot."

She did the maths and came up with four, "Who also beat you up."

"That's only a small part of it."

"Tell you what."

"What?"

"Go to the police, it's what they're there for."

"Your powers of deduction should have concluded that there are reasons for not doing that."

"This is getting worse by the minute."

He sighed, "Yeah, it's just like another Chrissy Haddon story, only this time the innocents are confronted with personal ruin rather than sexual abuse, but there are similarities."

Pat was lost for words. They had both gone 'off piste' with Chrissy Haddon and saved her life by doing so. She considered the options. Her request for information *might* not be picked up; after all, emails numbered thousands these days and were never checked unless an officer became the subject of an investigation by the independent police complaints commission. But there was no *might* about Harding, who would continue badgering her until someone in the office noticed. Last but not least, he was still a fellow member of Graham's Gang. She was still angry though, "A case."

"Pardon?"

"I said a case, not just a bottle."

She couldn't see him sag with relief, but she heard it in his voice, "Done!"

There followed something she had spent years wanting to say, "You are still a major shit, sir, retired."

***

Whilst the new bottles had yet to arrive the existing stocks were enough to keep them busy for the following two days. Progress was extraordinarily slow. With Anton still sucking on a siphon tube that was less than a centimetre wide, the transfer of cognac was agonisingly slow. Adam then inserted the corks by hand, before adding the foil and pushing the top of the bottle into the collar of a machine that rattled and shook alarmingly. The motor sparked ominously and the bottles had to be gripped firmly. It took an age to crimp the foil on and Adam fully expected to see a few bottle necks snapped off. By the end of each day his back and arms were aching terribly.

The following day was a Saturday and declared to be a day off. Adam intended to lie-in until lunch, when he would eat the two sausage rolls that waited for him, in the fridge. It was not to be. Anton began by knocking the door gently, but gradually, the beat and force increased until Adam had no choice. Whoever was down there wasn't going to give in. He left the door open and turned back towards the kettle without a word. Anton stepped in and closed the door gently, "I am sorry if I woke you my friend."

Adam said under his breath, "Me too." More audibly, he said, "What can I do for you?"

Anton sat down at the table, after noting that two mugs had been pulled out of the cupboard, "Fabian telephoned me this morning." He added timidly, "At ten-o-clock. He'd tried your telephone but it was switched off."

Adam sat opposite while they waited for the kettle to boil, "Go on."

"He has some news about Pichon's land and wants you to telephone him."

"Why didn't he tell you?"

Anton shrugged, "He knows you better."

Adam reached for his telephone, "You make the coffee and I'll make the call."

Fabian sounded excited, "Ah, Adam, the *Mairie's* office have written to me, with a copy of Pichon's holding. The original land has been in his family for generations, but they bought the neighbour's farm in nineteen forty three. The person at the Mairie's office put a note with it, explaining that the price paid is usually shown, but in this case it is missing."

Adam puffed out his cheeks and blew, "Doesn't give us a lot to go on then."

"Ah, but there is! You see; the document shows who sold the farm to them." He struggled with the pronunciation, "It was the 'Militärverwaltung, or Military Administration."

"That's interesting, how would the Germans gain owner-ship of land?"

Anton had been listening closely and began to wave his arms. "Adam told Fabian to hold on and listened as Anton explained, "The Germans shot the British aircrew there and the farmer and his family disappeared."

Adam turned the telephone back around and spoke into it, "Did you hear that?"

Fabian confirmed that he had, but the detectives mind forged on, "So they sold the land to the Pichon's for an undisclosed sum. We need to know more about that. Would you mind digging around please Fabian, my French isn't up to it, obviously."

When the call ended Adam waved a finger in the air, "We need to speak with either that Gestapo officer or his family."

Out of nowhere a thought sprang to Anton's mind, "When did you say you had a flight home booked for?"

Adam leapt out of his chair and tore the ticket out of his travel bag. He read it before waving it in the air, "It was for the eighteenth, six bloody days ago!"

In Bordeaux, Challans had finally been discharged from hospital. He'd lost eight kilos and his confidence. Laden with medication and dry dressings, they had taken a taxi home from the hospital, but now he sheltered in the apartment with his wife and child, unable to go out and refusing to answer the telephone. She held him often and at least he was eating, but he needed two things to recover completely; counselling and news of Pichon's demise.

Meanwhile, back at Waltham Parva, the other members of Club Cognac were blissfully unaware of the escalating crisis. Sue had telephoned Anton several times, but Adam had sworn him to silence, saying, "I don't want anyone else hurt when they get over here and the last thing I need is a posse of amateurs."

He'd reached an impasse though and hated it. Worse, he was having to *rely* on amateurs, while directing things at arm's length. If he'd been able to speak French, or the whole thing had been in England, he would have been chasing the leads himself. They weren't all amateurs though; the single professional telephoned him four days later, on Wednesday.

"Is there any stock left?"

The caller ID indicated that it was a withheld number, but he recognised her voice immediately, "I've put the last case to one side."

She huffed, "Glad to hear it, I've earned it."

His pulse picked up and he grabbed the pen and notepad, "Do tell."

"The nearest Wiesenthal Centre is in Paris, but they were extremely helpful and efficient. It appears that your Gestapo chappie left Spain in a hurry and now goes by the name of Arnold Myers."

"Not much of a change then."

"Not in name, but certainly in location. The last known one is in the US, in a town called Feltzburg." She gave him the full address before, "Oh, there's another snippet too. So far as they're aware, he's still alive, but you'd better pull your finger out; he's ninety five years old."

He asked, "How do they know the recent stuff? Are they still pursuing him."

"No, I don't believe so, the latest information was provided by a local reporter who attempted to rekindle things, unsuccessfully as it happened, since the paper's editor wouldn't let it run. Even so, the people at the centre were very interested in what we were doing, particularly when I mentioned that a colleague's investigations into a recent crime appeared to have some connection with Meyer's activities in Bordeaux. They made me promise to let them have details when they can be released. *That* can be your job."

Adam was grinning broadly when he said, in a faux French accent, "But of course." He continued, "Pat, I can't thank you enough."

She huffed, "*That* was a given. Let me know how you get on and take good care of that case."

He hurried over to Penny and asked to use her computer. This time, she insisted on accompanying him. The *google* map search pinpointed the town, two hundred and thirteen miles northwest of Washington DC and a data search established that it was in the Allegheny mountains, which formed part of Appalachians.

Penny asked, "So what now?"

Adam stared at the screen as the seeds of a plan began to germinate, "I know someone over there who will be perfect for the job. I need to speak with him first and then Rambert."

"Why Rambert?"

He turned to face her, "He's going to fund my trip over there."

"Has he agreed to that?"

Adam grinned, "Not yet."

It was four-o-clock; ten am in Washington DC, which was perfect. He dashed over to the *gite* for his battered address book before hurrying up to Anton, who was in the still room, refilling the pot with wine, "I have some news at last, but first, may I use your telephone please?"

He 'fat fingered' the dial pad twice before getting through to the precinct and asking to speak with Frank German.

While waiting to be put through he decided that it would be good to speak to Detective Frank German of the Washington PD again. They had shared so many memories. Some had been less than perfect, admittedly, but the end result had been a good one. A really good one, with a seriously nasty piece of work banged up to rights.

It took a little time before the connection was made and Frank German answered crisply, "German, good morning."

"Frank, how the devil are you. It's Adam Harding, from England. Well, actually I'm speaking from France at the moment."

There was an uncomfortable silence, until finally, the American said, "Hello Adam, how are you?"

Adam responded heartily, "Fine thanks."

The reply was less than expected, "I'm sorry to hear that."

"Ha ha, it's good to know you don't harbour grudges."

"I remember something you said to the good senator and I've waited a long time to use it." He made a tortured attempt at an English accent, "Fuck off, there's a good chap."

"Please Frank, put things into perspective. We had a couple of crossed lines, admittedly, but didn't we get a result? Which I might add was a joint achievement, whatever you might say."

Though Adam didn't know it, the next extended pause was due to shocked disbelief and the American's desire to simply slam the telephone down, but in the end, he simply couldn't let that one go unanswered, "By 'crossed lines' I take it you're referring to the times you nearly cost me my career and the *result* you're speaking of was *in spite* of you rather than thanks to you. For my part, I reckon that the reason I'm not issuing parking tickets today is down to pure dumb luck."

Adam's temper flared, "Screw you yank, it was me who produced most of the evidence and received a beating and don't forget I saved Chrissy Haddon's life!"

"You compromised more evidence than you produced and you saved that girl's life after putting her in harm's way in the first place; as for the beating, tough!"

Mention of the beating brought something to mind and armed Adam's next response, "I know the real reason you're still feeling pissed about the affair. You didn't get a million dollars out of Haddon, but I did."

This time Frank sounded tired by it all, "Whatever, the only thing I have left to say to you is, goodbye." With that he put the receiver down gently before slamming the side of his fist on the desk. People sitting at nearby desks chose to ignore the first crash and the second, when a mug of coffee hit the floor. It had been enough to hear him mention the Brit's name. Frank seethed as memories returned, along with a gloomy prospect. He knew Harding well enough to know that he hadn't heard the last of it.

One of the mantras Adam had drilled into junior officers was that there was no such thing as a problem; it was simply a solution hiding. This one began with the need to speak with Chrissy Haddon, but without her telephone number, the only way he could do that quickly enough was by using a courier service. He hurried back to Penny who did the research and came up with details of the DHL office at Bordeaux airport. The lady there assured them that for one hundred and forty five Euros they would promise to deliver the letter within forty eight hours, provided of course, that they received it before ten that night. He checked Penny's road map and considered the options. Either he could spend six or seven hours driving there and back himself; always assuming that he didn't get lost, either en route or around the airport, or he could enlist someone's help.

Two hours later, he found Fabian waiting for him in the rest area on the A10 at Cézac, just north of Bordeaux. From there, while the priest headed for the airport, Adam cut across to the Rambert's house, reasoning that it would save him a longer round trip the following day. Even so, it was after eight when he turned into their driveway.

Margot welcomed him like an old friend and Phillipe seemed less anxious, now that he had Anton's authority to release copies of the bank statements. For the moment at least, Pichon was off his back.

In the kitchen, over a glass of wine, he brought them up to date with most of the news and prepared to make his request, but Margot interrupted, "You must be hungry. Let me prepare something for you."

He raised a hand, "No, that isn't necessary, but I *have* come here to ask for something."

She ignored him and went to the fridge; translating over her shoulder when Phillipe asked, "What is it you require?"

Adam took a breath, "It looks as though Meyer is still alive and I need to speak with him, face to face. We'd be wasting our time by writing to him or trying to converse on the telephone. Someone with his history isn't going to jot it all down and send it back to strangers and he wouldn't talk to them over the 'phone either."

Rambert recalled Adam's interrogation of Challans while he was in a hospital bed and readily acknowledged the wisdom of Adam's logic.

He nodded for Adam to continue, "Unfortunately, I don't have the means to pay for the trip." He didn't need to add that it wasn't his place to fund it either.

Rambert asked, "When do you intend to go?"

"I don't know yet. There are a few arrangements I need to make first. The earliest will be in one or two weeks time."

The banker nodded, "I will make the necessary arrangements and will book the flight for you when a date is known."

Margot now had a question of her own, "Will there be any risks involved, to you I mean?"

Adam said, "No, Meyer won't want to risk attracting attention to that part of his CV and he won't get the opportunity to prepare anything. This will be a surprise visit."

She placed a filled baguette in front of him, "And what about here? Will he contact Pichon do you think."

"He might, but I doubt it. What protection could Pichon offer to an American? He'll also understand the need to distance himself from criminal activity, provided he still knows what time of day it is. He is ninety five years old after all."

"But if he does have dementia, is there need for you to go?"

Adam needed to explain, "We could start asking questions from here but if he is compos mentis, we'll have given him the chance to prepare for our visit. As I said, it needs to startle him. Also, dementia sufferers have periods of great clarity, particularly when it comes to long term memories." He added a caveat, "But I'll grant you, it's a risk."

Rambert said something and Margot translated, "We have no choice." She waved a hand at the baguette, "Please, eat."

It was a cheese and lardon baguette, filled with slices of fragrant ham; an ensemble that beggared belief. While he ate they reviewed things once more but Adam soon headed back to Aurigny. It was after ten when he arrived at the *gite* and found the note that had been pushed under the door. It read;

Evening Holmes,

Anton's been down in a state of high anxiety. Apparently you disappeared without sharing the news with him, so I did it for you.

Standby for a ticking off when you go up there tomorrow.

Your obedient servant,

Watson.

All was well the following morning. Any irritation Anton had felt had been eased by Penny's briefing. Even so, a penance was called for and carried out that day, replacing support wires with Henri, after which, the penitent staggered back to his *gite* for a hot bath and tumbler full of scotch.

***

The couriers managed it in forty hours, give or take and it took Chrissy ten minutes to make the call. It was breakfast time there and nearing the end of lunchtime in Aurigny, where Adam and Anton were seated at the kitchen table. By combining the courier's forty eight hour assurance with the six hour time difference, Adam had expected to receive word that evening, and was startled when Anton began to wave the telephone receiver at him, frantically. Her voice had changed with maturity, but the accent was enough, "Hey Adam, how are you? What's wrong?"

He couldn't contain the laughter, "Chrissy, it's so good to hear your voice" He hurried on, "Listen love, this is going to take a while to explain so give me your number and I'll call back." In fact, there was an enormous amount of ground to cover, beginning with Club Cognac. He'd told her about the distillery in his letters, but not the reason for their involvement. While he tried to be concise and chronological, it took over an hour, during which Chrissy interrupted with questions of her own or calls for pauses while she caught up with note taking. Eventually, she was content and knew what was required of her.

Adam tried to offer guidance, "Remind them that Graham's Gang honoured their obligation and kept the scandal out of the papers. All we ask in return is a little assistance, so that I can interview Meyer, AKA Myers. There will be no repercussions for them, either in the US or Europe, we just need to obtain information. Be assertive, this is a small favour in the interest of a continued accord."

She chuckled, "I get the message and so will Uncle Toby. You lot will continue to keep quiet if they grant you this favour."

Adam cautioned, "I wouldn't put it quite as bluntly as that."

"Adam! I'm seventeen years old; I know better than that."

"Oops, sorry, I keep forgetting that you're an adult now."

"Apology accepted. Leave it with me."

He put the telephone receiver down and looked at Anton, who had heard half of the conversation, with a nervous regard for his telephone bill, "There's a chance; we just need to hope that this 'Uncle Toby' comes through."

He wondered if the US government still felt as vulnerable as it did in two thousand and six, when they were faced with a scandal that would have made World news. They had few friends then, many enemies and a great many critics, following the invasion of Iraq. Not much had changed and he hoped that the State Department would still be averse to bad publicity. A US senator jailed for the repeated rape of his twelve year old daughter might still be something they would like to keep under wraps.

Uncle Toby wasn't really an uncle, but he was a close enough friend to be called one. He was also a US senator, who now hated her father enough to do him harm. In the meantime, he would always do all that he could for Chrissy, who was now seated on the opposite side of his desk. He picked up the telephone and told his aide to make a call.

Ordinarily, he would have given the Washington police chief, who he knew quite well, a call, but the Senator was one of the few who knew all the facts that lay behind the Haddon saga, so he headed upwards, to the State department. After all, it was they who still owed a debt of thanks to Chrissy and her British friends and the request for assistance was entirely reasonable. He reasoned to himself that if the police chief tackled him on the matter it could be argued that since foreign nationals were involved, as well as Americans, the State Department sought control.

Within hours, he discovered that the State department had long memories too and were perfectly happy to assist. After all, they were only committing an officer for a couple of days. Containment was still an issue though, so they issued their orders to the police officer who'd been involved from the outset.

CHAPTER 13

Frank German stared at his computer screen even though the lettering had disappeared out of focus. Nausea accompanied his rising anger; it was déjà vu, of the very worst sort. Rather than re-focus and read the message again, he grabbed his jacket from the back of his chair and raced down the hall to the chief's office.

"Forget it, I can't do it. I know who this is for and I'm not doing it."

The chief didn't need to ask what the detective was referring to; the original message had been sent to him and he'd forwarded it on. Instead he spoke calmly, "You *can* do it and you will. These are not my orders; I'm just passing them on." He held up a hand as German attempted to speak, "Don't ask me who issued them or why, but I *can* tell you that they came out of the State department, from a height that should have left icicles on them, so, you *will* do exactly what this British guy wants you to, because if you fuck up, the powers that be will get to my ass before they get to yours." He allowed a moment before, "And you know how unhappy that will make me."

German gasped, "But sir, you don't know what this means."

The chief interrupted, "I *do* know what it means and so should you! When direct orders come down from the State department we *do not* ask questions, we *obey* them, or rather you do. Now get out of here and do as you're told!" He saw German hesitate and this time he raised his voice, "Now!" As German turned to go his chief had one new piece of news, "Oh, at least you won't be alone. That chap Harding is coming over, he'll be here day after tomorrow so find a hotel room for him will you. I'll let you have the flight details when I know them."

The chief knew all about the Haddon case, and had a degree of sympathy that could be measured by his pretence of not hearing his junior mutter, "Fuck off!" before slamming the door.

The Senator had called Chrissy with the news some hours earlier and she had put a call through to Adam immediately. He promptly called Rambert who went onto the *Air France* website to arrange the flight and delivered a copy of the electronic ticket to Anton's that evening. Adam was cooking that night, after a fashion and perhaps wisely, Rambert declined an invitation to join them for dinner. He explained how Adam would have to fly from Bordeaux two days later, on the early flight to Paris, in order to catch the one twenty five flight from there to Washington, which would arrive at three fifty five local time. As agreed, the return flight had been booked for four days later, though on a flexible ticket, in case more time was needed. The banker then handed over an international debit card, which had been credited with five thousand dollars.

Adam was startled, "That's very generous Phillipe, I'm sure I won't need to spend anything like that."

Rambert smiled and with a gesture that was wholly out of character he placed a hand on Adam's arm and sought Anton's help with the translation, "My friend, if you achieve our aims, please, keep the change." He asked how Adam would get to the airport and Anton didn't bother with the translation. Instead he said, "I will take him."

In accordance with Chrissy's instructions, they emailed the flight details through to the Washington PD, where Frank German responded by snarling at the computer screen, "Go screw yourself!" It was entirely in keeping with his past experiences and current expectations. The oaf was arriving on a Sunday; one of Frank's hallowed days off.

Later, Anton remembered something, "You will miss the others; they'll be here while you're away."

Adam slapped his forehead, "Bugger, I'd forgotten all about them." He thought for a moment, "Tell them I've gone on a road trip for a few days. On no account tell them the truth; I don't want loose tongues in the village. If Pichon gets wind of what we're doing God only knows what he'll do."

Anton asked, "What about Penny?"

Adam nodded, "I'll pop in tomorrow morning and warn her too."

Rambert telephoned Fabian from the car and brought him up to date. With no reciprocal news they soon signed off, after which the priest telephoned the Challans on his own initiative, for he sensed that Rambert would have vetoed the call if he'd known about it, with the same concerns that Adam had. The network was large enough for leaks to occur. Fabian didn't see it that way. In fact, he saw the Challans as a family now; young, frightened and ashamed. Two days earlier they had attended his church as a family and he had heard Challans' confession. Afterwards, he sat down and counselled them; something they desperately needed and as they left the young man repeated his promise to call if Pichon made contact again.

The following morning Guinness blocked the doorway until Adam surrendered up a biscuit. Crumbs flew out from the sides of the dog's mouth as it sidled to one side. Adam feigned concern, "So you're adding extortion to your repertoire now."

Dog and victim made their way over to Penny's house, where she invited him to join them for Breakfast. It was Saturday, so Tom was at home seated at the table in his dressing gown. Adam sat down and spoke to Penny as she pulled a mug out of the cupboard, "I've come over to tell you that I'll be away for a few days; in Washington DC in fact."

She sat down and held up a hand, "I've told Tom everything. We don't keep secrets from each other."

Adam couldn't decide whether it was an update or challenge; both, probably. He wasn't surprised, or concerned, "Good, but no further, please."

She smiled slightly, "No, of course."

"Actually, that is one of the reasons for this visit. I don't want anyone in Club Cognac to know anything. One word in the wrong ear could bring Pichon back with a vengeance, literally as it happens. I'm going to interrogate Mr Myers, AKA SS Obersturmführer Meyer, provided he still has his marbles left."

Penny said, "I figured that one out, after our searches on *google* maps."

"Yes well, I don't think Meyer will make contact with Pichon. After all, once I've finished with him I'll make it clear that no further action will be taken. I will also promise that if he speaks to anyone about this, a shed load of stuff most certainly *will* happen. In truth, at ninety five, I doubt that he'd be bothered enough to warn Pichon, *but* at the first sign of trouble you must go to the police."

Tom spoke quietly, "I understand. Because Pichon will feel threatened enough to see this as an endgame."

Adam nodded, "Exactly!"

His host had another thought, "If you're going on a road trip, won't your friends think it strange that you didn't take your car?"

"Ah, good point."

Tom grinned, "There, I've been of some use already. We'll hide it in our garage."

***

Kendall Spencer was frightened, angry and very drunk. They had let him go from the Park Street station after four hours of intense grilling. That bitch had finally decided to accuse him of rape. All the same, Asians, they treated white girls as easy prey, but heaven help a white man who diddles one of their own. The two coppers were young and wet behind the ears, but they had been arrogant too. They told him that there was no statute of limitations for rape and his accuser was both distraught and utterly convincing. He countered by saying that she'd been gagging for it and when challenged he assured them that she had definitely *not* been a virgin, far from it, which was probably why she'd taken so long to come up with such a preposterous accusation. They said many things and set lots of traps, but he welcomed one piece of news. She wasn't pregnant, and his own bodily fluids, along with any evidence of tissue damage, apart from the hymen, would have been long gone. He countered their accusations with demands to see physical evidence, arguing that otherwise, it was his words against hers.

When they produced an evidence bag containing a torn bra, images sprang back to mind, of her stuffing it into her handbag, while crying hysterically. Thank God she hadn't found her panties. He'd used them to clean himself, until he saw the blood and had thrown them behind the bar in disgust, only to retrieve them after she had gone.

Until then he'd been confident of a clear outcome but the sight of her underwear had unnerved him. Had they found prints on them, or traces of skin? In truth, he had no idea how telling such traces could be in a world of DNA testing but finally, he took them up on their offer of legal representation.

They left him alone then, until the appointed solicitor arrived an hour later and the first interview ended shortly after. They left him in no doubt that he'd be called back in again.

The solicitor had sounded almost confident, but then Kendall reasoned, they always did. He hurried home where he was relieved to find that Megan was out and there were still two bottles of scotch in the cupboard under the stairs. He turned the television on but barely saw the Saturday rugby match. Instead, he took a fearful journey back to that hideous interview room and two detectives who treated him with such disdain. They had described her family, who had been preparing for the marriage her father had worked so hard to arrange and had now cancelled. By all accounts, the cost of that was nothing compared to the familial shame. They began to call him names then; animal, sick, predatory and wanted to know how many others he'd raped. As the liquor gained a hold, his discomfiture turned into anger. He reminded himself that she'd been up for it, so what right did they have to treat him so disgracefully; all on the word of a silly, stupid teenager.

When Megan returned, early that evening, from 'visiting a friend', Kendall would have been startled by an inspection of his wife's panties. Not only were they sexier than he could have imagined, but they were damp and creased too, from her lover's extended foreplay. Sophie had been with her grandparents all afternoon, while she had been in a hotel bedroom with Simon Sheldon, having told them that she was off on a shopping trip. She was surprised to see Kendall; he'd been scheduled to work that day, but any attempt at conversation was met by slurred insults. With a mental shrug, she went into the kitchen to make a cup of tea; they had eaten at her parents so that Sophie could be bathed and put to bed in good time.

There, the measure of Kendall's mood was hurtfully evident. The three airline tickets, for her, Sophie and Tom had been torn from the notice board and ripped into small pieces before being dumped on the table. Her stomach contents roiled at the sight, but as she gathered up the pieces tears sprang forth. They could be re-printed easily, but the act had been so appallingly malicious. Sophie began to cry too and ran to her with outstretched arms, in a need for comfort, which forced Megan to set her own concerns to one side; for the moment, at least. First she had to reassure her little girl with the normality of a bath and bedtime story.

She stayed with Sophie, long after the child had fallen asleep, but eventually, she steeled herself for a confrontation. This time, she wasn't going to let it go without comment.

The television was on and he was still slumped in the armchair, staring at the screen; unseeing, "That was a bit childish Kendall, even for you."

He turned his head and tried to focus on her before sneering, "Go an' tell Daddy then."

She said, almost conversationally, "You really are a little shit aren't you? What was the whisky for, Dutch courage? After all, it takes a real man to tear up tickets out of spite."

"Shaddup bitch."

She headed towards the kitchen while saying, "That was so brave of you and maybe tomorrow you'll have enough guts to apologise. On the other hand, you can drink yourself to death for all I care."

Tears of anger and hurt flowed as she leaned on the counter, waiting for the kettle to boil. What on earth had she seen in this man?

Incredibly, he managed to stagger into the kitchen without being heard, thanks to the roar of the kettle, so that she almost yelped when he lurched into her personal space and snarled in her ear, "Fuckin' fat bitch; you're sexless too!"

She almost gagged on the whisky fumes, but her anger took hold, "Then why don't you go to work and fuck another barmaid, like you usually do."

He was startled for a moment, but too drunk to care about the consequences, "Too right. They've given me more pleasure than you ever did. Half the time I expected 'Daddy' to be hiding in the wardrobe."

Her brow furrowed, "You've always hated him haven't you, in spite of all the help he's given us. At least my parents did something with their lives instead of being a relief manager for a brewery."

He rolled his head to one side, "You're kiddin' me, right? They own a tatty little corner shop that's losing money."

She couldn't bear to hear her parents spoken about that way, "Listen, you creep, I still love and admire my father. That poor kid upstairs will soon come to know that she has a drunken lecher for a father."

He was losing the argument, mostly because it was becoming difficult to assemble his thoughts in a cogent manner. Finally, he settled for, "Sexless cow. You never were any good in bed, I know *that* now."

"Get out then! Go and live with one of them, for as long as it takes for her to realise what a cheap cheating slob you really are, or better still, go and rape one of them. A five year jail sentence would be *very* acceptable."

His eyes widened, "Who told you?"

Her jaw dropped, "My God, you actually have done." She pointed at the glass in his hand, "That's what all this is about isn't it. One of them has accused you of rape. So what now? Are you waiting for the police to come calling?"

The punch came out of nowhere, knocking her to the floor and dislodging two teeth. She shuffled backwards on her bottom, into the corner formed by cupboards as blood flooded her mouth. Her cries were barely recognisable, "I shawry, I shawry."

He pulled her to her feet by her hair, "I'll give you sorry alright." She was too stunned to resist and too frightened to call out, yet somehow, through the alcoholic haze, he realised that the marks on her cheek were too visual. Instead, he pinned her into the corner as he heaved punches into her abdomen until finally, she began to lose consciousness. It was enough then to let her go and watch her collapse to the floor. He called over his shoulder as he walked out, "Now think on, bitch."

Megan curled up into a ball in an attempt to manage the pain and stay conscious. There were no tears now, just a desperate need to recover, for Sophie's sake.

She came to properly, at two in the morning and lay listening for any movement. The television had been switched off and the silence was complete, save for the gentle pulse of the electronic wall clock. After two attempts to stand, she finally made it to her feet; gasping with the pain and hanging on to the counter for support. Her head fell forward as a wave of pain rippled through her abdomen, which was when she saw the pool of blood on the floor and felt the trickle of blood down one of her legs.

Whimpering, she clawed her way to the sink and dowsed her face with cold water. It did little for the pain but in time, she was able to string thoughts together. She needed medical help, that much was certain, but someone would need to look after Sophie and that couldn't be her parents. Her father would want to do Kendall harm and would probably be harmed in the process. Kendall could no longer be trusted, either drunk or sober, in case his violence extended that far. For that matter, was he still there? She prayed to God that he wasn't.

Annie gave in at around three. Whoever was calling wouldn't leave a message on the answer phone. They just kept cutting off when the connection was made and redialling. Her first thought was that it was an Indian call centre with a poor sense of time zones, but eventually, she wondered whether it was someone she knew, with a genuine emergency.

She barely recognised what was being said, let alone the voice, until finally the caller identified herself, "Annie, I'm so sorry, it's Megan, over the road. I've had an accident and there's no one to look after Sophie." There was a pause before, "Kendall is out."

Any vestiges of sleep disappeared, "What sort of accident? Do you need a doctor?" She realised then why Megan had called. It wasn't just to tell her about an accident; the poor woman needed help. She interrupted Megan's attempt to reply, "Wait! I'm coming over; give me a couple of minutes."

The pain and bleeding had subsided enough for Megan to begin cleaning up. She had left the front door on the latch and somehow managed to put enough hot water into a bucket by putting it on the floor beside the sink and using a pint jug. She knew that hospital treatment was required, but first, the blood had to be cleaned up. Sophie would be frightened enough to find that her mother was missing and traumatised by the sight of blood.

She had stripped off her sodden panties and stemmed the flow of blood from her vagina with a tea towel, before struggling upstairs to put on loose underwear. Kendall had left the house, thank God, but he could come back at any time, which is why she had telephoned Annie; the one person in the village who could intimidate him.

Annie found her kneeling on the floor, holding the counter top with one hand and trying to clean up the mess with the other. It was a ghastly sight, but nothing compared to the shock of seeing the face that turned to look at her. One side was a bruised, swollen mass, bloodied by a split lip.

"Oh my God Megan, what happened?"

Megan simply shook the bloody hand that held the cloth, "Just nee' to clean this up, ven go to hospital. Could you take care Sophie please?"

Annie took her beneath the arms and forced her up, into a chair, "Leave that to me. You need an ambulance my love. Wait there while I call one."

Megan called out, "No! No, no no. I don't wan' an ambulance."

Annie sat down and put an arm around the woman's shoulders, before saying gently, "How else are we going to get you to hospital." The obvious finally came to mind, "Where is Kendall."

Megan waved at her face and tears began to roll down her cheeks, "Gone; don't know where."

"Then we *have* to call an ambulance."

"No!" After a moment she said, "Taxi, I'll call a taxi."

Some of the injuries were obviously internal and there wasn't time to argue, "OK, stay there. Where is your telephone?" She had an account with a local, twenty four hour taxi firm, who promised to have a car there within fifteen minutes, time enough to smother the bleeding and make Megan look as respectable as possible. At that time of night the driver would almost certainly be the owner and the last thing they needed was for him to refuse transport because she looked set to stain the seats.

The wait also gave them time to deal with other issues. Annie jotted down what Sophie normally ate for breakfast before asking, "What do you want me to do if he comes back?"

Megan sounded tired, "Nothing. She gave Annie an address book, "My parent's number is in there, under Eccleston. Could you telephone them in the morning please; they'll take care of Sophie."

Annie was giving some thought to what might happen in the interim, "As soon as Sophie wakes I'll take her over to my house."

Megan looked back with an expression that melted Annie's heart, "Thank you Annie."

The taxi finally arrived at just after four; ninety minutes later, she was in the operating theatre.

***

"I wonder where Megan's off to at this time of night?" Bob continued, "That was Annie seeing her off, so I'd bet that Sophie is still in bed."

Carol waved as the taxi drove by, but Megan didn't respond, "Oh dear, I hope that nothing awful has happened."

Bob had already reached that conclusion, "I'm afraid it has. The question is whether it's Kendall or one of her parents."

"Should I pop down there and see, do you think?"

"Definitely not, besides, we should have been on the road by now and we haven't even picked Barbara up yet."

The rest of the group had already departed in good time to reach Portsmouth for the ferry. Bob, Carol and Barbara would have to forego the rendezvous at Chieveley Services to make up time, leaving Bob to grumble about the need to stop at a garage for a couple of cans of *Red Bull*. In the event, they were only four cars behind the others in the pre-boarding queue. All three cars were crammed with tools and paints, bodies and luggage, in similar fashion to most of the other cars waiting to board; the holiday makers wouldn't start rolling up for another three months.

***

Megan had told the junior doctor in casualty that she had fallen down the stairs; a story that was patently untrue, but his priority lay in getting her internal injuries attended to. The questions could come later.

She woke in the recovery room at nine that morning and lay quietly while taking stock of her surroundings and the tubes that formed tributaries into the one that was attached to the catheter which had been inserted into the back of her hand. Soon, a nurse appeared and checked Megan's temperature, pulse, blood pressure and oxygen level before removing the oxygen mask, "There, good as new."

It didn't feel that way to the patient, whose jaw ached dreadfully, but at least her abdomen felt OK. She pointed at her jaw, "What abou' ve teeff."

The nurse took a quick look, as though they might have re-appeared magically, before saying, "The surgeon had to remove two I'm afraid, but the soreness will soon pass." Megan pointed at her abdomen, unsure of how to frame the question, but the nurse baulked this time, "All sorted, the doctor will be in shortly to tell you about it."

"Why can't *you* tell me?"

The nurse waved a hand dismissively but smiled, "Just technical stuff; nothing to worry about, but I know he'll want to tell you himself. Meanwhile, your husband and father have been in. We told them that you wouldn't be able to see visitors until you were clear of the anaesthetic, so they should go home and come back after lunch."

The thought of seeing Kendall was more than she could cope with; she asked, "And did they?"

"Your husband did, but your father refused to budge, beyond going to the refectory for breakfast. The reason I know that much is because he insisted on giving us his mobile number, with strict instructions to telephone him if you *were* up to seeing a visitor."

Megan's eyes filled, "Please, send him in."

"I will do, I promise, as soon as the doctor has pronounced you fit. He'll be here shortly."

Sixty long minutes later, a junior doctor appeared at her bedside, while a nurse drew curtains around them. He checked her notes and carried out a cursory internal examination and glanced at her jaw before declaring himself to be satisfied, but his expression implied that there was bad news too, "Well Mrs Spencer, you *have* been in the wars. We had to remove two teeth, but these days the dentist will be able to offer a number of solutions to that. Your abdominal injuries were less of a problem than we had thought, surgically speaking, but I'm sorry to say that you lost the baby. In fact, you had already expelled..."

The confused shock on her face suggested that she hadn't known about the pregnancy, but he was more startled when she grabbed his arm and interrupted, "Don't tell my husband!"

"I'm sorry Mrs Spencer, he's your next of kin; we had no other option than to tell him." He didn't add that the breaking of such news to the one who had inflicted the injuries had given him some satisfaction, particularly when it had been received with such a look of horror. It was likely that neither of them had known about the pregnancy; the foetus was only a few weeks old, but that made the case even more poignant. She was so obviously a victim of domestic abuse; such an attack from anyone else wouldn't have prompted the frail fiction of falling down stairs.

Now, he was receiving mixed signals from the patient, who said with some urgency, "Is my father still here?"

"I believe so."

"Then please, I need to speak to him, urgently."

Tom was ushered in by the nurse, who had left the curtains in place. He sidled in to the bedside and stopped, before putting a hand to his mouth and struggling to fight back tears. One side of his daughter's face was a swollen, lop-sided and bruised mess; a dressing concealed the three stitches in her lip, "Oh my God Megan, my poor darling." He hurried forward and rested his head against the undamaged side of hers. After a few moments he drew a chair up and took her hand, "I want the truth now Megan, what happened? He did this to you, didn't he?"

She couldn't lie to her father; never had been able to, but there were more pressing concerns. Tears streamed from her eyes, "Oh Dad, I've been stupid."

He sat quietly, as she told him of a wasted desert of a marriage and Kendall's stream of infidelities, but he was startled to learn that she had a lover too. Her affair with Simon Sheldon had obviously come later and was, to some extent understandable, though he couldn't help but ask why they hadn't taken precautions. She shook her head slowly, "We did, but obviously, something went wrong."

It had been six weeks earlier, when the only thing they could think of was that a stone in her engagement ring had snagged the condom as she had slipped it onto his erection. Later, when he withdrew and found just the collar of unwound rubber around the base of his penis, they had laughed. It wasn't her most fertile period and besides, even lovers were entitled to a little luck.

Tom asked, "Did Kendall find out?"

She realised what he was suggesting and shook her head, "No, but the doctor here told him. He'll know it wasn't his, he hasn't been near me for years."

He looked puzzled, "So what brought this about?"

She seemed to deflate, but the urgency and gravity of the situation overrode the pain. Clear diction was vital, "It's been building up for a long time, but I think the cognac deal brought things to a head; that and an accusation of rape. I think the police are involved."

Tom gasped, "Oh my God, this is getting worse. How did you find out about this?"

He let it slip in the row we were having." After a moment's thought she explained, "When I got home from your place last night, he was slumped in his chair, utterly drunk. All I received were insults or names like 'bitch', which was par for the course when he was under the influence. Normally, I'd have let it ride but when I found our air tickets on the kitchen table, torn into little pieces I couldn't. It was such a malicious and cruel thing to do. So that was how the confrontation began, but only after I'd made sure that Sophie had fallen asleep. Dad, I'm frightened of him, particularly now that he knows about the baby."

He squeezed her hand gently, "Don't worry; I'll make sure that he isn't allowed in here. Afterwards, you and Sophie are coming home with me and your mum."

"I'm still frightened Dad, for all of us."

"Don't be, we'll report this to the police and get a restraining order on him."

"They don't work Dad, not for people like Kendall. The next time he got drunk, a restraining order wouldn't mean a thing."

Tom squeezed again, "It has to be better than doing nothing. If what you say is true, at least the order would see him jailed."

She shook her head, but said nothing. They sat in silence then, until a nurse came in to say that he should leave, so that the patient could rest. Megan had been thinking though, "Dad, would you do something for me, please?"

He sat back down, "Of course."

***

He telephoned the Leicestershire Police Headquarters at Enderby and as soon as he had explained the reason for his call they checked their database and referred him to the Park Street station. One of the appointed detectives listened carefully and took notes, even though the call was being recorded.

It took just two hours to obtain the search warrant.

Kendall thought he'd had enough shocks for one day, but realised the need for pretence, at least until she'd been discharged from hospital. The last thing he needed was for her to make a complaint and have him charged with assault. Something he felt sorry for and a little ashamed. Once they were alone together he could convince her that it would never happen again. As for the pregnancy, well, she *would* have some explaining to do for that.

The shock at being denied access to his wife's bedside did shock him into a show of mild belligerence, which the nurse answered by saying that his wife was feeling too ill to see anyone. It was a patent lie and Kendall made to push past her when a brick shipyard in a security guard's uniform stepped out of the office. They sized each other up and Kendall backed down, and out, to his car.

The first three miles of his drive home were lost in the steering wheel thumping, head shaking barrage of vitriol, until he noticed the occupants of a bus staring at him at a set of traffic lights on red. He calmed down then, but anxiety soon replaced the anger. Had she refused to see him because she'd informed the police? It would explain why the security man had been there. The rest of the journey was lost in a series of 'did she' or didn't she's' and 'what ifs', until he got out of the car. Then his concerns appeared to be validated when two police officers got out of the car parked a few yards away. By a cruel coincidence, they were the same two detectives who had questioned him about the rape.

As soon as they had entered the house, one handed over the search warrant and offered him an opportunity to read it, which he declined. But instead of heading for the kitchen, they went upstairs, into the main bedroom. It was as though they knew what they were looking for and where to go, particularly when they opened Megan's underwear drawer and withdrew a plastic bag. Kendall couldn't see what was in there, but after dropping it into an evidence bag one of them turned to him and said, "Kendall Spencer, I am arresting you on suspicion of rape." After being cautioned he watched, dumbfounded, as they handcuffed him, then the same detective asked, "Do you have anything to say?"

In spite of his confusion, Kendall had the wit to say, "I want a solicitor."

On the way out of the house, a passing thought occurred to him; where was Sophie. With some chagrin, he realised that she would be with her grandparents. This shitty life was closing in on him.

***

It was eleven that night when the Club Cognac construction team reached Aurigny. Penny had waited up for them and caught a faint tang of something unpleasant when they exchanged greetings the French way. Even Guinness was keeping his distance. It prompted her to ask how their journey had been.

Alan exclaimed, "Don't ask; it was one of the most hideous experiences of my life and the others feel the same way, apart from Barbara, who managed to get through the crossing without throwing up."

Normally one of the most cheerful of travelling companions, Barbara had witnessed the scale of their misery and wisely kept her head down, in the belief that even a hint of cheer would have resulted in the pack turning on her. Thankfully, they all rallied as soon as they disembarked, but by then fatigue had taken hold.

Instead of commiseration, Penny's response was almost scornful, "Don't tell me you came over on the catamaran?"

Carol wailed, "We thought it would be quicker."

Penny huffed, "It might be, but they don't call it the 'vomit comet' for nothing. You should have asked me."

There was nothing more to say on the subject; they were all too tired and smelly, so Penny escorted them to the *gites* before beating a retreat. Bob, Carol and Barbara were to share the largest, while the other two couples had one of their own. Adam had been lined up to share with Megan and her father when they flew over.

When Penny climbed into bed, Tom stirred and roused enough for her to place an order, "I think you'd better buy some air fresheners tomorrow love."

The seven travellers were still sound asleep at five the next morning, when Anton collected Adam. The darkness was complete and a harsh frost added to their discomfort. Neither felt inclined to chat at that hour, so they made the journey to Bordeaux airport in a companionable silence. The short hop to Paris *Charles de Gaulle* departed at ten thirty, leaving him a couple of hours to find his way to the international departures lounge. Thanks to weekend road closures for repairs rather than weekday jams, they lost almost an hour on the approach to the Bordeaux ring road, which caused Adam some anxiety, but at least Penny had printed off his boarding passes, so that he could go straight to the security checks. They shook hands at the departures drop-off zone and as Adam reached in to retrieve his case from the back seat, Anton said, "Bonne chance my friend and bon voyage." He watched Adam walk into the terminal and noted that the chubby detective already looked dishevelled, just how a long-haul traveller should look like, at the *end* of the journey.

***

George tapped on Penny's door at eight thirty the next morning, with two French sticks, a bag of croissants and a jar of jam in his hands. Her greeting was as warm as ever, "Hello, you look a lot fresher this morning."

He grinned and gestured to the fragrant shopping, "I am too, but I've just called at Adam's *gite* to invite him for breakfast and there's no sign of him."

Penny feigned surprise, "Didn't he tell you?"

"Tell us what?"

"He's gone off on a road trip for a few days; should be back at the end of the week."

George was taken aback, "When did he go?"

He was even more startled by the reply, "Around three hours ago."

Over breakfast, when they were huddled in a crush around one of the kitchen tables he passed on the news. They were all startled but it was Alan who put their thoughts into words, "That's a bit of an odd do; he knew we were arriving last night, so why take off when we were actually here, three hours before we get up?"

Carol went further, "Surely it wasn't because he wanted to duck out of the work?"

George had wondered the same, "Well, it certainly means that we're down by one."

Bob differed, "We would have been anyway. Remember, he'd arranged to go home a couple of weeks ago, originally. Still, I'm surprised he shot off without saying hello."

There was a consensus with that and a general discomfiture.

There were more pressing matters though. They were only there for three weeks, with a formidable list of works. Penny had arranged for an electrician to visit the house that morning, to check the wiring and the plumbing had already been given a clean bill of health. The rest would be down to the amateurs.

There had been no sign of any paperwork and when they arrived at the house there was no sign of Madame Nicolas. The keys had simply been left in the door and when they stepped inside there were two bottles of red wine and a note on the table. George translated the message, "Dear Ladies and Gentlemen, I hope you have happy times here. My husband has repaired the shutters and left some logs for you in the workshop. Madame Nicolas."

Carol and Barbara were standing huddled together in the damp cold and both cried out, "Hooray!"

Bob chuckled, "OK, while you lot unload the cars; I'll get the log burner going." He was astonished at how easily the fire caught and by the time all the materials had been carried into the workshop the whole ground floor of the house had taken on a new atmosphere. The appearance of a kettle and mugs added to their growing comfort.

Within an hour, they were all at work. The huge, ungainly bedroom furniture and rusty beds were dumped in the yard, quite literally, for they found that ejection from the first floor windows served to demolish much of it on impact with the ground below. The ladies then began stripping the wallpaper from the bedroom walls, while George and Alan began painting those downstairs, after giving them a cursory wipe down. They had decided that all walls should be white, in an attempt to lift the ambient gloom, but the roughly textured walls in the living room would have to stay as they were; having them skimmed smooth could wait. Tomorrow, or perhaps the following day, they would begin to assemble the kitchen units.

Meanwhile, Bob set about the dark oak dining furniture with paint stripper, as he had promised on their first visit.

The electrician arrived at eleven that morning and spent the whole time criticising the wiring and fittings. Words like *terrible* and *catastrophe* kept being repeated. He was particularly scathing about the practice of channelling cables down the exterior of walls in plastic ducting instead of chasing them into the plaster. An hour later, George stood nearby as the electrician retrieved a pad from his van and began to complete his report. It looked long and wordy enough to empty their bank account, but eventually the electrician tore the top copy out of the pad and handed it to George with, "That will be two hundred and fifty Euros if you please."

George was astonished, "It is OK?"

The French man looked as though he'd been asked a stupid question and shrugged, "Yes."

***

Adam arrived at Washington's Dulles Airport at four pm eastern time, but it took another fifty minutes to get through Homeland Security and Customs. The arrivals hall was busy, but he had no difficulty in recognising Frank German. The detective was still lean, dressed casually as always, in a blue duvet jacket and a black pair of *Chinos*. The expression on his face hadn't changed either, along with the mode of greeting, "What time of day do you think this is?" He didn't add that Sunday afternoon was a hallowed period, reserved for the family, because he didn't want to share that much with the Brit.

Adam didn't risk suffering the slight of having an offer of a handshake ignored, but he did smile, "Sorry chum, you'll have to sort that out with *Air France*."

German turned and walked briskly out of the building to the unmarked police car he'd left in the drop-off zone. Unsurprisingly, the locals hadn't put a ticket on the screen or towed it away and when German opened the trunk and stepped back to let Adam put his bag in he gestured to the last vestiges of bruising, left over from Pichon's attack, "Still making friends I see."

It took twenty minutes to make it into the city; for the most part in silence, until Adam broke it, "Frank, this visit should be short and sweet, but it would be much better if we could start over; draw a line in the sand. See, it's personal this time. A friend in France and a bunch of other innocents are being screwed over by a thug who we believe was party to war crimes. I want to put a stop to it."

They drove on for a few minutes before Frank said, "I'm glad to hear you say that it's personal. I checked you out yesterday and guess what? You're not even a serving officer anymore. I went back to the State Department and told them, but it didn't make any difference, so your dumb luck seems to be holding."

The attempt at sabotage was no less than Adam would have expected, so he let it go. Instead, he promised to tell the whole story the next day on their drive out to see Myers.

They had reserved a room for him at the *Quality Inn* on New York Avenue, just as they had the last time, though he felt sure that it had been called a *Comfort Inn* then. As they entered the lobby Frank bluntly advised that the Washington PD were not picking up the bill this time and as soon as Adam had checked in he said, "Right, I am going home to my family; I'll be back at eight in the morning, be ready."

Adam smiled gamely, "In the meantime, there is something you could do for me Frank."

The American didn't reply, but he did stay and watch the Brit lay his case on the floor and extract a bottle, which he handed over, "Please take good care of this and hide it somewhere. It's one of the finest cognacs you'll ever taste, so enjoy it alone or with very special friends."

In spite of his ill humour, Frank was surprised. So the fat man had thought to bring a peace offering. He gave a curt nod of thanks, "I'll see you in the morning."

Adam dumped his case in the room and did the maths. It was midnight in France. His head was telling him to go to bed, but his body was making greater demands. He hurried downstairs and caught the shuttle bus to Washington Union Station, where he bought the largest hot dog he could find.

Later that evening, Frank German retired to his study, where his taste buds underwent an epiphany; he'd never tasted a spirit like it. After pouring a second measure, he went onto the web and discovered that Napoléon cognacs in the Washington wine stores came in at over four hundred dollars. He took another sip and gazed at the nutty brown liquid before murmuring, "Well I'll be damned; he's got something right for once."

***

Megan was discharged from hospital that morning, after being examined by the surgeon, but her relief was marred by the news her father had to give her. He'd spoken to one of the detectives who told him that Kendall continued to deny any wrongdoing. He was scheduled to appear at the magistrate's court that morning and would almost certainly be granted bail. In the meantime, traces of semen had been found on the underpants and the blood was the same type as the girl's. They were confident that DNA testing would be conclusive and then, perhaps, Kendall's solicitor would persuade him to change his plea. Either way, he looked certain to be facing a custodial sentence.

As he wheeled Megan towards the hospital entrance, Tom was unequivocal, "You're coming home with me." At lunchtime he knew they had done the right thing. One of the detectives telephoned to confirm that Kendall had pleaded not guilty and was out on bail.

Kendall caught the bus home from St Margaret's bus station and thanked his lucky star that no-one met him on the two hundred yard walk from the bus stop to his cottage. As soon as he closed the door he tore off his clothes; all of them. The stench of disinfectant and cloying atmosphere of the cell was still with him and he swore to himself that he'd never wear those clothes again. There was still the best part of a bottle of scotch left and he poured a generous measure before hurrying upstairs and into the shower. He was still numbed by it all mentally, but relief of sorts came from gradually increasing the water temperature until his back had become reddened by the heat. After drying off, he sat on the edge of the bed and finally considered his lot. The DNA testing would damn him; he knew that now, so his only defence lay in the claim that she was a willing participant, but they had shown him the bloody underpants, which suggested otherwise. They had gone on to assure him that the amount of blood would demonstrate that she had been a virgin. When he tried to suggest that she'd been menstruating they had explained, with some scorn, that menstrual blood was very different to the regular sort. Worse, her family were saying that they feared for their daughter's mental health and the whole family were having difficulty in coming to terms with the shame of cancelling the marriage they had arranged. He had thought of saying that she had used him to avoid the arrangement, but the coppers said that they had witnessed her distress. Her mental breakdown or worse, suicide would add a new dimension to his dilemma.

Tears of self pity rolled down his cheeks, particularly when his own wife's double treachery sprang to mind. His thoughts flared into a white heat of anger that gave rise to a conviction that left him in no doubt; she had earned the beating; it had been inevitable and would've just been a matter of time.

By mid afternoon his fears had been eased by alcohol, though the crashing thump on the door startled him. When he opened the door to find Tom on the doorstep all he could think of saying was, "What the fuck do you want?"

Tom held up what looked like an open credit card wallet, which held a single document that had been folded neatly, to occupy both sides and said, "Read it." When it became clear that Kendall was having difficulty with that Tom explained, "It's my shotgun licence. I want you to know that if you ever come close to my house or family, I will kill you. Do you understand?"

Kendall had never received a death threat, but in spite of his alcoholic haze, he knew this one was genuine. Tom waited until he saw fear in the man's eyes before he was satisfied and with that he returned to the car and drove home.

***

At around the same time as Megan was being discharged from hospital Fabian received a telephone call from Mathieu Laroche, who didn't waste time with pleasantries, "Father, I'm afraid that we have not found the files for you, we are still searching, naturally; it is very embarrassing you know. But with your project in mind, I have done some digging for information about the Chief Rabbi. Naturally, that involved many documents to do with the Jewish transports and *voilà*! I found some shipment orders. Sadly none included the Chief Rabbi, *but* they were all signed by the German you sought information about, SS Obersturmführer Meyer.

"Do you mean shipment orders for the Jews?"

The archivist coughed before, "Erm, yes." After a moment he added, "It is not much, but at least it confirms his involvement, as no doubt you suspected."

Fabian couldn't believe his ears, "Monsieur Laroche, I am indebted to you. My research will involve many small steps and this is certainly one of them. Would it be possible to have copies of those orders please, for my personal use, as you know?"

Laroche paused, they were still restricted documents, yet there was no mention of French citizens, other than those poor wretches on the transports, who had been murdered anyway. The German was unimportant in the modern day scheme of things and he was almost certainly dead too. Besides, his professional embarrassment would be eased by meeting the priest's request. Eventually, he said, "Very well Father, I will attend to it myself, on the understanding that they will not be made public."

Fabian crossed his fingers instead of himself, "But of course Monsieur, not only will they never be published in France, I will ensure that they aren't in Rome either."

The head archivist remembered the priest saying that he might send a copy of his findings to the Vatican and was glad of the additional assurance.

As soon as the call ended, Fabian hurried into his study and sat in front of the computer, accompanied by the handful of butterflies in his stomach. Fifteen long minutes later a beep signalled the arrival of an email. A minute later he could barely believe his eyes. There were six of them, all with the Nazi letterhead and a flamboyant, illegible signature, but beneath each one the name had been typed, 'Ernst Meyer, SS Obersturmführer'. He telephoned Rambert immediately, whose initial delight soon turned to consternation as he realised how important they would be to Adam. He almost shouted, "Fabian, we have to get copies of them to Detective Harding; he's in America! I have to make some calls; I'll get back to you."

Two minutes later Anton recognised the anxiety and urgency in Rambert's voice, as he opened with, "Do you have a number for Monsieur Harding."

Anton shrugged, in spite of the lack of visual contact, "No, I only know that he is in Washington, why?"

"It's imperative that we speak to him, before he sees the German." Rambert went on to explain, as succinctly as possible and in doing so, passed on his anxiety in full measure. After a moment Anton thought out loud, "Perhaps Penny knows; she's been sharing the research. I'll go and see her."

Rambert signed off with, "Then hurry, please."

Penny didn't have a contact name or number either and when they tried his mobile a recorded voice advised them that the number was temporarily unavailable. But she did have a spare key to Adam's *gite,* which she yanked off a hook on the way to the door, Come on, we'll see if he left any notes behind." During the search, in which shirts, socks and underwear were summarily ejected from the drawers, Anton wondered whether they had the right to be there and said as much. Penny waved his concern off, "Nonsense, I'm his Watson."

Nevertheless, their search was fruitless, though it had given Penny time to think. They hurried back to the house and signed on to the web, armed with the knowledge that he was in Washington and keeping company with a detective. The search for a police station revealed that there were twenty eight departments; all autonomous and so far as she could tell, without the benefit of having a central headquarters. It was then that she recalled Adam's conversations with a former colleague, who'd been party to his last American adventure. Logic dictated that the Leicestershire police headquarters would have his records still and therefore the number of his former station.

Leicestershire Police Headquarters did know all that, naturally, but they refused to divulge any of the information, no matter how hard Penny tried. Finally, in exasperation, she said slowly and clearly, "Look, this is an emergency. Would you please give my number to the female colleague who assisted him some years ago with a case involving a US senator's daughter *and* the US State Department? I don't know her name, but I believe she still works at the same police station.

The man at the other end knew all about that episode, which had become a matter of lore in the Leicestershire force. He made no promises to the caller but as soon as the connection was broken he put a call through to Harding's old station and asked, "Is Pat Geary there please, or may I leave a message?"

Thirty minutes later Penny took the call, "Hello, this is Pat Geary, I understand you wish to speak with me."

Penny gripped the receiver so hard her knuckles whitened, "Oh, thank heavens. Look, we don't know each other, but my name is Penny Challis and I've been helping Adam Harding with some research. The thing is, I now have some documents that we must get to him, immediately, but he's in Washington and I don't have any way of contacting him. Please, please, do you have a number?"

Pat wasn't prepared to give out information so whimsically. Instead she said, "I need to know more; a lot more. Let's begin with these documents."

Penny was in too much of a hurry and she snorted, "That much detail isn't necessary at the moment!"

The reply was terse, "Let me be the judge of that."

In that moment, Penny realised that she was talking to a police officer, who wasn't about to dole out information to a stranger. She took a deep breath and began from the beginning.

Pat knew the bare bones of the story which were embedded in the tale she was hearing and served to authenticate the enquiry while providing a fascinating whole. Naturally, she knew exactly how to contact her former boss, but not until she'd heard every intriguing detail. Finally, she was entirely satisfied with the validity of the call and in spite of her disinclination to get involved, she knew that there was only one way to fire up Frank German's office.

Penny was interrupted mid-sentence, "OK, I believe you, but I doubt that you'll get far by 'phoning them yourself. They'll take a message and probably leave it on his desk, but from what you told me, Adam and Frank are already on their way to see this SS officer." After a pause, she said, "I can't believe I'm doing this, but I'll put a call through for you on an official basis. I'm not getting involved beyond that though. The message will simply be to contact you."

Pat calculated that it was eight am over there; time enough for the squad room to be fully manned and hopefully, early enough to catch Adam and Frank before they left. While dialling out she sniggered and spoke to herself, "So the old goat's managed to get mixed up in a whole load of dirty goings on."

It was not to be. She tried several times, with different strategies, but either Frank's line rang out without being answered or the other lines were busy. It was almost ten am Washington time before someone answered his telephone.

***

Adam was waiting in the hotel lobby when Frank strode in at eight prompt. This time he extended a hand, but there were no pleasantries. Instead, he pointed a thumb over his shoulder, "The car's outside."

Nevertheless, Adam decided that the greeting marked an improvement in their relationship, which was borne out as they approached the car and Frank pointed at Adam's jacket, "Is that all you have?" When it was confirmed he pointed at one of the two duvet jackets on the back seat and said, "Then you'll need that; it'll be cold up there."

Adam smiled, said thank you and thought, yes, things were definitely looking up.

An hour and a half later they had climbed into the

Appalachian mountain range. Whenever they crested a rise magnificent views appeared, with mountains that seemed to be floating on valleys of mist. What had been a cold damp day in Washington was now a hard frosty one that laced the forest with white. Adam marvelled at how quickly they had moved from an urban jungle into a natural and very beautiful wilderness. When he said as much Frank agreed, though with a caution, "Most of it is still pristine, but the coal mining has devastated some parts. They don't mine coal the way you did; here they slice the top off a mountain to get at the seam. Maybe four hundred feet of mountain top is dumped into the surrounding valleys. The damage is permanent and far reaching. Water courses and natural habitats have gone forever."

It was the longest speech Adam had ever heard from his companion and he sought to keep up a dialogue, "So why is it allowed?"

"Big money and politics mainly, along with a whole lot of lobbying." He glanced at Adam and with a wry grin, "'Course, that's something you'd know about."

"How so?"

"Well, I know *why* you did it but not how. One thing was for sure, I've never seen anyone put a firecracker up the State Department's ass the way you and your cronies did with the Haddon case."

Adam said, "Ahh, it's a long story."

German pointed ahead, "There's still a couple of hours to go, so try me."

So Adam told him all about the firecracker. Two hours later they pulled into a family diner on the outskirts of Feltzburg for brunch, where Adam ordered a *Rooty Tooty Fresh and Fruity* breakfast. Frank settled for a couple of bagels with smoked salmon and cream cheese. The place was completely timbered, with around a hundred covers, most of which were empty at that time of morning, twixt breakfast and lunch. As a result their meals soon arrived, causing Frank to gasp and Adam to stare in wonder at the '*Rooty Tooty*', which came on a large oval platter filled with several rashers of bacon, sausages, eggs, home-fries, mushrooms and a pile of pancakes that were laden with peach slices, topped with sprayed cream. The flask of maple syrup and two slices of toast arrived with a final flourish. At that point Frank felt compelled to ask, "How have you lived this long?"

Adam eventually emptied his mouth and mused, "Well in England, we don't do this sort of thing as well as you Americans, though I do often think of what Willie Nelson is supposed to have said. It went something like, 'If I'd known I was going to live this long, I'd have taken better care of myself'."

Frank chuckled, "Amen to that." Moments later, he got back down to business. The reason for their trip, "You'd better give me the low down on this Nazi and what has been going on in France."

Adam had almost finished his tale an hour later when Frank's telephone rang. The lunchtime diners were in so Adam couldn't quite hear what was said, but watched as Frank scribbled some notes down on a pad. When it was over Frank said, "A message has come in for you from a Pat Geary; telling you to call someone called Anton, immediately."

Adam quickly wiped his mouth with a napkin before, "Shit, it must be important for them to chase me over here. Is there somewhere I could make an international call from do you think?" When Frank handed over his mobile, Adam asked, "Won't that cost too much?"

Frank shrugged, "Listen, the last time you were over here you nearly cost me my career; this is nothing."

The call was a revelation, which he shared as soon as it was over. Anton had provided Fabian's number with the assurance that the priest would remain on standby for as long as it took to forward Laroche's email, but first they needed a computer and an address. "So," Adam concluded, "We need to find somewhere discreet enough to receive this stuff."

Frank didn't hesitate, "Then it's a no brainer, we'll call in at the local Sheriff's office."

When the bill came Frank pulled out his wallet but Adam held up a hand, "Uh uh, this is mine." As he counted out the notes, from the wad he'd taken out of an ATM at Union Station, he asked how much he should leave as a tip and as usual, was startled by the answer, "I'll never get used to the size of tips over here. In England, I'd be given the waitress's number if I gave her that much."

Frank just shrugged, "When in Rome."

Instead of her number, their waitress provided directions to the Sheriff's office and ten minutes later they parked in front of a single storey, red brick building that was fronted by a row of tall, arched windows and an enormous national flag. Frank said, "Wait here while I go and introduce myself to the sheriff, then I'll come and get you."

Adam watched his new pal go up the steps and move to one side as two officers made their exit. Their uniform was a dull grey/beige with dark brown epaulettes and pocket flaps, which he decided were a tad drab, even though they were heavily pressed and laden with small armouries. The brunch was beginning to sit heavily and his body put out calls for a doze as he allowed his gaze to wander around the surroundings. The police building looked out onto a town square filled with shops or offices; half of which were empty and he knew the station was on the southern side of the town square because the strip of lawn near the road was the only one free of frost. That was when he caught sight of four boards that had been posted on the lawn paired at an angle to catch the attention of passing motorists. They bore pictures of two men and captions urging the public to vote for one or the other as the next County Sheriff. One was in uniform, which suggested that he was already in the post and seeking re-election. Adam wondered how that would go down with the Leicestershire force and for that matter with the local populace, but suddenly, his eyes widened in shock. He murmured, "Oh Christ," and threw himself out of the car before hurrying into the building. The lobby was small and sparsely furnished, apart from the white counter which shielded the occupants of four desks from the public. Frank was standing on the outside of the counter, talking to the man whose picture was outside. Adam didn't waste time with niceties, "Frank, there's a call come through for you; it's urgent."

German looked puzzled, but then spoke to the Sheriff, "This is the colleague of mine I spoke about, Adam Harding."

Adam quickly shook the proffered hand before taking Frank by the arm and squeezing hard, "Nice to meet you. Sorry to interrupt, but it's urgent. We'll be back directly." By then he was pulling Frank towards the door, with enough force to get the message across. Once they were seated in the car Adam pointed at the election posters, "Look at the name!"

After a moment Frank murmured, "It might just be a coincidence."

"Yeah, but as policemen we don't believe in coincidences do we?" he hurried on, "How much did you tell him, like for example, who we've come to see?"

The American thought hard before shaking his head, "No, we'd only got as far as me asking to use his computer to receive an email. Up until then it had just been police talk."

Adam sank back in his seat, "Thank God. If he's who I think he is we'd have had company."

"So what now?"

They both looked around the square until German snapped his fingers and pointed at a realtor's office, "They'll have a computer and decent printer."

The Sheriff watched them get out of the car and walk across the square to Mike O'Neill's office, before he called over his shoulder, "Bradie, over here please." The deputy joined his boss who pointed at the car parked outside, "When those two fellas come back I want you to follow them and report back to me personally."

"OK sir."

"Oh, use the unmarked car and be discreet."

The Sheriff continued to stare out if the window; lost in thought. Why would they be needing an email from France in such a hurry and what was that hasty exit about?

He didn't believe in coincidences either.

Thirty minutes later, after the two men had driven off and he was satisfied that Bradie was tailing them the Sheriff walked over to the realtor's office and stepped inside, "Hey Mike, how are things?"

O'Neill stepped up to the counter and shook hands, "As quiet as ever I'm afraid. Still, I hope the same goes for you; how's Martha?"

"Good thanks, and still baking stuff I can't keep my hands off. Actually, I'm here in an official capacity regarding your recent visitors. I'd like to know what those two fellas wanted."

Mike was more than happy to oblige, "Well there's a thing. They were from the Washington PD; one of them showed me his badge, though come to think of it, I can't remember his name. They asked to use my computer to receive an email and when I said yes they noted down my email address and made a call. The message came through a few minutes later they printed off quite a few pages. I didn't get to see what was on them because the chubby guy stood by the printer and palmed each sheet as it came through."

The Sheriff pointed at the monitor on the desk and said, "Mind if we take a look?"

They called up the email programme, but there was no sign of the message in the inbox. Mike was mildly surprised, "They must have deleted it. No matter, let's have a look at the trash file." When there was no trace in there he turned to the Sheriff, "Well I'll be damned, they deleted it from there too. Are they on some sort of secret service mission do you think?"

The Sheriff patted him on the shoulder, "No, I guess they were just being careful. You know how it is."

***

The construction team of Club Cognac finished at six that night; tired but delighted with their progress. All the wallpaper had been stripped from the bedrooms, thanks largely to the seasonal damp and one bedroom had received a first coat of emulsion.

Carol and Jayne had left at four to do the shopping and by the time everyone assembled in the Lucas's kitchen for apéritifs, the air was filled with the aroma of bacon, or more specifically, lardons. Penny had furnished them with larger pans, capable of cooking for seven, which should have been eight if Anton had accepted their invitation, but he had declined, saying that he was expecting an important call from a friend.

The shopper's remit had been straightforward; simple fare with an indulgent pudding. Someone had shouted out then, "Don't forget the cheese!" The rationale had been logical; they were too tired and hungry to wait hours for anything sophisticated, but the result was perfect. A homemade carbonara sauce and pasta, accompanied by garlic bread and a well chilled *Chablis*, followed by cheese and shop bought rum babas. Afterwards, they were too tired to linger over cognacs and unwilling to risk the effects of caffeine by drinking coffee, particularly with the prospect of another early start, the next day.

Meanwhile, Rambert, Fabian and Anton sat up until the small hours, hoping for news from Washington.

***

Frank had printed off a local map before leaving Washington, rather than risk asking the locals for directions, but it still took fifteen minutes to find the place, in a suburbia that looked as though it had been built in the seventies. The house was a single storey ranch home, standing in a quarter of an acre or so of well tended lawns. Those and the brick construction set the place apart from the neighbouring properties that were either aluminium or vinyl sided in much smaller, less cared for plots.

Meyer answered the door and snapped, "Who are you; what do you want?" There was still a slight accent and a stance that hinted of a military background. He was tall, certainly over six feet and lean, with chiselled features that helped to exaggerate his roman nose. Adam decided that the only thing missing was a duelling scar. If it hadn't been for the deep lines around the eyes and liver spots that covered his balding head, strangers might have thought he was twenty years younger, but it was the eyes that caught Adam's attention. They were a cold bluish grey with a pitiless stare that was austere and intimidating. 'Yes', Adam thought, they're the eyes that watched Jewish women and children being crammed into cattle trucks, while you knew exactly where they were going.

Frank showed his badge and said, "Mr Myers?"

Meyer simply nodded and waited for more, "This is my colleague, Adam Harding; we would like to have a word with you please."

"What about?"

"We'd rather not explain on the doorstep; may we step inside please?"

Eventually, Meyer took a step back and gestured for them to do so, before directing them into a large lounge. One wall was covered by well stocked bookshelves and a large mahogany desk sat at the far end, in front of a picture window that looked out onto the rear lawn and a screen of mature trees. Meyer walked over to a wing backed armchair and waited for them to sit; Frank on the adjacent sofa and Adam on the opposite armchair. All were in the same burgundy leather. The suite must have cost a fortune, but like the carpet, it was showing signs of wear. Meyer seemed to be a man of few words. His first was simply, "Proceed."

Frank opened with, "I think it would be better for Mr Harding to explain the reason for this visit." He turned and held out a hand, palm upwards, "Over to you."

Adam had prepared for this, "Thank you for seeing us Mr Myers, because at the outset you may feel alarmed. Please don't be. All I ask for the moment is that you hear me out." He waited for an acknowledgement that didn't happen, so he ploughed on, "A Frenchman you were associated with during the war is blackmailing three people right now, because he wants to buy a neighbour's farm for a song. What we don't understand is how he came about the information he is using. Most of it involves wartime activities; collaboration and the like, which included you and my hope is that you can shed some light on things. See, certain files regarding German/French dealings have gone missing, which leads me to think that this man's name is mentioned too."

"You're English."

Adam nodded, "Correct."

"Then what are you doing here with a detective from Washington?"

"They very kindly offered assistance."

"Get out."

At that moment, as if on cue, they heard the front door close and seconds later, Shefiff Bernard Myers entered the room, "Hi pop, everything OK?"

Myer's face lit up, "Ah, my cavalry has arrived. These gentlemen were just leaving, perhaps you could show them off the premises."

The Sheriff extended an arm towards the door, "Gentlemen, it's time to leave."

Adam was the first to stand, knowing how much he was going to enjoy the rest of their visit, "No problem, I was just explaining to Herr Meyer how he could live out his days here, instead of in a French jail. What will happen now will be devastating to both of you, because it will be front page news within forty eight hours, well before your election day."

The Sheriff growled, "Are you threatening us?"

Adam shrugged, "Yes."

"Then how about I arrest you two now, for threatening an old man and a law officer? Let's see how that goes down with the Washington PD."

Frank was standing too by then, "And the State department; they sanctioned this visit. If you arrested us, your office will be swarming with Feds before you go home tonight, which will ensure that it's front page news tomorrow."

Adam turned to the old man and spoke reasonably, "The Wiesenthal Centre are still very interested in you Herr Meyer; enough to provid us with your current address. They are still miffed by the French authority's refusal to indict you on the grounds that they lacked evidence."

Meyer senior smirked, "Quite so."

Adam returned the expression, "Of course, they haven't seen these, yet." He pulled a sheaf of papers out of his inside pocket and handed one each, to father and son, "These are copies of the shipment orders for Jews, from the Bordeaux area, all signed by you. Of course, there will be more, now that we know where to find them."

Meyer glanced at the document and snarled, "You think anyone is interested in this now? It is history; ancient history and I am ninety five. They don't have long enough to take action against anyone my age."

Frank interrupted, while referring to a notepad he'd taken out of his pocket, "Actually, Herr Meyer, on the twentieth of February, this year, the German authorities arrested a man named Hans Albrecht on charges of being an accessory to the murder of at least three thousand people; Jews in fact. He is ninety four and was just a lowly *Unterscharführer*."

Adam stared at him agog, thinking 'where the fuck did that come from'?

Frank continued, "Thankfully, I'm religious enough to believe you'll soon be fed into a furnace of your own making, *after* the cremation, but in the meantime you may want to remain here and see your son continue being the Sheriff."

Meyer addressed his son, "Get them out of here now!"

"Wait a minute Dad, I want to hear what they have to say." He sat on the arm of the sofa and pointed at Adam, "You; tell me what you came here to say."

Adam repeated what he'd said to the old man and then moved on, "The Frenchman who is the subject of my interest is named Pichon. My only concern is putting a stop to what he's been doing; that is all. Your father can burn in hell for all I care, but this evidence won't see the light of day if he gives me enough to do the job. You see, we need to keep the black-mail secret, because too many good people would suffer if the information Pichon's using became public, so the aim is to make it too dangerous for him to continue."

The Sheriff scowled but said nothing for a minute or so, before he reached a decision, "What guarantee do we have that you won't go ahead and make this public anyway."

Adam said, "None, apart from my word, but then I *can* guarantee that it will become public if you don't help us." Adam smiled inwardly and thought, 'spoken like a true copper'.

"I need time to think about this and to speak with my father."

Frank interrupted, "No way. When we leave here we won't be coming back."

A thought occurred to the Sheriff, "Who sent you this stuff?"

Adam pulled out another sheet and handed it over; it read,

Bonne chance my friend. The head archivist has the originals and believes there are more. He will continue searching.

Cordialement,

Fabian.

It was enough, for the Sheriff, at least. He looked at his father, "You need to do this pop."

Meyer snarled, "Show me that!" He read it and continued in the same vein, "This could have been sent by a hoaxer, just like these two."

His son sounded resigned, "Look at the sender's details."

Meyer glanced at it and said, "So?"

"He's a Catholic priest! Do you think he'd be involved in some sort of scam?"

His father wasn't convinced, "I am not happy about this."

Bernard flexed his metaphoric muscles, "Then don't be, but I'm not willing to see these two walk out of here and ruin all of our lives. Think about Martha and the kids as well."

They sat in silence then, for several minutes. The old man's arrogance needed time to fracture. Finally, with eyes that had witnessed torture and barbarity with indifference, he glared at Adam, "What is it you want to know?"

Adam pulled out a notepad and began with, "OK, let's begin by establishing a fundamental truth. You are, or were, SS Obersturmf*ü*hrer Ernst Meyer."

The man seemed to straighten up in his chair, "And proud of it."

The Sheriff slipped off the arm of the sofa and sat beside Frank. This looked set to be discomforting.

Adam continued, "Then please tell me all you know about Pichon, from the beginning."

"Then you must be talking about Maurice Pichon, or is it his son? It's of no consequence, I am sure they have a lot in common."

It was revelatory from the beginning; the story Anton had told him about the German's seizure of the hidden cognac suggested that it had been a chance discovery; not the result of a betrayal. Generations had suffered since. But there was so much more, such as Pichon's purchase of his neighbour's farm, at a tenth of its value. Meyer didn't add that a similar amount had been paid to him personally, forming part of a much larger cache of illicit wealth, but he would die rather than reveal any details of that. Yet the more information the old man imparted, the easier it became, to such an extent that he closed with, "There was one thing. That farmer, the one who sheltered the British aircrew; we did what we had to do, but I remember one of his sons was a dimwit; a subnormal. The whole family went down except for him, though he took at least two bullets before disappearing out of the barn and into the wood like a frightened hare. None of us expected it but there was no time to carry out a search. He was dying anyway. I asked Pichon about him some months later and he confirmed that he'd found the youth and dumped him into a lake."

Harding looked up; his pulse racing, "I want that in a statement, now."

"No."

"Fine, I'm off to find a French reporter and he can come with me and the *Gendarmes* to drag every lake around that farm. Bodies bring a stink with them, in more ways than one.

As Harding and German rose to go the old man called out, "Wait!" He rose from his chair and stood erect, still with the dominating presence he'd have had as an SS officer, "You guarantee that this will never be made public?"

Harding said, "I do." While hoping he'd be proved a liar.

Forty minutes later, they left the house, with a signed statement from a loathsome and heinous old man.

Frank summed it up perfectly, "I feel soiled."

Back in Feltzburg, Bernard Myers felt the same way, for a short time, until he reasoned that the old man didn't have long left anyway, so what could be gained by a court case over an ancient history that just didn't matter anymore. Besides, as pop said, 'he did what he had to do'. They were just following orders, just like soldiers should. There was also the question of a significant estate, which included overseas investments, the details of which pop had kept secret. They'd become evident soon enough and now, pass down to him, without the drain of legal expenses. Nope, they had done the right thing. His decision had ensured that the family wealth would stay where it was and so would Felzburg's Sheriff.

An observer might have concluded, 'like father like son'.

After the initial review of the encounter, in which they shared the delight of a successful interview and disgust of the subject, little was said during the first half of the return journey. It had grown dark and patches of frost ventured out from the forest onto the tarmac, like unwelcome organisms. Accordingly, Frank drove with additional care. Suddenly, Adam remembered something, "How the hell did you come up with that gem of information about the prosecution of a war criminal, last month?"

"You mean indictment?"

Adam waved a hand, "Whatever."

"Well, in spite of my feelings about this visit, I was intrigued enough to do some research of my own. You hadn't given me a lot. In fact, all I knew for sure was that we would be interviewing a known war criminal who might know something about a bad guy in France. My first thought was that there couldn't be any German war criminals left alive, but I soon found out that there are and they are still being hunted. Which reminds me, will you pass those Nazi shipment orders on to the Wiesenthal Centre?"

Adam had been thinking about that, "No, I gave my word and besides, if Meyer's case became public I'm sure he'd find a way of taking my friends down with him too."

"So the thousands he sent to the gas chambers don't count?"

"They do Frank and always will, but they are dead, God help them. My concern is for the living innocents." After a moment's thought, he asked, "Are you casting a judgement then?"

Frank shook his head, "Just playing devil's advocate. It's your case, your call."

Adam wasn't finished, "Tell me what you would do."

"Me? I'll just pray for divine justice."

Frank's passenger turned his head to look out of the side window, so he was only just able to hear the muttered words, "Amen to that."

After a while, they began to talk about general things and for the first time, German spoke about his family and the things they liked to do. He even went on to explain the subtleties of American football, but Adam would have none of it. In his view Rugby was still the real man's sport; just as brutal but pacier, with a different regime of subtleties. They differed of course, but it was good natured. When Frank mentioned that ice hockey was another of his favourite sports they *were* in agreement; in that it had a unique brutality, the World over. The American then startled Adam by saying, "Why don't you stay over until the weekend. I'll take you to a game."

Adam was touched and tempted, but he had already decided what to do, "Thank you, but to be honest, I've decided to bring my return flight forward to tomorrow, if there's a seat available. The sooner we can sort Pichon out the better."

They finally reached the hotel at eight that evening, where Frank declined the offer of a drink, on the grounds of fatigue and a wish to get home to his family. Adam jested, "I'd have thought that today had been a short shift for a detective."

Frank grinned, "Whatever, I'll see you tomorrow morning. Telephone me when you've demolished another breakfast."

Adam tucked the document file he'd been given under his arm and had ambled halfway across the hotel lobby when a voice called out, "I hope you're not planning to sneak off to bed without saying hello."

He whirled around, "Chrissy, what are you doing here?"

Her long dark auburn hair reflected the overhead lights in waves and *how* she had grown. The young girl had become a very beautiful young woman, with considerable poise, he noted as she walked towards him, with extended arms. "It is so good to see you again Adam, or should I call you detective still?" They hugged tightly before he replied, "No, I'm just a mister now."

She smiled archly, "So why aren't you behaving like one?"

He shrugged, "I walked into this one by accident, one that should end happily now, thanks to you."

"Well provided you're not too tired, now's as good a time as any to bring me up to date." She pointed at the lounge area, "Fancy a drink."

He looked at her dubiously, "What's the drinking age here?"

She looked back from beneath her eyebrows, "Twenty one, which is why I've been supping diet coke all night." After a moment she teased him, "I wouldn't expect you to though; I doubt if you've taken the pledge, not after buying into a cognac distillery."

The waiter arrived and took their order for a diet coke and a *Boilermaker.* As he turned to go Adam lunged for the bar snacks menu and called out, "Hold on." After quick scan he opted for a club sandwich and fries and offered the menu to Chrissy who shook her head, "No thanks, I've eaten."

They settled back into their seats while Adam asked her about school, her mum and her driving licence which prompted him to ask, "Did you drive all the way up here?"

"It only took four and a half hours, that's less than you did today."

He didn't know how to answer that without sounding matronly so he moved on to safer ground, "So you've been tracking me then. Like, for example, how did you know I was staying here?"

"The uncle who sorted things out with the State Department for you kept me up to date with a lot of stuff, but then so did Pat, who didn't realise that she had competition now, in the person of a lady named Penny."

"I suppose you had a lot of catching up to do with Pat; you must have been startled to hear from her."

"Not at all, we've kept in touch over the years."

He noted her choice of phrase 'over the years' instead of 'since the case'. She must have thought of it too, because a moment later she said quietly, "I've been getting help dealing with what happened and it's OK, but Pat has been a good listener."

The only thing he could think to say was, so far as Chrissy was concerned, perfect, "I cherish your letters you know, more than you could imagine."

She came back to the present as the drinks arrived, "I've spoken to Penny as well, since you omitted to tell me about your travel arrangements. She told me to tell you that Watson says good luck Holmes."

He chuckled, "Now would be a good time to bring you up to date." It didn't take long; she already knew the background so there was only a need to detail their meeting with Meyer, though she was affected by the sight of a shipment order, "It's weird, but just holding this paper feels menacing."

Adam nodded and took it from her, "That's exactly how I felt." After sliding it back into the file he moved on, "I'll tell you a bit more about France."

She replied fluently, *"Peut-être que tu devrais le faire en Français ."* Perhaps you should do so in French."

He look nonplussed, so she waved a hand, "Forget it, I'm just showing off. Stick with English."

A thought suddenly occurred to him, "Shit, I was going to change my flight home to tomorrow."

She lunged into her bag and extracted an *Ipad*, "No problem, do you have your booking reference?"

He jumped up, "I will have, in a minute, it's in my room." When he returned, five minutes later, his food had arrived, which left them both with something to do. Chrissy took the form from him and set to work while he ate. After wrestling with the *Air France* website for fifteen minutes, she announced, "The only seats they have are in business class."

He grinned, "That sounds perfect." Then handed over his debit card.

The hop down to Bordeaux was neither changeable nor refundable, but there were plenty of seats at that time of year and he still had ample credit on the card.

Afterwards, over another beer, he told her more about Club Cognac and their adventures, but it was getting late and they were both tired. He asked, "When are you going back."

She rocked her head from side to side, "When you do, I guess."

Adam clapped his hands together, "Wonderful! The flight doesn't leave until six tomorrow night so we can spend the day together."

She grinned, "I was *so* hoping you would say that."

He made to rise, "In that case, I have to get some rest. How about we meet up for breakfast at eight?"

The following morning, while Chrissy considered the fresh fruit and cereals on offer, Adam hit the hot buffet, hard. She chortled at the sight of his plate but left it at that, though before commencing his attack, Adam handed over two sheets of paper, with an explanation, "I know I can trust you not to share that with anyone Chrissy, but if anything happens to the original I'd like to know there's a copy somewhere. It's a copy of the Nazi's statement, would you mind holding it for me please."

She took it from him and said, "Of course I will. Do you mind if I read it?"

He picked up his knife and fork, "No, go ahead."

When she finished reading her eyes looked haunted, "And you're going to let him off scot free?"

He repeated the explanation he'd given to Frank but could tell that she wasn't convinced. In the end he laid down terms, "Chrissy, you have to trust my judgement in this. Too many of my friends would suffer if we took this further. If you can't agree to my terms give me that statement back and we'll say no more about it."

She shook her head, "No, I'll do it, but I hate this man, even though I've never met him."

As soon as he finished breakfast Adam went back to his room and telephoned Frank German, who answered warmly, "Good morning chubby English person, how are things?"

"Excellent thanks, but there's been a development. Chrissy Haddon turned up last night and stayed over, so I have to ask what your plans were for today."

German said, "Well, it depended on whether you managed to change your flight, but if there was time, I'd planned on showing you around, but hey, I'd understand if you want to spend time with Chrissy." After a moment's thought, he said, "Mind, I'd be happy to show you both around, if you wanted."

It was an unexpected gift, "That sounds absolutely wonderful Frank, if it's OK with you."

Thirty minutes later Frank found them waiting in the lobby. He shook hands with Chrissy before asking, "I guess you've seen most of the capitol, so I hope this won't be a bore."

She shook her head, "Not at all, it'll be fun seeing it through Adam's eyes and besides, there's always something new to see."

There was too. After a whistle stop tour of the Lincoln, Jefferson and Vietnam memorials, they agreed to look for somewhere indoors. It was still cold, with a fine drizzle of rain that showed no sign of stopping. Chrissy's suggestion of the Smithsonian National Air and Space Museum proved popular with both men but it was soon evident that there was far too much for them to see in half a day, particularly when lunch at the

'Wright Place Food Court' beckoned and before long it was time to head for the airport. Chrissy hated goodbyes, particularly at airports, so she hugged Adam and said, "If I set off now I'll miss the rush hour and be home by eight, but take care." She stepped back so that he could clamber into the car and as he was closing the door, she added, "Oh, and make sure you nail that turkey." He was still grinning when they approached the airport.

As Frank handed Adam his case in the drop off zone he extended a hand, "I have two observations to make. This time I've come through one of your visits without needing medication *and* my career is intact; things are looking up. Have a safe trip home." Adam almost hugged him and was halfway towards the terminal entrance when he heard the American call out, "And that is a damned fine cognac!"

It was a first for him and thoroughly corrupting as he entered the business class channel and strode past the hundred or so cattle class travellers waiting to check in. He was the only one in line and the clerk was extremely pleasant; giving him directions to the business class lounge once he had slipped through the fast track security check. The lounge was a long affair, with a huge picture window on one side that looked out onto the tarmac and much of the other side was taken up with a buffet. The bar lay behind the reception desk and served up a very acceptable whisky sour. When the boarding message appeared he was aware of the envious looks as he strolled past the queue he *should* have been in and straight on board, where he was welcomed with a glass of champagne. This, he thought, is the life.

The food, wine and entertainment were wonderful and while the lie-flat seats were a novelty, he was too broad to fit comfortably within the niche. Instead, he dozed fitfully in the reclined position. On waking the next morning he had considered telephoning either Rambert, Fabian, Anton or of course Watson, but as time passed he'd come to realise how weak their position was. Caution was called for. They didn't have the force of law or anything that could incriminate Pichon directly; beyond his blackmailing, which lacked proof and had to remain a secret. Their only hope lay with the threat of exposing the Pichon's wartime activities. Collaboration was one thing, but the direct involvement with a war crime and the hitherto unknown responsibility for the German seizure of the area's cognac stocks, would make him a pariah, even though his father had been the guilty party. Modern generations were still affected by the loss of those stocks, while Pichon the younger thrived. Moreover, his attempts to buy Anton's land were as corrupt as his father's purchase of the other neighbour's farm. That, if nothing else, would mean that he had as much to lose as anyone, if things became public.

They would only get one chance with Pichon and that would have to be by surprise. Adam knew he was right not to telephone the others, in spite of the anxiety he was causing, because if Pichon ambushed anyone he would have little difficulty in intimidating them into leaking information. Anyway, he was heading back two days earlier than expected.

The flight landed at Paris Charles De Gaulle airport at seven forty five, leaving him ample time to make it across to domestic departures. The service to Bordeaux was a continuous shuttle and his reservation was for the twelve forty five departure. Thankfully, his transatlantic ticket entitled him to use the Business Class lounge, which made the wait more comfortable. It also allowed time for him to telephone Anton, who was as anxious as expected, "Adam! We have been worried. Is everything OK?"

"Yes, fine thanks. I'll explain everything when I see you."

Anton groaned, "But that will not be until Saturday, surely you can tell me something today."

"I intend to, if you could pick me up at the airport. The flight arrives in Bordeaux at two thirty."

"Where are you now?"

"I'm at Charles De Gaulle."

"Oh my goodness, you have come back early. Then I think it is bad news you've come home with."

"Not at all, but it will have to wait until we meet up; I'll explain everything then."

"Surely..."

Adam interrupted, "Nope, it'll have to wait, sorry."

CHAPTER 14

Thanks to a total disregard of speed limits, Anton and Penny were waiting for him in the arrivals hall. He shook hands with Anton and gave Penny a peck on the cheek, but she beckoned him back, "We're in France, give." With a tired smile he returned for a peck on the other cheek.

As they headed towards the car park Anton explained, "We will go to Fabian's house; Rambert is meeting us there." He tapped his chest in the vicinity of his heart, "The wait is not good for me, but I suppose you will want to tell us your story when we are all together."

Penny cut in, "Particularly since your marbles are still half-way across the Atlantic."

Adam nodded his thanks and asked, "Is there somewhere I can get a strong coffee?"

Rambert and Fabian had obviously been waiting for some time, judging from what was left in the wine bottle. Three more glasses had already been set out, but another bottle had to be opened. When they were all seated Fabian was the first to speak, "Welcome back Adam, we've all been anxious for news. Was the trip successful?"

Adam noted the implied criticism and nodded, "Yes, for the most part." He went on to chronicle the trip in detail, and for the most part the others sat in silence. The continued need for translation caused delays but finally, he closed by presenting them with Meyer's statement. A babble of voices mirrored their delight and shock, until Penny summed it up perfectly, "This makes it so real. It's hard to think of that sort of thing happening in our village." Thanks to the need for translation, Rambert was the last to see the document, with Fabian, but his delight was clear and it looked as though a great weight had been lifted from him. Sadly, it was time for a reality check.

Adam called them to order and continued, "In some ways the trip was successful and in others, less so." He looked at Fabian, "Those transport orders were pivotal, particularly in persuading his son to help and let's face it, we were bloody lucky to find Meyer alive still *and* compos mentis, but now that I've had chance to assess the information I realise that it may not be as effective as we'd hoped. That is why I didn't telephone you." He waved a hand at the file, "We now have conclusive proof of the worst sort of collaboration, but remember, that was Pichon's father. Albert was only a child at the time. Now, I am sure that if this was made public he'd become a pariah in the community, but few seem to like him anyway, so will he care?" He glanced at Rambert, "It would certainly be relevant if he was charged with blackmail, but that's the last thing we want."

Rambert's despair was painful to see as Fabian translated, "So what are you saying?"

"I'm saying that this needs some thought. We need to ambush him with this lot to begin with, to demonstrate that we have the resources and will to cause him grief and then we'll hit him with something he *will* fear. Meyer's statement proves that Pichon's purchase of the farm was illegal, in that the price was a tenth of what it should have been, as a reward for the betrayal of the previous owner and the allied aircrew. That would have been a dreadful injustice to the farmer's extended family, who'd been effectively disinherited by Pichon. The old man, granted, but Pichon junior won't want to risk losing that land by having the deal overturned."

Anton asked, "Won't these threats push him into carrying out his?"

Adam turned his mouth down, "It's possible, but I doubt it. If he did, it would be out of pure malice, but we now know enough to turn the tables on him. There will be nothing to gain if he goes down for blackmail while the lawyers pick over that land deal."

They were all subdued, when Fabian said, "Then it is risky, you think?"

Adam nodded, "I'm afraid so, but it will be a considered risk and I don't know of anything else we can do, other than carry on with things as they are." He held up a hand, "But, if any word of this gets out before we see him we'll lose the advantage of surprise."

Penny knew what was necessary, "Then perhaps the sooner we meet with him the better."

Anton asked, "When?"

Adam said, "Why not tomorrow? As Penny said, the sooner the better; it's the main reason for my early return."

"Then should we telephone first, to make an appointment."

Adam was appalled, "No way! As I said, we need to ambush him."

Anton was still worried, "But how will we know if he'll be in?"

"That's easy; we'll go at noon, when the whereabouts of every Frenchman is known."

Fabian asked, "Who should go do you think. Phillipe must, and so should you, but how many others?"

"Good point, if we go mob handed he'll put up the barricades. On the other hand, we'll need a translator."

Penny interrupted, "It's no good looking at me, I'd be no good if things become technical and anyway, I'd probably end up yelling."

Anton was equally reluctant, "I think he would be upset to see me there."

Adam turned to Fabian, "That leaves you. I must say, it wouldn't do any harm to have a man of the cloth with us, but how do you feel about it."

Fabian sighed, "I've committed several indiscretions in this affair and something tells me that there will be more if I accompany you, but I cannot refuse."

Predictably, Adam was appointed as spokesman for the confrontation and they agreed to meet at Anton's by eleven the next morning."

An hour into the journey back to Aurigny Adam yearned for the travelling to end, but the thought of his *gite* brought with it the realisation that Club Cognac were in place too. He groaned audibly, before tapping Penny on the shoulder, "Would you mind dropping me off at a hotel in Cognac and coming back for me in the morning? I can't cope with the others tonight."

Penny called over her shoulder, "I guessed as much and made sure the outside light on your *gite* won't come on. We'll just have to smuggle you in."

Adam sagged with relief, "Watson, I don't know what I'd do without you."

***

After only four days, they had transformed the farmhouse, though for the most part, the bedrooms had seen only cosmetic changes. Walls had received a second coat of white emulsion and most of the woodwork had been painted in gloss. Everyone thought that the place was taking on a light airy feeling, except for Barbara. She'd been delighted when they allocated the smallest bedroom to her, but she still thought that it looked a little clinical.

Bob had finished stripping and waxing the furniture, revealing the lovely honeyed hue of old oak. It earned universal praise, particularly when the twenty pounds he'd spent was measured against the cost of buying new stuff.

Meanwhile, Alan and George had assembled and fitted most of the kitchen units. The light cream doors and drawers added to the lightening effect of the white walls, but the dark green work surfaces provided a practical and pleasing contrast.

In light of such progress, they decided to bring the shopping expedition for furniture forward to Saturday, two days hence. That triggered another set of concerns about Adam's absence. Alan voiced the group sentiment, "If he can't be bothered to be here, he can't expect to have any say in the choice of furniture."

The next morning it was Alan's turn to go and buy the bread for breakfast and he returned with news, "I believe Adam is back."

Carol said, "How do you know? I was out there a moment ago and there's no sign of his car."

"Be that as it may, but Guinness was waiting at the Adam's door and I trust his judgement."

George grumbled, "Well I hope he's prepared to start work. I'm a bit disappointed to be honest."

There were murmurs of agreement before Alan was appointed as envoy and despatched while the others cleaned up after breakfast and prepared for another day's work. The dog was no longer stationed at the door, but Alan was confronted with a choice; should he be welcoming or critical. His courage failed when Adam opened the door almost immediately, with a cheerful, "Good morning sir."

Alan put on his best reptilian smile, "Morning to you Adam and welcome back; we'd thought you'd abandoned us." He stepped inside without offering his hand, prompting Adam to think 'how very unfrench and where the fuck did he get that smile from, the *Pound Shop?*' Nevertheless, he played along, "Coffee?"

"Thanks, I'd love one." Guinness offered up a token woof before returning to his bowl of cornflakes, sugar and milk, so Alan decided it was safe to sit down at the table and asked, "Have a good trip?

Adam spoke over his shoulder while making the coffees, "Not bad thanks, but it's good to be back."

"Well, as I said, we've missed you. Did you see or do anything special?"

"Oh this and that, but it was a bit too cold for sunbathing."

Alan wasn't going to leave it at that, "So you were down on the coast."

Adam was beginning to enjoy himself, "Pretty close for some of the time, but as I said, the Atlantic coast is not an ideal place to be at this time of year."

"So presumably you visited things instead; anything in particular?"

"Nothing to write home about I'm afraid; a museum or two, a few memorials and three restaurants a day. All of it foreign stuff."

Alan tried again, "Come on mate, give me some specifics."

Adam chuckled, "It will have to wait until we're all together. That will stop me from becoming a repetitive bore. Anyway, what about you lot; how's the house coming along?"

Alan seethed inside, 'Chubby Chops' either had a lousy trip or he was lying. Either way, he obviously had no intention of divulging any of the details, at least for the moment. Perhaps the women would have better luck with an interrogation. In the meantime he described their progress while Adam offered up praise and admiration, just as one should. After that Adam stood and excused himself, "Sorry, just need to visit the loo. Travel always wrecks my metabolism."

Left alone, Alan scanned the kitchen for any clues. All the surfaces were bare and there was no sign of any luggage. Finally, he crept across to the litter bin and peered inside. There were only two things in there, which he grabbed and glanced at before stuffing them into his pocket. His pulse was racing as he hurried back to his seat, whispering to himself, "Well, well, you've been telling fibs Mr Harding." He couldn't wait to have a closer look, so as soon as Adam returned he finished his coffee and stood to leave, but not before asking, "So, are you joining us today?"

Adam seemed slightly distracted, "This afternoon perhaps, I've promised to help Anton with something this morning."

"Ah well, we can live in hope. We'll see you eventually, I'm sure. Must be off now though; the others will be waiting for me."

Adam watched him walk out of sight before addressing Guinness, "That man can be a pillock at times." He felt certain the dog nodded in agreement.

They *were* waiting too, beside the cars and since he was one of the drivers the scraps he had palmed would have to wait until they reached the farmhouse, when the rest would want to know what he'd found out.

As soon as they arrived he was asked for details and he described Adam's disingenuous refusal to impart any information, before extracting two boarding passes from his pocket, "I don't know what the hell is going on but I do know that Adam and probably Penny have been lying to us." He waved the passes in the air, "These are for a flight from Washington DC to Bordeaux, via Paris."

Barbara put a hand to her mouth, "Oh how exciting! Do you think he's a spy?"

George chortled, "That was one hell of a road trip."

Amy turned on him, "This isn't funny. What if it has something to do with the distillery? If it does we should be told about it."

Alan was reminded of something, "Actually, his reason for not coming here this morning was because he was doing something for Anton."

Amy held both hands out, palms upward, "See what I mean?"

George asked, "So what do we do about it? Confront him and demand answers? After all he's supposed to be a member of this group, but instead of helping us he buggered off to the States; oh and lied to us, to boot."

Bob held up his hands, "Whoa, we do nothing! Adam must have his reasons for not telling us and I for one will respect them. Mark my words, he'll tell us when he feels able."

George was already nodding, "I agree, if he chooses not to tell us it's because it's none of our business and before we haul him over the coals for not helping here, we need to remind ourselves that he shouldn't have been here anyway. If you remember, he should have flown home two or three weeks ago."

Alan wasn't enjoying life out on a limb, with only Amy on side, though he did have a parting shot, "Well let's just hope it doesn't have anything to do with us, there's a great deal of money at stake."

Bob had been holding the boarding passes and put them in his pocket, "I dare say we'll find out soon enough."

***

Pichon's farmhouse lay at the end of a two hundred metre track that ran along a valley, between tall hedgerows. The grass on the sides and centre of the track showed the beginnings of spring growth and had obviously been cut when necessary. Occasional breaks in the screens revealed pastureland; empty of livestock at that time of year and in the middle distance, the ground rose sharply and was covered in vines. Halfway along they pulled off the track to allow a cabbed pick up with four men in it to pass by, in the opposite direction, which alerted Adam to something he hadn't considered and he voiced relief, "At least he doesn't invite his men to join him for lunch."

The stone farmhouse and outbuildings were not particularly well cared for, with bare, weathered shutters at the windows and coarse roof tiles that were pocked with moss. The yard itself had been concreted and was relatively clean, with a roadway that led out and around the original buildings in a concentric circle, which gave access to a number of very large, modern buildings that formed two separate halves. One held livestock, hay and feeds while the other, sited some distance away, housed the distillery and cognac stocks.

Adam had spent the morning preparing for the confrontation, which would include the item he carried in the rucksack he'd borrowed from Penny. The file was tucked under his arm.

Pichon answered the door and glared at Rambert, "What are you doing here?" He nodded at Fabian, "And who is he?" Before they had chance to answer he went on, "Fuck off and come back..." He quickly changed his mind and instead of saying 'after lunch', he snarled, "If and when I tell you to."

Fabian translated and Adam smiled pleasantly, "No."

That gave Pichon pause, it had been a long time since anybody had answered him with such insolence and confidence. He didn't hesitate to turn around and go back inside, just as

Adam had said he would, following Rambert's experience and Fabian had been briefed on what to say. They guessed that the shotgun would be close at hand and there wouldn't be time for a translation, "If you so much as touch a gun it will be treated as an armed threat against a police officer."

Pichon slowed and then finally turned back to point at Adam, "Him?"

Fabian followed the script, "A English police officer, admittedly, but he has many friends at the local *Gendarmerie* who would be very angry."

Pichon smirked, "Then how about I shoot all three of you and bury your bodies in the woods?"

The priest had run out of script and *ad libbed*, "They know we are here."

"So no doubt you've told them all about the reason you are here?"

"No, but other, more important agencies know why." He quickly translated for Adam, adding, "I will leave mention of the US State Department and Wiesenthal Centre to you."

Pichon recognised the latter name with a germ of concern and his suspicions were confirmed when Adam said, SS Obersturmführer Meyer sends his worst regards."

The villain's mind was in turmoil, though he showed no sign of it when he turned around and walked inside, leaving the door open for them to follow.

A dried sausage, French stick and a piece of cheese had been left on the table, with a half eaten portion on a plate, beside a squat glass of red wine. The farmer sat down and began to eat while pointedly ignoring the visitors, who in time sat uninvited. Adam reached across and snatched the serrated knife off Pichon's plate. Startled, the farmer took a moment to register what had happened and he lunged for the utensil, just as Adam threw it across the room, "No weapons if you please." He pointed at a brown stain in the table top, "I take it that is where you skewered poor Challans's hand ." In the absence of a response he said, "No matter, forensics would soon determine that. I'd burn the thing if I were you."

Pichon still didn't show any reaction, but he was unnerved. Somehow, they had closed a loop around him. He growled, "Get on with it!"

Adam reached down and withdrew a chromed wrench from the rucksack before placing out of the owner's reach, "I've brought this back; which reminds me, how's your arm?"

The man glanced at the wrench but ignored the question and returned his attention to the food. They watched as he broke off pieces off the bread and cheese and stuffed them into his mouth. He chewed the food slowly and appeared to enjoy it, but Adam knew better, after a lifetime of reading body signals. The man wouldn't look up because he knew that his eyes would betray him.

Adam continued, as if it was of no consequence, "Records are like a spider's web. The information you thought you'd destroyed lay at the centre of many strands, some of which we now have." After Fabian's translation he went on, "Your father's penchant for treachery appears to be genetic, but at least, so far, you've only been responsible for the death of a cat, not a whole French family and allied aircrew. You have tried to emulate him though, haven't you, by stealing a neighbour's land."

Pichon listened to the translation and continued to eat, even though he could no longer taste anything.

Adam ploughed on, noting with some satisfaction that the man's face had paled before reddening, "Of course, we now know the truth about how your father kept his stock of cognac, when everyone else in this area had theirs confiscated. Nothing *you* could be held to account for, obviously, apart from the generations who are still suffering the consequences. In fact, I'd bet the whole cognac industry would be interested in the news, including your buyers."

They waited then, in silence, until the farmer placed both elbows on the table and sneered, "If that is all you have, English, get out of here and discover who has the most to lose."

Fabian interrupted, "I can speak for one of your victims.

Challans met with his superior three days ago and told him everything, knowing that at best, he would be allowed to resign. Thankfully, I was able to put a case forward for clemency and no other action will be taken. I was also able to persuade the head archivist not to report your involvement to the *Gendarmes,* for the time being." His translation came as fresh and startling news, but Adam was impressed by the priest's timing and sense of theatre. Even so, he realised that the people around him seemed to be making a habit of dropping bombshells.

Pichon jabbed at finger at Rambert, "But that's not for you I suspect. Loss of your job and prestige would be more than you could bear." He then snarled at Adam, "So, am I to suppose you planned to intimidate me with all that? Pah! You are pathetic."

Adam handed over a copy a Jewish transport order, "We won't but this will. See, the Wiesenthal Centre provided us with details of Meyer's current whereabouts on condition we shared anything we find with them. If they get these your Nazi chum will be extradited. Once that is done the French press and public opinion will gut you like a herring."

The farmer stared at the document as if he was reading it, but just three features were all that was necessary to startle him; the Nazi logo, the word *Jüde* and the name at the bottom, but not nearly as much as what followed. Adam extracted another document from his file and continued, "I met with SS Obersturmführer Meyer this week; 'course he doesn't go by that name now but he's a spritely ninety five year old, with the same disdain for your family that he had when you were collaborating." He passed the document over, "This is a copy of the statement he gave me, witnessed by a US police officer who was acting under the auspices of the US State Department." Since it was in English, he passed another copy to Fabian to read, in French and then watched the victim closely.

It was a catalogue of signals that couldn't lie; subtle changes in breathing, hand movements and body posture, all spoke of fear, but belligerence soon prevailed, "You think that this frightens me? Then go and do your worst; I've never cared about my reputation and have no fear, my buyers wouldn't dare to offend me."

Adam smiled once more, "But you haven't heard the worst yet."

After translation, Pichon sighed heavily, as though the whole thing had become a bore, and spoke to Fabian, "Just tell him to get on with it and then get out of here."

"Well, see, now that we've established how your family came by a third of the land you own a whole new horizon lies ahead, beginning with a feature in one of the Sunday papers perhaps. Don't forget, the press love crusades, which in this case will entail tracing the people who *should* have inherited your neighbour's farm. His extended family, however distant will take an action against you, on the grounds that the land was obtained illegally at a contrived price. At best, they'll come after you for the difference, re-valued to today's prices and at worst, they'll want the lot back, with compensation. Mind, I'm no expert in those things."

Pichon's lip curled up as he attempted to speak, but Adam snarled this time, "Shut up and listen! Your claim of ownership is based on murder, betrayal, war crimes, fraud and collaboration. Think on Sonny Jim." He wondered how that would translate.

Finally, the farmer was silenced; he stared at the table and the documents for a minute, though it felt a lot longer. Eventually, he looked up, "What is it you want?"

Fabian took control, "We want you to cease all contact with those you tried to blackmail, it's that simple."

"In exchange for what?"

Fabian shrugged, "For our silence, what else."

"And what can you offer to guarantee that?"

Rambert spoke for the first time, "My word."

Pichon sneered, "The word of a banker." The three allies remained silent as he considered the options. There seemed to be no choice, "Very well, I agree, now get out of my sight."

Adam held up a hand, "First, I want a written statement from you to that effect."

Pichon leapt up, so violently that his chair was knocked

over, "Never! I've given you my word, now get out before you go too far!"

Adam knew that their chances of getting what would be, in effect, a confession were slim, but they had achieved their aims. He nodded to the others and provided an inadvertent alliteration, "That'll do, we'll leave him to stew."

He did have a parting shot though, "Before we go, I want you to know that the English group who have invested in Michaud's distillery have power of veto to the sale of anything they don't agree with. I will also urge them to create a covenant on the land, as soon as possible, prohibiting the sale of anything to you or anyone connected with you."

Pichon listened to the car doors closing, the engine being started and the shift in gears as they drove down the track, *his* track, through *his* land. He thought then of Michaud's tract and seethed; so much time and money, for nothing.

∗∗∗

They returned to Anton's for a late lunch and an interrogation by both Penny and Anton who were desperate for news. Little had been said on the journey for it seemed that each man wanted to be left alone with his thoughts as their adrenalin levels fell away, until that is, something sprang to Adam's mind. He called over to Fabian, "That was a bit late to share that news about Challans; it was effective though."

Fabian coughed, "It was a difficult situation for me. The Challans family have become regular members of my congregation and he asked me to speak with the head archivist on his behalf. Making that confession was a brave thing to do, but a wise one too, as things turned out, because it took away any power Pichon had over him. I say brave, because he could have been arrested for what he did. Thankfully, the head archivist was swayed by what I had to say and settled for the acceptance of a resignation. Unfortunately, my plea for clemency involved telling him the truth behind my research. It was a very difficult meeting until I pointed out that my requests for information were authentic and the only reason I hadn't been entirely candid was to protect innocents. I also pointed out that the material he gave me remained secret."

Adam asked, "So that was it?"

"No, he told me that if I had been an employee, he would have dismissed me on the spot. It was very embarrassing."

All three of them discovered that they had an appetite and for the most part, answered a stream of questions with food in their mouths. Toasts were made and spirits climbed, but Adam began to flag. The food, wine and jet lag, combined with the low that follows a high stress encounter left him barely able to keep his eyes open. He rose from the table unsteadily, "Sorry guys, I'm going back to the *gite* for some Z'ds."

They all made solicitous comments but Rambert hurriedly insisted that they dine at his place that night, adding that Margot wanted to hear all about the Washington trip first hand.

Adam was woken by the alarm clock at five and collected shortly after by Anton. He was pleased to see that Tom had been included in the invitation and they drove out of the drive in Anton's car, thirty minutes before the Club Cognac members drove into it. The shopping trip had been entirely successful though their absentee member had featured strongly in their discussions, until a consensus determined that they should find out what the hell was going on and clear the air, that very evening. In spite of that cloud hanging over them, their spirits were high and two cars were filled with flat pack chests of drawers and bedside tables. The beds, wardrobes and kitchen appliances were being delivered on Tuesday and the carpet shop promised to cover the bedroom floors within the next week.

Adam's car was parked outside so Alan was despatched to pass on their invitation to join them for either apéritifs or a meal. He was told to make that a demand if the invitation wasn't accepted.

He walked back in, half an hour later, flapping his arms in frustration, "He's not there, either that or he isn't answering the door, so I went to Penny's house and then to Anton's to see if they could shed any light on the matter, but they're not in either."

Carol piped up, "Don't forget that it was Penny who told us he was on a road trip."

In the silence that followed, all their high spirits from shopping fell away, in the face of growing doubts and suspicions.

***

Adam was startled when Margot delivered four kisses on the cheeks instead of the two he'd become accustomed to. As they made their way into the lounge Anton explained, with a broad grin, "Two are for friends and four are for very special friends."

The meal was a superb balance between sensible volume and breathtaking flavours, accompanied by wine that treated the palate and throat with a velvet grace. Though the others had heard most of the story they listened to it once more, with delight, after Margot had insisted on hearing it for herself. This time Adam embellished it with some anecdotes and a little of the background to Frank German's antipathy and how it changed through the road trip.

For most of those present, it represented an epiphany. They had all been guilty, at varying levels, of seeing this overweight and shabbily dressed man as one of life's lesser people, yet here he was, modestly describing how he secured the support of the US State Department. Moreover, he'd gone to Washington DC, achieved the impossible and returned within three days. Rambert and Fabian had discussed the meeting with Pichon, with a growing sense of wonder. It had been like watching a predator take down its prey. Only Penny had always seen the inner strength and determination in Adam, but then she reminded herself, Watson always had been an admirer.

When he finished, Margot stood and beckoned for him to do so as well, before she advanced and hugged him tightly. When she broke away her eyes were glistening, "We shall always be in your debt."

Adam held up a finger and addressed Phillipe, "Speaking of debt, I need to give this back to you."

As he drew the international debit card from his wallet Rambert began shaking his head, "No, my friend, I told you that if the trip was a success you could keep whatever is left on it."

Adam laid the card on the table, "No need thanks, I've already taken my bonus. The only seat they had available for the return flight was in business class. That is a *very* civilised way to travel you know."

***

When George returned with breakfast the next morning the group were beside themselves with worry, particularly when he said, "There's no sign of activity at his *gite*."

Alan asked, "Is he even there?"

"Oh yes, I'm certain of that, the dog is stationed at the door again. I shoved a note under his door and put another on his windscreen for good measure."

Jayne groaned, "What else can we do?"

Bob answered her, "Exactly what we are doing, but perhaps one of us should go back there every half an hour until we finally catch him."

George said, "Absolutely, and we're not going to the farmhouse today until we do."

Twenty minutes later there was a rap on the door. Carol gasped when she opened it, but Adam was sporting a bright smile, "I've brought Guinness along for a spot of breakfast, if that's alright." When he stepped inside the atmosphere was dense enough to be sliced; he felt like a bacon sandwich at a *Bar Mitzvah*. Undeterred, he helped himself to a croissant and accepted an offer of a coffee. In the deafening silence that followed, each waited for another to begin, until Adam saved them the trouble, "I have rather a lot of news for you, which until yesterday could have been bad, but is now wholly good. Secrecy has been key to the whole thing, which is why you have been kept in the dark; sorry. I promise though, that when you hear the whole story you'll understand."

George asked, "When will that be?"

"Tomorrow, after Annie and Sue get here. I think it would be best if I tell you all together."

Carol had waited too long, "Please Adam, surely you can tell us something."

He thought for a moment before deciding to whet their appetites, "Suffice it to say that while you were in England I had a nose mashed, two eyes blacked and would have had a few ribs broken had it not been for Guinness, who put the attacker in hospital. I also secured help from the US State Department in interviewing someone over there, which was a pivotal point in the scheme of things."

They were all stunned into silence, apart from Barbara, who clapped her hands in delight, "Oh my, I told you he was a spy!"

Adam laughed out loud as he passed another piece of lightly buttered toast down to Guinness, "Well, you can make your own judgements tomorrow. In the meantime, I hope I've allayed your worries."

Bob chortled with relief, "I'm not worried anymore, but I can't wait to hear the whole story."

George cut in, "We've been worried and that's a fact, but now that you're here, how are you with flat pack furniture?"

It was Adam's turn to chuckle, "Not good; I was much better at being a copper."

***

Annie and Sue didn't make the same mistake as the others. Instead they caught the overnight ferry from Portsmouth to St Malo; the one that stayed in the water and had stabilisers. They drove straight to Anton's at his insistence and arrived in time for lunch. Quite unexpectedly, the anxieties of the previous month surfaced when he saw Sue, who thought that his welcome was a tad extreme when tears rolled down his face as he kissed her.

During lunch she noticed that he fidgeted and failed to

hold down conversations that extended beyond the banal, until eventually, she said, "Anton, is everything alright? Nothing's happened has it?"

The lie that lay on the tip of his tongue vanished when he looked at those eyes and thought better of it. She would know he was lying and would react badly. Instead, he said, "Everything is fine now, but we have experienced some difficulties."

"What, with the distillation?"

"No, no, that is fine, but I cannot tell you anything I'm afraid."

"Why not?"

"Because Adam will tell you later this afternoon; a special meeting has been arranged for everyone to attend. It was postponed until you got here."

Sue had no intention of waiting that long, but was startled by the steel in his voice when he told her that he had no intention of telling her any more. The exchanges began to become heated until Annie interrupted, "Sis, give the poor man a break. For whatever reason, he's been sworn to secrecy so you will have to respect that." She turned to Anton, "What time is this meeting?"

"Four pm, at Penny's house."

She glanced at her watch, "That's less than two hours away and we have to unpack, so any storytelling would have to wait anyway."

Sue sulked over her *Chocolat Viennois*.

The *constructeurs* Club Cognac had spent the morning assembling furniture, apart from Barbara who had her own agenda and pot of vermillion paint. Adam expressed genuine surprise when he was given a tour, followed by a *Phillips* screwdriver and a heavy box bearing a picture of a bedside table. Bob leaned over and whispered, "Don't worry, we can call this one yours, so if you make a balls up it won't matter."

Adam looked affronted, "What happened to, 'if you need help just ask'?"

Bob grinned, "Oh, there's that too; good thinking."

At around eleven, a shriek and dreadful crashing sound came from Barbara's room. She had announced that she wanted to work alone and had closed the door, but clearly, something had happened to warrant ignoring that instruction. Bob was first through the door, but nothing could have prepared him for the scene he was confronted with. Barbara was on the floor, between two overturned stepladders. She'd been winded by the fall and was gasping for breath like a landed fish, but he was taken aback when he realised that she was also stark naked and covered in red paint. The paint tin lay to one side, but the splatter of red paint that ran across the floor and up the opposite wall made it look like a crime scene. Carol had pushed him out of the way and rushed to Barbara's aid as his eyes were drawn to the wall she had been working on. The red paint on a white wall was a stark contrast, particularly when it had been used to make an impression of a spread-eagled female form in lurid detail. Two hand marks bracketed what must have been the tip of her nose and pouting lips and as his eyes drifted down the wall he saw that her shoulders had made fainter marks than the two breasts; even the aureoles were clearly distinguished. She must have pushed against the wall then, he deduced, from rounded compression of her belly, bordered by a sprinkling of hair marks which preceded the blotch left by her pubis. Thighs and knees were the only other parts of her anatomy to have made contact with the wall. Jayne and Amy had pushed past him to assist Carol, while the other men piled in behind to consider the image. Barbara was sitting up by then and began to explain, "The walls were so plain you see and I've always wanted to do that. When I thought it was done I pushed away from the wall to avoid leaving any smears, but I managed to push the stepladders over too." A thought then occurred to her, "You did say this was my room, didn't you?"

Carol could barely contain her laughter, but did so by dint of directing faux anger at the men, "Stop gawking you lot. Go and get some buckets of hot water, some sponges and a towel." She saw Barbara's look of horror and explained, "We need to mop up the spilt paint." The men hurried out, as though they had been caught peering into a ladies changing room, but as soon as the door closed she glanced at Jayne and Amy and they all collapsed in laughter. Barbara smiled in relief and had hoped to ask them for an opinion, both of her bodily impression and plans to paint sunflowers on the other walls, but her clean up team had become quite hysterical.

Downstairs, the men remained startled, until Alan made an observation, "You know, if I didn't know that had been done by a sixty odd year old I'd think that was a pretty erotic sight."

George looked startled, "Good Lord, come to think of it, you're right!

***

Since Penny's lounge was the largest available, they chose it as the venue. It was full and the guests were lubricated. When they had arrived, Penny noticed Barbara's new complexion and red fringe, but when asked if she'd had an accident the elderly artist had smiled sweetly, "No matter, it'll wash off, eventually, but do you have a hard chair by any chance? I wouldn't want to ruin your covers."

Very soon, it was time to get started. By prior arrangement, Penny was the first to speak and the chatter abruptly ceased when she stood up, "Hi guys, it's always good to see you, but not very good when I have to apologise for telling fibs. For that I am sorry, but I'll leave it to Adam to explain why it was necessary."

He began with the bank's threats, which they all knew about, but then he moved on to Rambert's confessional visit. From then on they sat in rapt silence. The story was so unbelievable, yet they had been a vital part of it.

Towards the end, Barbara continued to stare adoringly at Adam as she leaned over and whispered into Carol's ear, "I wish I was twenty years younger." Bob overheard her and slapped down the images that came to mind with a mental edict, 'Don't go there!'

Inevitably, someone asked about the former case, that had enabled him to secure help from the Americans, but he waved it off, "We don't have time for that one and you probably wouldn't believe it anyway."

There were lots of questions at the end, but most of them required a repeat of stuff he'd already talked about, as if they needed to hear things for a second time and the questions would continue for days. Finally, things wound down and Adam closed with a recommendation, "You may want to have our French lawyer draft up a covenant, prohibiting the sale of anything to Pichon, provided of course, that Anton agrees."

Anton did not, but he chose not to say so outright; instead, he mumbled something about waiting for a while, to see if Pichon had mended his ways.

George stood up, "Well, Adam, I'm confounded. We all thought you were up to no good, to be perfectly honest, but instead, we owe you a debt of thanks." There were murmurs of agreement until Bob called out, "So will you be up for assembling wardrobes when they arrive tomorrow then?"

Adam grimaced, "Regrettably, yes."

Annie and Sue declined separate invitations from Penny and the crowd to dine with them, saying that there was too much to do at the house and, Annie added archly, "Sue has a prior engagement." Anton studied his shoe laces while the others looked over and grinned, but they did let him off without comments.

Afterwards, the two sisters ambled back to the house and found a bowl of eggs and a basket containing a variety of vegetables on their doorstep, with a note, '*Welcome, from Marie Anne*'. *A* sheet of paper lay beneath the vegetables, bearing the recipe for cheese pastries.

When they'd arrived earlier, the place had been cold and a little stark, but now the heating had transformed it back into the cosy cottage they had originally fallen in love with. Unpacking was a pleasure; they had brought boxes of personal things, such as family photographs, ornaments and knick knacks that helped to put a personal stamp on the place. Soon though, and long before they found places for everything, it was time to walk over to join Anton, who was preparing a meal and had insisted on Annie joining them.

On their way there, Annie voiced a concern, "You know, we can't *keep* exploiting his hospitality, particularly now that we have a place we could entertain in. There must have been times when he thought we were moving in."

Sue had thought the same, but from a different perspective, "Well he wouldn't be wrong."

"What do you mean?"

"That's exactly what I'm going to do."

"Does he know that?"

Sue grinned cheekily, "Not yet."

After a lengthy pause Annie asked, "Do you mean during visits, or permanently."

"I haven't decided yet."

Which took Annie by surprise and for the rest of the walk she tried to gauge her own feelings on the matter. It wasn't as though they lived in each other's pockets back home and it would only take a few hours for one to reach the other by plane, but would that be close enough? She hadn't found an answer by the time they reached Anton's but she did watch them embrace and kiss, before each wrapped an arm around the other's waist while examining the food being cooked on the hob. Annie's doubts disappeared as another far more important mantra came to mind, which she whispered under her breath, "Just be happy."

The men were plain embarrassing that evening, an assessment all sober spouses make of drunken men folk and true to the norms, their ladies went to bed with a parting shot, "Don't forget you've got wardrobes to assemble tomorrow."

Yet the next morning, to everyone's surprise, they discovered that the terms of delivery included assembly. Bob, George and Alan became so embarrassed that they finished unloading the van and carted the packaging away. The three delivery men were experts too, and French, which is why they completed the job before noon. None of them made comment about Barbara's artwork, but when the opportunity arose, each of them took a picture using their mobile telephones. One of the images went viral, within a week.

Afterwards, the Club Cognac team toured the house with an air satisfaction and surprise. There was still work to do, but suddenly the place could be lived in, or at least it would be in two days time, after the carpets had been fitted on the stairs and in the bedrooms. Downstairs, the dull brown tiles would have to do, but at least the light coloured kitchen was complete, with a shiny white cooker and refrigerator, which left them with another priority and the prospect of another day off from manual work. Before moving in they would need cutlery, crockery saucepans, bowls, serving dishes, mixers, bedside lamps and so much more. The list seemed endless, so much so that they decided to shop at one of the hypermarkets in Cognac, the very next day.

Adam joined them, but only because Anton had offered him another day out with Henri, though he was glad when the shopping was done. The club members queued up at the same checkout, with three trolleys, stacked high with everything from table mats to light shades and they were too busy gossiping to notice that the till was manned by a young trainee, being instructed by a supervisor. The poor girl's jaw dropped when she realised that all three trolleys were to be checked out together. Bob saw her consternation and looked at the supervisor, "Oops."

The older woman clapped her hands and laughed, "Bravo!" Fifteen minutes later the screen displayed a total of over eleven hundred Euros and the girl sagged with relief but as they walked away Bob looked back and she gave him a little wave. They loaded all four cars before retiring to the store's cafeteria for lunch and a review of the print out from the till. Annie had accompanied them out of curiosity and to help with translation, but Sue stayed with Anton, to make plans for a celebration.

That year's distillation would be over in less than ten days time and he decided to mark the occasion with a party, which would require a major clean up of his dining room which was stale and dusty through lack of use while the kitchen, in Sue's opinion, was stale and grubby from regular use.

They didn't get much done that day though. With everyone in Cognac, a daytime romp in bed was far more appealing. The recent abstinence called for an encore after lunch, followed by a deliciously cosy nap together. Three visitors called in for a tour; all of them were British and all thought that the sign that Sue had taped to the door was the Frenchman's flawed attempt at English. It read;

DUE TO FORESEEN CIRCUMSTANCES WE WILL BE CLOSED THIS AFTERNOON

The following morning Anton received a telephone call that served to confirm that the Pichon threat was finally over. It was Rambert, "Anton my friend, I have some good news. This morning Pichon closed his account with us; he's gone back to his old bank."

Another celebration was called for, albeit with just two others this time; Annie and Sue. He went into the larder and then joined Sue, who was waxing the dining room table. Waving the champagne bottle in the air, he called out, "Tonight, we have another celebration!"

That same morning, Annie called in to have a coffee with Marie Anne, who showed her the shiny red rotavator they had bought and the piece of ground they had practiced on. Even Jean Claude advanced to peck her on each cheek and he smiled; at least that was Annie's interpretation of the movement beneath his walrus moustache. The new *entente cordiale* was confirmed later that day, as he delivered a warm carcase of a hare. When he saw her look of consternation, he just nodded and walked away with it, without a word, leaving her convinced that she'd caused offence. But he returned ten minutes later, with the same hare, skinned and gutted. He was startled and secretly delighted when she hugged him. She was still at a loss at what to do with it though and telephoned Sue for advice, who referred the enquiry to Anton. He leapt at the chance to get his hands on it and cook for them once again.

As usual, Annie walked home alone that night. There was no cloud and the sky was spectacularly jewelled, so she lingered for a while outside, but there was a sharp frost and she soon stepped over her threshold, into the enveloping warmth of the kitchen. The feeling of peace and well being was too good to cut short, so she made a hot cocoa and poured out a small measure of cognac. A few minutes later, when seated at the table, she raised up her glass and said, "To belle France."

The club members moved into their farmhouse on Saturday, still with lots of work to be done, but the place was now eminently habitable; an outstanding achievement in just twelve days. The only member without a bedroom was Adam, who declined the offer of the sofa bed they had bought for the living room, in favour of the space and comfort of his *gite*. The others expressed concern and regret that nothing more could be done, though Barbara did entertain a fleeting thought that was both fanciful and impractical, given that she only had a single bed. For his part, Adam welcomed the excuse to spend time away from them; it simply wasn't his bag.

CHAPTER 15

Pichon telephoned at four on Monday afternoon, "Hello Anton, how are you?"

Anton didn't recognise the voice at first and asked, "Hello, who is this please?"

"It's Albert, Albert Pichon."

Anton's tone became guarded, though he remained polite, "What can I do for you?" The reply startled him.

"A great deal actually; I want to ask for your forgiveness." After a tiny pause he hurried on, "I realise how much there is to forgive and I have to try and make good, somehow. I've changed Anton, believe me. Those friends of yours told me so much about myself and what I'd done, that I was left with a great deal to think about. Most of all I've been stupid, by trying to honour my father's wishes.

We've been neighbours for so long and we should have helped each other through the years; instead, I did all I could to hinder you. Father always coveted your land you know and he made me promise, time and time again that I would do all that I could to get it. I realised just how warped my father had become when your English friend showed me the statement written by a Nazi officer; the one who had dealings with my father. I knew about the cognac, of course, but believe it or not, I didn't know that we had acquired the neighbour's farm in such a bad way. It was that information which made me realise how easily I allowed myself to become warped as well.

Now, I wish to make new promises, to you *and* your new partners."

Finally, there was a pause, but Anton couldn't believe his ears and the only thing he could think to say was, "That is good news."

Pichon allowed a few moments until it was clear that Anton had nothing more to say and then he continued, "You know that piece of pasture, a couple of hectares in the southern corner, next to the field of yours with a stand of birches?"

"Yes."

"It's yours; a gift from a pathetic old man."

"But I couldn't possibly accept that Albert."

"Please do, I want it to mark a new beginning between us. There is so much more I want to say and so much I need to beg forgiveness for. It would please me beyond measure if you were to accept it."

Anton shook his head incredulously, yet he so wanted to believe what he'd heard, "I don't know what to say Albert. This is unexpected, to say the least."

Pichon chuckled, a sound that really did seem to signal a difference, "In truth, I feel the same way. Look, it's been a difficult few days for me and talking on the telephone like this is not ideal. Can we meet up somewhere and talk face to face?"

"But of course. Here, or at your place."

Pichon sighed loudly, "Neither, if you don't mind, I have men here and you have your English friends there, along with a steady stream of customers. Much of what I have to tell you I'd rather not be heard by others. Perhaps we could meet in a bar somewhere, without people around who know us."

Anton didn't particularly fancy driving some distance to find such a bar, but there was so much at stake and his old enemy sounded so genuine. Moreover, he wasn't the sort of man to give land away without good reason. Once again, though he didn't intend it, his tone was still guarded, "If that is what you want."

Pichon seemed to sense the ambivalence and suggested an

alternative, "Or if you'd prefer, why don't we meet up on the cattle bridge. We can sit down and chat there in private."

That sounded a much better idea and the meeting place lay on the border between their lands, which sounded so appropriate. The bridge, of long reinforced concrete beams had been laid across the stream decades earlier, when their parents had rented the adjacent pastures off each other as circumstances demanded. Unable to take vehicles, it had lain there unused, ever since the Michaud's had stopped rearing cattle.

Anton was comforted by the choice, "Very well, when would you like to meet?"

"How about tomorrow morning, at ten? Afterwards, if you wish, come back to my place for lunch; I'd love to show you around."

"That sounds wonderful; I'll look forward to it."

Pichon sounded emotional, "Thank you Anton, it is time for peace between us."

Anton hung up the telephone and clasped his hands together tightly, beneath his chin. If only they *could* become good neighbours with friendship taking the place of enmity. He would take the pastureland, if Albert insisted, it would be rude to refuse such a peace offering, but without the need for pasture he would rent it back to Albert, free of charge. Yes, that was the answer to that one.

Then the question of the covenant came to mind. In light of what had just happened, it would have to wait because very probably, it wouldn't be necessary.

Annie and Sue had gone shopping and he had been invited to join them at Penny's for a meal that evening. He checked his watch and calculated that he had over an hour to wait before sharing the news with someone. He could hardly wait.

Penny was the first one to prick at his bubble, over apéritifs, though Annie and Sue thought it was wonderful news while Tom reserved judgement. Penny on the other hand telephoned Adam, who was munching his way through a couple of sausage rolls.

"Holmes, you'd better get over here."

He noted the absence of pleasantries and decided that he wouldn't have shared them anyway, not with hot food growing cold, "Why?"

"Just a gut feeling, but I need your support."

"Is it about Pichon?"

"Yes, but that is all I'm telling you on the telephone."

"Can it wait a while?"

"No, our meal will go cold, or dry."

He began to sound irritated, "That is happening to my food, right now."

"What are you eating?"

He paused, before confessing, "Sausage rolls."

"I thought as much. In that case you need to come over immediately, while we're having aperitifs, there's plenty of food to feed one more."

Three minutes later he was banging on the Challis's door and fifteen minutes later he was digesting a scotch and canapés while trying to do the same with Anton's story. When it was over Penny said, "Well? What do you think?"

Adam didn't hesitate, "It stinks. People like that don't change."

Sue joined in, "I disagree. The World has seen lots of epiphanies, where people have changed."

Adam shrugged, "People like *Scrooge* you mean? I was a copper for thirty odd years; it teaches you stuff."

The conversation continued through the meal, but no amount of warnings could sway Anton. Eventually, he held up both hands, "Enough, please, you have to understand what this means to me. I am going."

Penny addressed Adam, "Do you think Anton could be in danger?"

Adam shook his head, "No, I doubt it. Pichon will know that Anton has told us about the meeting, but if I'm right he might try to pull a stunt, such as bullying Anton into signing something. That's why one of us needs to go with him. Pichon can like it or lump it."

"No!" Anton was sounding petulant, "I gave him my word that I would be on my own and he did likewise."

Adam noted the determination, "If I was still active I'd at least 'wire' you, so we'd have the conversation recorded."

Penny said, "We can do that! Anton, pass me your telephone." As he was doing so she explained, "All we have to do is get Anton to press the dial button on this before Pichon is in sight. We'll have already put one of our numbers in there so we can all listen in."

Anton asked, whose telephone shall we use?"

"It doesn't matter, provided it's fully charged." She glanced at Anton, "The same goes for yours too."

Adam had his doubts, "So are you suggesting that Anton waves that thing in front of Pichon, like an outside broadcaster?"

"No, of course not, he'll have it tucked into his top pocket."

Anton and Sue were promptly sent outside to try it, by him calling Penny's mobile and speaking normally at varying distances. All agreed that it was effective for up to five metres, in spite of being hidden in his pocket.

The question of whose telephone to use at the listening end was resolved when Adam thought to ask, "Can anyone record stuff on their phone?"

Sue held her new *Iphone* up, "This one does, though I've never used it."

"Great, well if you would learn how between now and tomorrow morning, we'll use yours." He turned to Penny, "Look, I realise that this is overkill, probably, but would you see if Hubert would join us please. If nothing untoward happens I'm sure he'll be discreet, but I'd rather be on the safe side."

Later, as they were getting into their coats Adam thought of one more thing, "Best if we don't mention this to the others; not until we know what was said. Some of the stuff he shares might cause panic."

***

The low key meeting ahead was at odds with the one that

occurred in Anton's kitchen at nine the next morning. There was quite a gathering, with Annie, Sue, Penny Adam and Henri, who had been told to stay indoors that morning. Hubert had telephoned to say that he was on his way.

They had discovered that whilst the telephone in the top pocket idea worked with a sports jacket, it didn't with a heavy winter coat, which only had heavily insulated side pockets. There had been another frost the night before and when Anton insisted on wearing the lighter jacket Sue made him put on an additional sweater and told him to keep things brief. The lunch and tour would have to wait for another day.

Finally, Anton strode out of the gate and onto his land, a little piqued by the anxiety their precautions had brought about. The others sat around Anton's kitchen table waiting anxiously in complete silence. Their ten minute wait seemed much longer and Adam considered chasing after his friend, until suddenly Sue's telephone rang; startling them all. She switched the speaker and recording application on before setting it down at the centre of the table. To begin with, all they could hear was a faint rustling, but quite suddenly, they heard Anton call out, "Bonjour Albert."

Pichon returned the greeting, with a broad grin. He was already on the moss-covered bridge, with a shotgun, broken open over one arm and the body of a cock pheasant in the opposite hand. He nodded towards the bird, "There isn't much to be had at the moment." To Anton's huge relief Pichon moved in a way that caused the gun to roll slightly; enough to show that there were no cartridges loaded, "I've given up for the day."

They had closed the gap between them by then and shook hands.

Anton then allowed the other to start, "Thank you for coming Anton, you cannot know how much this means to me."

Anton smiled, "And for me too."

"Here, have this for tonight." He thrust the bird forward so that Anton had no choice but to accept it, but the string around its legs wasn't tied off properly and the carcase dropped to the ground. When he bent down to pick it up Pichon snapped the barrel shut and whipped the stock around in a single smooth action, to smash against the side of Anton's head.

In the kitchen they couldn't make out what that sound was, but they did hear a splash and the concern began to set in, though it was eased slightly when they heard Pichon say, in a conversational tone, "Sit down my friend." They decided that Anton must have must have been slow to respond because a moment later, they heard the man say tersely, "Sit." .

Anton felt the crushing blow, but had no idea how he came to be kneeling in the stream. Black speckles clouded his vision and he felt blood running down the side of his head and along his chin before dripping into the icy water. He was barely aware of the figure that stepped down the bank and too dazed to say anything, but he did look up when a voice told him to sit. Pichon loaded two shells into his shotgun and snapped it shut before pointing the gun at Anton and saying sharply, "Sit!"

Anton teetered on the edge of consciousness, but the icy water served to revive him slightly as he rolled over into the sitting position. He considered the dreadful menace represented by the open gun barrels, now just three feet away, before he looked up at his attacker and asked, "Why?

Pichon laughed, "This is so fitting. I took your brother's ear off with this, just up there." He swivelled the gun to point upstream and continued, "He swerved to try and save himself and drove straight over the bank. The tractor rolled over and finished the job for me. Papa always said that with only one son left, the Michaud place would be ours as soon as your father passed on. You've been more tenacious than we gave you credit for."

Anton's mind reeled, in spite of the dreadful ache at the side of his head he tried to rationalise what he heard. "But you shot at him. If you had killed him the police would have suspected you more than anyone else."

"All they would have found would be a tractor, up there, in the middle of the vines, without a body to inspect. They would never have found one either. He could even have been a run-away; it happens all the time. I'd have dumped his body in the lake, three kilometres away. I must say though, things turned out neater than I could have hoped for. I was even one of the group that dragged him out from beneath the tractor, by which time the stream had stripped away any evidence of a gunshot wound. I had to be sure though.

Hubert was scribbling notes as fast as he could, though his heart was racing. How could it be that he was listening to a murderer's confession? His thirty three year career had just taken a violent turn for the worse.

Adam was startled too, though the information was taking longer to reach him because of the need for translation. Each revelation was announced in advance, by the expression on Penny's face. She, like him was becoming concerned.

The water was bitterly cold and Anton was beginning to lose feeling in his legs, but the next instruction signalled the end play, "Lie down!"

He stuttered, "No!"

"Now! it's your choice, either be cold or feel your guts torn apart with shot. If you make me do that I'll just dump your remains in the lake. You'll have company too. Father dumped a simpleton in there after the Germans had shot him. I was with him that day. The oaf couldn't swim, so we were saved the trouble of using a concrete block." He spoke reasonably then, "This way will be painless and they'll assume that you slipped off the bridge and concussed yourself. Fear not, I'll come along shortly and 'discover' your corpse."

Their eyes met as Pichon raised his gun and aimed at Anton's midriff. One frightened pair confronted by a psychopath's, "Down, now!"

Anton let himself fall back into the water, until his elbows met the gravel bed to give him enough support to keep his head above water. The iphone in his top pocket ceased to transmit anything but the sound of running water.

The moment Penny heard mention of guts being torn apart

she turned to Adam in horror, "He's going to shoot him. Oh my God, do something."

Adam yelled back, "Where's the bridge?"

She wailed, "I don't know!"

"Where's Henri?"

In that moment they heard the scream of an engine and saw a flash of white as the van flew out of the yard.

The little white van tore down the lane for half a kilometre before it swerved into a field of vines that ran down into the valley. It hit the rise off the road with enough force to launch the front wheels into the air, before they crashed back down to cause terminal damage to the suspension. Henri lost control for a moment and shied away as the front wing was crumpled by half a dozen vines, but then he depressed the clutch and allowed the steep slope to carry him on. At the bottom, a hedgerow formed a dog leg; to the left and then right, before reaching the stream and bridge. He slipped the stick into third gear and stamped on the accelerator as he reached the first turn.

The riverbank and hedgerow screened the sound of his approach for a while, but eventually Pichon heard the rumbling of the van's freewheeling approach over rough ground. He snarled at Anton, "Stay there!" and began to scramble up the bank, just as the sound of a racing engine began. When the van appeared, he began to wave frantically, as if he were signalling for help and smiled with fake relief as it drew closer. The noise dropped just yards away and the vehicle slowed as it drew near. When it was just yards away he let both arms drop to his sides, just as the lower gear was engaged and the accelerator was stamped to the floor. The battered little van leapt at him like a starved predator.

The crack of his femur snapping could be heard over the engine as the vehicle was driven into him, flicking his weight up over the bonnet before his skull smashed against the top edge of the windscreen, leaving a mass of blood, hair and brain tissue there before the twitching body was launched into the stream, to land beside Anton.

Henri ignored Pichon's body as he dragged Anton out, shouting at him to stay awake. His boss was blue and incoherent; unable to do anything for himself anymore and had to be dropped on the ground so that the back doors to the van could be opened. His deadweight was then bundled into the back, for a bruising race up the hill.

Back at the yard, Henri signalled urgently for Adam to help lift Anton out of the vehicle and into the still room, where he flicked open the furnace door and sat Anton down in the rush of hot air. Sue was told to go and get towels and blankets as the two men stripped the sodden clothes off and after giving him a vigorous rubbing down they wrapped blankets around his shoulders. The chest and legs were left bare, since the blast of heat was doing more than blankets ever could. Satisfied that they had done all they could for the moment, Henri sat on the floor and shuffled up to Anton's back, in order to hold him in position and continue shouting into his ear.

At one point Adam pointed at Henri's sodden trousers and offered to take his place, but the old man shook his head vigorously and he did the same a short while later when Sue sought to do the same, but eventually, the *Gendarmes* and ambulance arrived. The medics checked Anton over and decided to leave him where he was for a short while longer. He was talking easily by then, though there was still the question of shock and concussion. In due course he was persuaded to accompany them to hospital, swathed in *space blankets*. Sue travelled with him and Henri was isolated in the dining room with a *gendarme*, until the senior officer returned from the crime scene, which was not until after Pichon's body was taken away. Eventually, he went into the dining room to question Henri, who refused to say a word without Adam being present. In the absence of a police interpreter, Penny was admitted too.

Henri spoke quietly, at a measured pace, "He was my sister's eldest; a bit simple, but cheerful and strong. He was too cheerful for his own good during the occupation because he would march behind the German troops or mimic them saluting; that sort of thing. The Germans thought he was aping them and they arrested him two or three times. My sister was frantic with worry. They lived in the thirty kilometre coastal zone which was full of Germans and they had to have special passes. Non residents weren't allowed in there at all so when they confiscated his pass my sister had no choice but to send him out here, to work on a farm. She thought he would be safer away from the Allied bombing anyway, so she never forgave herself when they told her he'd been executed for helping Allied airmen. We all thought it led to her death. Food was short anyway, but she just seemed to waste away. It was a bad death; cancer they thought, but by then the Allies were over here and the Germans cared only for themselves."

As Penny translated, images of Meyers 'simpleton' running away with two bullet wounds only to be drowned at the hands of a Frenchman overwhelmed her. Adam took a hand and squeezed it gently.

EPILOGUE

Henri was arrested and taken away, but his lawyer moved his testimony away from the act of revenge against Pichon to one of rescue; of Anton. The fact that he had worked for Anton for most of his life served to reinforce that as a motive. Additionally, Henri was persuaded to keep quiet and not argue when his lawyer suggested that Pichon might have been pointing the gun at the van and the impact was no more than an act of self defence. The recording certainly proved that he had already threatened Anton with it and the police report recorded that it was loaded.

In the end, the case for either murder or manslaughter wilted under the weight of opposing evidence and the Public Prosecutor dismissed it.

By then, all the Club Cognac members had gone home, with plans to return in the summer. Sue still wasn't a member but she did stay behind and moved in with Anton, so she was there the day Henri ambled in for breakfast, as though nothing had happened.

Two weeks later he took them to the same spot he had shown Adam. Now though, a new granite stone had been set into the ground, next to the original.

Anton translated the inscription,

"Tribute to the Charente patriots who paid with their lives to help English aviators. Executed on the fifteenth of August nineteen forty three.

Beneath the inscription lay the names of the farmer,

Fournier, his wife and children, but at the bottom lay the name of another lad with a different surname.

Anton paid a team of divers to search Pichon's lake and they found the body. Once again, the *Gendarmes* took control and forensics did their job. The autopsy showed evidence of two bullet wounds and a DNA match provided final confirmation of lineage. By then, the story had been passed on by so many that the funeral was attended by the press and scores of people from the surrounding villages, along with the surviving members of the lad's family.

It was a special day and the first time Anton had ever seen Henri show emotion.

Later, one reporter summed up the horror perfectly,

Many were killed during the occupation and this casualty might have simply been one more statistic, had it not been for the hideous way in which his life was ended, by a fellow Frenchman.

***

Two months later Penny strolled down to their orchard, to bask in the dappled light that shone through the magnificent blossoms. It was a private pilgrimage she made each year but this one was interrupted when Guinness gave a warning bark. She was startled enough to cry out when the postman, Sebastian, appeared from the direction of the house, but his approach was diffident and anxiety clear when he said quickly, "I am sorry Madame, I didn't mean to alarm you. Your husband told me where to find you."

He was the same self-effacing man she had known all along and feeling silly, she hurried forward and kissed him on each cheek, "That's OK Sebastian, I just didn't expect to see you down here."

He shrugged, "I needed to speak with you, personally."

She smiled, "No problem, let's go back to the house and have a coffee."

"No, thank you." He drew an opened envelope out of his bag, "Do you remember me telling you that the old man Pichon beat me, because he thought I had stolen a letter that had been sent to him?"

"Yes, that was the day you warned me about the current Pichon."

He held the envelope forward for her to take, "This is the letter."

She pulled out the single sheet of paper it contained and felt revulsion at the sight of the Nazi logo. It was the first letter from SS Obersturmführer Meyer in Bordeaux, offering Pichon his neighbour's farm for a pittance.

Sebastian fidgeted with anxiety, "I have kept it secret for so many years. Perhaps, even now, I could be sacked, arrested even, but I had to share it with someone. It has stayed with me since then, like a curse."

Penny always carried a box of matches with her, since so many appliances were powered by propane gas. They both watched as the old paper caught light and in no time, she released the blackened leaf to flutter gently to the ground. She looked up at him and said, "Let that be an end to it Sebastian. No one will ever know about it."

He rocked from one foot to the other before nodding emphatically and making his way back to the van.

***

When Adam and Annie eventually told them the rest of the story, at a Friday coffee morning some time later, George lamented the fact that they were always the last to know anything. Even then, after apologies had been made and accepted, they were sworn to secrecy at Rambert's insistence. Barbara turned to Bob, "That is such a pity, you could have written a book about it."

They did receive recognition in other ways though. George finally persuaded his wine merchant to place an order, albeit a good deal smaller than the one from Nightingales, but they made good that shortfall in a splendid fashion, by urging one of their new clients to buy a bottle of Anton's forty year old. The man had gone to them with a dilemma, in that he'd accepted a dinner invitation from Sandra Bowley, the *Times* wine critic and was understandably terrified of having his choice of wine scorned.

The following morning Sandra contacted the wine merchant who promptly sent a complimentary bottle over, after telling her about Club Cognac. He didn't know a great deal but there was enough for her to know that it was newsworthy and two months later their story became a major feature in the *Sunday Times,* which included photographs of the farmhouse, Anton with Sue in the still room and a charming group picture alongside a row of vines, photo-bombed spectacularly by a grinning Guinness.

Other books by the same Author

A Child's Eye View

Graham Parsons is a very ordinary chap, with a safe, if slightly dull, sort of life.

But that changes when he witnesses the manslaughter of a young boy, Christopher. Whilst holding the child Graham experiences a profound out of body experience but before he can even question it he suffers a life-threatening attack which leaves him with permanent disabilities.

His recovery is accompanied by a telepathic connection with children who need help. An affinity which threatens his sanity, marriage and eventually, his life.

His new life begins with a fearful and confused denial that takes him to the edge of reason, until eventually he is forced to accept his remarkable gift, employing it with a charming modesty and care that disarms doubters and helps to salvage blighted young lives. His simple, candid honesty wins the friendship and support of four people from very different backgrounds. Christopher's mother, a GP, a child protection officer and a detective sergeant.

Graham's Gang

Graham Parsons has finally come to terms with his special gift; a telepathic affinity with children who need help. But sometimes his efforts to help them are accompanied by calamity.

A small group of supporters know his secret and try to protect him, but just how effective can Nancy, his partner, a GP, a social worker and an overweight detective be?

They are joined by a wealthy businessman named Harvey Calder after he and his wife discover Graham's involvement in the saving of their granddaughter's life. Forever indebted they decide to give Graham, Nancy and their foster child, Jimmy, a holiday of a lifetime.

But 'Life' takes on a whole new meaning when Graham confronts an American, set to become a US Senator, who will do anything to discredit and remove a threat.

Graham's false imprisonment does just that and the situation seems to be back under control.

But no-one has told the Senator about the Hell's angel, 'Big Bob'.

Help Out House

Graham is back in England, a fugitive from US law and threatened by a vengeful Senator and extradition.

His life goes on hold, in an anxious twilight, while in the US, Chrissy Haddon and her mother are forced to confront their own demons of abuse and alcoholism.

Is it time for Senator Haddon to answer for his crimes?

Meanwhile, the 'Gang' rally to Graham's side once more, gathering help and support on both sides of the Atlantic. Some of it is extraordinary, but like Graham, with his telepathic affinity with children who need help, those around him know that others would think their story was no more than fiction.

Just when things seem to be falling apart, help comes from an unexpected source, when the US State Department are persuaded to join in.

Meanwhile, in Leicester, Lori is a frightened fifteen year old, trapped in a world of drugs and prostitution. Yet in that darkness shines a glimmer of spirit. Only she knows her real name in Marya, until the day she sends a message to Graham. A message that will trigger a dreadful reaction and cause Graham to suffer one of his worst nightmares.

The Tack Chest

The cover of my latest novel, entitled 'THE TACK CHEST' depicts a shire horse beautifully groomed and standing beside a black lacquered chest bearing two trophies. Her name was Dolly Grey and the man holding her was my great uncle Jack.

That much is fact and they inspired me to write this work of fiction - a gentle story of farming from around 1920 to 1960 based locally, in the Hartshill, Mancetter and Atherstone areas.

It begins with the discovery of that chest, many years later, when the family matriarch dies and the discovery of a secret hoard within prompts an odyssey of discovery that shocks everyone.

Oh, did I say gentle? Well, there were the explosives, scandals, crime and classified weaponry along with secret loves and a World War Two guerrilla unit. All startling surprises to a family who thought their father was just, well, - Dad, who grew tomatoes.

My Dead Friend Terry

After twenty nine years as an independent financial adviser, I thought I knew enough to get by. My clients had, for the most part, enjoyed steady and relatively low risk growth to their portfolios, as had mine.

That was until I began to receive Skype messages from a dead friend. An extremely odd affair, given the circumstances, but the stock market tips they included were incredible, along with the riches that followed.

But all things come with a price, which in this case, looked set to be my life.

I had no idea that I'd become a tool and target of some of the most potent intelligence agencies in the World.

All I had was Smudge, a retired SAS Sergeant and together, we embarked on a mutual quest to stay alive.

The Carpenter's Gift

Arnie Osborne is a sixty eight year old florist, and alone, save for the beautiful companions in his shop. The business is barely viable, thanks to the superstores and would have disappeared long ago if it hadn't been so close to the hospital.

He knows he has cause to feel bitter, but then there are the children. The ones who don't realise they're about to be orphaned, knowing only that they want to take a gift in with them. It is enough to keep him going, to justify dragging his creaky old bones out of bed each morning.

Until he has the nightmare.